D1446420

HARROWGATE

KATE MARUYAMA

47N⬛RTH

Text copyright © 2013 by Kate Maruyama

DREAM OPERATOR By David Byrne, Courtesy Moldy Fig Music

Published by 47North – Seattle, Washington

ISBN-13: 9781477807651
ISBN-10: 1477807659
Library of Congress Control Number: 2013936769

For Ko, the best thing ever

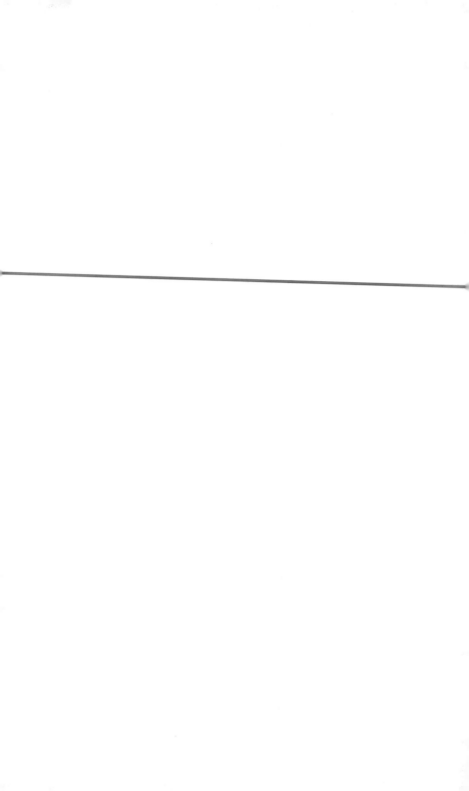

HARROWGATE

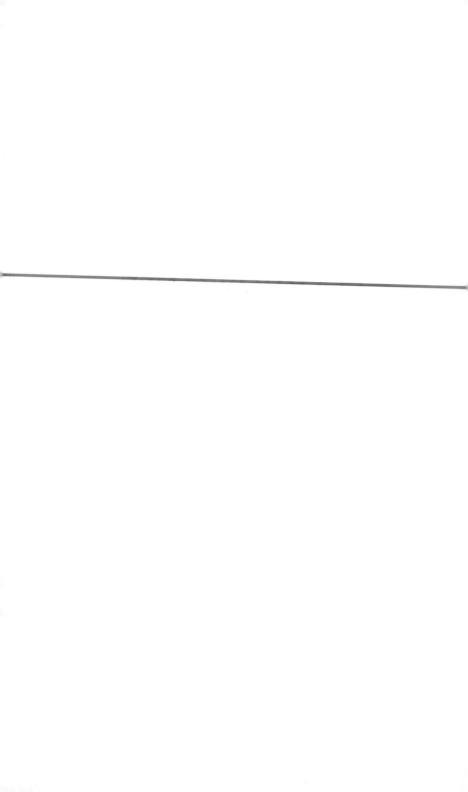

ONE

M ichael shifts in the cab seat, which causes his leather jacket to creak uncomfortably. How long has it been? Sarah called a week ago last Friday. He's tired of sitting. His left leg has gone numb again and the occasional shooting pain in his lower back has grown into a ceaseless throb. The cab smells of a brand new pine-scented air freshener, a claustrophobic spoof of an open-air scent. He's almost home. Why doesn't she answer the phone? Why can't he get a hold of anyone? The rain comes down so hard outside that he can't see where they are. This trip has been less a journey than an odyssey: hike to jeep to base to helicopter to plane to plane to plane to cab. His work as an environmental geologist takes him to pristine locations in the farthest reaches of Canada, but this appealing aspect of his work has now turned into the nightmare keeping him from his pregnant wife.

Sarah called a week ago last Friday, but how early does that make the baby?

Michael tries breathing deeply. What started as a low hum of anxiety when he got on the first plane has become a clamor of worries since he reached New York. He tried calling Sarah's sister Anna from Nome. No luck. Answering machine. He left messages, "Call me. You know the number. Is Sarah okay?"

If the baby is too early, there will be problems, complications. *No, don't think complications. It sounds too awful.* There will be concern about underdeveloped lungs. Will the baby be on a respirator? How is Sarah, having done all this without him? A wave of guilt comes over him, so he goes back to calculating the time. A week ago last Friday makes it almost two weeks. And he hasn't been able to get her on the phone. He jiggles his leg and stomps his foot a few times, hoping to bring it back to life.

The cab driver has been muttering to himself for about two miles now. He's an older white guy with a strong Bronx accent. He looks like a character lifted from a 1940s movie. Thomas Mitchell might play him, Ernest Borgnine if it were the fifties. There's anger in his tone, so Michael doesn't talk to him; he's got enough crazy, he doesn't need someone else's. A week ago last Friday would have been the twenty-second of April . . . thirty-four weeks. Thirty-five the following Monday. Thirty-five is so much safer than thirty-four.

They're stuck in the Midtown Tunnel and things aren't moving. He's trying hard to remember the part of the book about the development of the fetus's lungs. There was an all-clear week. Was it six weeks before the birth or thirty-six weeks of gestation? Why hadn't he read that part more closely?

He and Sarah frequently referred to the pregnant woman's bible, *What to Expect when You're Expecting*, to check the baby's development. Pea size. Kidney bean. Apple. Grapefruit. Sarah called it her mutating garden. The mention of the word "mutating" always made Michael uncomfortable.

Pregnant, Sarah was so changed and new in an alarming, but beautiful way. Her tall, slim body had filled out, giving her more presence. Her usually pale skin glowed a peachy-amber and her straight, dirty-blonde hair got fuller, almost curly. The angles of her face, which he always thought betrayed the sharpness of her humor, softened (the humor did not) and her green eyes seemed to grow bigger and warmer. Her gaze, which before darted from one thought to the next, now held people with a steady, intense, electric energy. The overall effect made her Sarah to the tenth power. Michael was a little jealous watching her go through this transformative experience without him. Even her sounds changed: a new, deeper timbre to her laugh, snoring when she hadn't before. Her sudden hungers and abrupt moods made him uneasy; she could be immediately overwhelmed by any emotion from sadness to hilarity or fear.

Maybe she knew something would go wrong and that's why she changed her mind about me leaving?

The cabbie asks, "So where on the Upper West Side?"

Michael says, "Riverside Drive and Seventy-Sixth Street."

The driver turns to glare at him a moment. "What's the matter with you?"

Michael says, "Excuse me?"

"You've been squirming in the seat since you got in the cab. You jonesing or something? Because I don't drive to deals."

Michael laughs nervously and, self-conscious, stills his leg, "No. No. I just had a baby."

The driver's not impressed.

Michael grins. "I . . . my wife had a baby boy." At least she should have. She was in labor, it's a boy, that's all he knows. *Don't think like that.* Of course she had the baby. Women have been doing it for years.

In an odd monotone, the driver says, "Well congratulations and good luck with that."

Michael drops the conversation.

Why can't he reach her?

He was so far out in the bush, it was two days before he even realized he'd lost signal. The last time they talked, she missed him, but she was fine. She was going to stay with her sister Anna, so he needn't bother calling for a few days. He worried, but reminded himself that she was safe. They were prepared for this possibility and Sarah said that she could manage for a week out of touch. The baby wasn't due for six weeks . . . a month and a half.

He missed her like crazy, but this trip was a trade-off. Management at the Department of Conservation would get him home three weeks before she was due and then he could have two full months of paternity leave. This job was a constant negotiation; Christmas in exchange for Thanksgiving, Thanksgiving for the week of the Fourth. Geologists weren't meant to have lives; they should be devoted to their science. Two months off was unheard of. Sarah said they should jump at the chance.

Right before he left, she'd had a change of heart. "Don't go."

He laughed, pulling her into him, kissing her ridiculously pregnant-thick hair. "I wish I didn't have to."

She wouldn't relax into the hug and pushed him away. "I feel like. I don't know. Something might go wrong." She looked genuinely frightened, which unnerved him. She was always so calm.

He said, "What could possibly go wrong?"

"Just don't go, okay?" She was so serious that he laughed.

She relaxed a bit and hugged him. She said it must have been the hormones talking, and he left.

Maybe she knew something was going to happen.

Michael checked in each day until the weekend. He should have listened to his instincts. Caroline, his field-trip partner for five years now, is always better at seeing the big picture. Broad-faced, hilarious and strong-minded, she's a steadying influence in his life. Everything was telling him to go back to base, to call home, but Caroline teased him. "Hey, Papa, the male of the species isn't really necessary for the birth part. Unless of course he's the doctor."

Two days out, take some core samples, two days back. They were already out there, it would be foolish not to finish their work.

The geological arm of the Department of Conservation was particularly interested in the results of this trip: if they didn't find evidence of oil, they could save the entire area from drilling. Caroline stayed on at base to finish up their logs, but Michael used the transport of the core samples as his early ticket home. Planes don't appear in the wilderness for over-anxious fathers-to-be. When the department heard he had the samples, they were happy to pay the expense to get him out of there.

Once in cell phone range, he tried Sarah and Anna with no luck. He dialed Sarah's number every hour after that. Anna's number every other. The hospital they planned on had no record of her checking in, and there was no answer at the apartment. He left only two desperate *call me* messages with Sarah's mother. He didn't want to freak her out for no reason. Everything might be fine. He finally got through to Sarah's cell when he boarded the plane in Seattle.

"Michael?" Anna answered her sister's phone. *Why?* She sounded very far away. Probably the weather.

Michael said, "Anna?"

She said, "Michael, where are you?" Did she sound concerned? She was dropping out and interference made it hard to judge tone of voice.

He said, "Is Sarah okay? Is the baby okay?"

"Michael, can you hear me? Sarah—"

The stewardess interrupted and Michael couldn't hear the rest of her sentence. "Sir, you're going to have to turn off your phone."

"Just a minute!" Then, distraught, into the phone, "Anna?"

He couldn't tell if she was laughing or crying when the phone cut out on its own, the battery dead.

———

The baby is crying. Again. Sarah's curled up on the sofa, trying to ignore its howls. She can't look at him anymore, his little pink face screwed up, his fists waving furiously in the air. He is a one-man revolution. She's done everything she can, nursed him, sung to him, paced the apartment with him, and yet he cries, incessant, unrelenting. He cries so passionately that she worries his chest will burst, his head fall off. She lies on the sofa watching the lacy bassinette shudder, the occasional angry fist visible above its edge.

Michael was supposed to be here; helping, tending, keeping her from losing her mind. But he's not here and she's alone with this wailing creature who is supposedly her offspring.

She's given up. What's the point, anyway? He'll cry. And then maybe he'll stop. Eventually. Anything she does in the meantime doesn't seem to have any effect on him one way or the other.

There's a knock and Sarah hears the front door open and close gently. Thank God, Greta's here again to help. Sarah's grateful for a different face; different from the troll-like open-mouthed toothless yawper. She also knows that she's been caught red-handed, not tending to her child. She's too tired to do anything but feel enormous guilt, and she turns her head away.

She'd been dead set against getting a doula. Something about having a stranger come into your home to "help" you with your newborn baby seemed intrusive and off-putting. She would manage on her own; people have done it since . . . there were people. But when Sarah found herself here, alone with this yowling thing, no Michael, completely lost and unable to redefine her new world, Greta's appearance seemed a godsend.

There's something comforting and earthy about this woman. When she enters the room, her heavy form, organic perfume and authoritative strength fill the air like a warm hug. Greta goes to the child. Sarah should feel more protective. She's read about that hormonal reaction you're supposed to have when other people touch your infant. But she feels only relief for someone else taking charge, somebody else being liable for this child's needs.

The baby stops crying.

Greta clucks at the baby and asks Sarah, as if about the weather, "Have you named him?" Greta has a strong, grandmotherly, New York accent. Her tone makes Sarah feel comfortable. At home.

Sarah can't manage to turn her head yet. "Yes." The moment she does, she will have agreed to this huge responsibility.

Greta says, "Good."

Sarah feels Greta move over next to her. She cringes as she hears the snuffling child that the woman lowers into her arms. Greta takes Sarah's arms with a gentle force, helping her to encircle the baby, hold him securely. Sarah can smell his wet, milky neediness. He's quiet now.

"Sarah." Greta is more than saying her name. Sarah's being summoned, commanded. "Sarah, take your baby. Talk to him."

Sarah won't turn her head yet. She doesn't have to. When she does, she'll be stuck.

But Greta's tone lulls her and fills her with warmth and purpose. "Talk to your baby. Call him by name. He is yours and he is here and you are here and nothing else matters. Love your baby, Sarah. It is all he exists for."

Sarah looks down at the infant sucking on his fist. He opens his eyes and looks at her. They're large, wide-set, enormous, black pupils set in a border of dark blue, and the only human thing in his squished up still-fetal face. There he is. Not just a crying creature. But Tim. Tim is here.

She puts her pinkie in his other cat's tongue-sized hand. He grips it with surprising strength for one so small. She smiles at the boy and starts to cry.

However lost she feels, she knows that she's home.

———

By the time they pull up to the curb, the windows of the taxi have fogged up from the moisture on Michael's clothing. He takes a deep breath. Feeling frantic isn't helping anyone, but he can't stop his heart pounding. Anna's voice resounds in his head, "Sarah . . . " What did she mean? "Sarah *wants to talk to you.*" "Sarah's *right here.*" "Sarah *can't speak, she's had a stroke.*" "Sarah *has painted the baby's bedroom pink!*" It was probably nothing. Looking anxious is not the way to meet his son.

Michael gets out. The streets are wet and he can hear the sound of water running in the gutters. Things smell fresh and dirty at the same time. City after rain. A few blocks east there would be restaurant odors mixed in. But here it's residential: wet litter and leaves mixed with fresh air and car exhaust.

The Harrowgate looms above him. "Look at it," Sarah always says. "Looming is what it does best." An early twentieth-century building, it has doglike gargoyles watching from above the second floor and limestone facing up to around the fourth floor, where incongruously plain brick starts, continuing all the way to the roof. The building is filled with architectural details like crown moldings, marble foyers, too-small service kitchens and ancient plumbing. Sarah fell in love with the architecture, even though Michael was plagued by the building's problems: persistently drippy faucets, occasional chunks of paint and plaster falling off the ceiling, and old wiring that would short out his computer. But he loves it, too. It's home, even if today the gargoyles look more menacing against the sullen sky.

The cab driver helps Michael get his things out of the trunk. He doesn't hold back his resentment, pointedly dropping the sample case onto the ground. He looks at Michael, challenging him to complain. It's best not to engage. Better to back off, give him his space and flee. Michael hands him the cash.

Saying nothing, the driver gets back into the cab and peels out of the spot in front of the building. Michael grabs his things as best he can and books for the front door.

There's a new doorman. "Can I help you?"

He says, "Michael Gould. Where's Charles?"

"Mr. Gould. Right. I'm Phil. Let me help you with your things, sir." Phil stares at Michael nervously, as if searching his face for a clue to something. He picks up Michael's luggage and walks it to the elevator for him.

"Thanks." Michael presses the button. It's taking forever, but the fourteen floors to his apartment mean that he won't get there faster by running.

The doorman stands next to him. "You have three boxes of mail, sir. Would you like me to bring them up?" His eagerness to help gets on Michael's nerves. Three boxes. Sarah's probably been too distracted to pick up the mail.

"No, thanks. I'll get it later." Three boxes. How long was she in the hospital?

The doorman isn't moving. Michael snaps, "I got it from here." The cab driver got to him. He tries a gentler, "Thank you."

Phil doesn't seem to mind. He just laughs nervously and goes back to his post.

It takes ages, but the elevator comes. That final moment when the porthole window lights up and the door grinds open is interminable. Michael pushes inside, closing the gate. He's never known the elevator to be this slow. He punches the button for the fourteenth floor and it lurches to life again. There are no thirteenth floors in much of Manhattan; it would be bad luck.

5 . . . 6 . . . 7 . . . 8 . . .

Even at the end of the day, fighting a full bladder and a raging headache, the elevator has never taken this long.

12 . . . 14 . . .

Michael wants to break the doors open, but the elevator will not be rushed. When it opens enough to squeeze through, he fights his way out and stumbles toward the door of their apartment. He hammers on it.

"Sarah! Sarah!" He stops himself. Baby. Waking the baby. He grins. He steps back, breathes, rings the doorbell. After losing his house keys in various remote locations, Sarah doesn't let him travel with them anymore.

She's not answering. He knocks, softly, but steadily. *Can she even walk? Can people answer the front door when they've just had a baby? What if she's in the middle of nursing?* The door opens a crack, the guard chain still on. Sarah looks like she's been through a war. She's pale and tired. He should have been there for her. It takes her a moment to focus on him.

"Sarah?"

Her eyes light up with surprise. "Michael." She sounds incredulous. She closes the door to take the chain off and opens it again. "I didn't know." She falls against him and starts to cry.

He buries his face in her hair. It's so good to hold her, to finally have her safe in his arms. "Shh, shh. It's okay, honey, I'm home." She smells like herself, but with a foreign added odor: a milky sourness with an undertone of powdery lotion. He realizes that it's the smell of *baby*. His heart beats a little faster.

He says, "Where is he?"

She smiles and leads him by the hand into the nursery. More guilt as he realizes he'd only just gotten it painted before he had to go on his trip. The crib was in pieces when he left, the changing table still in its box. Now, all is assembled, including a mobile and some pictures on the walls. With the daybed in the corner, arrayed with brightly colored truck pillows and stuffed animals, it looks like a real baby's room. He trembles as she leads him to the crib; he hooks his hands in his pockets to steady himself. He peeks over the edge of the rail, its bars obscured by a bumper covered in pictures of cars.

There he is. He doesn't look premature. He looks like a fully formed newborn. But what does Michael know?

"Tim?"

She laughs. "Of course. Timothy Wilder Gould."

He stares at the baby, arms splayed over his head, little chest rising and falling, face twitching. Tim looks like some wizened old man, his features still skinny, his brow furrowed. Newborns are notoriously ugly, but Tim is the most beautiful baby Michael has ever seen. Tim's face contorts into a wretched frown and he purses his lips, the aged man now discontent. Michael asks, "Is he okay?"

Sarah comes in next to him and watches the baby. She laughs. "Gas. He makes the most horrid expressions all day. I've read that it's what they do."

He teases her. "Been doing your research?" She was always so professional-minded; this new role of mother is amusing to him.

"A little." She smiles.

He looks at her pinched face; she's aged a few years since he saw her last. "I'm so sorry I wasn't here, was it awful? Did you do your breathing? Did you get the drugs? I told you, you should get the drugs." But his questions bring a look of panic and her eyes well up. Was it so horrible?

"Honey?"

She searches his face and stifles a sob.

"Honey? What happened? Did something happen?"

She raises his hand to his chest, stopping him. "Is it okay? Is it okay if I don't want to talk about it right now?"

It was awful. He should have been here. He pulls her to him and rocks her a little. "Shh, shh. Of course." He looks down and sees Tim there, his little chest rising and falling. Michael reaches his hand into the crib to touch Tim's belly, to feel that breath.

Sarah releases herself from Michael's hold and grabs his arm, pulling it back so quickly it startles him. "No. You'll wake him." She's got a tone in her voice he's never heard before: frantic, worried.

"Can't I . . . " He can't articulate it, other than making grabbing motions with his hands. He wants to hold the baby, eat him up.

She says, "You have no idea how long it took me to get him down for a nap. *Later.*" She pulls him by the elbow, trying to lead him away from the crib. But when Michael looks back at the baby, it feels wrong, somehow, to leave him.

He pulls free of Sarah and walks up to the crib, watches the baby's wise little face, his stretching hands. He says, "Hey, little man." The baby's clearly in a deep sleep now. Michael instinctively reaches out his hand again.

"Michael!"

Michael stings at being scolded.

He follows Sarah out of the room and into their bedroom. She folds a pile of baby clothes. He paces at the foot of the bed, trying to keep the anger out of his voice. "It's the first time I've seen him."

She snaps a baby blanket in the air and folds it sharply. This isn't like her. Sarah's always been the even-keeled one of the relationship. She would be there with a wry smile that let him know in an instant he was being ridiculous. She was the soother.

"You were gone so long." She's appeasing him now.

He says, "It was only a couple of weeks."

"You have no idea how it's been, how isolating. I feel like I exist to lactate and to get that child to sleep."

Michael laughs. Sarah shoots him a glare. He says, "Honey, I wanted to see him."

She says, "And then he has gas. If he has gas, he cries, and the crying, Michael, it goes on all night. And I love him so much, I can't take it when I can't fix it."

"Babies cry."

She drops what she's folding in defeat. Michael goes to her and wraps his arms around her. "I'm so sorry, honey."

She says, "You don't know what I've been through."

He rocks her gently. "I'm here now." He hates how deeply upset she is.

She pulls away from him gently. She says, "And the worst thing?"

He strokes her face. "What, baby? Shh . . . "

"I can't find my sense of humor. Anywhere." He laughs. She smiles and says, "I've looked in the fridge, in the laundry room, under the sofa."

He says, "Did you check my underwear drawer?" She musters a laugh. He knows he has her. "'Cause that's a funny place."

They will be okay.

———

They were friends first. Well, to start with, Sarah was more of a pest than a friend.

At the time, Michael was deeply involved with an earth-mother type named Naomi who was ruling his life the fall of his senior year at Georgetown, dosing him with equal parts ginseng tea and echinacea. Michael and Naomi had pretty great sex, which kept him involved in the relationship longer than he should have been. In the spring of his junior year, he fell in with her peasant skirts, form-hugging tops, and giant earrings, wrapped up in an essential oil of vanilla cloud. She read all sorts of books on sex, from the *Kama Sutra* and *The Joy of Sex* to some obscure texts translated from Sanskrit, and was eager to try out her newfound knowledge. She found Michael an ardent student and a willing slave. Up until he met her, sex had been pretty unimaginative; missionary, girl on top, occasionally implementing different pieces of furniture. But Naomi was willing to try anything, and while the candle wax and handcuffs period was more uncomfortable than fun, there was always something new waiting around the corner.

He was sitting in his first class of Geology 101 when Sarah blew into his life. A required science course Michael had neglected his first three years—pretty sad for a geology major—he needed it to graduate.

Sarah's sly voice startled him out of his morning stupor. "So, you gonna help me?" He looked up past the faded jeans directly in front of him and saw a pretty girl looking down at him with a wicked smile.

He said, "Help you what?" He was irritated by the angle his neck had to maintain to keep looking at her. She finally squatted down in front of his desk. She was less severe-looking at this angle, pretty in a fresh-scrubbed way. She had a pale complexion and freckles, a redness that threatened to rise at the least embarrassment. Her sharp nose and chin gave her a Puckish quality. One look into her quick eyes and Michael knew he'd have to stay on his toes with her. Her manner made him desperate to come up with something clever to say, which made him feel decidedly *not* clever. Her long blonde hair folded over on her head in an elastic at an odd angle, some stray hairs hanging loose. This and her lack of makeup revealed someone who didn't give much care to her appearance. He found this attractive, perhaps because of the time-consuming, ritualistic care Naomi took with her grooming.

She said, "I need tutoring for this class. You're a geology major."

He asked, "Tutoring for Rocks for Jocks?"

"Do I look like a jock?" She smiled. Michael instantly liked that smile: challenging, but honest.

He said, "I've got a full course load this semester. I can't."

But she kept asking. And he kept turning her down. It became a jokey routine before class started each session. When she brought him a batch of chocolate chip cookies, he finally caved.

Sarah was a city girl, which intimidated the rural Michael. Her wry jokes frequently went over his head, making him wonder if the serious Naomi had sucked dry his capacity for humor. It didn't take long for Michael to find his funny again and he looked forward to their study sessions more each time they met. Sarah was the ideal buddy, listening to his issues, laughing at his jokes, rolling her eyes when he was being an ass. He didn't think of her romantically then. He acknowledged that he found her attractive, but he had the sexual part of his life sewn up. Sarah fulfilled an intellectual role in his life that Naomi didn't. He was quite happy for a time, keeping these two lives separate and he talked himself out of his growing attraction to Sarah.

It was soon after a study session that included a near-kiss and Michael's almost-confession of love that Sarah started seeing a humorless (she lovingly referred to him as "humor-free") pre-law Adonis. Michael was relieved he hadn't declared himself, and their friendship took a new turn. Sarah and Michael started sharing stories of romantic traumas, from conversational misunderstandings to sexual escapades. He found it refreshing to talk about his love life with a girl.

Then, in one of those weekend-long Greek dramas that can only happen at college, Sarah and Michael hooked up, their respective partners erupted, clothes were rent (Naomi), tears were shed (pre-law Adonis), sage was burned (Naomi, again), and Michael and Sarah moved on. Michael found, to his great delight, that his sexual internship with Naomi paid off when it was taken into the realm of true love-making.

The fact that he loved Sarah more completely than anyone he'd ever met sent Michael into a brief panic; that kind of certainty is terrifying at the tender age of twenty-one. But Sarah calmly reassured him: they made sense. She knew him in a way that let him know he wasn't a complete alien. He belonged here, in this life, with her.

———

Michael is surprised when Sarah leads him to the bedroom. She has that look in her eyes. She slowly unbuttons his shirt and loosens his belt. He thinks for a moment that he might be getting what they have always jokingly referred to as "service," but she takes off her clothes and pulls him into bed on top of her.

He kisses her hungrily. It's been so long. Months now. He stops to look at her face, so worn and tired before, now momentarily lit with the flush of desire. She grins wickedly.

He says, "Are you sure? I mean, isn't it too soon?" He has so many questions. About the birth. Was it hard? Is she okay? It can't possibly have been long enough since the birth, she'd need to heal. He's aroused, which makes him ashamed. "Isn't it too soon?"

"The doctors say it's fine."

He strokes her hair. It's been awhile since she washed it, but he's so starved for her that it only seems to intensify his desire. She smells more like Sarah. For the longest time the enormous and awkward buoy of a belly had separated them. Now he can embrace all of her. The belly has deflated, and though there's more of it than there was before she was pregnant, it feels good to hold all of her again. Out of habit, he leans back on one elbow to survey the rest of her and she catches his chin. "No, don't look. I'm horrid. Close your eyes." He does and he feels her get up from the bed for a moment, and hears her draw the curtains. She turns off the light. It's already dark from the late afternoon rain, so when he opens his eyes again, the room is dim and he can hardly see her.

She says, "I said close 'em!"

He laughs, closing his eyes, and soon she's on top of him.

Michael finds himself joyously sinking into the familiar. Sarah moans, whispering, "I can't believe you're here."

All the strangeness falls away. It's just the two of them now; no baby, no worries, no separation.

Sarah stays awake and watches Michael sleep. She smoothes his hair back from his forehead, where it has fallen in his eyes. He's always had ridiculously long lashes and when he sleeps, he looks like some sort of fierce, scruffy angel reclining. Fallen angel. His brown hair has gotten shaggy again and he has a thread or two of gray in his sideburns, but his face is etched and peaceful in the light from the street. She loves him when he goes all outdoorsy, flannel and boots and walking like he owns the earth on which he treads. She feels sorry for him when he changes so drastically for work: he gets his hair shorn and puts on his suit, depleted.

She can't believe he's here.

It's different. The sex. She's been told that it sometimes changes after a birth, so on some level, she'd expected it to change. But she can't feel everything she used to. Those old feelings deep inside her are something she can't quite reach, no matter how she tries. This makes her sad, further evidence of the shift she's experiencing. There are some things she's going to have to let go of in her new reality.

She'll have to ask Greta what this means. But she'll do it tomorrow. For now, here is Michael and she can smell him, the Michael of him. She's so enthralled by the very here-ness of him, and he feels so miraculous, she can't get enough of touching him. As he sleeps, she strokes his chest with the palm of her hand, feeling his weight, the power of his lungs as they rise and fall. She holds her hand over his heart and feels the thumping of life within him. Michael. She leaves her hand where it is and settles in next to him, falling into the first relaxed sleep she's had in what feels like forever.

───────

Michael wakes a few hours later and stares at the familiar orange-shadowed glow of the streetlights across the ceiling. They feel like *them* again as they lie here in the dark. Sarah sleeps peacefully, and with all the stress gone from her face, she looks much more like herself. He strokes her hair, then the freckles on the back of her arm. Her face is still puffy, and there are brow furrows that weren't there before. Her belly is softer, fuller, but from Sarah's descriptions, he thought there would be an "extra person" worth of skin lying between them. He touches it gently, the vacated house where Tim once dwelled; he expects a hollowness, but it's supple, hers again. Sarah groans softly and rolls over. Michael realizes that he's wide awake and the only thing he can give his wife now is undisturbed sleep. He sneaks out of bed and pulls on a sweatshirt.

He tries to avoid the squeaky floorboards; he doesn't want anything disturbing the peace of their home right now. He smiles, wondering if Tim will be avoiding the same floorboards when he sneaks home too late as a teenager.

Michael has to readjust every time he re-enters apartment life. After climbing mountains and covering great stretches of countryside, his strides need to be smaller, his arms need tucking in. For the first week home, he usually whacks his hands against doorjambs, slams his knees into table edges, lurches into walls. Sneaking over the floorboards makes him overly conscious of the enormity of his body in this boxed-in space.

Michael stops outside Tim's door for a moment and sees his curtain blowing, the window open. It's cold. Too cold. Michael shivers as he creeps into the room. He tries to stay out of the line of vision of the crib, even though newborns can't see more than three feet in front of them.

When he gets to the window, he finds it's curiously colder inside than out. The breeze blowing off the river is usually warm this time of year. He pulls on the sash of the six-feet-high window. It's stuck. He knows that you have to pull and push . . . push to get it unstuck, pull to ensure that it doesn't crash down on the fingers. Suffering from years of paint and missing sash weights, the window finally rumbles down, making entirely too much noise, but Michael catches it before it hits the bottom. He stops, stock still for a moment, listening, but hears only the baby breathing. He gently closes the window that last notch.

The quilt, colorful with crudely drawn cars on it, hangs on the side of the crib.

Michael creeps forward and slips the quilt off the edge of the crib. It's worth the risk. It's surely more likely that the baby will wake if he's cold. He leans over the baby and is startled to find his eyes open. Tim is completely awake and he's looking right at his father with more focus than Michael thought he'd be capable of at this age. Tim smiles. Isn't it too early for him to smile? Michael's elated. Look at this. His boy! The first time the boy has laid eyes on him and Tim seems to know him; recognition flickers in that wise, old-man gaze.

When he grows up, will he have Michael's short temper or his mother's patience? Will he be good at sports like Sarah and her sister or a total geek like his father? Will he be good at music? What if he wants to be a baseball star? Can Michael cope with a jock? He laughs to himself. He will be Tim. That is the only thing for certain.

"Hi there," he whispers. "Hi, little man, I'm your dad."

The baby kicks, thrashing his arms in the air, smiling.

"Hi! Oh, look at you." He reaches his arms into the crib and rubs the boy's belly. "Look at *you*."

He puts his finger into one of the boy's grasping hands, which closes around it. Tim screams as if in pain, and launches into a horrible jerking cry.

"Shh. shh. No, no . . . " The baby is quiet for a terrible second, sucking in his breath, summoning deep inside him for his next ear-splitting scream. Michael scrambles and picks him up, holding him against his shoulder. But the baby thrashes, bashing his head against Michael; he won't settle. Michael cups Tim's tiny back with his hand, holding him steady. His head is bobbing dangerously. He pounds his forehead violently on his father's clavicle.

"*What* are you doing?" Sarah shrieks from the doorway behind him.

She storms toward him, a look of anger on her face he hasn't ever seen before, and she snatches Tim from his arms. The moment Tim is in his mother's arms, his screaming turns to a softer crying. "Shh, shh, little one." The crying turns to soft hiccups.

Michael says, "I'm sorry. He was crying."

Sarah, "Didn't I tell you not to pick him up?"

He's starting to get pissed off. "No, you didn't. You said not to wake him up. He was already awake."

"What were you doing in here?" she hisses, careful not to raise her voice.

But his voice is rising now. "The window was open. It was *freezing*."

"He needs fresh air."

"I thought he could use his quilt."

"Have you not heard of crib death?" She glares at him accusingly. The room feels even colder, like a strong draft has blown through.

Michael says, "Oh for chrissake, he's not going to die from that quilt. It's no thicker than a blanket."

Sarah soothes Tim. "Shh. Shh." He's stopped crying, but Sarah is still fuming. "You don't touch him, do you understand?"

Michael says, "He's my son." He doesn't understand why he has to tell her this. How can she forbid him from touching his own child?

Sarah says, "Who's been here for him every moment since he's been born?"

"You still can't . . . "

"Can't what?" she says in the same tone.

He holds up his hands, exasperated. Anything he wants to say is not going to help. He walks out, slamming the door. The baby starts crying again. Okay, bad move, but Jesus, that is *not* Sarah in there. How did he get so suddenly put on the outside? Is this punishment for the trip or is this the way things are going to be? How can he learn to care for Tim if she won't even give him a chance?

As he heads to his office through the kitchen, he notices an oppressive stench. The smell of garbage that's been sitting for quite a long time. Michael opens the cabinet door under the kitchen sink and a brick of odor hits him. There are more flies in that small space than he's ever seen inside the apartment. He quickly cinches the bag and lifts the entire can out to take it to the garbage chute; it's not worth the risk of the bag breaking. *How hard is it to take out the goddamned garbage?* He's always taking care of the stuff that should be glaringly obvious to her: the empty toilet paper holder, the overloaded clothes basket, the endless pile of papers and unopened junk mail on the dining room table. Three boxes. She didn't even bother to fetch the mail this time.

He catches himself. He's burning on pure anger now. Sarah probably hasn't been able to take a shower, let alone take out the garbage, since she got home. He hears Sarah singing soothingly to the boy down the hall. He knows she doesn't intend it, but her singing sounds self-consciously motherly. Forced.

"*Every dream has a name, and names tell your story, this song is your dream . . .* " The Talking Heads. He used to sing it to her when they were first living together. He feels a pang of jealousy; the song is no longer theirs, but the baby's.

Michael opens the heavy fire door to the kitchen as quietly as he can and inserts a step stool to hold it open. He hoists the trashcan over the stool and through the door, heaving it down the worn red-carpeted hallway, past the elevator.

The flickering light at the end of the hall casts an odd glow on the garbage chute door, adding to Michael's jet-lagged, post–argument uneasiness. He laughs at himself for being foolish and pulls the heavy chute door open. He stares into the blackness for a moment, mesmerized. He's heard about these new baby blues, that it's hard on the father, the disruption of his ordered universe. It's hard on the mother, as well, but she expects her world to change with the birth of a new child. The father is sideswiped. Michael's not that fifties guy who expects the pipe, slippers, and Martini at the end of the day, but he hasn't ever been in a place where he doesn't know what to expect in his own home. And with Sarah, he never thought he'd signed up for the unstable shrew he just saw in her.

Okay, unfair.

———

Sarah jerks awake, sitting up in bed. It takes her a sleepy moment to recognize that the violent sound that woke her is the baby crying. Adrenaline surges, her heart is beating wildly and she's breathing heavily. It's only a crying baby. This reaction to the sound of Tim's cry is also supposed to be natural for the mother of a newborn, but she hates it. Nature implanted this reaction to get her to the baby faster, but all it does is make her angry for having been woken so roughly, resentful that she has to take care of something. And it's always followed by guilt for that anger and resentment.

She sits for a moment, trying to wake up and get a grip. She sees that Michael's gone. She remembers their fight and the fact that he left the room, but beyond that things are fuzzy. She knows that she tended to Tim, put him down to sleep, and went back to bed. Why didn't she look for Michael? Was she too angry? She shouldn't have been so hard on him.

Michael was here. She knows he was here. But it's been days— three?—since she's seen him. And where is Greta? Greta hasn't come since he got here.

Maybe he's in with the baby. Sarah gets out of bed and runs down the hallway. She finds Tim alone in his crib, awake, kicking and crying. She picks him up. He wobbles and jerks around, looking for the comfort of the breast. She shoves her finger in his mouth to buy time as she looks around the apartment. The power of the baby's suck on her finger is staggering, and she feels the new familiar prickle on the sides of her breasts as her milk comes in and dampens the front of her nightgown. She doesn't understand why she can feel some things so acutely and yet something like sex is so far away.

She'll probably have to tell Michael everything, but she doesn't know if she's allowed. She'll ask Greta.

Greta helped her keep Tim. She doesn't know how exactly.

She doesn't like to think about it . . . it frightens her when she does. But she has so many questions. Like, why does Tim scream when his father touches him?

And where has Michael gone?

Maybe he found out what happened and left.

———

The echoing rattle inside the chute of trash from another floor makes Michael realize he's been staring into the black hole for some time, holding the chute open. He must be tired, to be submerged in thought so completely. He bends over to lift the garbage up, wondering if the bag will break or if he should dump the contents from the bag for a better fit. He chooses the whole bag and hefts it.

"The gates of *Hell*!" A voice booms from behind him, so deep and resonant it seems supernatural. Michael drops the empty trashcan, which thuds dully on the carpet. As if for comic effect, the garbage bag picks that moment to slide slowly down the chute.

A man laughs. "You were so . . . absorbed. It was hard to resist."

Michael turns around and sees a bespectacled, middle-aged man of Dickensian girth wearing a worn cardigan and a bow tie. Polka dots on the tie, stripes on the shirt. Peculiar attire for this hour of the night. Michael realizes his jaw has dropped; he closes his mouth abruptly and holds out his hand. "Michael Gould. 14A."

On hearing his name, the man sobers instantly. "Oh. I'm so sorry." He pauses as if searching for something to say. He then shakes Michael's hand vigorously. "Doctor Thomas James, down in D there."

Michael asks, "Sorry?"

"That I startled you. Inappropriate."

There's a quiet moment, which makes Michael nervous. He forces a question, "Did you just move in?"

Dr. James chuckles, "Not just."

"I've been gone for a few weeks and it seems like a lot has happened."

The doctor says, "Ah, time creeps oddly, I find. Excellent to meet you. If you'll excuse me." He holds up his own small leaky paper bag of garbage, gesturing toward the chute.

"Of course. Sorry." Michael stands aside absently, staring into space as Dr. James completes his task.

The doctor asks, "Mr. Gould? Are you all right?"

"Sorry. I'm tired . . . housework's piling up."

A cloud of concern briefly crosses Dr. James's face as if he doesn't understand. He clears his throat. "Ah. Adjustments."

"You could say so."

Dr. James musters a smile. "You'll be fine, fine. It takes time." He shambles off but then pauses thoughtfully, turning, "If you need anything, Michael, I'm just down the hall. I'm a shrink, you know. My door is always open."

Michael's embarrassed. Does he look that bad off?

"Uh . . . thanks," he says to the doctor's retreating back.

Odd man, but Michael's grateful for the distraction. He had been planning to walk the streets until he cooled down. But his anger has abated. He feels he can go back in and face Sarah, no matter her mood. There's no way she's stayed that venomous. It's just not like her.

He opens the kitchen door cautiously, so the stool won't slide and scrape the floor. He closes it just as carefully. It's one of those enormously heavy New York doors that can only close with a *ka-chunk*. He stops for a moment and listens. The baby has stopped crying, but Michael hears another noise from the living room. He walks in and realizes that it's Sarah, muttering to herself. He can't make out the words. Sarah's sitting on the sofa, knees curled up to her head, rocking.

She looks up, as if she's surprised to see him standing there. He doesn't know why she looks embarrassed.

He has no idea what to say. "Uh . . . hi."

She smiles nervously. "Hi."

"Yeah."

"I thought you'd left me." This doesn't sound like Sarah's usual sarcasm. It sounds like she means it—which unsettles him more than the shrieking.

He decides to pretend that it was her usual sarcasm: neither of them is thinking straight right now. He walks over to the sofa and plops down next to her, far enough away to give her some space. He says, "Nope. 'Fraid you're stuck with me."

It's not like she was going to smile and they'd go back to normal again, but he's surprised when she doesn't respond and folds her head into her arms. He sighs and settles into the sofa, rubbing her back with his hand.

TWO

He's just drifting off when Sarah wakes him. "Michael?"

"Yeah?"

"You awake?"

He rubs his face. "*Mmphth*. Yeah. Yeah, sure."

She's lying on her stomach with her chin propped in her hands, staring at him. "I'm worried."

Maybe there is really something going on, something that would explain all of her irrational reactions, her sudden moods. Maybe it's more than just having had a baby.

"About what?" He traces his finger on the outside of her freckled arm.

"That you won't like me anymore."

Oh. This is hormones. He has to play this right. "What are you talking about? I like you *always*. I like you whatever happens." He rolls on his side and kisses her nose. He smoothes down the worry lines on her forehead with his fingers.

"I'm a mother now."

He laughs. "Yes, you are."

"I'm not . . . I don't know how to explain." She looks like she's weighing her words so carefully, thinking of what to say. He's surprised when all that comes out is, "I'm not who I *was*."

He hopes he's not too tired to process whatever it is she needs from him. He says, "Okay."

"I'm not the lawyer, the problem solver, the clever one. I'm not even *funny* anymore. I'm not the woman you fell in love with. I don't even know what I *am*."

"Hmmm." He peers closely at her face. "Freckles? Check. Snoring? Well, I can vouch for that from last night. Oh, and the final proof: that half-smile when you're annoyed with me." The half-smile grows into a real one. He's relieved. "Oh, wait. Nope there it is, I see that sense of humor, see it? It's in that smile. The funny's not far behind. I guarantee you that you are the woman I fell in love with."

But her smile falls quickly into worry again. "All I do is carry that infant around and feed him. And I can't even do that right."

"Shh, shh." He leans in and kisses her eyes, one by one. "It's a change, that's all."

She says, "It's a big, big change." There is a weight to her tone that goes beyond her words.

"We'll get through it, honey."

She rolls on her back and sighs in frustration. "Well, we'll see."

There's no talking her out of it now; he's never been able to argue her out of a line of thinking once she got going. He's learned in these cases to just be there for her in a quiet way. He rolls over, resting a reassuring arm on her, and falls asleep before he means to.

———

Sarah stands nervously in the kitchen while Michael sleeps. She fills the kettle with water, puts it on the stove over a full flame and opens the cabinet to get down the coffee. She'll make coffee. She can't have coffee, of course, but it's the sort of thing you make when you have company. Right? Greta's supposed to come over, and while Sarah knows she'll have some answers to her growing number of questions, she's worried what Greta will think of Michael. She left a note for Sarah saying she'd be by tonight after Michael was asleep.

They've built a comfortable friendship, Greta, Sarah, and the baby. She wants terribly for Michael to like her, but she also feels guilty, as if letting Greta into their little family was a betrayal of some sort. Cheating. But Michael was gone. And she didn't know if he was coming back. And she needed help. And Greta always knows things. Like what to do next. And why the baby doesn't like Michael touching him. And why she's so afraid.

There's a metallic ticking noise and Sarah looks over to see that all of the water in the kettle has boiled away. The metal is heating up and creaking. She quickly turns off the stove. She's been doing this lately, losing time to her thoughts. This new world is so tricky.

Does Greta even drink coffee? She doesn't remember. She puts the coffee back and turns around to find Greta standing behind her. The older woman has a nervous energy about her, a fire in her eyes. She smiles and clasps Sarah's shoulders in excitement, squeezing. "Your husband is here!"

Sarah catches the sense of excitement. "I know!"

Greta says, "This is a very, very good thing."

But is it? Sarah has so many questions, she can't seem to get them in order fast enough to ask them. "How could we . . . ? We made love. I didn't think we'd be able to do that."

Greta smiles and hugs Sarah. "Oh my, honey, and you're on the right track already." Is she supposed to be doing something on this track she's on?

Greta's breathless, bustling about as she talks. "I was hoping. I left you alone for a time, hoping." She goes to the stove, takes the kettle off and fills it in the sink. "It's been so very, very long since I've seen this. You have to know, this situation is rare. You're a very lucky woman."

"I didn't think I'd ever see him again."

Greta lights the flame under the kettle and turns to her, saying, "But he's here. He's here. And having intercourse cinched the deal. I know it did. Keep that physical contact close, hon. That's so important. And the baby. Can Tim see his daddy?"

"He's been crying, screaming when Michael touches him. Is he bad for him or frightening?"

"Oh, no, no, no, no. This is good! He can see him! He just has to get to know him. Babies don't do well with new people. It takes time. But Sarah"—Greta looks at her directly, as if issuing a command—"This is important. It is absolutely essential that the child get to know his father. That the father get to know his son. Do you understand this?"

She doesn't, but she feels Greta wanting her to und complies. "I guess so."

"Get Michael involved in Tim's life as deeply and as quickly as you can."

Sarah doesn't like how manipulative this sounds. It's never been her way to "manage" her man. But she says, "Okay."

"You might be able to live and grow together . . . as a family." Greta's face softens and she smiles, beaming, "Oh, the possibilities." She gets a rapturous look in her eyes. "The possibilities."

The sounds of car horns and jackhammers echo up from the street and wake Michael. He hauls himself out of bed and throws on his sweatshirt and jeans. The air seems closer, more stifling, from the way the sounds get trapped and ricochet around the room to the smell of car exhaust that never completely leaves the apartment. It's such a contrast to the open spaces, rustling trees, trickling water, enormous places in which sounds and wind have room to move. He knows that this disorientation goes both ways, that when traveling anywhere in nature—deserts, mountains, forests—he feels bereft, as if all humanity has left him. As if the spaces are too wide to live in.

In the hallway, Michael hears voices coming from the kitchen. Sarah's laughter lightens his heart immediately, but then he hears a stranger laugh—someone older, with a huskier voice and a strong New York accent. Probably a woman. Michael pauses outside the door, listening for a moment. Despite being in a different room, he smells a waft of perfume: a heavy patchouli with some floral undercurrent that lies somewhere between gardenia and creosote. It reminds him of Naomi, but gone off. The result is an aura of odor, a malevolence.

"I'm not quite sure how to proceed. I mean, is it okay?" Sarah sounds anxious.

The aggressive, gratingly warm voice says, "Don't look a gift horse in the mouth, love. Just be. You know? Be and *enjoy*."

Sarah says, "Oh, wait a minute, honey, there's something I wanted to show you." Her voice is so light and she's using such a familiar term for this unknown person.

Michael finds Sarah talking to a heavy-set woman he's never seen before. He doesn't usually have violent reactions to new people, but beyond the smell, something about this person's presence rubs him the wrong way. She's probably in her late fifties, with that close-cropped salt-and-pepper gray hair and that many layered "international" look favored by many aging hippies. She's wearing a Mexican peasant skirt and a Chinese jacket, topped with some chunky amber jewelry with wooden beads. Someone should not fill a room so aggressively, so earthily, in so many different textures. Yet Sarah's happy and seems more relaxed around this person than Michael has seen her in his short time home.

He musters some cheer. "Good morning . . . "

Sarah's face lights up when she sees him. "Good morning! Michael, this is . . . "

"Greta Ohmann, 13D. Sarah and I met a few days after you left, and since then, we've been like a couple of schoolgirls."

The idea of Sarah as one of a couple of schoolgirls is so nonsensical that he snorts. He's met with no encouragement, so he sobers for their benefit.

He extends a hand. "I'm Michael Gould."

Greta takes Michael's hand amid a clatter of multicultural bangles and holds it in hers in a lingering, intrusive way. Her palm is warm and fleshy. He tries to extract it, but Greta doesn't let go. Trying to complete the correct sequence of handshake to get his hand back, Michael shakes hers again, saying, "Nice to meet you."

Greta clings, saying, "God you look awful." She bulldozes on, not giving him a chance to react. "You have no idea how glad I am that you're here." She pauses, looking at him quizzically. She turns his hand sideways, weighing it in hers, measuring him up. He opens his mouth to say something but can't think of anything appropriate.

Greta releases his hand as if she were waiting for it to be her choice instead of his. "Sarah has missed you so and she's been through so much, with everything." She leans in close, her perfume choking him. Her tone is that of a confidential gossip. Her cold gray eyes hold his and he's afraid to look away. "It was a very difficult labor, you know."

Michael realizes that this awful woman is privy not only to something he shouldn't have missed but also something he hasn't yet discussed with his wife. This stranger is too intimate with the details of Tim's birth.

Greta moves to the counter and gets down a mug. She pours some coffee and hands it to him. "Black, right?" *How does she know?* She goes into the silver drawer and gets out a spoon. She opens another cabinet, gets down the sugar, and spoons some into her own coffee. He doesn't like how this woman moves about his kitchen as if it belongs to her. He notices, with some irritation, that she's drinking out of the DADDY mug that Sarah gave to him to announce her pregnancy.

Greta says, as if solving some problem Michael doesn't know about, "I think the trick here would be to keep you two close. As close as you were before"—she sips her coffee, which feels like a cheap, theatrical pause, and stares at Michael—"before the baby." How many details of his life has Sarah shared with this woman? Michael is seething. Has Sarah hired a couple's counselor? Did they need one? How could she not discuss this with him?

Greta, as if she's come to some sort of conclusion, announces, "She really needs to work on her *muladhara chakra*." She throws a conspiratorial smile to Sarah who timidly returns it, "Or so I keep telling her. A little sexual healing oughta help that right along." This woman has to go. He has no idea how she charmed her way into Sarah's good will, but she does *not* belong here. He's home now, he'll take care of this.

Icily, Michael says, "Thank you for your concern, but that's none of your business." Surely he's right to be angry? Sarah's giving him a look he can't interpret.

Greta laughs, grabbing her things to go as if she can hear Michael thinking *Leave now.* "Oh, honey, you'll get used to me. I promise. Soon enough we'll be like old friends. I'd better go and leave you two lovebirds to it." She doesn't put the mug down.

Sarah starts to walk her to the door, but Greta waves her off. "Oh no, dear, I'll let myself out." She turns to Sarah and says, "I'll see *you* later."

Sarah leans in and kisses her on the cheek saying, "I look forward to it." Such warmth and familiarity with someone Sarah met only two weeks ago isn't normal. It just isn't. Sarah says, "Bye," and squeezes Greta's hand meaningfully. "And thanks."

"No problem hon." Greta gives Sarah a pointed look with her steely gray eyes. "You two get *busy*." She sashays out the door.

Michael looks after her incredulously as his DADDY mug leaves the apartment for parts unknown. "Who the hell *is* that woman?"

The fondness in Sarah's face falls into a frown at his anger, and she doesn't respond.

He retreats to the kitchen to drink his coffee.

Sarah sits down across from him. She has a glow about her, a mild gleam in her eyes. He'd like to think it was because of last night's sex, but he has a growing fear that it's because of her time with Greta. This is the look that she used to get when discussing a particularly exciting case. His jealousy feels too familiar. This is a thrill about a part of her life that doesn't include him. But his jealousy fades when he sees her worried expression.

"She's great," Sarah says. "She's great." Not with an air of contentment, but warning him not to argue. This galls him further.

He says, "She took my mug."

Sarah laughs, chiding him. "She'll bring it back."

He says, "How did she become so familiar so fast?"

"You were gone." He can tell she feels bad the moment she's said it. "I'm sorry. Greta came up with some banana bread and baby advice and we sort of went from there."

"Don't you think it's a little weird how she just moved in?"

She goes on the defensive. "She was a lactation consultant and a doula for years. Now she . . . she . . . " Sarah trails off.

Michael sighs and stops. His anger isn't helping things and clearly Sarah got something she needed from this woman. Something he wasn't there to give her.

He takes the moment to lighten things. "So this woman I don't even know has seen your breasts?"

She shoves him on the shoulder. "It's not like that."

"You *hate* doulas."

"I never said I hated them."

"Yes you did." He catches himself. His DADDY mug, this new woman. The raw jealousy and irritation he feels are like something out of the fourth grade.

They pause. Sarah looks at him a moment, smiling, amused by his jealousy. She knows him too well. A sudden, worried look crosses her face. Her eyes well up with tears.

Michael says, "Honey, are you okay?"

She laughs, wiping her eyes. "Hormones. Crazy." She looks at him again and cups his face in her hands. "I'm so glad you're here." She kisses him.

When they pull apart, Michael checks his watch.

She says, "Are you expecting someone?" That nervous tone is back.

"The messenger's supposed to come at ten for the samples from my trip. I should take them downtown myself, but they offered."

Sarah looks around at the mess of a room anxiously and smoothes her hair.

He knows what she's thinking and says, "It's a messenger, honey. He doesn't care what things look like."

She says, "I can't. We can't have anyone see the apartment. And" —she searches for something and the tone in her voice when she comes up with it makes it sound like a child making up a lie—"the baby's not supposed to be around anyone new just yet." He looks at her in disbelief. She adds a hasty, "Germs."

He asks, "What about Herr Greta, there?"

"She's a doula, honey; babies are her business. Please, Michael, no one in the apartment, not yet."

He says, "I'll leave it by the front door."

"In the hallway, with a note?" she says, hopeful.

"This stuff has come too far to be left in the hallway. I'll leave it by the door." He sees that she isn't calming down and fear is growing in her eyes. She has the look of a cornered animal. He finds himself saying anything just to get that look off her face. "I will wait until he rings. I will open the door only enough to push the case out. I will close it quickly."

She appears relieved. Tim squalls from directly behind them, making Michael jump. Sarah seems undisturbed. He realizes that the baby monitor is on the counter. Sarah grabs his hand, a mischievous smile creeping across her face. "I've been talking with Greta and she says it's okay if you hold the baby." She pulls him out of his chair and leads him down the hallway.

Michael sputters in indignation. *Why wouldn't it be?* Greta dwells in and rules the realm of baby, where clearly, he has not yet been initiated.

"He was having stranger anxiety. Once he gets used to you, he'll be fine." Her tone is soothing, as if she's speaking to a child; this bothers him.

"I don't understand."

In the nursery, Tim's little fists shake and his feet kick and he's an unnatural shade of red. His cries are so deep they seem to shake his body, too big to be created by something so tiny.

Sarah says, "Go ahead, pick him up." She hangs a burp rag over Michael's shoulder. He picks up the squirming thing in his arms. He's so little and fragile, yet so violent. Michael tries to nestle the baby's head against the burp rag. The child starts beating his head against his father's chest, like a bird looking for something.

Sarah says, "Oh, he's hungry." She sounds so matter-of-fact, as if this infant child bashing his face into people like a blind lunatic is a normal thing.

Such a feeling of helplessness rises in Michael that he needs to hand the child off. Now.

But before he can, Sarah moves over to a bottle warmer and pulls out a clear plastic bottle. He looks at her, confused.

She says, "I pumped."

Ick. It's his first reaction but he doesn't say it. He takes the bottle, warm with a liquid that came from his wife. Throughout their lovemaking and all of their illnesses, he thought they'd experienced all the fluids each had to offer, but clearly not. Instinctively, he turns the bottle upside down into the feeding position. Drops of this mysterious liquid cling to the plastic after the rest has moved down to the nipple. It oozes slowly away from the sides like a viscous oil. A fine, grainy residue remains once the liquid has moved on. Chalk dust. Milk dust. Future bones.

Michael cradles the thrashing boy in the crook of his arm.

Sarah says, "Watch his head." She helps Michael guide the bottle to the baby's mouth. Tim starts to suck greedily, in alarming gulps. Michael looks to Sarah, panicked that the child will drown, but she's unconcerned. She nudges Michael's shoulders and pushes him back toward the rocker next to the crib. He sits down and the gulps relax into a rhythmic sucking. The baby grabs onto his father's pinkie and his wise eyes roll back into his head, like a user going into a heroin haze, clearly in heaven over this ambrosia.

Sarah says, "He likes our song. You know, the one you used to sing to me? That dream one."

Michael starts singing to the baby, his voice startling him in this new space, the rocking chair in his child's nursery. *"When you were little, you dreamed you were big, you must have been something, a real tiny kid. You wish you were me, I wish I was you . . . "*

This is so weird. This is so great. Sarah pets Michael's hair gently, stroking the side of his face. Michael feels that she's happy and this calms him. All of the strangeness and irritability he'd been feeling melt away and he falls into the wonder snuggling down in his arms.

———

There's a knock at the door, but Sarah doesn't get that spinning feeling this time. No growing darkness. No cold. This person won't come in. She lets Michael go take care of it—he has to give them something. She doesn't re-member what, but she knows she was okay with it. Mostly, she remembers that for right now, he won't leave.

He'll find out about her eventually, but the longer she can keep him around, the more she can get him attached to Tim, the more likely he'll choose to stay once he does find out. He doesn't know Tim yet. She has to facilitate that. Watching Michael feed the baby filled her with such joy, she almost forgot how they got here. She could pretend for a moment that she'd lived. That she and Tim and Michael were starting out their new life together. They are, but it's different from what she'd imagined.

"Don't look a gift horse in the mouth." Greta was right. It's better this way.

When the messenger comes, Michael absent-mindedly shoves the case out the door and closes it, eager to get back to this newfound world. Sarah's weirdness over the exchange seems nothing but an unpleasant memory. He heads into the nursery, where he finds himself confronted with his first diaper change. He's not prepared for this. He doesn't know what he expected from baby poop, but it certainly wasn't this thick, nasty mustard sauce that has filled every nook and corner of the diaper. It has a vague vinegar smell. Just as he starts to wipe at it, more starts coming out of the child's behind, like someone is squeezing a tube of toothpaste way too fast. He's horrified. "Oh. Oh, God, that's awful. Honey!" He yells for help even though Sarah's right behind him.

She laughs as she steps in and quickly closes the diaper over the boy, whose red face is contorted from the effort. She refastens the Velcro, announcing, "Disaster averted." That first bottle did it. Sarah's becoming more relaxed. Less edgy.

Michael sees that the stuff has started coming out the legs of the diaper. "I don't know about that." He looks up at his wife who has a patient, amused look on her face. She's rubbing the boy's belly and clucking to him. There's a "mom" look in her eyes. Part weary, part patient, all kind. It's odd to see something completely different and new in this person he knows better than anyone. Even when she was uber-Sarah, pregnant queen of the universe, this side of her didn't exist yet.

A strand of her hair comes loose and curls around her cheek. She hasn't got a stitch of makeup on, but he doesn't think he's ever seen her more beautiful. Her green eyes shine bluish in the morning light and he can count the feathers in her irises. The angles of her face are soft and there are tiny smile lines around her eyes. And here they both are,

Michael and Sarah, hovering over this erratic, charming, revolting, amazing and appalling creature that is their son.

Sarah's suddenly all business. "I think he's done." The diaper has to weigh over a pound. Michael, armed with a wipe, goes in, but doesn't know quite where to start. Sarah stands back, folding her arms as a sign that she isn't going to help.

He implores, "Oh, come on."

"Listen, Mister, I mastered it on my own. You can start from scratch, too." She sits down, rocking nonchalantly. She snorts as he goes through five wipes without blinking. He does not seem to be making a dent in the sludge.

He's exasperated. "Wouldn't it be easier to give him a bath?" She laughs.

Michael's up to fifteen wipes by the time he's done. But now he's enjoying it. Tim looks up at him, quizzical, little crossed eyes, his eyebrows forming a fuzzy, nearly naked caterpillar across his brow. Michael's gradually becoming accustomed to his son's tiny body, but his skin is red and scaly with a yellowish hue to it. His nose seems to be covered with tiny raised yellow bumps that look like scales on a lizard. "Is he . . . supposed to be this color?"

She laughs again. "You are funny."

Michael says, "I mean, he doesn't look like he's got real skin yet. Does he need lotion or something?"

Sarah gets up and puts her arm around her husband, looking at Tim who squirms happily atop the changing table. "He is funny-looking. But it's normal. That peaches and cream complexion only comes with time." She reaches across the changing table for a white strap with a plastic clip. There's a matching one on the front; she fastens it like a seat belt across the baby's belly.

Michael says, "What, is he driving somewhere?"

She says, "Have to get in the habit. In a few months, he'll be able to roll off."

"Where did you get all this stuff? Did they give you courses before you left the hospital?"

She says, "I didn't have anything to do but read books. It made me less nervous while you were gone." Michael knows she's not trying to give him a guilt trip, but still, it stings.

They lay Tim in the middle of the giant bed in their room, surround him with pillows, and put on some Mozart, which is supposed to develop the baby's math skills. Michael looks at the beautiful, helpless, troll-like creature that is his son and doubts his mathematical abilities. But the music is soothing and breathes living air back into the apartment. The music makes him feel less cut off from the world.

He should call into work. He'll do it tomorrow. Caroline will take care of the report. He needs to call Caroline, too. He hasn't even charged his phone yet.

They're so comfortable here and he was supposed to take paternity leave anyway.

Sarah curls up on one side of Tim, Michael on the other. She looks at Michael and strokes his face. This is more like what he'd been waiting for. Not the discord and alienation. Tim lets out one final squawk and kicks his legs before settling in and sucking his fist. His eyes drift back in his head and he closes them. As if Sarah's still connected to Tim by an umbilical cord, her eyes droop as well, her breathing grows regular, and she falls asleep.

Michael watches them. After a few minutes, Sarah's eyes dart back and forth beneath her closed lids, but her expression remains peaceful. Tim solves the problems of the world with starts and grunts, while his lips make sucking sounds that let his father know his dreams are at least nourishing. Michael wonders if their dreams are connected, too.

He marvels at them until the warmth from the sunlight streaming in the open window, the music and the spring air lull him into a doze.

There's a knock at the front door and Michael wakes. It's getting dark outside. He feels a chill and pulls a blanket up over Sarah and Tim, who sleep on.

The second knock is louder. Michael rubs his eyes and scrambles down the hall as quickly as he can, weighing which will be louder: a shout of "Coming!" or another knock. He gets to the door in time and opens it. It squeaks with an infuriatingly loud groan in their echoing hallway.

It's Mrs. Grady from downstairs, holding a casserole dish. Her thick bifocals magnify a worried look. She's wearing a gold-and-green-paisley housecoat, which probably dates back to the early sixties. The pink slippers, judging by the amount of dirt on them, are maybe only a few years old.

Michael says, "Hi there." He's trying to sound as if he hasn't just woken up. It's not working.

Mrs. Grady says, "See, I knew you were home early. No one was expecting you for another week and they said your phone wasn't going through, but I knew you were home." She pushes the glass casserole dish, crumpled, probably re-used tin foil clinging to its edges, into his hands. It's cold from the fridge.

Then she says something odd: "You poor thing." Her glasses give Michael the feeling he's being investigated with a magnifying glass. He self-consciously straightens his hair; he must look a fright. He can see Mrs. Grady decide against saying something meaningful. Instead, all business, she says, "Forty-five minutes at three-fifty should do it."

"I'm sorry?"

"If you like, cut it up and put it in Tupperware in the freezer to last you longer. You look like you haven't had a proper meal in weeks." Her words catch in her throat and she puts her hand on his forearm,

"God bless you, Michael." Her eyes fill with tears. Michael has a random fear that he's starting to have this effect on everyone.

He says, "Uh, thank you. Are you okay, Mrs. Grady?"

Her chin rises in a pout of concern one would give a child; it becomes apparent that she's left her dentures out. She raises her hand to Michael's face and clicks softly with her tongue. She turns to go and he can hear her muttering to herself and sniffling as she shuffles down the hall.

"Michael?" It's Sarah. She's awake.

He closes the door quickly, feeling caught. He wants to avoid whatever craziness Sarah was having yesterday and a quick shutting of the door seems like the answer.

She comes down the hallway and slips her arms around him, kissing him on the shoulder. She says, "Why'd you get up? It was so snuggly in there."

He says, "Mrs. Grady brought us a"—he holds it up and sees cheese and red sauce through the side of the glass—"lasagna?"

He feels her hands go stiff and she steps back. "Really."

Either some feud has developed with their old-lady neighbor while he was gone or Sarah has gotten weird about company. Michael figures it's the latter.

"I don't understand, honey, am I supposed to not answer the door because we have a baby? Because I read all the same books you did and I didn't read anything about shutting out the world."

Sarah laughs nervously, but he can tell that she's performing for his benefit. She asks her next question carefully, "What did she say?"

He says, "Not much. Just directions for how to cook it. Then she started to cry." He muses over this last part, but then realizes he should have left it out.

Sarah doesn't say anything. Michael hears Tim's voice from the other room. Not a cry, but the early staccato *huh-huh-huh* that means crying is about to happen.

But Sarah stands there, clearly still stewing. Michael tries to keep it light. "Weddings and babies. My grandmother used to cry at grammar school graduations."

This seems to satisfy her. "Right. I'd better . . . " And she's off down the hallway. It seems like he doesn't even know what he's trying to accomplish when he talks to her anymore. But if she leaves a conversation soothed, he feels he's done his job. *Why?*

The phone rings. Sarah flinches as if she's heard gunfire. Michael heads to the telephone, but Sarah whispers, her voice sounding downright creepy in their high-ceilinged hallway. "Don't answer it."

Michael says, "Oh, *really*." This is their stock, "I'm going to do it anyway" phrase. He heads toward the phone. He doesn't hear her follow him, so he's surprised to find her hand clamp onto his before he can reach the telephone. Her hand is icy cold.

She's looking at the caller I.D. She says, "It's Anna."

"Since when are you not talking to your sister?"

"Don't answer it."

He looks at her, worried.

She rolls her eyes to assuage his fear, but he knows she's hiding something. *But why?* She says, "Honey, we had a huge fight. It's nothing. We're not talking. But it's nothing. I don't want you to get in the middle of it." She looks at him too anxiously, waiting for his reaction. When he lifts his hand from the phone he sees her relax. Then the machine kicks in.

Hi, it's Sarah. And Michael. We're not here right now, but please leave a message. The end of the message is Sarah laughing. Michael had tickled her at the time.

He smiles at this. "We need to change the message. It's not only Sarah and Michael anymore." *Beep.*

"Hi, Michael? It's Anna." She sounds anxious. "Are you home yet? Your cell phone isn't working for some reason and . . . I need you to call me the minute you get back. Please." Her voice cracks as she starts crying. "Oh. God. I'm sorry. That message." *Click.*

Michael says, "She sounds upset."

"I'll call her tomorrow," Sarah says flatly.

He's surprised by her callousness. "What could you possibly have fought about that would be that bad?"

She sounds regretful. "I love her so much."

"Then call her!"

"I want to. But I can't. I can't."

She heads off down the hall. Tim has given up his "huh-huh" and gone quiet again; maybe he comforted himself back to sleep.

Sarah and Anna have always been pretty intense together, but they haven't fought in years. Michael will talk to Sarah about it tomorrow. He takes the lasagna to the kitchen and puts it in the oven, turning it to three-fifty. He can't remember the last time he ate anything more than cereal. It will be good to have something homemade.

Tim's cry echoes down the hallway. The first cry doesn't have her racing to him, only waking and sitting up. Her heart still pounds more quickly, and she's wide awake, but it isn't as alarming as in the past. Michael rolls over in his sleep. She wonders if he dreams.

Her own dreams have become different. Even though her pregnant dreams were strange, they were still based in reality. Her dreams now are abstractions. Some filled with darkness and fear. Others with light, color, and a growing hope. And always the talking. Someone talking but she can't quite hear them. She tries so hard to make it out, but whenever she gets close, it fades, or Tim cries.

She goes to Tim. His cry is more cranky than distressed. She lifts him over her shoulder, moves across the room and sits in the rocker, bringing him to her breast. The handy nursing gown makes for easy access, two hidden slits down the front reminding her of her primary job. That first suction and letting down of milk is still sudden and painful. There's a sharp pull around her nipple as he latches on, the prickling creeping down the sides of her breasts as her milk comes in. She read and heard about how nursing is the most wholesome, wonderful thing a mother can do, but Sarah feels like Tim's parasitic suckling can only be unnatural. Once they settle in together they're okay, but Tim doesn't stare at her with his loving, clear eyes as he does when they're playing together. He's gone off to the land of milk, where he dwells alone.

And Sarah's left to think. Which is not a good thing.

The thing Sarah didn't count on was other people. This afternoon she felt hopeful about keeping the truth from Michael. They could build a little cocoon and get to know each other as a family. But with the call from Anna and Mrs. Grady's need to needle her way into every neighbor's life with her fucking lasagna, she knows the outside world won't stay away for long. They'll all start calling and wanting to come over—her sister, her mother, Michael's mother. Oh, God, their friends.

Sarah feels a stab of fear followed by a tingle at the back of her scalp. She's suddenly cold and the edges of the room fade into darkness. Tim has a startled look on his face and she realizes that she's breathing too quickly. She needs to calm down for the baby. She starts to sing, "Every dream has a name, and names tell your story. This song is your dream . . . "

After a moment, Tim is soothed, the room comes back into focus, and Sarah is present again.

As she sings, she remembers Greta's words, All that matters is that you are here with your baby. And she has to keep Michael close. Just two things to remember. She can keep track of two things. She used to be in charge of entire cases, held entire law books in her head. She could summon deep wells of knowledge to bring into arguments in front of a judge and a jury.

Tim's blinking, drowsy. Sarah lays him in his crib where he snuggles down, his head falling to the side. He stares at the pattern on the bassinet, soothing himself to sleep. Sarah heads back to bed. She's bone tired. She doesn't think she's ever been so tired. She's lost the sensation of tasting, and a lot of the sensation of touch, so why is she so exhausted in such a body-bound way?

By the time Michael's finished changing Tim's diaper later that night, he realizes the baby won't make it to dawn without needing another one. Which they don't have. So, with Sarah sleeping peacefully, Michael grabs some clothes out of the bathroom and slips them on in the hall. Slamming his elbow into the wall, he stifles a curse. He's still too big for this narrow space. He picks up his wallet, shoves the entire crumpled plastic diaper package into his pocket for reference and sneaks out the front door.

He's gone. Sarah wasn't supposed to let him leave.

Michael's lost in thought as he steps onto the elevator and presses the button.

A woman says, "And where are you going at this hour?" He wheels around to see Greta standing behind him. He doesn't remember anyone being on the elevator when he got on.

"Uh, hi. Diapers."

She has a smile on her face, but anger over something flickers in her eyes. He doesn't understand. Maybe she had a fight with the mister. Does Greta have a mister?

She says, "You shouldn't leave your wife, you know. She had a hard time of it. She's in a fragile state."

Who the hell is this woman? Michael says, "We're out of diapers. I need to get some more."

There's a pause, but Michael finds himself fuming at the intrusion. The elevator stops on the fourth floor. Greta gets off and turns around, holding the door open. She looks at him steadily and says, "Stay close to your wife, Michael. This has all been very hard on her."

He holds her gaze and says steadily, "I'm going to go get some diapers now. You have a good night." As the door closes, he can see she's shaking her head as she shuffles off down the hall.

Michael has been inside the apartment for so long that he's invigorated by just the sound of his footsteps on the marble floor of the empty lobby. As he steps outside, the cool, night air is downright liberating. There's a light breeze off the river, and things are as quiet as they can be only at this time of night in Manhattan, and then, only in certain neighborhoods. He heads down toward the Duane Reade on Broadway. The city that never sleeps seems to be in slumber now, not even a cab to be seen. The breeze picks up as he passes a transplanted maple sticking up out of cigarette stub-littered, wrought iron grating. It won't ever grow to its potential. The grate itself isn't optimistic, leaving room for a trunk only a foot across. But he finds solace in the sound of its rustling leaves. Sarah has always been a city girl. Michael immediately loved her sharpness, her humor, her ability to find a great restaurant in any urban neighborhood. He challenged her on this one, taking her to lost neighborhoods in Chicago, Boston, Philadelphia. But Sarah would always find a place, whether a mom-and-pop restaurant, a sandwich stand, or a chain that happened to be famous for one specific dish. They haven't had a bad meal yet.

Michael grew up in a dumpy little town in New Jersey that didn't have much to offer by way of urbane culture. There was a terrible Chinese restaurant called Yum-Yum next to the local bowling alley; there was a small library and a grocery store and a run-down pharmacy his parents jokingly called Mr. Gower's. Anything else and you'd have to go to the next town over. But none of this mattered, because for Michael, life was the outdoors. When he was a boy, the only thing that would pull him into the house from the woods in summer was food and drink. He spent hours exploring, collecting rocks or perched under a favorite tree, reading a book. Giant maples that had room to breathe, not these lackluster ailing street types. *We'll take Tim hiking. Maybe we'll get a cabin for summer. A boy needs to run, explore.*

The lights on Broadway are unforgiving compared to the quiet of the side streets. Once inside the pharmacy, Michael blinks like a startled frog. He goes up and down the aisles and finds himself in the shaving section. He laughs, realizing that this is the only section of the store he's familiar with. This and feminine products, when Sarah was stuck at work and needed *supplies*. Otherwise, she always did the shopping.

He walks along the aisles reading his choices, *Antacids, Analgesics,* and eventually finds his way to the baby aisle. Everything is lit up with colors: bright plastic tubs of wipes, yellow baby shampoo, green bottles of soap shaped like fish, pacifiers and teething rings. The diapers loom in stacks, an array of red and purple and teal packages. The variety is enough to overwhelm the ordinary man, but Michael came prepared. He pulls out the crumpled purple wrapper from his pocket and finds the corresponding package of new ones. *N.* For *newborn.* For *new.* He picks up two packages of wipe refills for good measure.

Sarah paces the apartment, gnawing on her nails, trying not to hear Tim screaming in the nursery. He won't stop.

Michael was here. She knows he was here. They made love. And his clothes are on the floor where he shed them. She can't have confused that. But he's gone. For ages, he's been gone, and she can't figure out where to.

Tim's been crying. A lot. It's not that needy newborn crying, but an angry cry. He knows Michael's gone. She tried feeding him. He won't take the breast. Burping him. But nothing helps. He's turned into this wretched little ball of red and wet, thrashing in his crib. She curses the high ceilings of the apartment for making his cries echo in jerky, repetitive, Hnyeah! Hnyeah! Hnyeah! It's frightening and he's not letting up. She's crawling out of her skin.

Maybe Michael got tired of them. Maybe he can't face the idea of caring for a baby. Greta said that making love "cinched the deal."

She cinched the deal.

And he left. And she doesn't like how cold it's getting and how strange and how the baby won't stop crying.

She has to go to the baby. It's the only job she has.

Michael's so focused on unlocking the door quietly that when he swings it open to find Sarah standing there, seething, he drops the bag of diapers.

Sarah's hair is in disarray; half of it has fallen out of its clip and hangs in hanks around her neck, the other half is still up, making her look disjointed. Her face is frightening, her pupils enormous and the rings under her eyes brought into relief by the light from the hallway. Her cheekbones stand out like shelves.

"Where the *hell* were you?" She's not yelling, she's hissing a whisper, but she might as well be yelling.

Michael realizes there aren't any lights on in the apartment. And Sarah's wearing an ugly, cornflower-blue jersey nursing nightgown, and judging by the freezing temperature in the room, it isn't healthy for her to be so exposed. Her legs look unnaturally pale and spindly.

When he pulls himself together enough to talk, Michael says, "We were out of diapers." He scrambles to pick up the packages and close the door before the neighbors see this wraith giving a pale impression of his wife. The door closes, plunging them into shadow.

He says, "What are you doing here in the dark?

She snarls, "You were gone for *weeks*! What was I supposed to think?"

The orange streetlamps shine up through the windows, casting odd shadows on the walls. He knows his apartment well enough to get around in this dim light, but Sarah's condition frightens him into turning on the light.

"Weeks?"

Sarah turns away from him as if he'd said something stupid. She looks worse in the light. This doesn't look like a change that can have come over his pliant, weary but glowing wife in half an hour. It's more like she's been in prison for a few months, doing hard labor. Her chest is heaving, making the pits in her neck above her clavicles go deep and shallow in turns, which makes her look even more gaunt.

"You need to get a blanket or something," he says. "Honey, is the heat even on in here?" The thermostat is turned up to seventy, but the temperature reads fifty-five. He taps on it. What a time for the goddamned heat to go out. "Shit. Is the baby warm enough?"

Sarah turns on him. "How can you act like *nothing* happened? Where have you been?"

He walks over to her. She's shaking with rage. He doesn't know how she got so disheveled since this sunshiny afternoon. He grabs a blanket from the sofa and wraps it around her shoulders, pulling her in for a hug. She's freezing.

She breathes into his neck, "I don't understand." He sinks onto the sofa, holding her, thinking that maybe Greta was right, he shouldn't have left. Is this postpartum depression? He heard things could get weird with chemical changes after childbirth. Maybe this is just that.

He kisses her. She's shaking, but starts to calm. He starts talking into her hair in a soothing voice as if to the baby. "I was gone twenty minutes, honey. We were totally out of diapers and I didn't want to be shorthanded at four in the morning, so I went to get some more. I came back as soon as I could. You're fine. We're fine. You probably just woke up disoriented. I'm so sorry, I should have left a note."

The radiator starts to clank, maybe just the heat kicking in.

He says, "There, now. Is the baby warm enough?"

"The baby is warm enough." She says this impatiently as if it never should have been a concern. This puzzles him. Things that seemed important no longer are and things that meant nothing have taken on life-shaking proportions. Sarah says, "I didn't know if you were coming back."

He looks into her eyes, which seems to calm her. "I always come back. Across continents and oceans I come back. I can't help it. It's a compulsion."

She's beyond a laugh, but has relaxed now. He pulls the blanket more tightly around her and rubs warmth back into her limbs.

THREE

Michael and Tim are sleeping, but Sarah knows by the pressure and heat in her breasts that he's past due for a feeding. She knows it's pointless to try to sleep, so she paces the living room. For the first time, her body is crying for Tim and not the reverse.

How is she supposed to keep Michael close when he keeps disappearing? She never knows how long he'll be gone, or if he'll come back. She has never before been so completely at a loss for answers. She always had answers. She was the one people turned to for answers and when she didn't know something, she knew where to look it up. There was nothing she couldn't handle. But this—the way she is so completely lost in this new world—this unmoors her.

Greta materializes next to her, wearing a concerned pout. It should be galling, but it seems genuine. She puts her hand up to Sarah's face and says, "It's going to be okay." This is comforting, but Sarah's unnerved by the fact that Greta knew she was worried.

Greta gently pushes past her and plants herself on the sofa with a foof. She pats the sofa next to her. Sarah sits. It feels good to sit. What she can feel *and can't feel is a tricky area of her new existence that she tries not to question. While she can sense the comfort in sitting, the sofa is farther away from her. She runs her bare feet along the fringed edge of the carpet, but she can't quite touch it. Something whispers across her toes, or maybe she's just remembering how it used to feel.*

Sarah says, "I don't know how to keep him with me."

"You're doing fine."

"But he left and was gone for ages."

Greta says, "He comes back. You just need to work a little harder at keeping him here."

Shame rises to Sarah's cheeks. Greta's words remind Sarah of her mother's passive-aggressive mode of criticizing her. Sarah says, "He snuck out on me. In the night. How was I supposed to help that? We were out of diapers. Of course he went to get some."

Greta chuckles, amused. She rubs Sarah's back in small circles. It's warming, and good to feel something real. Despite herself, Sarah relaxes. Greta says, "You need to keep him with you. You need to keep him with the baby." The resonance of Greta's voice makes Sarah feel blanketed in calm. "Sarah. The longer you keep him with you, the longer you keep Tim with him, the more likely all of you can be together."

"But we are together."

Greta smiles. "I mean together for good."

Forever? It sounds frightening and inviting at the same time. Greta pulls out a rectangular tin and hands it to Sarah, who takes it uncertainly. Greta says, "Give this to him every evening before bed. And every morning when he wakes up."

"The baby?"

Greta laughs. Why is she always so certain when Sarah is so confused? Greta says, "No, honey, to Michael."

"Why does Michael need this?"

"It will help. Keep him near."

Sarah weighs the cold metal tin in her hand. The tin is dark green, worn around the edges and sticky with kitchen grime. Whenever Greta gives her something, it feels more real than anything else around her. She says, "I don't understand."

"Honey, Michael is helping keep Tim with us." Sarah doesn't like the use of the word "us." Greta's eyes light up. She looks full of a mother's pride as she says, "He's growing! Have you seen how he grows?"

Do other babies not grow? Isn't that what babies do? Sarah starts worrying again and a cold rock of panic seizes her chest. What does Greta mean, "They don't stay?" Where would he go? Is he not supposed to grow?

But Greta starts talking in that voice that draws fuzziness over the worry. "You will work to keep Michael with you, as best you can. The closer you keep him, the better your chances are. The tea will help. Once in the morning. Once in the evening. All that matters is that you are with your baby and your husband."

Michael makes sure to spell it out for her this time. He's going out. He will get some groceries. He will be back. She acts as if she doesn't understand why he's making such a big deal out of food. This nursing mother who should be eating everything under the sun.

Sarah took a shower this morning and her wet hair is pulled back. It emphasizes the shadows of exhaustion on her face, but at least her washed hair and scrubbed skin make her look like she's back in the realm of sanity. She's wearing a silk shirt and a pair of business trousers.

Michael attempts nonchalance. "You going somewhere, honey? You're all dressed up."

She ignores his question and says, "You don't need to go out." She seems so together, so matter-of-fact, as if last night never happened.

He says, "I want to be sure you understand."

She wells up a bit. "Don't talk to me like I'm a child. Stay home. We'll order in."

He tries very hard not to roll his eyes. "There are no groceries here, honey. You haven't had anything fresh since I got home. I'm afraid to even look in the refrigerator. We need to do some serious shopping. I'll be gone only half an hour. Now what do you need?"

Sarah throws out one more protest. "You don't *have* to go out." She sounds melodramatic. She sinks to the sofa in defeat; the momentary hold she had on reality is leaving her again. Michael can feel it.

He sits down next to her and looks over at Tim, who's sleeping happily in his swing. The plastic arm rocks slowly, giving off a very faint rhythm as the motor goes around. It can't be good for the kid's sleep, all that movement. There's a safety arm holding Tim in, as if he's locked in for an amusement park ride: one that would likely take him upside down, because it clicks shut not only across the baby but between his legs. There's a plastic rattle hanging from the crossbar, which clacks slightly with each backswing. *Clack. Clack. Clack.* An unnerving metronome to their conversation.

Michael rubs Sarah's back, carefully asking again, "Honey? What can I get for you at the store?"

He's never had such trouble understanding her before. It used to be that when they were headed into an argument, he sensed where it was going. Now he has no idea, so he waits for her to talk.

She's exasperated, but it beats angry. "I don't even know what to say anymore."

Michael sees that with each backward clack, the swing wobbles. He walks around it to investigate and says, "Sweetie, I'm asking what kind of food you'd like to eat. You know." He closes his eyes and makes a tasting noise with his mouth. This is a joke between them. One of them will make a tasting noise. *Smack, smack, smack . . . mmmm . . . pizza,* as if tasting what he or she would like to be eating at that moment.

She puts her hands to her face. "I don't know!" There's a comic tone to her voice that lets Michael know that she understands she's being ridiculous.

He laughs softly. "Do you want to come with me? We could try out that Baby Bjorn carrier strappy thingy. Maybe a walk would do you some good."

She gives him a look as if he's suggested roasting the baby on a spit for dinner. "I . . . I can't believe you'd even say that."

One leg of the swing isn't fully pushed into its holder. Michael grasps it and slides it in, realizing that the apparatus was merely resting on the edge of the tube for the stand and the entire thing was in danger of capsizing with every swing. He's angry that Sarah missed this, then angry that he didn't check it. But he keeps his voice cheerful. "I've seen newborns out all the time with their moms."

"I can't, Michael. I can't." She says this last part with an end-of-discussion resolve. Apparently there's no argument.

He tries to speak clearly. "Then tell me, honey, what you'd like to eat. You've got to keep your milk up and I've hardly seen you eat anything since you got home."

"Greta's been bringing me infant-friendly meals." This sounds too awful to be a lie, but something about the way she says it doesn't ring right.

Michael says, "Well, I'm home now, honey. I'm going to the grocery store. I'm buying things." But she's not looking at him. He turns to a forced casual voice and holds up an imaginary order form and pencil, putting on a cheesy French accent in a feeble attempt at comic relief. "What can I get for the lady zis evening?"

She throws her arms up. "Whatever you want to get is fine. I. Don't. Care."

"Fine." He grabs his coat and heads to the door. He stops at the table to pick up his phone, but he still hasn't charged it. How could he not have charged his stupid phone? He'd heard that all thought goes out the door when a newborn enters the house, but he didn't believe it until now. He plugs it into the cord by the front table. He has to call Caroline to tell her the samples got there. She'll be back in a few days, and since she's handling the report on her own, the least he can do is check in. And he could use a good talk with her. Caroline's humor and common sense will provide some perspective.

Sarah says, "Don't go."

Michael turns around and, for good measure, throws out an "I love you." It is more a reminder than a heartfelt comment, as if the fact itself should make things better. He leaves her sitting on the sofa, staring vacantly at the boy in the swing. At least the swing is stable now.

Clack.

Clack.

Clunk. The door closes heavily behind him, the carpeted quiet of the hallway mercifully obliterating the clacking of the swing. He feels relief for leaving and then guilt for that relief.

———

Sarah tried. She did try. What could she do? Throw her arms around his legs and weep? Obviously the tea wasn't going to work after only one cup in the morning. And all of her power for argument, which had made her such a brilliant litigator, has been reduced to "You don't have to go. We don't need anything. Don't go."

She should have freaked out, pulled a knife, threatened to harm the baby. Okay, not good ideas, but all something, *something more than "Don't go."*

They could have ordered groceries. Idiot. She never said that. She should have said that.

The trip to Duane Reade for diapers was three weeks. How long will this outing take?

———

He's beginning to worry that the food thing might be about body image. Sarah made such a big deal of gaining weight for the baby, how much she gained each week and where on her body it showed. She was a professional woman with a lean, suited look, and this loss of control got to her. Knowing how Sarah hates to lose control, and knowing how out of control her life has become worries Michael. Not eating is a definite control thing. Of course she's been eating *something*, but a nursing woman is supposed to have an insatiable appetite; she's supposed to consume food with a newfound obsession.

He'll buy some fruit. The apples in the bowl have gone brown. He'll buy some sort of soy protein something and tasty things she can eat while she's nursing. He'll get some basics, chicken, beef, some fish. He doesn't understand how two days have passed, and aside from plunking Mrs. Grady's lasagna in the oven, he's barely been in the kitchen. He feels a pang of guilt as he realizes that he left the meat lasagna in the oven last night after eating only one slice. It's spoiled by now. He has to get a handle; groceries are a start.

But once he gets to the elevator, his resolve weakens. He pauses before pushing the button. Looking down the hall, he sees Dr. James's door ajar.

"I'm a shrink, you know."

It would be a safe place to talk about Sarah. He doesn't want to worry their friends. He's thought of calling at least Chuck and Dan, or Sarah's best friend from college, but he hasn't, for fear that they'd want to come over. He can't have them see Sarah this way. She's not ready yet.

He walks toward the door and hears two voices arguing. One is that of a distressed younger man. Dr. James's reply is steady and calming, but patronizing. Michael turns back toward the elevator when the psychiatrist's door opens.

The doctor says, "Ah! Mr. Gould. I'll be with you in a moment." As if he were expecting him.

Shit. Stuck.

Michael waits, trying to look everywhere else but at the uncomfortably intimate scene going on behind the door.

He hears a bratty, impatient, boyish cry. "God, you're such an asshole!"

Dr. James is whispering as if he doesn't want Michael to overhear the conversation. "Milo."

Milo's not playing and is theatrically loud for Michael's benefit. "Let me *by*."

There's an odd, hard-plastic rustle, like a shower curtain being pushed back. Something has physically stopped the boy from moving. Is he wearing a hazmat suit? Milo lets out the frustrated sigh of impatience teenagers usually reserve for their parents.

Dr. James chides, still whispering, "You *will* come to our next session."

Still full volume, Milo replies, "I don't have to fucking listen to you anymore, you *freak*."

"I cannot let you go unless you agree."

There's a pause as he considers. Dr. James is holding the door and Michael can see only his back, but he imagines some sort of staredown is taking place. He wants to interrupt and excuse himself. He wants to slink away. But neither feels like the right thing to do.

The doctor's voice takes on a whispered scolding tone that reminds Michael uncomfortably of Sarah. "Do you agree?"

Michael begins to wonder if Dr. James is even a decent shrink.

Apparently Milo has agreed in some way, because Dr. James swings the door open, revealing a scrawny, tear-stained boy of about fifteen. Incongruously, Dr. James holds up a phone and waves it at Michael. "I'm sorry, I'm on the phone." He puts it to his ear.

When Milo sees Michael, he sneers a victorious smile and says with a European horror movie accent, "Next victim, Doctor." He cackles afterward for effect. His black hair is spiked and his heavy black eyeliner and mascara have run around his enormous brown eyes. He has crushed-petal lips smeared with red lipstick. He looks as if he were born pouting. He wears all black under a clear plastic raincoat. Not a hazmat suit.

The doctor says at a normal volume, "Take care of yourself." He says this in a warning tone, rather than with any good will. He's obviously speaking to Milo, and Michael wonders what the person on the other end of the phone must think. Milo squeezes past the baffled Michael. The doctor stares at Michael, concerned for a moment. Michael turns to look at Milo standing at the elevator, and then back to the doctor who's eyeing him with something like terrified surprise.

The doctor says, "You saw that?" He's probably embarrassed, but his tone implies something more that Michael can't quite discern.

Michael says, "Uh . . . I'm sorry."

Dr. James sounds incredulous. "You saw that."

"I tried to stand back, but the hallway's so small and . . . " He doesn't have anything resembling an answer and starts to get angry that the doctor put him in this situation and is now calling him out on it.

The doctor says, "Please, come in." He smiles warmly and seems anxious to talk. He puts the phone back in its charger without saying goodbye to the person on the other end.

Michael steps into the warm, sunny apartment and realizes he's been freezing since he got home. He needs to talk to the super; there's definitely something wrong with the heat in their apartment.

Michael says, "I'm sorry, I didn't mean to interrupt."

"Nonsense, he was leaving anyway." Dr. James moves a pile of books out of a chair and motions Michael to sit. He seems agitated. "This is most incredible. Sit. Please."

"I'm only going to stay a minute. I . . . " He doesn't know how to start. "I wanted to introduce myself. Formally." But he finds himself sitting anyway.

Dr. James chuckles. "Don't worry, we'll keep this informal. I never charge for consults." He smiles, like Michael won't get the joke.

Michael shifts in his seat. The room is filled with bookshelves, overflowing with paperbacks, hardcovers, old, new, stacked sideways and every which way. There are odd objects stuffed among the books. Some dust-collectors and small-ish pieces of art. But he smiles as he sees a bottle of antacids stacked next to a leather-bound *The Freud Reader*, old mail shoved in among some paperbacks. It's comforting to know a real person lives here. Michael breathes out for what seems the first time in a while. The knot in his chest that he didn't know he had releases a little.

Dr. James puts a cup of coffee on the table in front of him. Michael looks around disoriented, unsure from where he conjured it. Dr. James chuckles. "It's not drugged, I promise. Cream or sugar?"

"Oh, no, black is fine. Of course. I didn't mean . . . " Nothing's coming out right. "I'm just worried."

"About the coffee?" Dr. James lowers himself into a comfortable-looking, leather Morris chair, which sighs under its familiar burden.

Michael's just not in the mood. He wonders if, like Sarah, he's lost his sense of humor.

The doctor seems to understand. "I apologize. My little jokes aren't hitting, are they? How are you holding up, Michael?"

The doctor's manner is warmer and more welcoming than it was in the dark hallway the other night. His eyes, previously obscured by his small, round, horn-rimmed glasses, are blue and watery, but clear and honest. His face is florid and wide, framed by gray sideburns that fade up into reddish-brown hair. He has the presence of an old friend, or at least that of a character actor who always plays the old friend in movie after movie.

Michael feels comfortable enough to talk. "I'm a bit lost. I can't quite get a handle on anything."

The doctor nods understandingly.

"I haven't even called the family yet. I don't think I can face them."

"This is all normal. These are stages you know." The doctor looks like he's solving a logarithm with most of his brain while the listening, professional shrink half has gone on autopilot.

Michael says, "I mean, I can face them, I don't think I can let them see *her* yet." This seems to get the doctor's attention. Michael is sheepish. "New baby. Things get . . . strange."

Dr. James looks concerned and somewhat uncomprehending. But he waits for Michael.

Michael realizes he's been getting ahead of himself. "I'm sorry." This is the first non-Sarah person he's talked to since he's been back. He offers his hand. "Yeah, um. Hi. Michael Gould. I live down the hall. We just had a baby. Well, Sarah did. Sarah's my wife. A boy. Tim."

The doctor leans forward a bit, studying Michael intently over the top of his glasses. "Congratulations." He says this with little emotion. It's probably a shrink thing, being a mirror and such.

Michael starts scrambling, "And it's great. He's totally incredible. And helpless. But my wife . . . " This is stupid. Why is he here? He has to get groceries. "I'm sorry, I don't even know you." He takes a deep breath and starts to stand, then sinks back down. He feels dizzy. Probably sleep deprivation.

Dr. James leans forward, earnest. "Now, now. I told you I'm the hall shrink. Door's open anytime and I believe I told you that. Relax. Continue."

Michael leans back, grateful for another moment to sit. "I'm not sure why I'm here. I've been so . . . at odds. I don't know where I fit in. My wife's moods are, like, off the charts. She used to be the stable one; she was always so . . . in charge. But now I don't know what to expect from one minute to another. I'm worried she's become imbalanced. Do you think she has postpartum depression? Is it too soon for that?"

Dr. James waves his hand, laughing. "Now. One of you at a time, please. You're the one who's here." He trails off for a moment, thinking. Then, appearing to have figured something out, he proceeds, "It's common for new fathers to feel alienated, overwhelmed, off balance."

This comforts Michael. He's not crazy. Maybe she's not crazy, either.

Dr. James continues, "Your wife may have been sure of herself before this point, but a new child is an all-consuming thing and adjustment is hard on both parents." He pauses for a long moment, searching for the right thing to say. "Bear with her while she figures things out." Dr. James leans forward and puts his hand on Michael's arm. "You'll know when you can help her." He sits back again.

Michael stares at the doctor in disbelief. Is the man waiting for a response? He could have gotten that advice out of a quarter fortune-teller.

Dr. James merely gazes back at him, still waiting. Maybe this is how therapy works. You pay $250 an hour and they let you come to your own decisions.

The silence becomes awkward, so Michael gulps one last sip of coffee under Dr. James's expectant gaze. "Well, I've got to get groceries. We're out of everything and my wife definitely isn't eating right." He gets up to go.

"Michael." He has a warning look in his eyes. "Pay attention."

"Sorry?"

"The time isn't right yet and I know that. But promise me you'll *pay attention*. Watch and listen. It will come clear." He's serious, furtive, as if he has imparted wisdom that will save Michael from a terrible fate. Only the weight with which he says it doesn't translate. *Pay attention.*

"Okaaay." Michael grabs his jacket and puts it on, backing toward the door. He steps forward and abruptly shakes the doctor's hand. "Thanks for the coffee."

Dr. James grasps his hand firmly, flashes him a grin. "You'll be fine, Michael Gould. You're made of good stuff, I can tell." He claps him on the shoulder and releases him, walking him to the door. "Do me a favor will you?"

Michael says, "Sir?"

"Check in on me in a few days. I might need it."

"Uh . . . sure."

The man gives him one more slap on the back as he escorts him into the hallway. Michael heads to the elevator, and by the time he looks back, the door is closing.

The elevator opens on the first floor and Michael finds himself face to face with Greta. The damn woman is everywhere. But as he just sought advice from a cryptic shrink, maybe he should be more understanding of Sarah turning to the aging hippie from downstairs.

He gives her a polite smile and steps out of the elevator, but she steps in front of him.

Michael says, "Excuse me."

"Where are you going?"

"Out." He steps around her, brushing her abruptly with his shoulder.

She calls after him, "You seem to be in the habit of leaving."

Shame slams his chest. He's not sure why this woman he hardly knows can do this to him, but it makes him more resentful of her. They need groceries. He doesn't look back as he says, "See you around."

He's been gone for three? Four weeks now. Tim's been without his father for four weeks because of something Sarah forgot to say. She can't remember what she forgot to say, but the guilt of forgetting overwhelms her. It's all been a blur of diapers and Tim and time passing and losing hours. She can't get a handle on her days, can't quite reach them. And with all of this time passing, she feels the hope of their all being together diminishing. She can't keep him here. She can't think about it too much; it makes her dizzy. She focuses on the sofa, looking at its weave and threads. She strokes it with her fingers, but finds she can't feel it in the same way she used to. Like she's had a body-wide injection of Novocain.

She misses feeling everything about her days from that first moment she'd step out of the building into the morning, when the sounds and smells of the city would hit her. The cold would prickle her nose, or the oppressive heat would weigh her down. The smells of exhaust and early-morning coffee would react differently with the air depending on the season. The noise of the city traffic and construction echoed differently with each season as well: a close, claustrophobic sound with the snow, an echo after rain, relentless in the heat.

She misses the smile from the waitress at the local diner who knew, after three years of her daily patronage, to have her cup of coffee and a bagel waiting for her at exactly 7:32 a.m. Add a $2 tip, and it was still less than a cup of coffee and a bagel at Starbucks. And she got that smile. She misses the morning greetings from her partners at the office, the bits of business that connected her with people, with purpose. She misses being able to solve people's problems using her knowledge of the law.

The worst is, even in this confined apartment, she can't feel anything the same way she used to: the slip of clothing on her skin, the weight of carrying something, the cold of a glass or the heat of a pan.

She misses—is heartsick for—the feel of the wood floors under her bare feet. She knows she's walking, but she used to feel *so much, everything: the rise of certain floorboards, the cold that clung to the plaster of the walls, the wool runner halfway down the hall which hurt her sensitive feet first thing in the morning, but became a pleasant sensation later in the day. She yearns for it like a forgotten poem that she's certain once used to move her to tears.*

Maybe she should have told him she died. If she told him, Michael would realize how awful it is when he leaves. Then he wouldn't go. Because he loves her.

Or he'd move on. Maybe he's already found out and he's moved on.

Weeks. Or not. It's so hard to tell. But if it has been real weeks, it's enough time for him to have found out and left. Or maybe he went back to his job. Maybe they sent him across the globe to get over her. He could be taking core samples in Azerbaijan and she wouldn't know.

She can't think like this or she'll go mad.

Tim's not crying today. Sarah worries he's forgetting his father. They were supposed to bond. When Greta came by after Michael left again, she didn't scold Sarah; she just gave her a withering look of disapproval. Sarah felt like she failed her. Now she feels like she's failed Tim. Michael.

She paces the floor in front of the couch, picking at her fingers. If she can pinch them hard enough, she can get in touch. The pain reminds her of things. Things that seem to get foggier, farther away, the longer she's here.

When she sees Michael again, she'll work harder at taking care of him. She feels so out of touch. She doesn't know if he's been eating. There was lasagna, but that must be gone by now. If she can make tea, she can cook. She'll work a little harder to pay attention. She'll make him a nice dinner. Or lunch. Or whatever meal it is when he finally makes up his mind to come home.

Tim starts crying. This calms her a little. She goes to him. If it's just the two of them, she's going to make every moment together count.

———

Tofu, Vanilla Tofutti, apples, oranges, pears, strawberries sinfully out of season but gorgeous looking. The apples are from New Zealand; Sarah will kill him, but it seems less important to buy local today. Soy cheese. Bread. Whole wheat crackers with some sort of pesto spread. Pasta. Spaghetti sauce. Rice. Brown rice. Chicken. Steak. Frozen salmon patties. Pizza dough to go with the soy cheese. Soup. Olives. Garlic. Garlic-flavored oil. Sarah told him gas-producing food passes to the child through breast milk and can make a baby colicky. Steak. Asparagus. Asparagus isn't gassy, is it? Granola. Granola bars. Dried fruit and walnuts. Herbal tea. Almond milk. Various frozen individual dishes for himself, including burritos and anything he can find with cheese. He'll eat enough dairy for the whole family. The cart is full by the time he wheels it to the front of the Fairway and he laughs, hoping his two over-sized canvas bags will be able to hold it all . . . and that he'll be able to carry them for the four-block walk home. The fresh air has cleared his head a little. He still feels a little dizzy, but it's more like that spotty weakness at the end of a long cold.

By the time he gets to the building, he's slogging forward like a Yeti.

Phil comes to the door and asks, "Can I help you, Mr. Gould?"

"Got it!" Michael lurches across the marble floor toward the elevator, Phil dancing around him like an anxious sheepdog.

"Are you sure, sir? I could take one of them."

"I've got momentum on my side, Phil, so stand back."

"I left your mail outside your door, sir. I hope that's okay."

"It's fine."

Michael gets to the elevator and the doorman has still not left his side. They stand waiting for the elevator together. Michael looks over to him wondering why the guy is there. Phil seems to be searching for words, working up the nerve. Is he going to ask for a loan? A personal favor? A date?

Phil asks, "So, um, all the groceries, Mr. Gould. Is it time now?"

Michael says, "I'm sorry?"

Phil clears his throat, rephrasing. He sounds grave and concerned. "How many will you be expecting, sir?"

Michael looks at his load as the elevator dings. He laughs. "Oh, no, this is just for us." Phil looks confused. Michael shrugs as he steps into the elevator. "Never shop hungry, I guess." The doors close and he sees Phil wander off, shaking his head, disapproving of some thing or another. Doormen always have an opinion.

Michael's alarmed to find the door to the apartment ajar and to hear strange women's voices coming from inside. One of them is sobbing and it doesn't sound like Sarah. As he goes in, he quietly slides the bags across the floor into the corner. He then reaches for the boxes of mail outside the door and slides them in after. They're full. He realizes Sarah hasn't left the apartment at all since she got home. This and her reluctance to go for a walk can only mean acute agoraphobia. This is more than average postpartum.

A woman is speaking between sobs, and it's not Sarah or Greta.

"I can't seem to find the joy anymore, you know? I try and I try to be grateful that I am here with my baby and it's everything I dreamed, but it's not what I expected, you know?" She breaks off with a very wet, mucous-y inhale.

Michael pokes his head around the corner into the room. He is bewildered by the sight of five women sitting in his living room, each holding small babies in their arms. The woman who's speaking sits in the armchair facing the sofa. She's heavy, has the standard blonde mom-bob, which is clearly unwashed, and she's wearing a large, green sweatshirt that reads JUICY across the chest. Michael thinks briefly that she does look juicy in a leaky, overflowing sort of way—an over-ripe pear. She looks like she's been crying for a while and is rocking her baby and squeezing it almost too hard. She cries into its neck. The child indulges her, squirming uncomfortably but not fussing.

Michael's surprised to see how together Sarah looks. Her hair, already dry, is pulled back into a comfortably tidy bun and she has changed into a skirt and loose blouse. Tim must have spit up on her other outfit. The frightening creature from last night has fully receded, and while her face is still drawn and tired, she looks oddly at peace. More like the real Sarah.

Greta's sitting between two women on the sofa, presiding like an ominous cloud. She looks at Juicy concerned, nodding.

The sound of her voice penetrates the room with the resonance of a priest and forms a dark, heavy rock in the pit of Michael's stomach.

"Thank you, Maureen. Ladies, what we need to remember is that you and your babies come first. Your other concerns are,"—her hand flutters off to her left like an escaping bird—"Nothing. You are here.

Your babies are here. That is love. And it is this love that we need to nurture, not with sadness, but—"

Sarah's voice breaks Greta's speech. "Michael!"

The older woman looks up at him suddenly with malice in her eyes. But the malice clears quickly, leaving the smug smile that he'd encountered upon their first meeting. Greta announces him. "Ladies, may I present Michael Gould, Sarah's husband, who loves her enough to be here with us."

The women murmur among themselves as if someone famous has walked into the room. Michael looks at Sarah, questioningly. She says, "These are"—she searches for something to call them—"These are other. Mommies."

The word sounds so foreign coming from her.

Greta rises from the chair, asserting her control over the situation. "These are Sarah's friends." She says pointedly, "New mothers need a lot of support, you know." Michael tries to think of an appropriate response, but Greta turns to the room. "Girls, that means it's time for us to go." There's something wrong with the power she holds over these women.

"Oh, no, Greta, that's okay." Sarah's clearly embarrassed.

Greta says, "We've taken enough of your time and your husband is home, darling. Go to him."

Sarah rises from her chair, hitches the sleeping Tim into one arm, and crosses the floor to greet Michael. As she kisses him on the cheek, Michael has a sinking feeling that, for the first time in their marriage, she doesn't mean it. This is a ceremonial show of affection, like the kiss an elected official gives her spouse on the podium at a rally. Sarah grasps his shoulder a little too hard as she whispers into his ear, "I didn't know when you were coming back."

He speaks softly, but can't keep the impatience out of his voice. "I went grocery shopping, honey. Remember?"

The women have started squeezing past them out the door. Maureen goes first and Michael catches a glimpse of the child she clutches, unnaturally pale and still. Michael has a morbid flash, wondering if maybe she squeezed him to death, but the infant yawns, bringing him back to reality.

A particularly dour, pinched-looking woman with black, short hair and eyes with deep rings under them shuffles past, hunched over her child, who is wrapped in an ancient shawl. The woman is an anachronism, from her nun-like shoes to her Depression-patterned, cotton shirt-dress. Michael catches a glimpse of blood on the infant's forehead, a deep and nasty-looking gash. He leans in for a closer look, but Greta sweeps between him and the woman. She warns him with her the eyes, saying, "Forceps injury. Takes awhile to heal. Michael, your wife needs you. You need to stay with her more. She can't do it all alone."

He says, again, "I just went to get groceries." It sounds increasingly absurd each time he says it.

But she's out the door, followed by the rest of the mothers, most of whom Sarah kissed good-bye. The elevator opens as Greta announces, "I have a batch of banana bread fresh out of the oven, ladies. You're welcome to join me downstairs."

There are happy murmurs and the oppressive air of the group's sadness seems to evaporate. The newly buoyant cocktail party disappears as the elevator door closes, the crammed box taking them away to continue whatever it was they were working on.

Michael looks at Sarah, who watches after them, both wistful and embarrassed. Is he allowed to ask her about these women? Or will it turn into a fight like the one about Greta?

She turns and puts a sleeping Tim into his bouncy chair. This is yet another peculiar baby device that litters their apartment. The swing, the Diaper Genie: this new dimension of plastic and brightly colored fabrics has taken over. The bouncy chair is a vibrant, butterfly-fabric reclining seat resting on a heavy, gauge-wire frame, which bounces lightly when the baby kicks. Sarah turns on the motor at the bottom of the bouncy seat, which causes the baby to vibrate on the fragile wire frame, his cheeks quivering with the gentle rhythm. Michael smiles for a moment at his jiggling, growing boy, then takes the bags of groceries into the kitchen. Sarah follows.

Michael opens the cabinet and starts to fish things out of the bag. He says, "Let me get this, honey."

She steps forward, as if her presence will stop him. She says, "No, it's no trouble."

He heads toward the fridge. She cuts him off.

Sarah looks him in the eye, searching for the right thing to say, the magic formula. "Sweetie, I need to . . . I haven't even been out yet, so . . . can I do this? Please?"

He looks at her a moment, and then steps back, hands up. It was more irritation than he'd wanted to show, so he waits for a negative response.

But Sarah turns on the flame under the kettle and then calmly moves to putting things away.

Michael sits. He has to ask her about the mommies group. Is it some kind of support group or club? What does she get out of it? Why are they so odd and why Greta is so . . . enormous? He gets the feeling that Greta wants something from these women. That she's not there solely out of a positive nurturing spirit. How did Sarah meet her? Was it a message board thing? Are these seeping, sopping women sufficient company for his wife who used to run with the bulls, taking lunches and meetings? Each question he formulates in his mind elicits an imaginary curt or angered response so he bites his tongue.

As if she's heard him, she speaks up. "A lot of new moms suffer from postpartum depression." *Don't say anything. This is where you listen. Listen to her.* "Greta's been so great at getting us on the right track to being . . . happy moms. It's overwhelming, you know. The sudden unemployment, the lack of that work atmosphere, and on top of it, this tiny thing that you love so much, but don't know how to take care of." She pauses.

He will listen. He lifts the vase from the center of the kitchen table. It's empty and filled with browning, stagnant water. He doesn't think it's had any flowers in it since the daisies he brought home a few months ago. There's a dark ring under the vase where it stuck to the table and some old toast crumbs under that. Their home is getting disgusting around the edges, like his grandmother's house in her later years. He remembers the sickening feeling of emptying a glass of lemonade only to see the brown scum sticking to the bottom of the glass that hadn't been properly washed. Is their apartment going to be like this from now on or is this a phase? Maybe people age considerably once they have kids, only he'd imagined it took a bit longer. He can't remember his house ever being this gross when he was growing up.

Sarah says, "It's hard, Michael, but I'm trying."

Pay attention. He remembers now that those were Dr. James's words, "Pay attention."

He says, "I know, honey." This is a good place to talk. She's listening, too. "Are your friends helping you?" The word friends sounds so hollow, these sad women he's never seen before, who know so much about his life. They're sharing such intimate stuff, do they talk about sex?

She smiles, apparently relieved that he asked. "You don't know how much." She gets their battered stockpot out of the cabinet under the stove and puts it on top. Popcorn, soup—this had been their first pot and had functioned even as a frying pan for an awkward week when they first moved in together. A proper frying pan was Michael's first purchase for the place. Sarah turns off the kettle and pours the boiling water into two mugs next to the stove. It feels nice having her perform a comfortable task.

He gets to his feet. "Is Tim good for a while? Are you good for a while? I haven't had a minute . . . " He nods toward his office, a small room off the kitchen.

Sarah says, "Sure, honey. I'm cooking tonight. You have 'til dinner."

He steps up behind her, puts his arms around her, and kisses her on the neck. "Mmmm." He can feel a smile form on her cheek. She taps his arm with a wooden spoon. "Now run along, I've got to get cooking."

He says, "Ma Kettle. Where's your rolling pin?"

"Don't make me find it." She hands him a mug of tea and he gives her one more squeeze before heading off to his office.

FOUR

Aside from litigating, cooking is the only other thing Sarah can do well. On Friday nights she'd come home from work, put on some music—sometimes classical, more often bands from her twenties, when she and Michael met. She'd pour a glass of wine and start preparing a meal. The motion of getting things out of the fridge and the cabinet, the rhythm of chopping, the smell of garlic hitting hot oil, the simple comfort in the order of building a sauce or a soup or combining flavors that go well together would remove all of the week's calls and stress and briefs and people who needed things from her, and put her in a mellow zone she owned. When she was cooking, she had landed.

But as time passes, Sarah has more and more trouble seeing and touching certain things. Objects are easier. The stockpot looks familiar, sounds familiar, despite the fact that she can't feel it in the same way, its cold metal body, its warm, worn, plastic handles, melted on one side from being left on the stove too long in her pregnant absent-mindedness.

She works very hard and tries to concentrate. She's determined to re-master at least one old skill. But when she goes to the fridge, she finds things *hard to grasp. She doesn't feel the cold from the fridge like she used to, either. The light that comes from inside is too bright and the food looks blurry. She knows where the vegetable drawer is and she opens it, reaching in. How do you start this? Onion. There's half an onion. And garlic. Maybe she can sneak more vegetables into the recipe. Michael looks so thin and she hasn't been taking care of him. He needs a nutritious meal. Carrots. Celery. Good start.*

Michael opens his office door, which bangs against a pile of cardboard boxes. The back portion of the tiny room is crammed with crap they'd taken out of the den to convert it into Tim's nursery. Michael moved his entertainment center into one side of the office, which used to hold a comfortable but unsightly chair. The comfortable chair went to the street, much to Sarah's relief.

This is the room of margin, where everything that is not about *them* ends up. Books from college, back-issues of geological magazines, his neon Schlitz sign. He laughs when he sees it, as it had been a major point of argument when they first shacked up and represented Michael's bachelorhood. He remembers at the time holding the firm belief that if he let go of this sign, boosted from a friend's college dorm room, he'd be giving in to a bourgeois lifestyle. He doesn't even like Schlitz. He tugs on the metal-beaded chain in the sign's frame and the neon light casts a sickly yellow glow over the room.

He pulls the dust cover off his desktop and turns it on; it's a Mac and boots up with a deafening *bronnnnng*. He'd had his music up pretty loud the last time he used it. He takes a sip of tea. It's hot and good. There are some spices he knows in it and an additional, earthy note he can't place. Whatever new brand this is, there's something deeply comforting about it. He tries to clear away the piles of books from the sofa. Does he really need his Italian dictionary or his yet unread book of Proust he'd bought to impress a girl in college? These came off the shelf in the den where they'd served a purpose, furnishing the room; it looked more like a home with books lining the shelves. Now, the den a nursery, the books thrown on the sofa have been reduced to crap. Why do they have so much crap?

When they moved in eight years ago, they had only some cardboard boxes, a sofa he'd adopted from his former housemates, and a bed Sarah's grandmother had given them. And of course, the Schlitz sign.

The bed was the most expensive thing in the house: a late-nineteenth-century antique monstrosity, a large, square, molded headboard indented with two rectangles, each with carved bunting draping its cornices. There was a lot of consternation about getting it up the stairs of the apartment building; it was far too big for the elevator. Michael and his two roommates, Chuck and Dan, had wrangled it up each leg of the stairway, then had to lift it flat over the banister to get it to the next curve. It was too large to make the corners. This seemed like a great solution at first, but by the fifth time they hefted it, they knew the ten remaining floors were going to be near impossible.

Chuck grunted, "How many more fucking floors?"

Michael said, "One less than the last time you asked."

Sarah intervened, bringing them some beer. She had a purple handkerchief around her hair, a smudge of dirt on her nose, and a "what now?" look on her face. Michael loved her so much and he still couldn't believe they were finally moving in together. More than the commitment, the possibility of fucking it up terrified him. Living with him every day, she'd see all the safely hidden details that he'd kept from her over the years. He'd make a conscious effort not to floss in bed, but what if he did something really stupid in front of her? What if she found out his sick addiction to reality TV? Or his need for crappy guy food? She was such a health nut; how would they get around his customary pizza/wing combo on Monday nights?

The beer gave Chuck the strength of ten men. Okay, maybe a guy and a half, but eventually they got the slab of wood up to the apartment and put the bed together.

They made love on that enormous monstrosity of a bed in their otherwise empty bedroom that afternoon, the dust from the prior owners lurking in the corners, the electricity not turned on yet, the dusk setting in. Michael woke in the middle of the night to find Sarah watching him by the light of the street lamps coming in through the naked windows. He knew he was home. The creeping fears he had about shacking up were completely gone. He remembers thinking, *This makes sense.* More than anything in his life so far, moving in with Sarah made sense.

"Best thing ever?" Sarah asked, her brow furrowed with worry. How could she possibly worry?

He said, "Best thing ever." He kissed her as if to punctuate it.

———

Now cardboard boxes, a sofa, and a bed have somehow multiplied or mutated into acres of crap, from the crusty vase on the kitchen table to the postcards from years ago, which still sit, determined and inexplicable, in the alcove next to the front door. He will throw the Schlitz sign out tomorrow. He's over it.

But maybe it's worth something. He'll sell it on eBay instead.

Michael looks over at his e-mail box, which has popped open. There are five hundred unread e-mails. He sighs, sits in the chair and starts from the top. Lots of work crap. There's a new laziness which has come with the baby. Part of him wants to get back to work, but another part of him is tempted to go lie on the sofa and stare at the boy's jiggling cheeks.

He scrolls through a few ads for Viagra but then begins to see a lot of e-mails that say, "I'm sorry." He highlights them all, thinking they're spam, but when he sees the addresses, he realizes that he recognizes one. He opens an e-mail from Chuck that reads, "I'm so sorry man. Let me know if there's anything I can do." Then he opens another from Dan, who now lives in Iowa. "Michael. This sucks. Call me if you need anything."

He starts to panic. What sucks? What has he missed? "Honey?" he hollers, but he knows she can't hear him with the door closed.

He clicks open another e-mail, but the computer freezes and suddenly powers off. His surge protector starts beeping.

"Goddamn it!"

The power in the room is still on, so it's probably the outlet fuse.

What the hell were they sorry about?

Did something happen Sarah didn't tell him about? Is his mother ill or something? Is something up at his job? He picks up the phone to call work, but he remembers that it's Sunday; they won't be in. He dials Caroline's number.

It goes to voicemail. He says, "Um. Caroline, it's Michael. Call me." He realizes he sounds too anxious, so he adds, "Just want to touch base," in a manner meant to be nonchalant, but it just comes out weird.

Why wouldn't Sarah tell him if something happened? Did she not tell him because she didn't want people coming over? Had she become a complete agoraphobe? Why hadn't any of his family called—about anything? He wasn't supposed to be home for a few more days yet, but they would have checked in with Sarah by now. Maybe that's why she and Anna were fighting. He feels like a bad husband for not being more in tune, but clearly something big has happened and Sarah's keeping it from him. He heads out into the kitchen, fuming. His head whirls and he stops in the doorjamb to steady himself. Eyes closed, he says, "Honey, what the hell is going on?"

No answer. He opens his eyes. Sarah's chopping something on the cutting board. He notices vaguely that she's changed her clothes and is wearing the peach batik dress that she always hated. He's too upset to ask her about it. She's humming to herself, an old They Might Be

Giants song from when they were first dating. The one about the dinner bell.

Michael asks, "Honey, did something happen?"

"What do you mean?"

"I don't know, something you haven't told me about. Something important. I got all these e-mails . . . " He trails off.

Michael realizes that something is very wrong. The anger leaves him and is quickly replaced by a growing uneasiness. "Honey?" There's an awful smell in the air, rotting vegetables with the undertone of refrigeration, and when Michael processes this, he realizes that the knife Sarah is using isn't making the right sort of noise on the cutting board. The knife goes through what sounds like a sticky sludge and skids across the worn wooden surface.

Sarah vaguely replies, "What's bugging you, sweetie?"

To keep her talking, he says, "I got some weird e-mails. I wondered if you forgot to tell me . . . " he trails off.

Sarah takes whatever she has cut on the board and lifts it over to the stockpot. Michael sees a brown gooey mess that makes a sickening *squish* as it lands in the bottom of the pot, sizzling in the heat.

He steps forward, standing behind her. "What're you making?"

She says, "A little stew. It's been so long since I cooked. It feels good." He bends over the pot and draws his head back; the heat of the pot is intensifying the odor. This is something rotten.

Michael moves over to the fridge as she prattles on. "I thought I'd make that Chile Colorado that you liked so much. With the ancho chiles? I don't have any avocados for guacamole, but I probably couldn't cope with the raw onion, anyway. Luckily Tim's gas seems to be passing. Pun fully intended . . . " Her voice is bright and chipper, which only exacerbates the sinking feeling in his stomach.

He notices that the groceries are still in their bags on the ground. He holds his hand on the fridge for a moment.

The fridge is covered with ultrasounds of Tim in various stages. Kidney bean. Grapefruit. Mutating garden. There's a picture of Tim that he hadn't seen, in Sarah's last weeks of pregnancy. It's one of those creepy 3-D ultrasounds, with a ghostly image of his beautiful boy's face: white and shadow, cheeks, nose, lips, eyes closed. Even in utero he can see Tim. His heart swells with love, and fear. Because of the way the 3-D ultrasound works, in layers, a section of his forehead is missing, as if sliced off, leaving a dark shadow.

Sarah absently says, "You need something, sweetie?" The mire in the pot is starting to bubble and the smell is becoming putrid. Michael opens the refrigerator and is hit with an even stronger odor: rotting vegetables, mold, mildew, and the foul and persistent note of rancid meat. Bags that once held produce hold brown mush, some of them leaking. There's a plate of something unrecognizable covered with mold, and there, on the top shelf, a chicken in a pan, left to marinate about three weeks ago, the source of an overwhelming portion of the stench. It has turned a grisly blue-gray brown in color. He closes the fridge.

He looks back at Sarah, cheerfully going about her business. *Christ.* He didn't see it before; he thought she was adjusting, temperamental. But this is beyond that. This is unhinged.

Michael says, "Baby. Um. Let's order in tonight." He walks up to her and looks at the side of her face, the fact that she's clearly not processing any of this. He pushes her hair away and pulls her to him, holding her. With his other hand, he turns off the burner. He sways with her slightly. He never swayed before Tim, but now it seems natural.

She pushes him away playfully, saying, "What's wrong with you? You look all serious. You've got that"—she pokes a finger in between his eyebrows—"You know, that crease in your forehead. I love cooking, honey. I miss it. Let me."

It's moderately comforting that she seems cheerful, but it's only an indicator of how far from reality she's strayed. If she's this crazy, how safe is Tim? Is she going to eat something rancid and get sick? Is she going to feed something to the baby? Is he going to have to commit her or can they get help at home? How will he take care of the baby alone?

He says, "Sarah, honey, we're ordering in tonight."

She's getting cross. "Sweetie, there's nothing fit to order in. All the food is too gassy."

He says, "The deli. Nothing bad there. Matzoh ball soup. Potato knish. Yum."

Her eyes well up with tears. "Why won't you let me *cook*?" She sounds like a child about to have a tantrum.

It's his job to fend it off. What answer will keep her from going completely off the handle? *Think quickly.* He says, "Tomorrow. It's late anyway and I've got to clean out the fridge. It's been a while." *How can you not smell that? You used to get nauseous at the smell of Cheerios, how can you not smell* that?

There's a knock at the door.

———

No. It's too soon. She needs to explain but the room is going spinny and shimmery. She hasn't told him that she loves him, that she's sorry, that maybe if she'd gone into the hospital that first day—when she found it hard to breathe— maybe then it wouldn't have happened. She thought it was just the baby cram- ming up against her lungs. Shortness of breath is common in pregnancy.

The worry fills her with dread and as the dread grows, the room fades. She bites her hand to get a handle on the present. The room goes clear again.

There is another knock. She feels cold and her knees are shaking. She can't get a grip.

Not yet. *Maybe she can stop him. Stop it.*

———

Michael turns around and yelps because Sarah's in his face, the knife still in her hand, her eyes flashing. She hisses, "Don't answer it!"

She isn't threatening him with the knife; but it adds to the menacing picture.

This is worse than he thought. Much worse. He clears his throat. "Don't worry. I'll send them away."

He turns away because he can't look at her now. The rancid chicken mixes with the smell of her shampoo: Pantene. The vegetables. He eyes the stove as he passes it and walks down the hallway.

The doorbell rings and then there is pounding on the door. It isn't very hard, it's just steady.

Sarah's in front of him. *How?*

"Don't answer it!" She's breathing heavily and the air has gone frigid. Rings under the eyes, pupils enormous, hair suddenly askew, she resembles the specter he came home to last night.

He reassures her, "I'll send whoever it is away."

But Sarah's distraught. "It's Anna! Please. Don't answer it."

They aren't speaking. She probably tried to help. Anna can help. He says, "I'll send her away."

But Sarah's off down the hallway. The pounding on the door has gotten harder and he can hear a small feminine voice in the hallway. "Michael! I know you're in there, now open up!"

Michael opens the door. Anna is standing there: Sarah painted with a different palette. Her hair is dark brown and hangs in a curly mass around her head. Her skin is ivory and unfreckled. If one saw the two on a sunny day, Anna would be the one you'd pick as the evil twin. With her coloring, the angles from Sarah's face reflected in her own become more foreboding, distraught. It takes people awhile to get to know Anna because her dark brown eyes look either threatening or angry. Her brow is now furrowed with worry, giving her the determined look of a college activist. Hell no, she won't go. She rushes into Michael's arms and holds him tight, squeezing him in a hug that verges on painful. She begins to cry.

Anna. It's all over now. No amount of tea or persuasion can keep the rest from following: family, friends, condolences. Sarah goes to Tim who is crying. She picks him up out of his crib and sinks to the floor, waiting to disappear. Waiting to go back to the Dark.

Anna asks, "How long have you been back?"

Wow. It's worse than he thought. He says, "Two days."

"Oh, God, Michael. Nobody saw it coming. There was nothing they could do. Her heart had been growing all that time. It's not something they watch for but still, it happens. I don't understand that part."

Is a growing heart some sort of euphemism for going crazy? He doesn't understand. Anna's sobbing. What had Sarah done to her? It must have been dramatic.

Anna stops for a moment, distracted. "God, what's that smell?"

She moves toward the kitchen. He stops her. "A lot of the stuff in the fridge went off. I'm cleaning it out. Sorry."

She pulls away from him and looks at him intensely, concerned. "I've been trying to call. God, and then your cell phone. I mean what the *fuck*, Michael?" He can see by the look on her face that he's causing her alarm. As if speaking to an aged person, delivering bad news in a calming tone, she says, "It was congestive heart failure. It sometimes happens. With pregnant women." She seems to be talking to herself now. "I mean, how can it just sometimes happen and nobody was monitoring it? I don't know. It just did."

What? He says, "What?"

She looks at him, concerned, and gently pulls him back toward the sofa. She sits him down.

Michael looks at the bouncy chair at his feet, empty but still vibrating, the plastic toys on the mobile jangling crossly. Sarah probably took Tim so she wouldn't have to face Anna. *But.* Maybe the congestive heart failure made her go crazy. His thoughts are sucker punches and each one makes less sense.

Anna keeps talking. She won't give him a minute to think. "The baby didn't have a chance. We lost *both* of them, Michael. Both of them. How is that fair?"

He feels his soul fall out from under him, his chest compressing beneath an enormous, unbearable weight. Anna says, "I'm so sorry." Her sobs tell the truth, what he should have known. What's been in front of him since he got home. *Sarah.*

He can't breathe. He looks at the empty bouncy chair. The folded Onesies in the corner of the sofa. He smells the overwhelming odor of dead food. This doesn't make any sense.

His words sound hollow as they echo off the high ceiling. "Tim, what about Tim?" *No. Please, God, no.*

She says, "Who's Tim?" Anna's face falls when she realizes. "You named him. Shit."

"What?" He looks at her, furious, "Tell me what. *Exactly.* Happened."

Anna looks alarmed by his expression. She says, "Oh, God. You didn't know." She speaks carefully. "They tried to do an emergency C-section, but they couldn't stabilize her and they couldn't stabilize him and it all happened so fast and it was so fucking pointless and all the doctors and they still couldn't . . . " She trails off as she looks around the room. "Michael. How long have you been home?"

He's slid off the sofa onto the floor and is sitting on his knees, feet splayed behind him like a child, his arms on either side of him, help-less. He's staring at the fringe on the edge of their carpet, which has been pushed the wrong way. He tries to breathe.

Then he starts to yell. It starts somewhere in his bowels and comes up, building strength. He yells, drowning out the buzz of the bouncy chair, drowning out whatever the hell Anna is saying to him, to obliterate the runaway thoughts plowing through his mind, digging trenches that seem to fill only with blackness.

Michael's yell rips into Sarah. It hurts so much. More than labor, and that was the worst pain she thought she could feel.

I'm so sorry. If I had gone to the doctor when my breathing felt short. If I'd had a checkup. I'm so sorry.

She did everything she was supposed to do for a healthy delivery. She stopped working. The shopping for the baby was done well before it would be a strain on her. The only thing she had left to do was to bring this boy into the world.

She kisses his soft, sweet-smelling head and begins to cry.

She's still here. That yell from Michael echoed so loudly that it should have made it all go away.

But her back is still against the crib, she can feel its bars hard against her spine. The baby is in her lap. She can smell the strong day-old-diaper stench coming from the Diaper Genie. She's still here and they'll get through it. When she lost her father and nearly fell to pieces, Michael's love and humor got her through it.

And at least he knows now. No more lies.

Michael stops and breathes. He has no choice. The yell accomplished nothing. Anna's still there—freaked out, but still there. She has her hand on his knee, searching his eyes for some sign of life. He wishes she wouldn't find it. He wishes that he'd yelled himself into oblivion.

But there he is. And Sarah isn't. And Tim isn't.

Anna turns off the bouncy chair. "How long have you been home?"

He says, "I don't. I don't know . . . maybe . . ." He squints, trying to think. "Two days?"

She says, "Why didn't you pick up the phone?"

"Don't answer it." Of course. Anna and Sarah didn't fight. But, she couldn't answer it, because she couldn't answer it. And she couldn't have him answer it. Because then he would know.

He hears Tim squawk. It echoes in the room. He looks up and inhales. There's Sarah, standing in the doorway to the nursery. She's rocking the boy and furtively putting a pacifier in his mouth to keep him quiet. She mouths something to Michael:

Get rid of her.

FIVE

When they were in grad school, Sarah and Michael didn't talk much about their studies. Their apartment was an oasis of friends, food, old jokes and comfort. So when Sarah finally passed her bar exam and went out to Cipriani to celebrate with Michael, she was stunned when they were ushered into a back room with a table full of friends and family. Michael had thrown her a party.

Pleased, she said, "What did you do?"

He murmured in her ear, "You got a law degree! That's a big deal!"

He was so insanely proud of her and she took great strength from that pride. The first time she appeared before a judge, Michael took the day off work and snuck in the back of the courtroom to be there for her. She was nervous as all hell, but with Michael behind her she gained the courage to do pretty damn well.

Sarah had grown up listening to her mother, who was the genius of the subtle put-down, so at first she was flustered by her husband's constant praise. When they were with friends, he'd refer to her as, "My genius litigator wife," or ask people, "Have you met my gorgeous lawyer wife?" He complimented her to the point of bashfulness.

How proud could he possibly be of this new version of her? His successful wife had failed at giving birth and now seemed to be failing at being dead. And what would her mother say?

In her former life, Sarah would have been able to get rid of Anna. She loves her so much, but her sister is the queen of bad timing.

She can see her sister now . . . sort of. Anna looks blurry, like a reflection of herself cast onto a liquid being. She shimmers a little when she moves and when she turns, just so, Sarah can barely make her out. Anna's voice sounds faint, shadowy, and irritating, like a movie not turned up loud enough.

Michael is so upset. Don't worry, I'm right here.

His knowing isn't the problem. Anna is the problem right now. She has to leave. Her shimmering form and her distorted voice make Sarah feel woozy and she has the closest thing she's felt to a headache since she died. She kisses Tim's head and sways, but the entire room is starting to shimmer around Anna and Michael is the only thing she can see clearly.

Anna shows no desire to leave and Michael can't focus enough to make it happen.

She says, "Let me help you with the kitchen."

He can't process any of this. It hurts too much and there's Sarah, looking impatient, holding his boy. Is that his boy? He needs time to think. He looks up at Anna, imploring.

Sarah prompts him, "You need to be alone." The crazy lady is the only one thinking straight right now. But she's not crazy. She's dead.

No.

Michael stutters, "I . . . I need—"

Anna interrupts. "I'll get the garbage bags." She heads toward the kitchen. It's one thing to smell it, but he knows that if she sees the pot with the muck burned to the bottom, she won't leave.

"No!" his voice sounds comically tragic. Lear, near the end. Blinded. But it stops her.

Anna turns around, not understanding.

He searches for a believable reason and finally says, "I need to be alone." Sarah mouths it along with him, like a teacher offstage feeding lines to a kid in a school play. She seems farther away, or she's moved into a shadow.

Michael hasn't moved from his spot on the floor where he sits in a puddle, suffering from a mortal blow to the chest.

Then Sarah's gone again, and he knows she's taken the boy. He hopes to the nursery, but it doesn't feel that way. She seems . . . absent. He wants her here. Right?

But he has to make himself move, or Anna won't leave. He gets to his feet, which feels like moving heavy machinery. A backhoe; one lever works the legs, another the arms. The room spins when he stands, but he knows that human contact is needed for Anna to leave. He stumbles forward and tries very hard not to look like a zombie. He puts his hand on Anna's shoulder and says, "Please. Give me some time."

Her brow is furrowed, just like Sarah's, and her eyes search him intently for signs of sanity, capability. She's making up her mind. He's trying to let her.

She says, "You need help in the kitchen."

He answers, "I need something to do."

She gets that. "You'll call me."

He says, "Tomorrow."

She looks at him, threatening, "Tonight."

Michael musters the sanest voice he can summon. "Tomorrow. I promise."

Anna huffs, shrugs, and grabs her bag to go.

When he closes the door, he stops for a moment and listens to the empty apartment. He turns to look. Everything is the way it was, the bouncy chair, the piles of laundry, the swing. Maybe he imagined her. Maybe he imagined them both. Maybe he's gone completely mad.

But she can't be gone. She was here and Tim was here and look at all this stuff. He reaches in the dirty laundry basket and pulls out a Onesie and smells it. He can't smell baby. That distinctive smell of Tim. Did he make it up? He reaches in and pulls out a used burp rag. Aside from being wrinkled, it looks completely unused. He smells it. Nothing but the package it came in.

He walks down the hall to the nursery, slowly at first and then faster. He thinks he hears a rustle and calls out, "Sarah?"

The nursery is emptier for the echo. His heart starts beating faster. If he did imagine her, then it means that he can't see her again, and if he can't see her again . . . but does he really want to see her? Is it really her?

He rushes into his bedroom. The sheets are still a mess from last night. Last night. Before. "Sarah?"

He demands again, sharply this time, "Sarah."

He runs back down the hallway, his bare feet slapping against the wood floor. He looks into the living room. He had looked there before. But she moves so quickly now. She moves. If she *is*, she moves. But *she* might not be.

He yells, "Sarah!" He ducks into the kitchen. The rotting smell is still there. The stockpot is on the stove. He approaches it cautiously, a ticking bomb. The goo has burned to the sides of the pot; viscous bubbles have formed and popped, leaving pockmarks. He opens the fridge. There's the rotting mess. Still there. That's real. But what isn't? He heads to the nursery.

He should have seen it earlier. When you look closely, it's everywhere. Not only the rotting food, which he'll clean out later. But her clothes. There was something weird about her clothes. And when she changed them: randomly. In one day she'd go from being disheveled in her nursing gown to wearing something bizarre, like for the office. He thought that she was changing a lot because of the milk. Ruining shirts. Was his mind inventing all of those strange outfits?

He should have known from her reaction to his leaving. And her obsessiveness. And weirdness. It must be weird to be dead. Is it weird to be dead? Is this something you're allowed to ask the dead? And what about all of those mothers . . . are they dead, too?

In the nursery, the wipes container is still open, one exposed and drying out. The smell of Desitin is in the air. But no smell of baby poop. There'd been a faint smell this morning, and, despite its name, the Diaper Genie isn't that good. He opens the top of the cylindrical container, an absurd time capsule to the morning. To when he didn't know.

Michael pulls and pulls at the linked sausage of plastic-wrapped diapers but still doesn't smell anything. He finds one toward the bottom, bulging with a lot of wipes. That first diaper he changed. He rips it open.

Sarah laughs. "What are you doing?" Her voice produces a cold pebble of fear in his stomach. He knows this is not really Sarah, but she acts like everything is normal and she's walked in on her husband doing the silliest thing ever. The day-old vinegar shit odor surrounds him in a sudden cloud. It wasn't nice smelling to begin with, but give it some time to fester and it becomes unconscionable. Did it smell when Sarah wasn't here or is the stink because he just ripped it open?

Now that she's here, he's not sure he wants her here. He doesn't want her to go, but he's frightened. He doesn't turn around. Seeing her might make it all real. Or might make her disappear. Or maybe he'll see the dead side of her.

"Nothing." He covers quickly, like a small boy caught doing something he shouldn't. "Changing the Diaper Genie." He needs time to think.

"Well if you do it from the top, you'll have a mess. Look at you!" She laughs and walks over to him, taking the sausage and gently shoving it back in.

He's surprised to see Tim sleeping peacefully in his crib. His fear dissolves into a mix of joy and a sorrow so acute that his eyes sting with tears. He goes to his boy and lays his hand on his chest. That breathing. "Oh, look at him," he murmurs. He has to stop crying. Now. He has to think. He can't think with her here, but he doesn't want her to leave.

Sarah's behind him, her arms around his waist, her cheek on his shoulder. She's warm. She's there. She is real. And this rising and falling underneath his hand. This is real. And Tim's real, down to his baby smell.

Michael doesn't think; he breathes. He feels his son's heart beating in a quick flutter, his wife's chest breathing against his back. He starts to feel calm and this perplexes him. *She's dead, what are you doing?* And this son. This son he wouldn't have met. *Look at him.*

She talks, her breath hot against his back. "I'm sorry." He knows she's about to cry.

Sorry she died? Sorry she didn't tell him? Sorry about the rotten food?

Michael says, "I don't understand."

She sounds embarrassed when she explains, "I thought maybe if I pretended. I mean, you didn't seem to notice, so maybe we could be . . . normal for a little while?"

Normal. The sudden cold. Her looking horrible. Her lack of a grasp on reality.

He turns around and her arms don't leave his waist. He puts one arm around her, never taking his hand off the terry-cloth, warm belly of his baby. He kisses the top of her head. He smells Sarah. It's Sarah. It's no less her than yesterday. He doesn't want to cry. He doesn't want to upset her.

Trying not to sound desperate, he asks, "What are we going to do?"

She says, "I don't know. I don't know how it works. I don't know how long it's going to last."

He squeezes her, looking at the boy. "Was I really gone for weeks?"

She says, "I didn't know if you'd left me. If maybe you knew, but." She starts to laugh.

"What?"

She says, "I kinda thought you wouldn't be able to afford an empty apartment. You'd have to come home eventually."

He smiles. "Now there's faith."

She adds, "Plus, you left all your gear here."

"I wouldn't leave you, you know." But he's not entirely sure that's true. He holds her more firmly. Grasps the boy's wriggling belly. They aren't alive, but they are *here*.

She squeezes him. "I know."

He feels he's going to cry. "I'm sorry. That I wasn't here for you." *When you died.* "I'm so sorry."

Sarah soothes him. "It doesn't matter anymore. You're here. You won't leave. I don't want to talk about it now. Let's enjoy it. Being together."

She kisses him to silence him, but he doesn't need silencing. He can't talk about it any more. He's spent. She looks him sternly in the eyes: *Now, follow my lead.* "He's asleep for a while now." She takes him by the hand to lead him out of the room.

He stops for a moment. If he follows her, he's agreeing to something he isn't sure about yet. But the alternative would be to leave. He could go stay with someone else for a while. He could go into mourning for his wife and his baby. The baby he'd never met.

Sarah tugs his hand. "C'mon. Let's wash up."

And it's the baby he can't walk away from. And it's Sarah he can't say good-bye to. She leads him into the bathroom to wash their hands. The poop. Michael catches his reflection in the harsh light of the bathroom, which makes his head reel. The warmth of the water makes him aware that his hands were cold and clammy. He looks pale, drawn, his five o'clock shadow turning into the beginnings of a beard. He hasn't shaved since he got home. Out in the wilderness he'd managed to shave, but here, here things were sliding. Was that gray in his hair before all this happened? And Sarah. Glowing, luminous. The color has returned to her face. She's still wearing that peach batik dress. The one he'd bought for her from a street vendor last spring. At the time, she claimed it was too "hippie" for her tailored tastes, but he cajoled her into wearing it on the odd Sunday. Was she wearing it now to please him or was he somehow conjuring up what he wanted to see her wear? *Don't think like that. That is Sarah.*

He surveys himself in the mirror. "I look like a ghoul." *Wrong thing to say.*

She smiles, kissing his shoulder. "They say it's the first thing that goes out the window when you have a baby. Bathing."

He says, "And shaving, apparently."

She laughs and pulls him toward the shower, which she turns on.

He doesn't know if he's ready for this. Now that he knows, it's different. He warns her, "Sleep when the baby sleeps."

She has that mischievous look in her eyes that he knows so well. "That baby sleeps a *lot.*" She's got the shower good and steamy. She starts to take off his clothes. He steps back nervously and does it himself. They were fine last night, before he knew, there's no reason they shouldn't be now.

She begins to unbutton her dress. He finds himself staring as if at the unveiling of the results of a science experiment. This is the first time he's seen her naked in the light. The last time he saw her alive, her belly was swollen, with an alarming web of bright-red stretch marks running up and down, starting at the navel and circulating outward in oblong patterns. Michael had thought her belly looked like that of a red snapper; he could almost count the scales delineated by the criss-crossing of deep crimson lines.

Her dress drops to the floor. Michael tries not to look distressed, but it is unsettling. Sarah's belly is much like he'd felt it the other night . . . slightly bigger than before she was pregnant, but small again, hers. The stretch marks are there, but clustered closer together.

And they're black. A spider web tattoo creeps around her belly button as if closing in on something. He knows this isn't right. But nothing is right now, is it? There aren't doctors for this type of thing. He can't think this way; this is his wife. Whatever changes she's going through, she's still Sarah and they belong together.

She knows he's staring and she slips off her underwear, getting into the shower. When he gets in, she's facing away from him. He turns her around and sees that she's crying. He tries to kiss it away.

She says, "I'm horrible."

"No, no." He takes her face in his hands and makes her look at him. "Do you know how amazing you are?" He kisses each of her eyes. The water drops, the skin of her face, the saltiness of her tears, she's here.

She laughs a little. "Why are you always so sweet when I'm so miserable?"

He says, "Because it's the best thing ever." She laughs. The more she laughs, the more real she is. The more he can forget.

She looks at him doubtfully. "Really? Still?"

"Always." Of course he can do this. This is Sarah. He takes her in his arms, the water getting into his eyes, but he doesn't care. It's them again. Soaking wet, but just them. As they used to be. Again he pushes away the reality and sinks into the thing that's there for the taking. Real enough.

That night, while Sarah's sleeping, Michael sneaks into the kitchen and throws out everything from the fridge. If he's going to do this, he's going to do it right. Two garbage bags full of rancid meat and rotting food, curdled milk, and a few unidentifiable bags of mold or brown liquid. The ruined stockpot clatters hollowly all the way down the garbage chute. The realness of its sound fades, leaving him in an empty hallway.

He goes back to the kitchen and notices that the odor hasn't cleared yet. He's grateful for the stench; not everything should leave so suddenly. Sarah's still in bed, sleeping. *Thank God.* Michael removes his trousers, creeps into the bed and wraps his arms around her.

───────

After the shower, they make love for a second time in the bed. Sarah was grateful before, but they had this secret between them, this enormous lie. It's still not like it used to be, but it's as close as she can get to Michael in this new life. The smell of him, the contact makes her feel safe . . . alive.

Sarah turns her head to the side. A shadow in the corner of the room stops her.

Michael says, "What? Am I hurting you?"

"No."

Greta is here. Watching. Taking stock. This is wrong, they hadn't discussed this. Sarah tries to glare at her to make her go away, but Greta looks steadily on, interested, implacable.

The closeness, the safeness of being with Michael has fallen away. In its place comes uncertainty. She breathes and closes her eyes, trying to focus her entire being on Michael. It works enough to reduce her panic, but when Michael comes, she opens her eyes.

Greta is still there.

───────

Michael blinks awake in the morning to find Sarah sleeping next to him. Her hair hasn't quite dried in the night and it gives off a damp, clean smell. She has a crust in the corner of one eye and snorts in her sleep. She's *there.* He hears the baby start to cry. Tim's there. Maybe it's a reverse nightmare: Anna, the bad dream.

There's a knock on the door. It's tentative at first and then less so. Michael rolls over and faces the door, gathering the strength to answer it. There's a cold breeze at his back and he rolls over to look at Sarah.

She's gone.

The baby noises have stopped, like someone turned them off. The emptiness of the room closes in on him. He's learning that she's dead all over again. But the knocking is like a hammer now.

Anna.

"Christ, I'm coming!" he hollers, although he knows it's no good, those heavy New York doors, the carpeted hallway outside. It takes all of his strength to get out of bed, when it would be so much easier to curl up and stay there forever.

———

As soon as Sarah heard the loud pounding, things got cold and frantic . . . and then silent. And now she's here. In this other place. In the Dark. She's been here before.

This is where she came after . . . when the machines stopped beeping and all of those people surrounding her in the hospital disappeared. They were panicked, shouting. There was a loud roaring noise and then silence.

Total silence. And darkness. Absolute and complete. Time passed. Then a baby was crying. A woman's voice called in a different language, chanting in an ancient, throbbing rhythm. The voice was commanding. Other women joined in, talking, talking, talking, and their voices became a pulling clamor. The next thing she knew, she was in her apartment and Tim was there.

She's come here since then. When people come over, she is sent here with Tim. It doesn't frighten her when she's here with him, as she knows it will pass. But Tim's not with her this time and she panics. The only noise she hears comes from herself. Everything is blackness. She hears her breath increase and an unconscious, anxious grunt escapes, startling her.

Think. *Tim is with her, usually.* Stop breathing a moment, listen. *It takes her a moment to slow her breath enough to stop it and she hears a sucking noise and a contented baby sigh. He's here. He's just sleeping. She breathes again, anxious, and weeps. She thought this was it. When it comes, when it's time for her to go, will it be like this?* Poof? *And blackness? She gets down on her knees and crawls forward. This is the first time she's paid attention to what's beneath her in this place. It's always blackness, and silence, except for the noises made by Tim, and by her. She's cold. But as she crawls along the floor—no, ground—she feels hard, uneven rock. She stops a moment and holds her breath.*

She hears Tim's familiar Uh-uh-uh. *That noise he makes when he's gearing up to cry. She never thought she'd be grateful to hear it. She crawls farther, feeling her way. The rock is uneven but has no texture beyond that. Like a smooth sandstone, it has no particles, no dirt, not much variation. It lacks that earthy presence of Place. It hurts her knees. She doesn't mind, it's nice to feel something.*

Tim's noises turn into a cry, but she's there in time to pick him up and hold him to her. As she turns to take him up in her arms she sees that a tree has appeared behind her. While lit by an invisible source, it casts no light for her to see Tim by, making the blackness in which she's submerged more severe. It's a handsome, full-grown maple, thick with dark, summer-green leaves that blow in a breeze she can neither feel nor hear. She gets to her feet and walks toward the tree, but no matter how long she walks, she can't get any closer. After trying for a time to get to it, she sits down on the smooth stone. As she feeds Tim she watches the tree. She's relieved to have something to look at, but finds its presence deeply disturbing.

———

Michael throws on a sweatshirt; his boxers suffice as he's only going to send the visitor away.

When he looks through the peephole, he sees aged, bespectacled owl eyes peering back at him. Mrs. Grady. Oh. That was a sympathy lasagna. The crying.

He opens the door a crack. "Uh, hi, Mrs. Grady. Um . . . this isn't the best time, you know?"

She blinks behind her glasses. She's wearing her teeth this morning and looks rather natty in her pressed white trousers and her crisp green-and-white striped shirt.

She pushes on the door. Michael stops it with his foot, but she keeps pushing. It seems farcical, blocking this old woman's entrance, but when Michael hears a heavy glass clunk against the door he yields to her covered casserole dish. It's one of those Corningware numbers from the seventies, with the brown-and-orange pattern on the side mostly worn off from years in the dishwasher. Through the steamed glass top, Michael can see white goo. Likely tuna.

Michael tries to hide himself behind the door while he takes the casserole from Mrs. Grady. It's still warm.

"Um, thank you, Mrs. Grady. You're too generous, you didn't have to . . ."

She's gruff in her answer: "You have to eat."

He can see her peering around the corner of the door. He can't let her see the living room until he's cleaned it out. There are still piles of freshly folded Onesies on the sofa. The bouncy chair. The swing. Evidence of a wife and child who are supposed to be dead. He clears his throat as if to draw attention to his state of undress.

Mrs. Grady looks him up and down. "Don't worry. Nothing I haven't seen before. Do you need some help cleaning up or something?"

Michael's at a loss. He tries to distract her with a fumbling compliment. "You look all dressed up today."

She brightens. "I'm going to the club!"

Michael mimics her enthusiasm, "That's great! I need to get into the shower, Mrs. Grady. Have to keep going, you know. Thanks so much for the . . . " He proffers the dish.

She says, "Turkey casserole." Not tuna.

He says, "Thank you. I think I've got the cooking under control, Ma'am."

She investigates his face for signs of grief. He looks at the ground, to give her what she wants without letting her in. She coughs and says, her voice cracking, "You take care now, boy."

He nods at her with a false appreciativeness and feels suddenly devious. He's relieved when she turns to go. He sees Dr. James open his door at the end of the hall. The doctor starts for a moment, as if caught in the middle of something. He waves tentatively, but seems distracted.

"Doc*tor*," Milo's voice bellows from within. Michael notices with curiosity that Dr. James is wearing a slinky, black, silk pair of pajamas with a matching paisley silk robe. Michael checks his watch. It's 8 a.m. Michael's beginning to think that Dr. James's relationship with Milo is not strictly clinical.

He nods to him politely and closes the door. The safety of the apartment is much more appealing now.

———

Sarah doesn't know how much time has passed, but she's beyond thinking about it. Tim seems happy. The tree's leaves seem to be getting lighter in color and more fragile, like in spring. Or she's stared at it so long she's imagined it. She tries not to think too hard about it and feeds Tim whenever he fusses. The specter of Greta watching her with Michael has faded, like a nightmare. Greta didn't mean any harm, she's just a little . . . strange. She will tell her not to do that again. It will be fine.

Sarah recites Greta's words. "All that matters is that you are with your baby. All that matters is that you are with your baby." Her voice has no defined space to echo off. It sits there, muffled, like a conversation on a snowy day. But these words hold comfort. She curls up around Tim and they sleep on the cold, hard stone.

She wakes when he fusses again. She doesn't dream here. It's waking Dark and the blackness of sleep. The waking Dark is disquieting and endless with waiting, so she sings him part of his lullaby. "Hard to forget, hard to go on, when you fall asleep, you're out on your own." Her voice, the words comfort her, and she continues, "Let go of your life, grab onto my hand, here in the clouds, where we'll understand." She can't see Tim's face, but he kicks his feet so happily that she knows he's smiling.

Upon waking after one of these many sleeps, she hears that ancient language again. A woman chanting. Greta calls her name out of somewhere beyond the darkness, "Sarah." She sounds so calm, so authoritative. "Sarah."

Sarah picks up Tim and rises to her feet. She feels a pulling deep in her belly and finds herself standing in her kitchen, clutching Tim. She blinks in the light. Greta's standing over the stove and catches the kettle as it starts to whistle. It's night. It takes Sarah a moment to realize that the bright light hurting her eyes is from the street outside the window. The light in the kitchen is off.

The agony of waiting is released now that she's back.

She lets out a moan that surprises her in the tangible space of the small kitchen

Greta clucks to her. "Shh. It's okay. Shh." She hands her a cup of tea, dipping the bag a few more times.

This tea is the only thing in this life that she can taste. Sort of. It's strong, comforting, spicy, but she can't identify what kind of spice. Did she give Michael tea today? She was supposed to. How long has it been? Did the same amount of time pass for him?

Sarah asks, "How long was I gone?"

Greta's voice is as comforting as the smell of the tea. "No matter. You're home."

Sarah's arm starts to hurt. She kisses Tim and bumps her nose. He's taller. And heavier. She shifts him in her arms so he rests, straddling her stomach. She looks at him and he meets her face with a calm, steady gaze. He's at least three months older and his shoulder is poking out of the top of his Onesie. How could she not feel that in the Dark? She says again, "How long was I gone?"

99

Greta turns to her and takes the baby, smiling and lifting him high in the air. He kicks and giggles as she lowers him to her hip. "Look at how big you are!" With her free hand, she puts the tea into Sarah's hands and pushes her gently toward the chair behind her, where she sits down. Greta gently orders her. "Drink."

Sarah takes a sip, looking at her boy, his straight back, his hair, which has grown longer and curly. His Onesie is stretched over his form and tight around his belly. How did this happen? The time in the Dark felt endless, but not months endless. Days endless, maybe. But Tim has clearly grown by months. She asks, "What was that place?"

Greta answers, "Drink it all up, honey. No matter."

Sarah says, "There's this tree . . . " She sips the hot, fragrant tea and feels her fear subside, the Dark fade and comfort grow. She's no longer worried about Tim's size. She was going to ask Greta something—what was it?

Greta says, "That's not a good place to go, Sarah. It happens when the real world comes in too fast. A person comes into your apartment. You can get lost there. You need to be careful."

Sarah's feeling sleepy. A person. Her voice comes out more anxious and argumentative than she wants. "But Anna was here, that didn't happen."

Greta's voice becomes rhythmic, like it does when the other mothers are there. "It doesn't matter Sarah. All that matters is that you are here, at home, with your baby. And your husband."

Sarah starts to feel better. The questions are receding.

Greta says, "Now, let's get this boy into some clothes that fit him better, shall we?"

———

Michael hears women laughing in the kitchen. Again.

No. No. She can't be a part of this reality. Now that he knows Sarah is dead wouldn't she be . . . no longer needed? He stops at the door to the kitchen. The gravelly tone in Greta's voice sends prickles up his neck.

Greta says, "There's the boy. Ohhh, look at him grow." The drawn-out tone of her "ohhh" lets Michael know that she's picked the baby up. *Don't touch my child.* He marvels at this new instinct that did not exist before this week. Papa bear.

He barges into the room and tries to sound cheerful. "Greta, where'd you come from?" Sarah looks nervous at Michael's entrance, like she's been caught. She blinks rapidly and forces a smile.

Greta also has a forced edge to her cheerfulness. She seems unhappy with Michael, as if he's done something wrong that she'll punish him for later. But she chirps brightly, "I'm only one story down, you know. I hiked up the back stairs." She turns to Tim's little face and puts her forehead against his. "I popped in the back door, didn't I? Didn't I?" Her Southeast Asian earrings jangle when she shakes her head and her stack of wooden African bracelets clank. The warm, fleshy smell of her perfume fills the air, poofed out from her clothing by any movement.

Michael is revolted and ignores her answer. He needs to get the baby away from her.

He says, "Good morning, Tim! Good morning, buddy!" He reaches out and gently takes him. He meets with a moment's resistance and a flash of anger from Greta, but she relents and soon the wiggling boy is safely in his arms. Tim's heavier than he was yesterday and has filled out a little more. His hair has grown into curls. He shoves his fist in his mouth and giggles at the sight of his father. He's wearing little blue, terry-cloth footie jammies with stripey arms. He's the epitome of baby. Is he growing faster? They always say that they grow "too fast," but he wasn't giggling yesterday and he wasn't this heavy. Michael swings him into the crook of his arm; he's definitely bigger. He shifts the baby to his hip where he's more comfortable to hold.

Tim can hold his head up now; his back and his neck are stronger. He is *really* growing. At a faster rate than time is passing. What is he, two, three months older than he was when they put him to bed? Michael knows that Sarah's changed by all of this, but he hadn't thought of the effect on Tim.

He looks at Sarah who moves cagily about the kitchen pretending to busy herself with the cups in the sink. She's riding out the awkwardness of this gathering with a hostess's smile pasted on her face. She looks like she might pull some hors d'oeuvres out of the oven: cheese puffs, crab cakes.

Tim squeals, pulling at the collar of Michael's sweatshirt and whacking him in the face with his wet little fist. Michael grabs the fist and kisses it. There's joy in this baby. Michael had taken pleasure in a passive squirming bundle of helpless infant, but this baby is a whole person, joyful, active under his own power.

Michael sees Sarah smiling at them, admiringly. He catches her eye and grins. This is too great.

Greta looks like a displaced grandparent, a bit indignant. She tries to take control of the room. "It seems we have some things to talk about."

Michael's not biting. "Really? What?" He has so many questions to ask her. But because it's what she wants, he won't ask. If he asks too many questions, he won't be able to enjoy this new Tim, who makes eyes at him and laughs and drools. And, besides, he's not sure he wants to hear any of the answers she has to give. He does not want this woman to be part of their strange new life.

Michael starts swaying with the baby. Sarah laughs.

Greta says, "Things have changed. We should talk about ground rules." There's a parental firmness to her tone.

Don't lose your temper. Losing your temper with this woman won't get you anywhere. Here's Sarah. Here's Tim. Move carefully.

He keeps it breezy. "We're okay." He blows on Tim's neck. The baby squeals with laughter. "Aren't we, buddy? Yeah, we're okay."

Sarah looks at Michael with a tolerant shrug. What can she do? It's Greta. Michael can almost hear thunder building in the older woman. "It's not that *simple*," she hisses. "The first thing: you need to stop leaving. It's very hard on your wife when you leave, don't you see that?"

Michael says, "You've told me this. I don't even know what you're doing here."

Greta says, "I am the one who is making it possible for you to spend more time with your wife and baby." The way she says it, she's putting herself in charge. Michael doesn't remember giving her permission. He sees Sarah pacing with worry. Is Greta really a necessary part of this equation?

Michael says, "But who *are* you? Why are you in our lives? What do you want from us?"

Greta opens her mouth to answer, but her chin waggles. Like a child coming up with a lie, she's taking her time. "I'm a minister to needy moms."

Michael scoffs. There will be no straight answers. He remembers a meeting with an equally reticent oil company board. His boss told him, "Information is power." And Greta seems to be holding on to hers.

Sarah and Michael exchange glances and he can see that his wife is making a decision. Still the hostess, she walks up to Greta, throws her arms around her, and gives her a long kiss on the cheek. "Thanks for coming by, Greta. We're so happy to see you. I think you were right, we need some bonding time."

Greta hasn't taken her eyes off Michael. Sarah whispers something in her ear. Michael can feel Greta's need to control things, and that need worries him. But she, too, makes some sort of decision and calms. She paints a smile on her face so incongruous that it looks like a pained grimace. She disappears. A faint black puff of dust hangs in the air and then evaporates.

Michael knows that his wife and baby are dead. He knows things aren't going to work the same way anymore. But this ridiculously supernatural moment jars him. Why did she walk out the door before and disappear now? As if to counter with earthliness, Tim's trying to stuff Michael's sweatshirt into his mouth. Michael starts bobbing him around on his hip. He tries to formulate a question that won't offend, but only says, "I don't understand who she is."

Sarah says, "She's Greta. She's been helping me." That testiness has returned to her voice. She turns to the counter and gets a cup of tea, which she hands to him. When did she make that?

He takes the tea and puts it on to the counter next to him saying, "But is she . . ." *Dead?* "I mean . . . like you?"

"I don't know." She's getting that lost, frantic look in her eyes again.

Michael comforts her. "Oh, shh. Shh. I." But he's not letting it go. "She said ground rules. What *rules*? Is she in charge or something? And who are all of these other mothers?"

"I don't know. I know that she was the one with all the answers and she's been helping us. Michael, we have to be nice to her. She's going to make sure we can be together."

It's not like Sarah to be bullied. Michael says, "Who told you this? Did she tell you this? How do you know?"

"I got rid of her, didn't I? Isn't that what you wanted?"

He squeezes her. "I'm sorry. I want to protect you. I don't like . . . " He stops and thinks a moment. He can't fix this all now. "I want to make sure we can stay together. This woman . . . she . . . she doesn't like me."

Sarah snorts a mucous-y laugh. "You always think my friends don't like you."

But this is different, the control Greta tries to wield, the way she fills a room, manipulates it. *What does she want from us?* Michael keeps it light with a juvenile, teasing, "Do not."

She laughs and wipes her face. "Do, too." She looks at Tim and lays her hand on his belly as if she's taking in his weight, his form.

Sarah has such love in her eyes, such adoration, that Michael feels a twinge of jealousy.

He says, "By the way, there's something hinky with our new neighbor." He's not sure why it came out. Maybe a need for regular conversation.

She says, "Mrs. Stanton?"

"No, no, the new guy. Dr. James."

She looks at him blankly.

He says, "The shrink? Just moved in? Older gentleman." Sarah has no idea what he's talking about. "He moved in recently. You've probably been too . . . busy. But he's got this patient, he can't be more than fourteen years old. There's something a little off about him."

"He's a psychiatric patient, honey." She's always been so reasonable.

"I suppose you're right." He says, "Something felt . . . I'm not entirely sure they're not having an affair."

She says, "Who?"

"The doctor and his fourteen-year-old patient."

"And what brought you to that conclusion?" Always the lawyer.

"Well, I can't be sure."

There's a twinkle in her eye. "Hall gossip. Who'da thunk?" She hands the tea to him again. "Now drink your tea, Mrs. Kravitz."

He takes the tea and sips it. It is hot and spicy good. Tim has nestled his head into the crook of his father's shoulder. Michael kisses the boy's hair. The smell of baby and baby shampoo. The smell of warmth and life.

SIX

The telephone has made Anna's voice even more strident, bossy. She says, "You're hiding from the world. You need to grieve and there are so many people here for you, Michael. So many people who love you." She's starting to remind him of Naomi from college, who always insisted they talk about her ideas about his feelings.

He says, "I don't need to . . . I. Anna, I'm fine. I need a little time." Sarah's eyes are on him and he doesn't know how to have his half of the conversation without upsetting her. The word "grieve" would definitely upset her. But she's changing Tim's diaper, huffing loudly and rolling her eyes over the conversation so far: the annoyed sister.

Anna says, "I'm coming over." She makes it sound like a threat.

"Don't come over. I said I need some time." Sarah always called Anna a pest, but this is getting ridiculous.

"I won't stay long, I want to check in on you." There's something desperately pushy in her tone. It's Veruca Salt-like: the decision has been made.

"Goddamn it, Anna. How clear can I make myself? I need to be alone."

"Michael, you need to *grieve*." She hangs up. Twenty minutes from her place to theirs, if he's lucky. He doesn't have much time.

Does he need to grieve?

They had Sarah cremated. They wanted to wait until Michael was home to have a proper funeral. This decision being made without him would have bothered Michael if Sarah were actually gone. But it's oddly helpful now. They'll hold off on the funeral until he's ready.

Michael scrambles to clean up the apartment and Sarah watches him cagily, like when he would pack for a field trip. They both knew he needed to travel for his work, and each time he went, Sarah tried very hard to pretend she didn't mind his long absences, despite the fact that she hated being alone. And he tried to pretend that he wasn't totally excited for the trip, even though every fiber of him was itching to climb, breathe clean air and leave the noise of the city behind.

Sarah sits and rocks the baby, cooing to him, watching Michael nervously out of the corner of her eye. And Michael isn't talking; he won't bring it up until he absolutely has to. So they do this dance of a lie, her pretending he's tidying the room, his pretending he doesn't care that she's pretending and that cleaning the room is just something that needs to be done.

He finds some used baby bottles; Sarah's been pumping so he can help with the feeding and he's let them pile up. While she's here, he has things to wash. When she goes, all signs of usage are gone. He can't really think about the why of this, but baby bottles of any kind are best not left to Anna's prying.

He heads down the hall to the kitchen to wash and his stomach lurches and the hall seems too bright. His shoulder skids against the wall and he dizzily realizes he's wobbled to the side. He stops for a moment. Maybe he should get to a doctor, it might be an inner ear thing he picked up on his trip.

When he gets to the kitchen, he realizes there isn't time to wash the bottles. He's relieved that he tackled the kitchen the night before. He opens the fridge to put them there, but Anna feels comfortable in this apartment and might help herself to something in the fridge. The dishwasher. Anna would never open the dishwasher. Or maybe she would. She's supposed to be coming to help him. He's grieving, right? He opts for the oblong shelf in the top of the broom closet and chucks the bottles in with a clatter just as there's a knock at the front door. He turns to answer it, but Sarah's there, her arms around him, whispering in his ear.

"I love you." She kisses his neck and he kisses her forehead. He's focusing on the way her part is crooked near the top of her head, and how there's a mole right there, where the part zigs; a brown milestone against the pale white road through the soft, yellow-brown waves of her hair. She evaporates and Michael lurches, having been left with only half a hug.

He groans, "No." It is a gut-deep plea. She's gone. And, as *there* as she was, she's twice as gone. It's all he can do not to collapse. Every time she leaves, he's back to sheer grief; that first moment he knew she'd been taken from him.

She isn't gone. She'll come back. She did before.

The knock is insistent. As he goes to answer the door, he realizes with some shame that he's dreaming up lies to fill his time with Anna.

Michael thinks about popping into the bathroom and checking himself in the mirror, but he's supposed to be grieving, right? As he opens the door, he whips the burp rag off of his shoulder and chucks it in a corner. It was soaked with a copious amount of spit-up. Whether it's there or not now is another question he doesn't want to think about.

Anna has a bag on her shoulder. It's full. It's going to be harder to get rid of her than he thought.

She says, "God, you look like shit."

"Nice to see you, too." He tries to sound comical, to make it light. "Uh, hi. Staying awhile?" But his tone doesn't come off right.

She pecks him roughly on the cheek and drops her bag inside the door. She looks around as if searching for signs of grief. She's taking his temperature. What stage is he at? Still denial or has he moved on to anger?

Anna asks, dripping with sympathy, "How you doin'?" Her tone sounds stilted; she's put it on and it's a poor fit. Michael thinks Anna may be having as much trouble as he is figuring out how to act. He notices that she looks worn around the edges and, for the first time since he's met her, she's wearing a lot of makeup. Cover-up. A mask for grief? The result is alarming, her eyes sharper, her cheeks more sunken. She is an altered version of herself.

He answers by rote, "Fine, thank you. You?" What's the correct response, given her perception of his reality? The question is how to fake this. But what exactly is he faking? His wife is here, but he has to pretend she isn't. How can he fake grief when real grief is standing in front of him?

She steps back and peers into his face, squinting suspiciously at him. She sniffs. "At least you haven't been drinking." She marches into the kitchen, to see the state of things; she goes directly to the refrigerator and opens it.

He says, "Please, make yourself at home." He's allowed to sound annoyed. He's grieving.

She says, "Have you eaten? We need to get you some lunch. Hong Kong Kitchen . . . " She heads toward the drawer that holds the takeout menus.

"It's ten in the morning."

She closes the drawer and starts to bustle about the kitchen. She gets his used coffee cup out of the sink and puts it in the dishwasher. He almost grins for not having put the baby bottles there.

Michael says, "What are you doing?"

"Helping out. I'm going to help out." It's apparent that she came up with the answer on her way here and will repeat it when necessary.

She does not sound convincing.

He asks, "And the bag is full of, what, cleaning supplies?"

"I'm going to stay with you. You shouldn't be alone." Her mouth is set. She won't look at him now. It's either because she's keeping something from him, or she's lying.

He says, "I'm fine."

Anna absently wipes the counter with a dishrag. The kitchen is pretty clean . . . he even tossed the vase, any evidence of decay. She snaps at him, "You're not fine." And her voice cracks. "I mean how could you be fine?"

Oh. This isn't about him. This makes it a little easier. He grabs Anna's shoulder and pulls her into a hug. She starts to cry and Michael feels his shirt get wet not only from tears but from the sobs coming out of her mouth in bursts of breath. "It's not fucking fair! It wasn't . . . " she mumbles incomprehensibly into his shoulder. He holds her and rocks her. Her grief surges, so huge, so uncontrollable, that it starts pulling his own grief to the surface. He feels like crying, too, but he sees Sarah standing in the doorway of his office, rocking the baby, impatient. She widens her eyes as if saying, "Get rid of her already!" Michael shrugs, what can he do?

Sarah rocks Tim. Michael rocks Anna.

This is weird.

———

She was in the Dark. And just as quickly, she wasn't.

But she can't cope with Anna's warbling, it makes her dizzy. She takes Tim through the kitchen. As she passes the flickering Anna, sitting at the table with the very-alive Michael, she feels a chill. She goes back into the nursery and sits down with Tim in the rocker. He's blowing raspberries. She mimics him when Greta's voice breaks in from behind her.

Greta says, "You have trouble, Sarah."

It startles her, and, as she sees Greta looking out the window, in shadow against what Anna imagines is sunlight, she knows that this effect was calculated.

Sarah keeps her voice steady. "It's my sister. I can't keep everyone away."

She can't do Greta today.

Greta says, "You need to work harder at this. Why didn't you tell him not to let her in?"

Sarah hates this feeling that it's all on her and that she's failing. She feels a sixth grade sort of shame creep up the back of her neck, but says, "I'm doing all I can." She leans forward and lays Tim on the floor. He rolls over onto his stomach and starts hitching along the rug. A new trick. It makes her smile.

Greta says, "You're not doing enough."

She feels Greta turn toward her. She will rise and face her. In life, in court, Sarah was someone to be reckoned with. She tries to summon a bit of that old strength. She says, "I'm still here. This visit from Anna can't be that bad."

Greta opens her mouth to say something, but rethinks. Why is she changing her tack? When an opposing lawyer does this in court, Sarah knows to go on alert.

Greta says, "The tea. Two doses a day?"

Doses. Sarah doesn't like the sound of that word. "What's in the tea, Greta?"

Greta says, "A combination of herbs to keep Michael . . . " She pauses. "Aware of you. The human mind has a tendency to move on, to grieve. After a while it makes it harder for the living to stay in touch. The tea makes him more open to the idea of you."

This sounds logical, but something about the careful delivery makes Sarah wary.

"What's your stake in this Greta?" The strength in her voice surprises her. It's been a while.

"What?" Greta looks equally surprised.

"What do you get out of this?"

Greta's voice is resonant and terrible. "Do you like where you go? That dark place? That takes you away from your husband?"

Just the mention of the Dark makes Sarah's heart constrict, her breath quicken.

Greta continues, "How did you come back? What did I give you that brought you back?"

There's something bigger going on, something that makes Sarah go cold and prickly.

Tea. The tea brought her back. But why is Greta so angry?

Tim starts to whine, distressed.

Greta glances down at him and breathes deeply. She changes suddenly to a soothing tone. "Sarah, you have a rare opportunity here. You can't let it be taken from you." Her tone smoothes out the wrinkles, assuages the fear. As quickly as it came, Sarah's panic abates and she feels calm and a little sleepy. "All that matters is that you keep your husband close. If he goes, how can we be sure what's become of him? You know he needs you. He'd be lost without you."

Michael would be lost without her.

———

It took one solid hour of grief counseling to get Anna to leave. This included a painful blow-by-blow recitation of Anna's last day with Sarah, which caused Michael's guilt for his absence to bubble up again. Only after Anna had what she termed, "a good long cry," was he able to get rid of her.

The phone starts ringing about ten minutes after she leaves. Michael wonders if Anna called in the troops, or if it's just that word has gotten out that he's home.

Sarah still seems to be gone; he doesn't know what to do with that.

Beep.

"Mike! It's Chuck. Yeah." There's a long pause. Saying the right thing was always a daily challenge for Chuck. Michael feels for his friend as he hears him squirm. He's relieved when he finally says, "This isn't answering machine material. Call me."

He washes Anna's water glass by hand, as it takes time. Sarah will come back in time, right?

Beep.

Caroline's voice is next. "Michael, I just got back. I just heard. Call me. Please." And he had wanted to talk to her about everything. But now he can't talk to anyone about any of this.

Beep.

"Michael, it's Ed." *Shit. Work.* He gets up to get the phone when he hears the rest. "We got the samples, so that must mean you're back. Look, you were taking two months paternity . . . uh . . . you were taking two months off. Take them. We don't need you back until you're ready to. Uh. I'm so sorry, Michael." Ed adds, oddly, as if reading it aloud, "All of our hearts go out to you in this time of need."

Michael picks up the burp rag from where he threw it by the door. He squeezes it in his hand; it's bone dry. It smells like fabric softener. They're gone. As if they were never here. He can't deal with this this coming and going.

Maybe that was the visit. Maybe Sarah heard Anna's story of her death and . . . moved on. Maybe not knowing what really happened was keeping her here.

Beep.

"Michael, it's Dan. Man, I can't believe this shit. I hear you're home, though. Give me a call. Let me know when the funeral is and I'll fly out. I wish. Dude, I wish there was something I could do."

He turns the volume down on the answering machine and the phone's ringer off. Now the only reminder that the world is swiftly closing in is the whirring of the machine as it clicks in.

Funeral. Fuck.

He sits on the sofa and the tears come. He can't stop them this time; they run out as if they'd been building up somewhere in his head the whole time Anna was here. He hasn't cried like this since he was a child. It takes control of him and his face feels like it might turn inside out. The absurd slurping and snorting must be coming from another source: it doesn't sound human.

Fuck.

He kicks the coffee table. This feels satisfying. It's an ugly, metal, claw-footed antique number that came from a deceased aunt soon after they were married. The only antique quality to it is that it's old. He kicks the table again and the metal feet rattle. He stands up and stomps his foot down on it, breaking off the edge. One of the nails catches his calf and grazes it.

"Fuck!" His voice echoes in the apartment, only to be interrupted by Sarah's laughter.

He looks up in disbelief, wiping his wet face in the crook of his shirtsleeve.

She says, "I think you killed it." She's grinning. How can she be so fucking *happy?*

He lets out a bear-like growl of anger.

She laughs louder. He can't help but smile. Here she is again. And if she's here . . .

He asks, "Where's the baby?" From despair to excitement in ten seconds flat. If they're here, whatever that means, at least he can spend more time with his boy. He has to see him.

She says, "He's sleeping."

Michael sprints down the hall.

Sarah calls after him, "Michael, don't wake him, I finally got him down for a nap."

He holler-whispers, "I'll be very gentle." He stops when he gets to the door of the nursery, breathing heavily, his head spinning. His nose whistles, reminding him that only a moment ago he was drowning and now he's here, expectant, overjoyed at seeing his boy. His Tim. Sarah follows him as he walks softly inside. The nursery smells like baby again. Tim is on his back, arms and legs splayed, fat cheeks red, sucking on his bottom lip. His downy, chestnut hair spreads in soft curls on the mattress and his lashes are heartbreakingly long. He's wearing some ridiculous red tie-dyed red footie jammies with stars on them.

Michael leans over.

Sarah whispers, warningly, "Michael!"

He pauses half an inch above the baby and inhales. It is all Tim. The baby thrashes in his sleep, whacking Michael in the cheek. It doesn't hurt so much as it startles him. Michael laughs while Tim settles, his fingers twitching, feeling the memory of his father's sharp stubble.

Michael turns to Sarah who's beaming. He goes to her and takes her in his arms, holding her. God, she smells good.

In a comic, hopeless tone she says into his chest, "The best thing ever?" They aren't going to talk about it, her being dead. But it's there.

He says, "The best thing ever." He'll take whatever he can get, for as long as he can. It beats the alternative.

It was enough to fall asleep with his face in her hair that night. Holding her. Trying very hard to think of nothing but being there, knowing Tim is sleeping peacefully in his crib.

But when Michael wakes in the morning, she's gone. He breathes deeply, trying not to panic. Maybe there's someone at the door. Maybe she's in the nursery. He knows she's not in the nursery. He can sense when she's there, when she's not. But he checks anyway. And no Tim.

She has only ever left before because someone arrived. But no one's here. So why would she leave? Was *that* it? The last of it? Was the passion of their lovemaking last night taken as some sort of good-bye?

He can't think this way every time she leaves. It's too exhausting.

He paces the living room for a moment. He sits on the sofa. He stands up and walks over to the window and looks out. Spring is going on in New York, fourteen floors below, beneath the pale-green, new leaves of the scattered trees. By the looks of the foot traffic, it's around ten o'clock and people are going about their business in a bewilderingly normal fashion.

Michael picks up the phone to call someone. He hangs up. He hasn't gotten the strength to respond to any of the twenty-four blinking phone messages left by people who need to comfort him. He should probably call his mother, who left at least eight of those messages. Tell her he's okay. He picks up the phone again. But if he calls her, he'll have to have that conversation and he'll have to lie to her and he can't do that yet. He hangs up. He picks it up again and stares at the numbers on its face, hears its accusing dial tone. There's no one he can talk to about this right now.

He goes to the kitchen to eat something. He grabs a greenish banana and opens it, but its green, sharp smell nauseates him. He can't eat. Nothing feels right. His limbs are twitching and his heart is pounding like it does when he has too much caffeine. He walks back to the nursery and peeks in again. No one is there. He knew this. He walks back to the front hall and looks at the phone.

He opens the front door.

But what if she comes back?

What if she doesn't?

He closes the door.

He opens it again and looks at Dr. James's door down the hall.

He trips the deadbolt to keep the door open and the door falls to with a dull clank as he walks down the long, carpeted hallway. He's too crazed to have to worry about keys.

Before he gets to Doctor James's door, Greta materializes in front of him, her eyes glinting accusingly. She says, "Where are you going?"

He keeps his eyes focused on the floor so he doesn't have to meet hers. "I'm checking in on a neighbor."

"I thought you weren't going to leave her."

"She's not *there*."

"Maybe she knew you were leaving."

He feels like she's fishing for some sort of argument. He won't give it to her. He shoulders past her.

Greta says, "You need to stay with your wife."

He turns around, expecting to see anger, but she smiles and says, "She doesn't do well while you're away. You'll see that soon enough." She dissipates.

He can't read into this or figure it out. But he can at least accomplish what he set out to do when he left the apartment. He knocks on the doctor's door.

———

Greta said it would be just a minute. She wanted to show Sarah something in her apartment. While Michael slept, Sarah took Tim out of his crib, draped him, still sleeping, over her shoulder and followed Greta to the front door. Her first step out of the apartment, she knew it wasn't going to work. She could hear the howl of the elevator shaft and everything got dim, hard to see. As she approached the elevator, the howl grew louder, echoing back a larger space than an elevator shaft, an all-consuming nothingness. The hall didn't look shimmery, like things had been in the apartment, but dark, oozing black. It was as if the Dark Place that she'd been pulled to before was coming to her, seeping out of the walls, floor and ceiling, devouring the hallway.

Greta was saying something to her, but all she could hear was that howl begin to shriek, and Tim woke up and squirmed, crying. She walked as far as the elevator, the door rolling open with the rumble of an arriving subway. The shriek then opened up into a sucking black din, and despite Greta's inaudible urgings, Sarah turned and ran back down the hall in the direction of her door. Sarah clenched her eyes shut, felt for the doorknob and scrambled to turn it. She opened the door and slipped in. Before she opened her eyes, she could see the light. Tim was hiccupping in that post-cry way, and everything was quiet again. And Michael was gone.

That was three months ago.

Greta has visited every day since then, soothing her, keeping her company. The mommies are sometimes with her and that's some comfort. Greta explained that it's different for every woman—time and space in this place—like pregnancy. Michael's involvement in her life has somehow bonded her to the apartment, not like the other mommies who come and go. Greta assures her that it's okay, she will always bring the mommies to Sarah's place so that she won't be alone. Greta told her that this frightening trip to the outside was a reminder.

Sarah can't help the creeping feeling that Greta took her away from ~~Michael on purpose; that she made her lose her hold on him.~~ *When Michael comes back, she cannot let him go again.*

———

Dr. James is dressed and alone.

Michael sits in the deep leather chair staring at his tea while the doctor watches him. But this time, the watching doesn't make him nervous. He tries to think of the right way to ask this. "Can we talk theoretically?"

The doctor answers, "Absolutely."

"Hypothetically?"

The doctor gently scolds him, "Michael."

Michael says, "Well you see. My wife. My baby I told you about?" He looks into Dr. James's eyes hoping he doesn't have to say it out loud. Even with Anna, he hasn't had to say it out loud yet.

Dr. James senses his discomfort and leaps in. "Mrs. Grady told me, Michael. I was so sorry to hear about your loss." He leans forward and peers at Michael over his glasses. There is genuine sadness in his eyes.

Something releases inside Michael and he says, "Only they're not gone." The words trip out without much forethought and lie there on the coffee table, waiting.

The doctor says, "I got that." Oh. So matter-of-fact. Michael looks at him uncomprehendingly.

The doctor explains, "Last time, when you told me. You talked as if they were here." There's a silence, but it's Michael waiting for the doctor this time. He's not sure how much they're allowed to talk about.

The older man clears his throat, takes off his glasses, and cleans them on his shirt in a self-conscious way: an actor waiting onstage for someone who's missed a cue. He puts the glasses back on and peers at Michael, who notices that the doctor has only succeeded in smearing them. He says, "Sometimes, they don't go." Dr. James puts this forth as a gentle offering, an agreement that they're now free to discuss this openly.

How does he know this? Understand? Michael doesn't care; he knows that this is the guy who gets it. He might have some answers. He asks, "Is it her? Or have I somehow conjured her up?"

The doctor asks, "Does it matter?"

No. It doesn't.

Michael says, "But she was gone this morning. When I came over here, the apartment was empty."

Dr. James smiles at his worry. "You'll know when she leaves for good. You'll know."

Michael asks, "And in the meantime?"

The doctor gets out of his chair, sighing like a much older man. "Don't look a gift horse in the mouth." This he says with an air of finality.

Greta had said that. Greta. How to ask about Greta? Michael formulates the question for a moment before he says, "Dr. James?"

"And try to get some sleep, Michael, and eat better. You look terrible."

"I think I've been fighting a bug." A bug. That's what it feels like. The dizziness, the cold sweats. But he's also been fighting his growing uneasiness with this specter of a woman in his wife's world who says she is somehow facilitating their ability to be together. The fear that each time Sarah disappears, it's for the last time. Friends and family and real life closing in. And something else . . . a darkness he can't put his finger on. The idea that this is all somehow wrong.

The doorbell buzzes. The doctor calls over his shoulder as he ambles toward the door. "My next appointment. I'm sorry, Michael. Please, come see me anytime." He seems anxious to get rid of him. Michael gets up and follows him down his narrow hallway.

Dr. James hesitates before the door. The entryway is close and has a very high ceiling. Michael's dizziness returns, a reverse vertigo. The buzzer rings again, startling both of them. It's longer this time. Someone's leaning on it.

Dr. James takes a deep breath, steeling himself, and opens the door.

Milo flashes his eyes theatrically and pushes past the both of them into the apartment. He says, "Ah! Company. Tell me, neighbor, does the doctor use the same techniques with you as he does with me? 'Cause let me tell you, they're working like a charm."

Dr. James cautions, "Milo . . . " That parental cautionary tone again as he closes the door.

Sarah's worried. Tim's been sluggish for days now. All he wants to do is sleep. If he were living, Sarah would think that he had the flu or a light fever. He hasn't any appetite. He won't even wake when she picks him up. She shakes him awake occasionally to make sure he's okay. His eyes blink open and focus on her for a moment before he goes back to sleep. He lies still in the bassinette. She needs to call Greta. Tim looks so small and vulnerable on his back in his red-and-white, tie-dyed footy jammies, his arms thrown over his head in surrender.

As if she were summoned, Greta appears. She steps in to look at the baby.

The worry in her voice startles Sarah. "How long has he been like this?"

"Three . . . four days now."

Greta pulls Sarah out of the way sharply and moves toward the baby. She says, "Call his name."

Now Sarah's worried. "Tim." This is more serious than she thought. Why didn't she call Greta sooner? Such a terrible mother, she didn't even think anything was wrong. How is she supposed to know how babies act here?

Greta barks, "Call him again. Louder."

Sarah says sharply, "Tim!" It's the closest thing to a scold she's ever directed toward her child.

Greta starts murmuring. The murmuring gets louder and stronger in an ancient language. The back of Sarah's scalp crackles as she recognizes its tones and rhythms. There's a strong musty, earthy smell in the air and the room around the baby is dark with a black cloud of silt. Tim sleeps on, unaware. Sarah knows Greta is there to help her child, but she can't stop the urge to pick him up, protect him, help him through this.

Greta's chanting increases and Sarah's need to interfere grows stronger. Wait.

She steps toward Greta.

There's something wrong here. Sarah grabs Greta's arm. Greta turns toward her, her eyes obsidian, fierce.

Sarah wakes up on the sofa. It's late afternoon and the sun shines in the window comfortably. She feels so sleepy.

The baby.

There's a squeal from somewhere on the floor. Sarah startles and sits up to find Tim on a blanket in the middle of the living room. He pulls on the feet of his brown polka-dotted footie jammies and squeals happily. He giggles. She smiles and goes to him. He's so happy, so vibrant.

What was she upset about? Something awful happened and she was worried about Tim.

She needed to protect him from something. There was . . .

But she can't remember. It must have been the residue of a nightmare. She's been having those lately.

When Michael gets back to his apartment, he finds the door closed. This makes him anxious, as he doesn't have a key. He buzzes the doorbell. Nothing. He hammers on the door.

Michael slumps with relief when he hears the catch turning.

Greta greets him with a scowl. She looks at him as if he's intruding. *It's my apartment, what are you looking at?*

Greta calls over her shoulder, "Sarah! Your wayward husband has returned." She turns to him and mutters angrily, "I told you not to leave. Now you'll see." Before he can object, she swishes into the living room to the chatter of what seems like a dozen concerned voices, "Where's he been?" "How can he think that . . . " and general tut-tutting.

Michael's stomach roils with the smell of Greta's dark, earthy perfume. Each time he smells it, it takes on a stronger . . . intent. It's the animal funk of her person surrounding all who are near her.

But Sarah left. She was gone. She might have been gone for good. And he needed answers. He doesn't want to go in, but any escape route is in full view of the living room. Sarah comes to meet him instead.

She's aged ten years since last night. Her face is haunted by shadow; her hair has gone lanky and her complexion is sallow, void of its usual pink pigment. Her teeth are gray, her mouth set and worried.

"Honey." He takes her face in his hands and strokes it. "Honey. I went down the hall. For like ten minutes. You were gone. What happened?"

She throws her arms around his waist and pulls him close, resting her cheek against his chest. "You were gone for months."

He doesn't understand. He holds her and finds there's less to her, as if some flesh has fallen away since last night. He sees her shoulder blades sticking through the back of her shirt. He can feel her tremulous worry and the desperation in her hands as they clutch his back.

He asks, "Is the baby okay?"

She snorts and starts to pull him toward the living room.

Michael says, "No, I don't want to interrupt your . . . "—he doesn't know what to call it— "meeting."

But she's insistent and her frailness makes him afraid that if he resists, her arm might tear off like the tail of a lizard he tried to catch as a child.

He finds himself in a room filled with the same women from the last . . . meeting. Juicy is there, although she's now called Guess. Maureen. A few familiar faces, a few new ones. One new woman sits in the corner looking out the window, lost.

The ladies call out in chorus, "Hello, Michael."

He says, "Ladies," as if he has merely walked in on a tea party, a girls' night in, a baby shower. A man who knows he's out of place.

Greta issues a command. "Michael, have a seat." He loathes her tone and looks to Sarah imploringly, but she won't meet his eyes.

He says, "Okay." He looks down, surprised to see a handful of babies sitting up on a blanket playing with things. One crawls away very quickly, and Sarah's up like a shot, chasing after him.

It's Tim.

He's crawling with a strange adeptness. Months have passed in a heartbeat. He has more hair, more expression, and he yelps in frustration and kicks his legs angrily when Sarah picks him up. He appears to be around eight months old. Sarah gently shushes him and blows on his neck to distract him. He giggles.

Greta's saying something to Michael, but he can't hear her over his wonder. Sarah sees his look and hands the baby to him. Michael feels the newfound strength in the boy's back. Tim stares at him, his head no longer waggles. His cheeks are rosy and healthy, his eyes full of intelligence and humor. The baby blows a raspberry and then laughs, wriggling, pounding Michael on the chest with the palm of his hand. *Ba-ba-ba-ba-ba!*

Michael's incredulous laugh wracks him like a sob. Tim puts his hand to Michael's mouth and he blows on it. The boy screeches happily like an exotic bird and explodes into giggles. Michael repeats it and he laughs again. The women around the room relax and coo at this interaction.

~~Greta speaks in a condescending tone, poisoning the moment.~~ "That's *much* better."

Maureen clears her throat and stammers a little. "Christine was about to answer my question about nursing."

Greta turns to Christine. "I think we had agreed that it is best to co-sleep with the baby until it's sleeping through the night, hadn't we?"

The woman by the window starts moaning, "No, no, no, no, no, no, no." She holds herself, rocking back and forth. Michael notices she's holding an infant. He's sure that she wasn't when he came in. "No, no, no, no, no, no, no."

The one who must be Christine barrels forward as if they're discussing the weather and ignores the misery in the corner. She's slim and very well put-together in jeans and a twinset. Her baby sleeps in a baby carrier on the floor, which she rocks gently with her foot. With her brown soccer-mom bob, she speaks officiously to the group in a tone that reminds Michael of the Lamaze class he took with Sarah. "Clearly you need to nurse the child on demand. The baby's thriving in your warmth and nearness and why else are we here but to be with our babies?"

Tim grabs Michael's hair and pulls on it. It's a very real pain, one that takes him back to his child and away from wondering about these women, whoever, *what*ever, they are.

Greta chimes in, "Christine is right, darling. Keep your babies near you and you can stay with your babies." So many things Greta says sound like polished slogans. How long has she been doing this? What exactly *is* she doing? *Don't think. Just don't think.*

The woman by the window wails this time. "No!"

Greta plows right over her. "Patrice, your case is very unusual. It hardly ever happens." There's murmuring in the background while Greta continues on as if discussing a ruined cake, or a lost dog. "Ladies, what Patrice neglected to tell you is that she accidentally smothered her infant while sleeping with her." Sympathetic noises travel around the room.

Christ, who are these women?

The woman shoves her hand into her mouth. The infant is now nowhere to be seen. She murmurs, "No, no, no, no, no, no, no."

Maureen gets up and goes to the woman, holding her.

Greta smiles as if proud of an alcoholic achieving her one-year chip, or of a handicapped person climbing Mount Everest. "And Patrice, ladies, took the bravest path imaginable. She *followed* her baby girl here. Rather than let her go into the unknown alone, she chose to be with her. And here you are, Patrice, you are here with your baby girl."

Michael looks over to find Patrice cradling her infant again, weeping with gladness as Maureen pets her shoulder, rocking her happily. This isn't right. This is clearly wrong. How can Greta praise a woman for killing herself? He feels a need to put a stop to all of this—wrongness—but has no idea how to even approach it.

He puts Tim down between his knees and the boy crawls toward the center of the blanket again. Michael does the only thing he knows how to do: he goes to Sarah and puts his arms around her, holding her tight. If she's going to be here with these monsters, she's not going to do it alone.

He notices Greta look over at them, an approving smile pasted on her face, her eyes communicating concern . . . or is it fear?

A knock at the door—and it's enough for Greta and the other women to fade from the room. He feels Sarah linger in his arms a moment longer, but then she's gone. He can still feel her warmth on his chest. There's another knock followed by a soul-piercing cry of abandonment.

It's coming from the baby carrier still in the middle of the floor. The other babies are gone. The plastic, molded carrier starts to rock on its own spookily, as if being shaken by a telekinetic power. But when Michael rises and walks around to the front of it, he sees that a baby, about three months old in footies with elephants all over them, is kicking, making the whole thing move.

Michael whispers soothingly. "Shh, shh, baby, shh . . . "

The crying increases and Michael wonders if the person behind the door can hear it.

"Shh, baby." Should he pick it up? He doesn't want to pick it up, this phantom baby. He tries not to think too much about his immediate revulsion in relation to Tim. The visitor has decided to hold the buzzer down, adding to the cacophony. The infant stops suddenly, sucking in air, summoning deep inside for untold screaming powers, and lets out an ear-splitting cry before fading away like the others.

A cry to wake the dead, Michael thinks as he opens the door.

A delivery guy stands there with a large bowl of jewel-toned flowers, roses, irises, and deep-red camellias among a splendid array of greenery. The basket is made from bits of bracken. It's beautiful and smells fresher than anything that's been in the apartment since he got home. Only when he sees the deep-purple ribbon around it does Michael realize he's looking at his first sympathy bouquet.

SEVEN

Tim's with Sarah in the Dark. She only got to see Michael for a moment and now here she is. She doesn't understand how time works.

She holds Tim to her belly and he snuggles into her shoulder.

The tree has no leaves now, as in midwinter. This makes her deeply uneasy.

What was she just feeling, sitting in her living room? It was something bad. It was dread and confusion jumbled in a murky stupor. She was glad the mommies were there, right? But they were so loud and so worried, all of that worry, all the time, surrounding her in what used to be her living room. Now that she's away from Greta, she's beginning to think. Only the edge of a thought, but a real thought. Greta's a comfort when Michael leaves, but when she first arrives, Sarah gets a thick feeling in her stomach, like her first waking of conscience as a child; when she was doing something wrong, but she didn't know exactly why it was wrong yet. This feeling usually passes, but when Michael came back this time, she felt it again.

Tim whines a bit and pulls on the short hairs at the back of her neck. It hurts, but she finds herself grateful for the sensation. It means that she's still *there and he is as well. And he's real. She sings, "Three angels above, the whole human race, they dream us to life, they dream me a face." But she falters. The words of the lullaby aren't comforting today.*

As quickly as she disappeared, she finds herself standing in her dining room, watching Michael smell a bouquet of flowers on the table. She's overcome by a feeling of wellness and love.

———

Michael hears Sarah's voice behind him. "Oh, these are lovely, who are they from?" He wheels around with something between a groan and a shout.

"The office," Michael says. He's lying more easily these days.

He watches as Sarah lowers Tim to the ground. Happy to find himself free, the baby begins to crawl across the floor.

Fortunately, Michael's managed to pluck off the dark purple ribbon and the bouquet looks a bit more festive. Not very baby-welcoming, but not horrible.

Sarah leans in and smells the flowers. Out of habit? Or can she truly smell them? Their green and woody fragrance fills the room with a breath of life that stirs Michael with nostalgia. He is overwhelmed by memories of past springs, long walks in the park with Sarah. When they'd meet for lunch by the duck pond in Central Park, he'd bring the falafel from their favorite cart, she'd bring the Orange Julius.

She doesn't ask to see the card, and he decides it's time to explore boundaries.

He says, "You know what? It's a beautiful day. Let's take Little Man out for a walk." Before the last word leaves his mouth, he can tell that this was the wrong thing to say. She gets nervous and starts fidgeting, touching each flower like a hummingbird. She's avoiding his eyes.

"Oh, no, I don't think . . . I don't . . . I don't think he's ready yet. You know? He's so little."

But he's not little. Anymore. He's huge. And crawling.

Michael says, "It's okay. It was just an idea." He doesn't feel so well, anyway. His mild headache has turned into pervasive pain. He doesn't think his head has been completely pain-free since he got home. He'll get to a doctor after.

After what? He can't think about a timeline without thinking about Sarah and Tim leaving.

He has to focus on his little family. For as long as he has them.

She looks at him anxiously. "And. I'm afraid. I don't think I *can*."

He gestures for her to continue. "Or . . . ?" Her grasp on reality seems so tenuous that he feels he should let her put her own words to things.

"I don't know. And I don't want to—"

He stops her. "Of course not." He feels bad for asking.

The nervousness isn't leaving her. She drifts over to the window and looks outside. Her hand rises to the glass but hovers just shy of it, as if she's afraid to touch it. She looks down at the street below.

She sounds surprised. "It's spring."

He walks up behind her, looking out the window with her. "Yep." He wraps his arms around her and holds her tight. She's chilly, but warms with his touch.

Sarah used to be the one dragging them out of the house on weekends, to gallery openings, readings, food fairs, performance art shows. She laughed at him when he wanted to stay home, order in, and watch movies. It saddens him to remember that she'd always say, *"Life's too short to miss out on any of this."*

The thinness hasn't gone away, but her color is back. Her hair's untidy, but beautiful as the light from outside shines through it. Michael could live and die by the curve of her neck. He kisses it.

Sarah asks, "When did that happen? Where did the time go?" It's a question people ask every day in mock surprise, but from Sarah it sounds baffled, desperate.

He turns her toward him and kisses her forehead. "It came after winter." Then her nose.

There's a pterodactyl-like squeal from the floor behind them. Tim is smacking his father's leg. Michael looks around to see Tim grinning up at him, drooling on his Onesie. The baby chirps when their eyes meet; that joy of recognition.

Michael laughs as tears flood his eyes. *Stop it.* He's like a hormonal teenage girl.

Tim, having gotten a good grasp with one hand, scoots forward, grabbing on to Michael's leg with his other. He's pulling himself up. It looks like he's using the weight of his head as a counterbalance for his behind, which clings to the floor, leaden in its diaper. With some huffing and pulling, Tim manages to pull himself forward on his knees, hanging on to the pants, wobbling back and forth. His head is teetering close to the floor, his bottom in the air. Michael leans over to rescue him, but stops when he hears Sarah say, "No. Wait."

The chubby hands walk up the pants, grasping new fabric, and after a precarious minute, Tim is standing. He laughs and bobs, keeping his grip on the jeans.

Sarah praises him. "Good boy! All by your lonesome! Mommy's so proud of you."

Oh, God. Don't think about it. Enjoy it. Michael squats down, holding Tim under his armpits. He kisses the boy on his wet cheek and Tim turns his drool-y mouth to try to meet his. After a wipe along his cheek leaves him soaked, Michael pulls away from the slobbery mess to see the baby, mouth open, break into a smile. He's been slimed and the boy gets the joke.

Michael wakes to find Sarah's arm around him, holding him close. He carefully extracts it, disheartened to find that it's lighter than it once was. More fragile. He slips out of bed and goes to the bathroom for a drink of water. He is always so thirsty these days. While he's up, he'll check on the boy.

Tim is asleep on his tummy. He's learned to roll over and this is his preferred position. Michael gently puts his hand on the boy's warm back to feel his breath. The crib creaks as he shifts and Michael grasps one side of it with his hand, moving it gently. It sways, extremely unstable. He grabs the other side to wiggle it further and his hand touches a plastic bag, taped to the bar. He pulls at it and tears it off. His hand recognizes bolts and screws, but he holds the bag to the light from the window to see. Unopened, it still has the instructions inside.

Michael turns on the overhead light, but dims it quickly. He crouches down and looks for the hole in the crib where the screw goes. He still can't see well, so he puts his finger in. It's empty. He's such an idiot for not checking it earlier. Especially after the swing. She didn't know she was cooking rotten vegetables, how would she be able put a crib together properly? His wife, the master of the universe, isn't the same. Her motor functions are clearly impaired. He should have known this, made sure things were safe. Michael finds the right bolt and its matching nut and starts to screw it in by hand. What else has she not been handling?

━━━━━━━

If they can stay this way, hide out, can they make a life together? She told Greta to stay away for a little while. She did it as kindly as she could and promised to keep giving Michael tea, but she could tell Greta was hurt. She has no concept of time when Michael's gone, but he's here now and they've spent two beautiful days together, morning to night, a routine, with naps and bedtime and story reading. With grown-up conversation, laughter, and lovemaking. Greta comes to watch once in a while. But she doesn't speak to them and she hasn't interfered in their lives in other ways for days, so Sarah simply ignores her. Greta's just another uncomfortable side effect of her current condition.

Like food. She doesn't know why she doesn't eat and why Tim does. Or why she can drink the tea that Greta gives her. But she can't eat real food and she yearns for it. When Michael eats, she tries to ignore it politely, to make herself scarce. Sometimes she looks the other way, like you do when someone is picking his nose, or scratching himself somewhere inappropriate. Michael will steal off to the kitchen and Sarah will make sure to busy herself in the nursery. She tries not to sulk. It's not his fault she can't eat. But she misses it. She can't smell everything anymore, but sometimes a scent will seep through. Garlic. Coffee. Like the edge of a memory of a dream about food.

Two amazing days, no Greta, just family. They are on the floor of the living room watching Tim cruise around the edge of the sofa to the chair, squealing. So close to walking already.

Michael leans in to blow on the boy's chubby neck, and Tim slimes his father's cheek. He leans back and laughs, a low, husky, baby laugh. Michael says, "Dude, we need to teach you how to kiss." Sarah laughs. But her laughter, the weight of life in Michael's arms, the slobbery, sweet smell of the baby, and the wetness on his cheek suddenly evaporate. Through the squealing and laughter, he has not heard the hammering at the door. Large fists, pounding.

Sarah is gone before he notices. The loss of Tim is a punch to the gut, causing Michael to grunt. He falls to his knees, unable to get his bearings. The door thunders again and he can hear the tenor of Dr. James yelling. He heaves himself up off the floor.

Greta materializes in front of the door, smoldering in anger. Dr. James is yelling and pounding on the other side.

Michael says, "Get out of the way."

"You can't let people in. Sarah's gone."

"Get out of the way."

"Do you want to keep your wife and child?"

Michael reaches out his hands to grab Greta's shoulders and physically move her. "Move." As soon as he closes his hands on the Chinese silk, Greta's shoulders grow ice cold and she evaporates, leaving a cloud of black dust. When Michael inhales, the dust prickles his eyes and the inside of his nose like snow. He opens the door.

Dr. James's shirt is covered with blood. There are patches on the front, soaked into peach-striped, oxford cloth; his arms have been painted with it. The metallic tinge of blood mixes with a strong smell of cologne. Dr. James has been weeping.

Michael resists the urge to close his door on whatever is going on out there.

The doctor wheezes, "Please," and then turns down the hallway, back toward his own apartment.

Sarah's already gone; he can't change that. He shouldn't leave.

But the blood. This is more than a casserole or groceries.

————————

Michael cautiously enters Dr. James's apartment through the open door. The living room is empty—and impeccably clean. A burgundy tablecloth covers the wooden coffee table and two candles burn on either side of an unopened bag from Burger King. Handpicked flowers are messily stuffed into a glass.

But where is Dr. James? Michael hesitates for a moment before stepping through the doctor's bedroom door. Here the scent of blood is stronger.

The bedroom is dark. The bed is made. Still no doctor. But the bathroom door is a rectangle of blinding light, and he thinks he hears sounds.

With growing dread, Michael enters the bathroom. He stares down, the intense glow of incandescent light against white-and-black tile hurting his head.

Slowly, he looks around as his eyes adjust. The walls are not covered with splatters of blood. No bloody footsteps on the black-and-white tile. But there, in the tub, lies Milo. Restful, arms at his side, head turned away, glassy eyes staring at the wall. Dr. James sits on the toilet cover, watching him.

If not for the blood on Dr. James's shirt Michael wouldn't, at first, have known that the boy was injured. It all has the appearance of some gruesome prank: white-gray makeup, funky contact lenses, a glassy stare. Milo's wearing a black trench coat, black turtleneck, black trousers. There's something red around his wrists. Without his sassy comebacks, Milo looks more like a vulnerable child than a teen. But the tub underneath Milo and his clothes are soaked with blood; the source seems to be the wrists, which are oddly wrapped in bright-red hand towels, also soaked; tin-soldier cuffs tacked onto a Goth comic book action figure.

Michael can't quite process what he's looking at. Is this something staged or is it real?

Dr. James says, flatly, "I tried to stop the bleeding. He won't listen. He never listens. He kills himself."

Kills himself? Why is he so calm? The doctor should be freaking out, raging, terrified, *something*. Michael says, "I don't understand. Did you call an ambulance? You have to call the police." Michael scrambles for his phone in his pocket, but it's not there.

The doctor laughs, shaking his head. "Don't call anyone, Michael, it won't do any good."

Michael stops, perched by the door. "Why the hell not?"

The doctor sighs, exhausted, and says, "I did call, the first time."

Michael says, "The *first* time?" Why is he so calm?

"I let it go too far. Once he declared a romantic . . . interest . . . in me, I should have found him alternative care. That's standard operating procedure. But I didn't. We had made such progress." He trails off. Shame burns in Michael's ears for having assumed the worst about this guy. "The joke? He threatened to kill himself when I suggested a new therapist. So this is better?"

He looks up at Michael, clearly upset, but not as upset as he should be. He should be frantic. "He does this. Over and over. He sneaks into my apartment and prepares a romantic meal. I arrived home . . . " He laughs hollowly and looks at Michael. "Hamburgers. And he cleaned the apartment. Did you see the flowers?" Michael nods.

Dr. James looks back at the boy in the tub. "When I told him that it was extremely inappropriate, that we needed to stop therapy, he excused himself to use the bathroom." He stops for a moment and then says, "And here we are."

Michael asks, "How long ago . . . did you find him? The first time?"

"Two years ago. It's like this and then after a week or so he shows up again, healthy, whole. We go through the whole thing all over again."

Michael stares at him blankly. Is there something he will be repeating with Sarah? Is there something he's supposed to do to help the doctor? He shakes his head, reeling from trying to sort out the details.

Dr. James looks at him, incredulous, impatient. "I thought you'd understand." He observes Michael a moment and then slides his glasses up to his forehead, rubbing his eyes.

"Dr. James?"

The doctor gets a distant look. "He says he goes back to his parents, too. I wonder what it is they need to endure over and over." He laughs. "I guess every man's hell is different."

Michael says, "Hell?"

"You didn't wonder why I understood about your little haunting?"

Wait, no. That's wrong. That's trite. It's not a haunting. She's real.

Michael says, "Milo's a ghost."

135

"I needed company tonight. I panicked. I called you too soon: I should have waited." He pats his blood-soaked sleeves and looks over to the bathtub, as if waiting for something to cook, or dry. "It'll be another minute. It's so hard . . . to explain. I didn't want to tell the story without you knowing this." He motions to the tub. "I fucked up horribly and inexcusably and I don't know when I'll stop paying for it. But the idea of someone else understanding it . . . " Michael's not talking. Milo is fading. In a moment the two men are alone together. For some reason, Milo's absence is not as violent as Sarah's when it occurs. Dr. James smacks his hands on his knees and gets to his feet. "I need a drink."

Michael follows him to the living room.

The doctor digs through the bottom drawer of his desk. He pulls out a bottle of J&B and two glasses. He says, "Can't display liquor in front of the minor patients." He laughs. He pours two shots and hands one to Michael, who's all too happy to take it. Michael stands opposite the desk and downs the shot. It burns his throat, which mercifully gives him something else to focus on, if just for a moment.

He has questions. But there's that worry. Five minutes in this apartment cost him three months last time. And there's Greta. What can he say to be able to leave?

He says, "I'm sorry."

The doctor says, "How many times is this now?"

Michael has to get out of here.

Dr. James gets a panicked look. "I lost count." He starts looking through his week-at-a-glance calendar on the desk, frantically flipping pages. "I'd been keeping track. I didn't want to write it down. I thought maybe that when it stopped mattering, it would stop happening." He stops flipping. He looks momentarily hopeful. "Which means maybe it will stop happening." He looks at Michael. "But it's happening for a reason, right? I can't believe there's no reason."

Michael starts to realize that Dr. James is lost, too, which makes him think of something he said earlier. *"I guess everyone's hell is different."* He says, "Wait a minute. What did you mean, your hell?" He thought the doctor was referring to Milo before, but now he knows he's talking about himself. His own hell. "Am I in a hell? Is it something I did?" Is he being punished for not being here for the birth? For her death? Panicked, he finds himself going through an absurd laundry list of lifetime wrongdoings before the doctor stops him, motioning to the chair.

"I'm sorry. I'm sorry." The doctor sits on the sofa. "Sit. Please. I'll explain."

Michael sits, but his leg starts jiggling. He needs these answers but he needs to get back before bad things start to happen.

The doctor sits opposite him, considering for a moment. "I. Am in hell. You, on the other hand. I don't know. I was curious the first time I knew you could see Milo. But then, when I realized you had your own ghost . . . " Michael winces. *"Visitor,* it made sense. You can see your"— he pauses to choose the next word—"Sarah. Maybe I can see her, I don't know, you keep her locked up."

Michael says, "She won't go out."

This interests him. "Maybe she can't."

"I tried to get her to go for a walk and it freaked her out."

The doctor thinks on this. "How did she die?"

The word "die" burns, as does Michael talking about it. It feels disloyal to speak of her in such a way. He slumps, talking to his shoes. "Congestive heart failure. She took the baby with her. I was out of town."

Something in the doctor lights up a little on hearing this. "She waited for you. You weren't there to say good-bye, so she waited."

Michael asks, "Why are you smiling?"

"It's the first good thing I've encountered in our predicament."

Michael remembers Milo's face, his red cuffs, his cloying remarks, and finds it hard to see himself in *"our* predicament." He's getting irritated and nervous and rises to his feet. He says, "I've been gone too long already."

Dr. James says, "You have time slippage?"

Michael sits again.

The doctor asks, "How much time gets lost?"

"Months."

The doctor thinks for a moment. "I suppose it's easy to keep track of with a baby. The baby ages?"

Michael nods and asks, "What does that mean?"

The doctor pours himself another shot, repeating the question, making it his own. "What does that mean?"

"Does it matter how long I'm gone? I was here five minutes the other day and three months passed." He says it again, thinking he didn't convey how horribly long that was. "Three months. He could crawl."

Dr. James says, "Yours live with you. Mine comes and goes. I remember *when* it is, though. How far in we are . . . were. I remembered from the appointments. The progress of his illness. It was so textbook, I should have known. I did know, on some level, I just thought this was different. That only *I* could help him. And *that* was a textbook savior complex." Michael doesn't have time for this, and as if sensing it, Dr. James catches himself and says, "But you, my friend. You have an exceptional experience. Have you thought that, if you'd been here for the . . . incident . . . if you'd been here, she may not have stayed?"

He hadn't thought of that. He can't. "How long will she stay?"

The doctor says, "You say this hopefully." He laughs. "I keep hoping mine will leave. But I do like hope. I don't know, my boy, I'm figuring it out as I go along." He drifts off for a moment, but remembers himself. He gets to his feet. "Now, get back to your wife. I've kept you too long already." He takes a shot and swallows hard, leaning in close. He says, "I don't think we found each other for no reason." Michael rises, waiting for some brilliant conclusion, an epiphany or at least some sort of solid answer. But the doctor says nothing. He leads Michael to the door, saying, "If you'll excuse me, I have some serious drinking to do."

Michael turns to him. He doesn't know what he's supposed to say. "Are you okay?"

Dr. James laughs again. "No." He closes the door.

It's been a while in the Dark. Time is elusive, but she knows a while has passed. She remembers as a child thinking that a "while" seemed like forever. She tries to tell herself that the blackness will pass. It does. The trick is not to let it get to you. Fortunately, Tim never seems to mind the coming and going part of their life. For a large part of the while she's been thinking about her childhood. If she can go to a specific place in her memory, it comforts her, and Michael can't be in that place for it to work. Memories of him only make her think about now, which is too hard to think about.

She watches the tree, which has a few brown leaves clinging to its otherwise bare branches. She's thinking about that morning she and Anna crashed the red wagon into a tree—it was smaller than this one. Or maybe it was the same size. Is this tree getting smaller? It was the cool part of a spring morning, when it's chilly enough for a sweater, but if you can sneak out of the house without one you might make summer come faster. They got their red Radio Flyer and set it on the sidewalk at the top of the hill. Sarah concentrates, trying to remember the feel of the cold, red wagon, the steepness of the incline, the smell of wet grass and earth and rust, and the smell of her sister's baby shampoo as she climbed into her lap.

There's a loud crash like a refrigerator falling fifty feet and landing right next to her and she's back. The living room looks the same. She thinks that the crash might have been the door closing. She doesn't bother looking for Michael; she knows he's gone. She goes to the sofa and curls Tim in her lap, kissing the top of his head. His hair is growing thicker.

That terrible pounding again. She clutches Tim, expecting to disappear, but hears a key in the lock. Oh. Pounding is knocking. Some things are exactly like they used to be and she can recognize them; where things are, what they look like. Other things have receded: smells, sensations. She knows she's sitting on the sofa but she can't feel it, the fabric, the give of the cushion, the lump of the hard, little, leather end pillow Helen brought back from Morocco. Sitting on sofa is not the same experience it once was.

Outside the window is also different, sometimes easy to see, sometimes faded or fuzzy. Sometimes not there.

Sound has changed altogether. Minor changes at first, but now it's a completely different thing. She's learned how to translate her new perception of sound in some cases. The high-pitched chainsaw noise is the telephone. The constant bass thunking that follows Michael wherever he goes is his heart beating. The refrigerator drop could have been the door slamming, but now she knows that the pounding is knocking. Sarah gets up off the sofa, balancing Tim on her hip. He screeches one of his suddenly joyful pterodactyl noises; it startles her. The real noise mixed in with the not-noise.

Anna is here in that shimmering, warbling, maddening not-here way. She has someone with her, Sarah can tell by the way her sister moves and the pattern of her voice that she's talking to someone, but Sarah can't see that someone. Anna is in and out, depending on which way she turns. Sarah walks up close to her and puts out her hand, but is too afraid to try and touch her. She loves her sister. She fought with her a lot, but Anna is one of the things that she really, truly misses. Almost more than food. Almost.

Sarah's startled as Anna flickers and disappears. But in a moment she's back, three feet away. Sarah still can't understand what she's saying. Or whom she's talking to. She's reminded of the adults in the Charlie Brown specials: blarp blah blarp blarp blarp. If only she could make out her words, the annoying irritation in her voice. Anna, the perpetually irritated rebellious teenager.

Anna puts something on the table. Sarah is startled as something appears right next to the something Anna put down. But the objects are shimmery, weird, and her eyes are hurting and it's making her nervous. She walks over to Anna, determined this time. Sarah squints and pushes her hand toward her sister's black curls, or the black shimmer at the back of where her neck should be. Her hand goes through and feels an echo of a sensation, a whisper across her wrist. She tries to grab the hair but cannot hold it, and Anna pulls away, startled. Her burble becomes louder.

Maybe Sarah could stop the shimmer and shake Anna out of her haze. She walks right up to her again and yells somewhere near where the shimmering object's head should be. "Annnaaaaaaaa!" Her voice echoes in the apartment and reminds her of yelling at her sister when they were teenagers. The shimmer stops where she is for a moment. Then moves away. Tim arches his back and points his toes, letting out another pterodactyl cry in answer to his mother's yell. Sarah sinks into the sofa in defeat.

———

When Michael gets back, he sees that the dining table is now laden with sympathy bouquets. Black ribbons, birds of paradise, deep-purple roses, fruit baskets. There's even a wreath. He panics a moment; has Sarah seen them? And how did they get here? Greta appears next to the table, preening. What is she so smug about? She says, "Get rid of them." She disappears just as quickly.

He jogs down the hall to the nursery calling out, "I'm sorry, I only stepped out for a minute."

He finds Anna standing over the crib. She's holding a handful of burp rags. He steps into the room and recognizes a familiar scent. *Obsession.* He turns around to find himself facing his mother, Helen, who has never stopped wearing the perfume he bought her when he was in high school. Her hair has been recently colored and cropped to a stylish bob and she's wearing a suit. An eclectic anachronism, she never travels without her suit or her worn cowboy boots. She's holding the little zebra from the mobile and crying. Helen goes to Michael and throws her arms around him, squeezing him tightly and rocking him. Through her perfume, Michael can smell airplane.

Rocking is something parents know. And, because he's now a parent, Michael finds himself rocking with his mother as she sobs into his shoulder. "Shh, shh, shh." He knows soothing now, too.

Anna is the annoyed sister who's caught him at something. "Michael, what are these?"

Burp rags, you idiot. Can't you smell them? "Rags. Dust rags. I mean. Not dust rags, but I was dusting with them." Anna's not buying it.

"Oh, Michael. Michael, honey." Helen pulls herself away from him so she can see him, take inventory. She looks into his eyes, worried. She raises her hand to his cheek and then to his brow and the back of his neck like she did when he was little and had a fever. "Honey, you don't look well."

Well, yeah, grieving, right?

"We called *several* times," Anna says. "It's freezing in here; you need to get your thermostat checked. I felt the worst chill in the living room."

Helen says, "Why didn't you call me, Michael?" Mothers have a way of eliciting guilt with simple questions; it takes years of practice to hone this craft.

Guilt. Now it's time to remember what to do. But he doesn't remember what to do. He looks around the room like a teenager whose parents have arrived home early after a party. Aside from the rags and the stuffed zebra Tim was playing with, not much is out of place. Sarah had just tidied. Sarah had just tidied. Sarah.

So his voice chokes at the right time. "I wasn't ready."

EIGHT

S arah saw Michael return and rose to meet him, but he didn't see her. He looked at the dining table and then went back to the nursery, where they are—Anna and whoever that not-person is. It made Sarah tired and dizzy, trying to look at Anna and trying to listen, so she took Tim into her bedroom and curled up around him on the bed.

Tim plays with the ties on her hippie dress, the peach batik, the gathered yoke neck and laces at the chest. It seems to be conducive to nursing and Michael loves it, so she wears it to please him. When did she ever wear anything specifically to please him? Motherhood is meant to bring out your femininity, but Sarah never thought it would turn her into a codependent, needy clinger. She used to be a captain of industry. Okay, a captain of the law. Or a captain of her work life, at least. She owned her office, she owned a desk. A phone. A purpose. This new reality fills her consciousness, as does the need to keep Tim and Michael near, but she misses living, she misses working, she misses people. She misses Anna and her mother. She misses her "good morning" from the doorman, from her waitress, from the doorman at work. She misses Angie, her assistant who kept things operating seamlessly, but was always ready with a quick comeback. She misses answering the phone and solving other people's problems.

Sarah wanted to take a year's leave of absence to get to know her child, so maybe she'd be missing these things anyway. But it would have been temporary. She would have gone back. In the meantime, she'd be able to call her colleagues, have lunch and catch up. She'd be able to call Angie and get the latest office gossip. Or Anna. Or her mom. She wants her mom. Her mom is a snooty drag sometimes, but she loves her. Much of who Sarah is comes of disagreeing with her socially conscious mother, Betsy. And, argue as they might, Sarah rests firmly in the knowledge that Betsy loves . . . loved . . . loves her. She can't think about this.

Tim bonks his head against her belly. She says, "Ouch! That hurt."

He does it again. She gently grabs his shoulders and sits him upright. He grins, ear to ear, and yells, "Ba!" Tim has such a smug look of pride in his eyes that Sarah laughs. He laughs, too. Babies can't talk and their laugh is smaller, but so human and intoxicating. Sarah laughs harder and Tim's husky laugh grows into giggles and squeals.

Greta's laughter startles Sarah.

She's sitting in the old leather chair in the corner, the well-worn brown one with the dark-wood frame. It was the only thing Sarah kept from her father when he died. The chair creaks when Greta shifts and Sarah thinks uncharitable thoughts about Greta's weight.

Greta says, "So."

Sarah, angered by the intrusion, but also something else she can't quite reach, snaps back. "So?"

Greta motions to the door with a wide sweep of her arm. "Life interferes."

Sarah tries to sound uninterested. "And?"

Greta shifts in her seat and leans back into the chair, sighing. She doesn't answer; she's exerting control by making Sarah talk next. Sarah's impatient, but Greta seems to know something that she's not telling her. She hates feeling manipulated, but she softens her voice and asks, "How can I stop people from coming?"

Greta's quiet for a long moment. Tim has rolled onto his back and is pulling the pillow over himself, wrestling with it. The pillow is winning. Sarah feels like Greta's working out a problem in her head. She's a bit surprised that for once, the woman doesn't have an immediate answer.

Sarah prods, "Greta?"

"I don't know if you can." Greta says her usual spiel as if she's reformulating it. "All that matters . . . " Sarah tries to tune it out, but the words have become a throbbing, nauseating part of her. When she's done, Greta goes quiet for a moment.

Tim pulls the pillow away from his face, discovering, once again, the joy of peek-a-boo. He squeals with laughter.

Greta finally speaks, and Sarah can tell by the breath she takes before she talks that she's changed her tack. "There are sympathy bouquets all over your dining table. People have started sending their condolences."

Sarah hadn't expected this. She feels cold and dizzy and frightened. She looks up to ask Greta what it means, what she should do, but she's gone. People can't just do that, take away the hold she has on her little family. Bouquets. Notes. Condolences. They're sorry. Sorry she's dead.

Tim giggles and that heady feeling recedes a little, but she's still frightened.

Michael wants Anna and Helen to leave, but hopes that more time spent with them now means that they might leave him alone later. Helen has been away too long and knows him too well to accept a quick good-bye. The lies are building. He feels a childish shame, but he's doing this for his family. Everything he's doing is to keep Sarah and Tim with him, and people have done worse to keep their families together. He knows that "together" means something different with Tim and Sarah, but it's all he's got.

He leads his guests into the kitchen, hoping that the act of making them tea will disguise his body language. His mother can always read him too easily.

Helen says, "How are you holding up, honey?" He doesn't know why his mother's comforting voice makes him want to cry, but it would be perfectly natural for him to totally lose it right now.

He clears his throat. "As well as can be expected." *Fill the kettle. Start by filling the kettle.*

She says, "Anna said you were doing all right, and I flew home as soon as I knew you were back. I kept calling."

Anna says, "He's not doing the phone these days." Now that Sarah's not here to annoy, Anna works on Michael.

His mother tries to smooth over Anna's sharp tone. "She picked me up at the airport and we came right here." She has something stored up to say; he can tell by her overly pleasant tone.

Michael asks, "How's London?" Is small talk allowed? *Turn the burner on. Get out the milk.*

He goes to the fridge and opens it wide, but quickly closes it almost all the way when he notices two bottles of breast milk in the shelf on the door. Well, they *were* bottles of breast milk. Now they look absurdly empty and clean, like they came with the fridge, like ice trays. Michael snakes his arm into the fridge and fetches out the mercifully narrow carton of milk.

Helen says, "London's . . . nice. Michael, we need to talk about the funeral."

Funeral. Fuck. This was gonna happen. You knew it was gonna happen.

Mugs. Get the mugs.

Now Anna starts, "We're doing it Saturday. Mom can't wait any longer."

Helen chimes in, "You have to understand how this is for Betsy. This is her daughter. She needs to lay her to rest."

Why does he feel like they're trying to talk him into breaking up with Sarah? Like they're her bitchy high school friends, off-loading a boyfriend with that "this is for your own good" tone.

Anna says, "No big deal. A bare bones funeral. Sarah wanted her ashes scattered . . . "

Michael says, "No."

Anna says, "It was her wish. She wanted her ashes scattered in The Cloisters where we used to play when we were little."

Michael snaps, "That was a promise she made to you when you were *twelve*."

Anna looks like she's been slapped.

He realizes he's been a little sharp, but if they scatter the ashes, will she be gone? For good?

She's not letting this one go. "She always said."

"She always said that you two made hundreds of pinkie promises when you were little and it's the sweetest thing I've ever heard, but I think this is up to me now."

Now he's pissed. Why can't they go away and leave them alone?

Anna stands, stunned. Helen walks up behind Michael and puts her arms around him, resting her head on his back. He succumbs for a moment, so she'll think she's doing some good, but then gently extracts himself and goes to the cabinet for the teapot.

They only have one. They got it while honeymooning in London. They spent all day in Camden Market looking for the perfect English teapot. White, simple, big enough to hold several cups, tall enough to keep from spilling out the lid when poured. They talked endlessly over that teapot; it was an obsession of Sarah's. Finding it in a little shop in Islington one day before their flight out was a major victory. She put it in her carry-on, wrapped in sweaters so it wouldn't be broken on the trip home.

A week later, they were hustling down Madison Avenue on the way to dinner at a friend's apartment. It was a gray November evening,

pissing rain, and Michael stopped, stock still, in front of the Crate &
Barrel. Looming there were shelves upon shelves of the same model of
teapot. His heart sank when he saw the display, wanting to protect
Sarah's obsession, her gratification over finding the right pot. He tried
to block her view of the window but it was too big and bright. All was
gray and dark outside and there was the dazzlingly lit display against a
brilliant-red background. He threaded his arm around her waist and
started steering her past it, when he saw her look up and catch a
glimpse. The moment of recognition, astonishment. Her face fell.
Then it lit up and she laughed.

Sarah said, "See! I told you it was the perfect fucking teapot!" She
shoved him in the chest and then pulled him in for a squeeze. Her hair
was wet and cold, her scalp warm underneath when he kissed her head.
He remembers feeling lucky he married her.

Helen uses her soothing mom voice, but the words slice right
through her tone. "Whatever you do with the ashes, honey, she has to
have a funeral. Too long has passed."

He hasn't had long enough. He won't be able to protect her from
this, either. Too many teapots.

He turns around to see Anna mouthing to Helen, "You tell him."
He says, "Tell me what?"

Helen looks at Anna and then says, "Michael, honey. Her mother
has bought coffins. And. Betsy is set on having a coffin for the baby."

Anna pushes the point home. "I didn't like it and I tried to talk
her out of it, but then when you said you'd named it, I thought maybe
you'd be okay."

Him. Named him. Fuck. Please leave. Leave now.

Helen says, "You can keep the ashes, honey. They're only coffins."

Only coffins. He doesn't move. His hands have moved to the counter and he's not sure if he wants to fall to the ground, slug Anna, or
collapse into his mother's arms and weep for days.

Helen tries to hug him, but he's worried he'll completely lose his
shit. He pulls away like a petulant teenager and moves to the table,

sitting in one of the chairs. There's Rosie the Riveter, stuck in her triumphant smile, "WE CAN DO IT!" A conspiracy of women doing what is needed.

There must be some magic spell that will make them go away. Who gives a fuck about coffins? Empty boxes. Doesn't matter. *Will it be white? Will it look tiny in that gigantic church?*

Is he worried that he'll cry at the funeral? He's supposed to cry. Now he's only worried about Sarah and where she and Tim are.

His voice is definitely cracking enough. "You guys. Fine. Okay. Whatever." This helps. The kettle whistles, giving him something to do. Relieved, he gets up to pour it.

Anna asks, "And the ashes?"

"Give that one up, Anna. What time?"

Helen smiles, tears coming to her eyes again. "My brave boy." That means so much more now that he has a boy of his own. So much about his mother means more, now that he knows that feeling, that pull, that need to do anything he can for his child. He tries not to think about the fact that he won't get to see Tim grow up. He tries to think of what to say.

Helen says, "It'll be at ten in the morning; the church is booked."

Pour the water. Change the subject. He says, "Where are you staying?"

The tea is brewing and Anna's moving back down the hall. Even though she might be headed for the bathroom, Michael follows her. He acts as if he had business at that end of the apartment.

Helen says. "The subletter miraculously bailed on the lease two weeks ago." She follows him, the end of an awkward parade. "I'm at 336. It's kind of a wreck, but it'll do. I can stay for up to a month, if you need me." The number for his grandmother's home became its name somewhere along the way. 336 Central Park West, 1920s. Two-bedroom apartment most definitely not overlooking the park.

Anna's heading back into the nursery. Michael's getting anxious. There's an awkward pause as she heads over to the bookshelf. He wonders if it's too soon to say good-bye; how soon would arouse suspicion.

A little too loudly, he speaks like a host at a party, "Well . . . you must be tired." What is Anna after?

His mother smiles at him; she knows her cue. She claps her hands on both of his shoulders and squeezes, looking at him warmly; he feels like he just aced a spelling test or something, uncertain of what kind of praise he's going to receive. She says, "Be strong, Michael, we'll get through this." She drops her arms and he goes in to kiss her, but she stops him, saying, "If I hug you I'll start crying again."

Anna is running her fingers along the bindings of the books on Tim's shelf. She pulls out a tattered copy of *Four Fur Feet* by Margaret Wise Brown. She tucks it under her arm.

Her fingers trail along until they find a first edition of *Where the Wild Things Are*. She takes that as well. Anger surges in Michael as he sees her searching for even more pieces of Sarah to take with her. *What if Tim gets old enough to read?*

"Anna," he says too sharply, he realizes. If he makes this an issue they'll stay longer.

Anna looks embarrassed, caught. "I . . . was going to . . . I'm sorry, but they were ours and I was thinking of my children . . . " She starts to put them back.

Michael relents. "No, it's okay." Anna's nowhere near having children and yet her imaginary future children are somehow challenging Tim's existence. Michael hates this.

Anna looks at him and vacillates for a moment before taking them down and grabbing two Beatrix Potter books while she's at it. She slips out of the room and heads toward the front door. Michael follows.

Helen turns to him as she passes, her brow furrowed with concern. She says, "I'll take you to dinner tomorrow night. You're losing weight."

He says, "I was in the field, Mom."

"All the more reason. Dawat. Tomorrow night."

Michael scrambles. "Can you . . . I'll be dealing with stuff around here. Can you bring takeout?" He knows what happens sometimes when he goes down the hall. He doesn't know what happens if he leaves the building for the time it would take to eat a meal. The funeral is still five days away. Maybe only five more days with Sarah and Tim. Maybe more, he doesn't know.

His mother regards him a moment and agrees with a nod, stepping out the door. Anna reaches in, pecks Michael on the cheek, dropping one of the small Beatrix Potter books. She scrambles for *The Tale of Jemima Puddle-Duck,* and slips out the door. Stupid book anyway. Dumb duck. The door slams shut with too much of an echo. Michael closes his eyes for a moment, not wanting to find the apartment empty. Not wanting to look.

Hands creep around his chest, holding his arms down. Sarah's doing a spooky voice, chanting rhythmically, *"He walked around the world on his four fur feet, his four fur feet, his four fur feet, he walked around the world on his four fur feet and never made a sound-O."* He spins around and catches her, tickling; she laughs.

"You're freaking me out, lady." He puts his arms around hers now, pinning her. Keeping her. How long can he keep her?

She laughs, trying to squirm free. "That book always creeped me out when I was little."

"Why did you put it on Tim's shelf?"

She shrugs. "Sentimentality."

He kisses her, not letting go. "I'm so glad to see you." He relaxes, pushing her away and looking her over. Not worse. Still skinny. Warming up. She's wearing the peach batik again and he can't help but think she wants something when she does that. Living Sarah refused to wear it so many times.

Sarah mirrors his concern, asking, "What?"

He asks, "How long has it been? For you, I mean." Met with her confused stare, he says, "How long have I been gone?"

She says, "You only just went out."

"I don't understand." He pulls her to him again, happy to hold her bony form.

"How long were you gone?" She asks this like she understands the question.

Milo. Dr. James. Anna. Mom. A thousand years? "Uh, like an hour?"

She looks up at him, frowning a question, but then shrugs. "It is what it is, honey."

Michael asks, "Where's Tim?"

"Sleeping." She hugs him tighter. "Let him sleep."

"How long have you been here?" He doesn't understand how she knew about *Four Fur Feet* or when she came back or what she overheard.

She says, "I don't know. Stop asking questions, you're making me nervous. What did my sister want? Aside from the books."

He feels he's balancing lies on both sides, and it's hard to keep track of how much information he should give, how much he's already given. He's glad she didn't hear everything. He doesn't want to talk about the funeral. Not yet. He'll tell her about it that day in case it's good-bye, but he doesn't want to worry her. He'll spend every minute with her until then.

He says, "Mom flew in, you know. She wanted to touch base."

"That's who it was." She traces her hand around his cheek, fondly. "Her boy."

He says, "It's different, isn't it? Now that we have Tim, everyone is different."

"Especially parents." She looks into space for a moment. "I don't think I could handle seeing my mother now."

He says, "She can't handle seeing me, so it works out for everyone."

"Can't get rid of my sister."

Michael smiles. "She loves you." He doesn't know how weird he's going to get when Sarah's gone for good. Maybe he'll get snippy and petty, too.

But Sarah's face has fallen. She looks surprised and a little distraught. Michael wheels around. The sympathy bouquets. More teapots.

Sarah moves toward them, her fingers pass lightly over them and her shoulders slump, defeated.

Michael says, "I'm sorry, they must have come . . . I bet Anna and my mom brought some. I. I'm sorry."

She touches one of the lilies and squeezes the petal between her fingers. She smiles, looking at Michael. "Nothing to be done, is there? I mean, it's there, isn't it?" She makes a Vanna White sweep of the table with her arms, and says grandiosely, "And it appears that you need sympathy." She starts to go through the cards, reading them aloud.

Her theatricality is thorny. "So sorry for your loss." She tosses it on the table. She pulls another one: "If there's anything I can do." She flicks it in the air and it lands on the rug. "Our hearts go out to you in this time of need." She pulls another one. "Call me." Her eyebrow goes up and she laughs. "My replacement's moving in."

He plays along warily. "Who is it?"

"Caroline." *What would she say about all of this?*

"Ha." Caroline's gay, so the joke works, but the edginess in Sarah's tone is increasing. He's not sure where she's headed, but it's nowhere good.

She reads, "We're sorry for your loss." *Flick.* "We are so sorry for your loss." She's angry now. "'We are *so* sorry for your loss. What did you lose, Michael, can I help you find it? Was it a ring? A puppy? A home?" She's getting hysterical and the temperature in the room has plummeted by at least twenty degrees. "*What* did you lose?" She pulls the cards out of all of the other arrangements without reading them, throwing them on the table.

She then starts pulling at flowers, their petals coming off in her hands, releasing their woody, floral odor. She seems to find that satisfying and pulls at more. Soon, she's reaching into the dark forest of sympathy bouquets and ripping heads off the flowers, fistful by fist-ful, throwing them into the air. Michael hears a sickly plinking. Some of the blossoms make a completely unexpected noise when they hit the table: they've frozen. Frost-covered stems remain.

Michael says, "Sarah."

All warmth has faded from her; her face has grayed with shadows and he sees that she's wearing the nursing gown again, the same one he saw her wear that night he came home from the grocery store. Her arms fall by her sides as she sits down in a chair, still.

He speaks sharply to her as if to a child. "Sarah." She looks up at him, glowering. She breathes heavily, the shadows in her clavicles grow-ing and receding. There's something in her eyes that was not there in life, a lurking darkness. He's frightened by this look. "Sarah!" His call leaves a breath of mist in the air. She's not answering him; she's looking right at him, her eyes focused on something beyond him in another place.

Does she slip away or does the world fall away? Sarah can't tell.

The flowers got her thinking. Thinking is not a good thing. All of these people sending sympathy bouquets like she isn't here anymore. Like she's gone. The room got shimmery and then dark and all she saw was the flow-ers, one after the other after the other, and she knew. And then even they disappeared and here she is, sitting. And there's nothing here. No tree. Only blackness. She's conscious that she's sitting, but she can't feel a chair beneath her. And Tim is nowhere to be found.

Greta said something. It was bad. Sarah's angry with her for saying it. She tries to remember in more detail. But it's hard.

This time, the Dark is terrifying. Like before, there's no sound. There's no light and the blackness presses in around her.

What if this is it? This Nothing? Where's Tim? She tries to scream, but she can't feel the breath to begin it. She does what she remembers are as the things you do to scream:, you breathe, you press hard with your diaphragm, you open your mouth. But she can't reach any part of those things. She's stuck.

She smells something, far away. It's sweet, comforting. A voice penetrates the blackness, and gets stronger.

———

Greta's there, holding a steaming cup of tea in her hands. "Now, now, dear, you stay a moment and drink this." Her tone is soothing, but tenuous, not unlike Helen's tone a few short minutes ago. Smoothing things over.

Michael's not sure if she walked into the room or appeared. But here she is. She walks between Sarah and Michael. He's ashamed that he's grateful for the separation. The room is warming up a little. Through Greta's oppressive perfume, Michael can smell the tea. Spices and herbs and hot and soothing. This is the tea that Sarah's been giving him. This is the tea he has been drinking non-stop. His stomach drops and he begins to sweat.

Greta says, "Drink, honey." Sarah looks at her and the focus comes back into her eyes. Recognition. Relief. Michael feels a pang of helplessness that he wasn't able to get that look back on his own. Sarah's sipping and warming. Greta turns to Michael angrily, "How long has she been like this?"

He says, "I. Just a minute. It was just a minute ago."

Greta looks at the table full of flowers. "Why did you let her see these?"

He says, "I didn't know they'd come and my mother was here." He doesn't speak further; any explanation won't make a dent in whatever the hell is going on. He doesn't care anymore. He wants answers.

Greta turns to Sarah and caresses her face. "Honey, you look exhausted, you should get to bed."

Sarah nods, the helpless patient.

Greta says, "Go on, now." The women exchange a warm glance and Sarah heads off down the hall, clutching her cup. Greta waits until she's safely gone and then turns to Michael, motioning wildly to the detritus on the table. "Get rid of this stuff. She doesn't need reminding." She leans in, threatening, "You need to keep her happy. I thought you knew that." She turns to go.

Don't go. It takes fighting past his growing hatred for Greta for him to call to her. "Wait." She stops a moment, her back to him, a classic stage move. The very fact of it makes him sick, but he plays along because she might be the only one with answers. "Can you? Please? I have questions."

As she turns to face him, Greta's triumphant, smug smile makes him want to slap her, but she's all he has right now.

She says, "I have questions, too."

Michael knows that he needs to play her game, at least for now. "Shoot."

"How much do you love your wife?"

"What the hell kind of question is that?"

Her voice remains maddeningly calm. "It's simple enough. How far would you be willing to go for her?" She sits herself in the dining chair, which squeaks under her weight.

Michael asks, "Who are you? How can you see her? Who are you?" *What are you?*

Greta chuckles. She looks him in the eye. "I'm here to help Sarah. I think you know that by now."

He asks, "Who are all of those other women?"

"Mothers under my care. That's all you really need to know."

"They're dead, too."

She says, "It's a hard time to die, being a parent of a little one. It goes against all of our greater instincts. How can we care for the child if we're dead? I simply offer counseling and comfort."

"Why?" *Why are you so creepy? What's in that tea? Why do I get the sense you want something from them? Why are you so happy when they're in your care?* But he asks, "Are you dead?"

Greta breathes in at this question. She then laughs, shaking her head. "Shouldn't we be talking about Sarah?"

He says, "How long is she here for?" He's so full of questions and he has this feeling Greta might disappear before he finishes asking them. He madly tries to organize them in his head. He wasted time asking her the questions that have been creeping him out rather than the ones relevant to Sarah. He repeats, "How long is she here for?"

She says, "That depends on you."

"What do you mean?"

She motions to the table full of flowers next to her. "We need to keep her happy. You haven't been keeping her happy." She turns to look at him. Michael sees a blackness in her eyes, similar to what he saw in Sarah's only a few minutes before.

Michael's getting tired of the same runaround. He says, "Why?"

She continues, "When she gets upset like that, it's harder for her to hang on; she might leave you."

Shit.

Greta says, "And when you *leave.* You can't leave. When you leave, you risk everything. She needs your presence to stay here. Your son needs your presence to stay here. Do you understand that, now?"

The time slipping. The boy growing.

"Tim may look strong, but he needs you, Michael, he needs you to stay strong."

Next question. What's the next question? He feels like he's stepped into an alley in a dodgy neighborhood to buy something illegal. Every moment of this conversation feels unsavory and wrong.

But he's only asking, he doesn't have to listen. And he has to ask. "How?"

"How what?" She knows what, he can see that she's relishing that he asked.

He sighs and then asks, "How do I keep her happy?"

She smiles as if she's won something and gets to her feet. "Keep things . . . normal. Like nothing has happened. Don't talk about what happened. Pretend she came home from the hospital and you're with your wife and son and enjoy it. This is her reality, having a baby and a husband. Don't let this"—she gestures to the table—"happen again. Keep the outside world out. Don't confuse her." She comes in close and touches his arm. "We want to keep your baby and wife with you as long as we can." Why does this sound like a threat? "Keep her safe."

"What's this tea? This tea you gave her and she keeps giving to me."

"You need the tea to keep them here."

It's not enough of an answer. "Why?"

Greta's growing impatient. She says, "It aids your connection."

Michael can't help but feel like he's been slipped some sort of soul-mickey, that he's given up something without his knowledge.

She's too close and her smell is oppressive, worn-out patchouli fragrance, unbathed flesh, heavy clothing that's been worn a few times. The room has warmed up again. There's an additional sweetly sickening odor that Michael can't put a finger on.

"You can't allow a funeral, Michael. You have to talk your mother and Sarah's sister out of it." She disappears, her words hanging in the air like the Cheshire Cat's smile.

It's too fast a blow, and her words carry too many variables for Michael to sort them out. Her saying this means that she was listening to his conversation with Helen and Anna. How often is she here—is she always here?

He can't stop the funeral. When people die, it's what comes next. Aside from birth, and actual death, it's probably the most unpreventable occurrence in a person's life. You're dead, people will do what they will. He can't take that from Sarah's family. They wouldn't allow it.

High-WASP, the Lowells observed the rites and rituals of their tribe with military precision. Michael and Sarah didn't have a wedding, so much as they were marched through one; guests, invitations, registries, seating, ceremony, reception, thank-you cards. He might be able to talk his mother out of a funeral, but the Lowells won't have it.

He knows Greta's motives aren't pure. She's somehow necessary to Sarah staying, but he can't let her govern his every decision. He doesn't know what the funeral will mean. Somehow Greta's implying that he could stop the funeral has opened up an entirely new area of guilt.

He has to stop thinking. He may only have a short time left with Sarah. He has to make the most of it.

He turns around and sees the flowers on the table. Time to toss them. He walks over and identifies the odor that he couldn't place before: the sickly sweet perfume odor of rotting flowers. All of them have turned black and spotted and their dirt is overgrown with a gray-green hairy mold. He goes to the kitchen for a trash bag.

———————————

Michael wakes up several times in the night curled around Sarah, who's breathing normally. She's warm in his arms. He buries his face in her neck and drifts off. The third time he wakes up, it's dawn and he can no longer sleep. Sarah's face is peaceful, but gaunt in the morning light.

Her breathing speeds up and her eyes shoot back and forth rapidly underneath her lids. What do the dead dream of? Life? Or is it something disturbing and new that the living can't even imagine? When she was pregnant, Michael was jealous of the life-altering experience that he couldn't truly be a part of. All of the changes Sarah's body was going through, all of the kicks and hiccups and private thoughts of carrying a child within her were Sarah's alone.

Michael's trip for work had taken him far from Sarah to a tectonic ledge in western Canada, overlooking a creek that roared through pine trees and fallen rocks below. On his first morning at the location, Michael stepped out on to the edge of the shelf to breathe in the morning dawn air. It was cold and crisp, the creek yielding a dampness that produced one of the cleanest smells he had ever experienced: loam, water-soaked granite, pine and a soul-pulling clear scent he couldn't quite make out. An eagle soared out of the trees and hovered over the creek, looking for prey, and Michael realized that this was something Sarah wouldn't experience. He could tell her about it, show her photographs, but it wouldn't in any way compare to the experience itself.

He looks at her now, twitching in a nightmare he can't be a part of, something larger that he will never fully comprehend. And he knows that what she's going through is terrifying and beyond his imagination and he can't help her.

She's whimpering. In their life before, she told him that when she's whimpering, she's usually screaming in her sleep. He would wake her up and rescue her. They would talk about the dream and laugh about it.

He knows they won't laugh about this dream later. He touches her gently on the arm.

Michael says, "Shh. Sarah, honey, you're dreaming."

She whimpers. "No. No, don't." She's fighting something and it's frightening her. She starts writhing.

"Sarah, wake up. You're having a nightmare."

She breathes heavily and frost comes out of her mouth. He feels her arms turn icy to his touch. He starts shaking her. "Sarah!"

She yells, "No!" Her eyes open. She's still breathing deeply, and freezing; his hands burn as if he's holding dry ice. Sarah's eyes are black and far away. It's the same look that he saw last night, only more intense. The whites of her eyes are still there, but her pupils have eaten her irises. The windows to her soul have steel shutters over them so dark that they reflect his fright. Her eyes are looking at him, but he knows she doesn't know him and she may not even see him.

He wants her back. "Sarah?" He needs her back. But she isn't here. A central part of her is missing. "Sarah?" He starts stroking her face, ignoring the burning in his hands.

He puts a blanket over her and touches her hair. "Honey?" He kisses the top of her head, icy hot to his lips. Desperately, with tears smarting his eyes, he sings to her. Their song. Tim's lullaby. *"When you were little, you dreamed you were big, you must have been something, a real tiny kid . . . "*

But she still isn't there. She's breathing heavily, her eyes looking at something terrible in the distance that Michael can't see. He looks in that direction and sees only a cracked and flaking patch of ceiling.

He sings louder with more urgency. *"You wish you were me, I wish I was you . . . "*

Tim starts crying from down the hall. Michael turns on the baby monitor and turns it up to full volume, holding it to Sarah's ear. Her breathing slows, her eyes clear. Her temperature warms.

"The baby." She looks panicked, but human again, and sits upright, rigid.

Michael says, "I'll get him, I'll get him, sweetie. Just stay."

In the nursery, Tim is standing up in his crib, bobbing and crying, tears streaming down his face. Michael picks him up and wraps his arms around the boy, squeezing him to his chest so as much of Tim is touching him as possible. The weight of him is hard to deny, the damp little squirmer. The boy stops crying and snuffles a bit as Michael carries him to his mother.

When he gets to their room he finds Sarah sleeping again. Curled up, undisturbed. The room is warm; her skin seems tight, but rosy and real-looking. Whatever had a hold of her is gone.

Michael sits on the bed, looking at his wife. Tim squirms in his arms and reaches for her. Michael puts him down between them. The baby crawls to his mother, patting her back. *Thump. Thump.* "Mama. Mama." His first word.

Michael says, "Sarah! Sarah, wake up, Tim is *talking* to you."

Sarah stretches and smiles. She opens her eyes and looks at Tim, who says, "Mama. Mamamamamamamamama."

He's pulling on her hair now. She pulls the boy to her and tries to snuggle him, but he's too busy and pushes her away. He slams his fists on her chest. "Mama."

My little family. So much life. But so much unknown. They can only hold on moment by moment, growing and being, disappearing, appearing, haunted by nightmares and that woman. Where could any of this possibly go? He wells up again.

Sarah looks up at Michael and grins. "Look at you, big softie."

He wipes away his tears as if he hasn't been crying. He wants to ask her, but doesn't want to remind her. "Sleep okay?"

She gets a distant look in her eyes. "Yeah. Okay, I guess."

The sunlight is spilling in through the windows. The clouds are puffy and white. The rock hasn't left his stomach, but Michael wishes the bed could be an island and nothing could touch it. There's a throbbing in his hand and he looks down at the inside of his pointer fingers and thumbs, where he'd shaken Sarah. They are burned red and blistered.

NINE

Michael's starting to have practical thoughts. It feels like yet another betrayal.

While Sarah's napping, he sits down to the first box of mail at the dining table and spreads it out in front of him. The pile of neglected envelopes can't be ignored any longer. Whatever happens, he doesn't want them turning off the electricity. While he's only been home a week, how long has she been gone? Two weeks? Three? Is there such a thing as too pregnant to do the bills? The sight of two different cable bills makes him nervous. When he and his mom were first on their own, getting the bills paid on time seemed to be a center of stress. Early in life, she sat him down and taught him how to stay ahead of creditors when there wasn't enough money, how to pay everything off when there was. His headache suddenly returns in pulsating throbs. He gets out the checkbook and starts to open the envelopes one by one. With two incomes, they're fortunate not to have to worry too much about bills, but the old anxiety comes back. Despite Helen's efforts there were always a few that slipped by. Their phone was an intermittent luxury during his middle school years.

Does he even need cable now? Sarah was the one hooked on HBO and Showtime. He could make do getting his news online and watching the networks. They haven't watched any television since he's been home, but what if she gets a sudden urge to see *Entourage?* How can he ask these questions about a ghost? If he thinks about each bill, he'll go crazy.

The credit card bill: Babies "R" Us, FAO Schwartz, the supermarket, for that chicken that was rotting in the fridge. A charge on the Amex from the hospital for $12.97. What could possibly have cost $12.97? The electric bill is next to nothing. He doesn't want to think about why. He pays every single bill he can: mortgage, co-op—*have they always paid this much in co-op fees or has there been a recent hike?* Sarah used to handle the bills. More credit cards. *We're clearly spending too much on groceries.* A sweaty haze consumes him and the bills glare at him. Insurance, gas, and then he turns to the pile of bills from the hospital. He doesn't have to read the details, but he knows that having creditors after him would definitely be worse.

She's dead. *Sarah is dead.* He says this to himself three times before he opens the first hospital bill. He tries to shuffle through it for the payment slip and tries to ignore all that is written there. The bill is two pages long and covered with text. *Anaesthesia, room charge, disposal fee.* Of course they have to write it in all caps: CONFIRMED DEAD.

Fuck.

And the charge for the death certificate. Certificates. Two of them. INFANT DECLARED DEAD ON DELIVERY.

Fuck. Find the slip, find the slip, find the slip. There it is. Because insurance, it cost him only two thousand, five hundred and twenty-seven dollars to lose his wife and son.

He writes the fucking check. He puts the hospital bills in the paid pile. They sit there. He catches the antiseptic blue logo of the hospital glaring at him. He pulls out the cable bill from the bottom of the pile and lays it across the envelopes like a tarp so he won't have to look at them. His heart's pounding in his chest and he feels like he can't breathe. But he's not going to give in to grief again. Not yet. She's still here. To keep her happy is to keep her here. He opens their investment statements.

Fidelity. In her name. Did she remember to sign it over to him? Is this going to be an issue later? It's only a couple of grand, but still. Sarah was like a squirrel with her investments, not wanting to put too much in any one place. Smith Barney, Citigroup, Chase. All in her name. Can he ask her before she goes or will his asking make her go faster? What is it exactly that *will* make her go? This line of thinking is making him nuts. He has to stop.

There's a knock at the door. It's only ten-thirty and his mother has always been pretty respectful of his space; she wouldn't come without calling. He can't imagine that Anna would come back.

He grabs the opened bills in one fist and shoves them into the drawer in the banquette, slamming it shut. There's another knock. Sarah hollers, "Honey, you going to get that?" This is odd, given her usual need to disappear. He goes to the door and hears another tentative knock. This time it doesn't stop, and this irritates him. Enough already.

He looks through the peephole. It's Dr. James. He's sweating and looks worried and is hunched sideways from the weight of a pile of books he's holding under one arm.

Dr. James speaks quietly, as if trying not to wake a baby. *Or the dead.* He's breathing heavily. "I've found something valuable. Not real answers. But maybe some insight. This is more complex than I'd thought . . . "

Michael is intrigued by the books, but is worried about Sarah. He says, "I don't think I can talk right now."

Sarah says, "Michael?" She's behind him. He's tempted to slam the door, but Dr. James has stepped onto the threshold.

The doctor inquires as if he's recognizing an old friend, "Sarah?"

She's not the least bit startled that he has addressed her and she puts on her best hostess smile. She steps forward and holds out her hand, "Doctor James, I presume."

Dr. James is cautious for a moment, but once he gets a hold of her hand, he grasps it firmly, shaking enthusiastically. He lights up. "I am so delighted to meet you."

He's in, the door's closed, and Michael sees that the books he holds in his hands are old, gilt-lettered and crumbling. One spine reads, *Ghosts, Then and Now* and, oddly, the older and crumblier of the two reads, *Modern Day Hauntings*. Fortunately Sarah's still looking at the doctor and not at what he's holding. Michael steps forward and takes the books. "Let me help you with your things." Michael chucks the books into the antique wooden cabinet by the door and has to slam the mahogany door shut twice to get them in, but by that time, Sarah and Dr. James are sitting on the sofa, talking in polite tones.

Don't say anything. For chrissake, don't say anything.

But the doctor seems to be keeping it social. "I see you get the northern light in this apartment. I envy you that—I like to paint in my spare time."

Sarah says, "Oh? What do you use?"

"Watercolors. I dabbled in oils but I couldn't get past the smell."

Sarah smiles. "I had to drop out of a painting class in college because of that smell."

They laugh.

Michael's climbing out of his skin. It makes no sense. How can these two just sit there and chat? What does the doctor want, anyway?

He's a shrink. Maybe he's trying to get her into a comfortable place before he springs something on her.

Michael clears his throat. "Um. Doctor James, is there anything we can do for you this morning?"

Sarah's embarrassed by his lack of tact. "Michael." She doesn't notice screws missing from a crib, but suddenly she's all about manners.

But Dr. James laughs. "I have nothing I *need*. We can talk about the . . . er . . . project we were working on later. Right now I'm delighting in your wife's company."

Okay. That's okay, then. Right?

Sarah says, "It's been so long since I've seen anyone. Or anyone's seen me." At first she sounds like the flustered housewife, but then it comes. "How is it that you can see me?"

What they can and cannot talk about exasperates Michael. They tiptoe around Greta, but Sarah can ask such a straightforward question so casually?

Dr. James takes her hand and looks into her eyes. "How could I not, dear?"

There's a pause. Michael hopes this was enough, but he sees by the questioning look on her face that it's not. Fortunately, the doctor steps up. "I don't know. I have someone else I can . . . see. Maybe that has something to do with it." Michael wishes now he hadn't told Sarah about his suspicion of Milo's relationship with the doctor. He doesn't really want to tell her about Milo's death, so he'd best leave it.

But the doctor's explanation seems to be enough for her. "Well, it is nice to sit and talk to someone." She says to Michael, "No offense, honey."

"None taken. I think." Michael says, "Can I get you some tea, Dr. James?" He's not about to take away Sarah's only human contact aside from himself.

Harmless enough. Michael goes to the kitchen and starts the kettle. He reaches into the cabinet for some tea. PG Tips, which they've been drinking since England. But he sees a dark-green, metal tin that looks like it's from an apothecary. Michael pulls it down and eases off the curved, rectangular lid with a suction-y *thwook*. The canister is filled with tea bags, hand-folded, yellowing, homemade-looking bags without strings or labels. No label under the tin, either. He smells it. It smells like the dried version of what he's been drinking—comforting, strong, and spicy.

The headaches. The cold sweats. This isn't something he picked up in Canada.

Greta is not a good person and this tea is definitely not wholesome, not good for him, but it helps him see Sarah. *Feel* Sarah, and Tim. It makes him more open to them. It keeps Sarah from drifting away. Or is Greta lying? Is it something different?

The tea rescued Sarah when he couldn't. He stands for a moment too long, staring into the dark cavity of the tin. His stomach feels uneasy, but he pulls out two bags and plops them into mugs. PG Tips for the doctor.

The doctor took his books when he said good-bye, conscientiously turning their spines in toward his body to shield them from Sarah, who insisted on walking him to the door. But he left with a pointed, "And I'll talk to you *later*, Michael."

Sarah was so brightened by tea with Dr. James, that Michael feels like he should call and cancel his mother for dinner. But when Helen calls from the restaurant for his order, he knows there's no way out of it. She is his mother. His wife has died. This needs to happen. It's all marching down on him, this unstoppable outside force. Then the funeral. Greta's pinning the responsibility for it on him makes it all worse. Can he call in sick for the funeral? Would that help?

He tries to cheat bedtime. Around five, he takes advantage of Sarah's hazy grasp on time. He starts yawning and stretching. He could let her disappear when his mother comes, but he hopes that if he can get her to sleep, she won't go. If she doesn't go, Tim won't go, and there won't be any danger of time slipping.

In the living room, Tim's in the Pack 'n Play, which is the modern version of a playpen, with padded edges and mesh sides. Sarah got tired of chasing him and the boy seems to be content sitting and playing with stacking cups. He can't stack them yet, but the brightly colored plastic cups make a great noise when clacked together.

Michael watches him for a moment before interfering. He's such a big boy already. Michael smiles grimly, remembering that parents always say time slips away when you have children. His case is the extreme version. One year in a week.

Michael crouches near the Pack 'n Play and gets his face down near Tim. He says, "Hey, buddy."

Tim shrieks happily when he sees his father's face. Michael moves his chin to rest on top of the playpen and Tim gets up to meet him. "Dada. Dadadadadadadada."

Second word. Michael sees a look of unadulterated joy in Tim's eyes as he squeals and pats his father's face with his soggy paws. "Dada. Dada. Dada!" He starts bobbing up and down with little grunts and his diaper ruckles as he does so. He knows Michael. By name now. The love that wells up in Michael for this little slobbery creature of intelligence is too much for him.

His voice cracks. "Hey, buddy. Dada." He grins, pointing to himself. "Dada." He points to Tim. "Timmy. Timmy."

Sarah says, "Hey, when did he become Timmy?" She's looking at them, smiling that smile, the one that came with the baby.

Michael reaches into the playpen and picks the boy up, raising him high in the air. He feels dizzy from the motion and brings him quickly down to his chest again. He breathes deeply, but tries to sound normal for Sarah. "Timmy. Don't you see it?"

"Dada. Dada. Mama. Mamamamamama." Tim looks from Sarah to Michael. He grabs his father's face in both hands, looking him soberly in the eyes, making a declaration, with gravity, "Dada." Michael stirs with pride as if he's been named or knighted or blessed, and he pulls Tim to him and hugs him, rocking him back and forth. If he could hug him into his chest, fill his body with the boy, he would. He struggles to remember that he had another agenda.

He says, "Time for your bath, little man."

Sarah says, "Already? He's only just eaten."

"Time slides by when your baby is talking and playing and, how did he get so big?"

Sarah smiles proudly, but a look of worry flickers across her face. Michael knows that when these thoughts come, it's best to have a change of scene. He hands the baby to Sarah, saying, "I'll run the bath. You get a towel and some jammies."

———

Michael and Sarah are in the bedroom, propped up on the bed reading books, when there's a knock on the door. All the yawning and stretching he could muster would not persuade Sarah to turn off the light. Tim's sleeping, safe in his room. Sarah looks up, alarmed. The temperature drops. Michael has to try.

He says, "You . . . I don't know how much control you have over it. But you don't have to go. It's only my mom. I couldn't send her away. She's brought dinner. Then she'll leave. Please don't go. Whenever you do . . . " He should stay away from details. But he doesn't want Tim to age, Sarah to feel lost. The tea was supposed to help. Maybe if he'd given her another cup before bed.

She's gone. The room is empty. Like that. The air becomes warm again. This should be comforting, but Michael sees the book, the frost thawing off its cover where Sarah's hands held it. The rumpled sheets. The dent in the stack of pillows where she was leaning is rising back into place, filling the void.

She was reading Wallace Stevens. In life, she always read poetry when she was troubled. It calmed her.

It takes all of his strength not to open the nursery door to check on the boy. He tells himself that it doesn't matter if Tim is there or not. If anything, opening the door might make Tim vanish, if he's there at all. And it's not something he can control.

Michael's appropriately upset when he gets to the door. Helen wears the look of determined cheerfulness that Michael knows she put on in the elevator on her way up. She's carrying two big fragrant, oil-spotted paper bags full of Indian food.

Over saag paneer and an amazing apricot lamb dish it takes the restaurant two days to prepare, they talk about other stuff. Helen's testing the waters, making sure he's okay.

She says, "So there's this fella . . . in London." She blushes.

Michael says, "Mom, what have you been up to?"

"His name is Tom, he's a retired chemist, and very sweet, really. Took me skeet shooting over the weekend."

"But you hate guns."

She smiles. "It was rather fun, ecktually."

"So you're going all English weekend in the country all of a sudden?" He does love the banter and he hasn't seen her in six months, but he gets the sense that this visit will be dangerously long for Sarah, wherever she's gone.

Helen goes into a monologue about how she and Tom met and how funny he is, and where her flat is in relation to his and by the time she gets to picnics on the common, Michael finds time has slowed to a crawl and his anxiousness has grown into a mild panic.

"Michael?"

He says, "I'm sorry."

"When I lost your father, I thought it was all over. Half of me wanted to go with him. The other half thought of you and that you still needed me. But for a long while, I existed in this place, this in-between place. I understand that it's part of the process and it sucks, honey, it does. And you have to dwell here for a while before you can move on. I want you to know that you're not alone here."

You don't know the half of it.

Helen continues. "And this may sound *totally* bizarre, but in a way? In a way your dad is with me still. Some days I think he's more with me than he was when he was alive."

He knows she doesn't mean *with* in a Sarah or Milo way. But that's a haunting of a type, isn't it?

He was only five when he lost his dad. He doesn't remember much beyond a dull, sad yearning that haunted his childhood. As much as he pined for him and despite a few distantly happy memories—a county fair where they got to feed the goats, one fantastic, surprise Halloween snow when his father took him out to explore the neighborhood, orange pumpkins bright against the white—he never really had a solid memory of who he was as a person.

He wonders how much Tim will remember of him.

When he sees his mother's eyes looking into the distance with a smiling sort of gratitude, filled with love, he knows that in some ways, his dad never did leave her.

She reaches over and grasps his hand. "I've been there, and any time you don't even know what to talk about, but you get that feeling, you can call me. I think you know that feeling."

Which of the many thousands of feelings that he's been going through is she referring to?

"Any time, you call me. Okay? And I'm as happy to talk about nothing as about something."

Helen always had that emotional pushiness, that need to make sure you got her point. It irritated the hell out of him during his teenage years, but right now he's grateful. He smiles at her and nods so that she knows it. To avoid crying, he sticks his fork into some tikka masala and wraps some naan around it.

Sarah didn't want to go, she tried not to. When he said, "Don't go," she looked at her Wallace Stevens and repeated to herself, "Kiss, cats: for the deer and the dachshund are one. Kiss, cats: for the deer and the dachshund are . . . "

It wasn't enough. She was gone. The Dark isn't as scary as last time. She doesn't know what brought her here, but she feels that she's here in a more concrete way. She scrapes her feet along the stone–like floor and they make noise. This is hopeful. She holds her breath, listening in the dark and hears a sleepy mumble. She senses Tim is here. It'll be okay.

The tree is oddly in an autumn phase, its gold and red and orange leaves blowing in a breeze she can neither feel nor hear. Something else is off and it takes her a moment to see that the leaves are falling up. Back onto the tree. She cannot think about what it might mean. It makes as much sense as her not being able to see Tim. Or the existence of this place at all.

Kiss, cats: for the deer and the dachshund are one. *She wishes she'd memorized the rest. It would be something to do. She gets down on her knees and, listening for Tim, makes her way toward him.*

When his mother leaves, Michael can't find Sarah. Or Tim. And all the fears come back and the certainty that he doesn't know anything about this world. Should he go see Dr. James since she's gone anyway? Last time it didn't affect time that much. He opens the door and looks down the hall at the doctor's door. Last time. But the time before, it had taken months away.

He remembers the promise he made himself, to stay in the apartment until the funeral. He closes the door. It's eleven; too late to call, anyway. He wishes the doctor hadn't taken his books with him. At least he could read. He could read until she returned, and at least feel like he was doing something for her, or about her.

He goes to the fridge; it's still full of food and, thanks to Mom being Mom, he now has about three days' worth of leftovers. He doesn't need to order groceries. He finished paying the bills and chucked them down the mail chute earlier. He has a pile of paperwork to get through in his office, but it seems that any time he even thinks about going over the statistics from his last trip, he goes back to the last trip, and missing her call, and coming home, and the fact that he wasn't here. He can't face it now. It's late, he should go to bed.

He checks the nursery. Twice. He paces the hall for ten minutes in a fevered vertigo and catches himself on a wall before he realizes that he isn't helping anyone. Finally, he does go to bed, curling himself around Sarah's pillow that no longer smells like her. Maybe there's time for a little grief.

———

It's been too long in the Dark. Maybe Sarah's being punished because she tried to cut Greta out.

Tim has started talking. Simple nursery rhymes. Small sentences.

It's been too long in this place. She knows from watching the tree. All of its autumn leaves re-stuck to its branches, turned dark green, then light, then shrunk to a bare froth of green fuzz before shrinking to red buds. Time in reverse seems longer. Only clearly it is moving forward at the same rate for Tim.

They sit in the Dark. Sleep in the Dark. Sometimes Tim toddles off, but he finds his way back to her. She's beginning to think he can see in this place, where she cannot.

Tim likes games of repetition. This is supposed to be typical for a two-year-old.

He says, "Dark, Mommy, Mommy, dark, Mommy, dark."

She says, "Yes, Tim, it is dark."

They've been here too long. Maybe Greta's punishing her.

Then he gets into the rhythm of the words for the fun of saying them: "Dark, Mommy, Mommy, Mommy, dark, Mommy, dark, Mommy . . . "

It's maddening. She thinks of every nursery rhyme she can to entertain him. Pease Porridge Hot. Roses are Red. Pat-a-cake. But after fifteen rounds of Three Little Kittens, Sarah's ready to scream. Only she can't. It would scare Tim. She tries to tell him stories, but he's not old enough to understand and he grows impatient and interrupts or wanders off. She loves him so dearly, but he's no conversationalist. She misses Michael. She misses grown-up conversation.

Greta's definitely punishing her. Sarah's beginning to hate her, but Greta is human contact and she has the power to pull Sarah out of this place.

This place. Is this worse than death? Could she and Tim be happy together in some sort of heaven now?

"Dark, Mommy. Dark."

What has she done to her boy?

The sound of Greta's voice from another room cuts through Michael's sleep and wakes him up. It's slow, sonorous, unrelenting. The sun is already high in the window. He's still dressed from the night before and his jeans are decidedly uncomfortable and slept-in. He goes to the bathroom to clean up before facing whatever awaits him.

———————

Greta eventually brought her back. Michael was nowhere to be found. Sarah didn't talk to Greta for a while. Greta left her alone, but gave her the impression she felt that the ball was in her court. This made Sarah want to shut her out entirely, but after a month of only herself and Tim and no sign of Michael, Sarah longed for some company. The mommies have come by, now and again. Sometimes Greta brings them, other times they materialize around her, one after the other. It's been almost a year since Michael left. She's starting to lose hope.

Greta's sitting on the sofa. She made them both tea this time. Sarah's had trouble getting a handle on the physical lately. Greta's prattling on in a soothing way about child development. Apparently a child of two learns a new word every two hours. Sarah wonders how one even measures that.

Sarah looks up to say something, but Maureen is sitting next to Greta, crying. Another woman appears in the chair by the window. Another in the desk chair. Another leaning against the sofa with her baby. Sarah startles. They're all new faces except for Maureen. She doesn't understand why the moms go when they go or where the new ones come from. She asked Greta once, but she said something about how they no longer needed her. They've moved on. This terrifies Sarah. She doesn't want to move on. She wants to stay with Tim. She wants Michael to come home.

But Maureen is here without her baby and she's crying. She looks like she's been crying for some time. Greta lets the mommies go on talking about weaning and she goes to Maureen, puts her arm around her shoulder and guides her out of the room. They walk into the kitchen and Sarah can hear Maureen sobbing and Greta's soothing tones. Then Maureen's voice goes up, agitated, panicked. Greta's tone doesn't change.

This is Sarah's apartment. Maybe she can help. She leaves Tim playing in the corner and walks toward the kitchen. She rounds the corner and sees Greta through the doorway as she takes Maureen into an embrace. Maureen relaxes a little, lets out a large sob and then surrenders to the hug. Sarah doesn't want to disturb the scene and is about to turn back to the living room when she sees Greta's arms tighten around Maureen. Maureen begins to struggle.

Greta says, "Shh, shh. Relax, Maureen. It will be easier. Your baby is in a better place now. It's best this way."

Maureen relaxes a little and Greta pulls her closer. Sarah is horrified to see that Maureen is being absorbed by Greta. The hug is consuming her. There's a strong smell of burning ozone and a poof of black dust and Maureen is gone. Greta turns around, her face smug and shiny, well fed. She sees Sarah. She looks alarmed for a moment and Sarah opens her mouth to speak, but there's a pounding in her head and everything goes black.

Sarah wakes up to find that she's sitting by the window. The mommies are in the midst of conversation. She must have dozed off. She doesn't know why she's so tired. Usually the mommies energize her a bit. But she feels sad, overwhelmingly sad, and there's a dark feeling she can't shake. Something bad will happen. Or happened, she's not sure. The sound of Greta's voice bears no comfort. Tim's laughter from across the room bears no comfort. There is only sadness and a slowly creeping dread.

Michael steels himself as he rounds the corner of the hallway into the living room. Sarah's sitting in a chair in the corner, looking out the window. She looks like she's been on a hunger strike for several months since she left Michael last night. He doesn't understand. He didn't leave the apartment. This isn't supposed to happen if he doesn't leave.

Michael's heart sinks to his stomach as he frantically searches the room for Tim. There are about ten women sitting around and Michael's startled to see that he doesn't recognize any of them. He doesn't know why this is frightening, but it is. There's a three-year-old squatted down next to the bookshelf, pulling the books off, one by one. A full head of curly brown hair. Part of him wants to scold the child or get its mother's attention, but there's too much to process. The other children in the room are babies. Some in carriers, some in fabric, hammock-like slings, strapped closely to their mothers. One or two are crawling.

As Greta drones on, Michael is disconcerted to see that she has somehow increased in size. Her mass has expanded on an elemental level. *Power* is the first word that comes to Michael's mind when he looks at her. The oppressive force has grown to a dominant one. Greta's face is firm, flushed and healthy; her eyes crackle as she continues her litany. The words are similar to what Michael has heard before, but her delivery is more forceful, as if she's reciting an incantation.

The words have gotten as grating as a repeated advertisement. "All that matters . . . babies . . . " But before, he hadn't noticed how these cheap slogans affected the women hearing them. As Greta rambles on, he sees some of the mothers hugging the babies to them. Tickling them with a dogged fervor to make them giggle. The mothers are feeding off Greta's energy and creating a new unsavory energy with their children. Michael feels strongly that he doesn't belong here.

She says, "When thoughts disturb or distract you. Recognize those thoughts, acknowledge them and show them the door . . . " What thoughts exactly is she warning them against? Or protecting herself from?

The three-year-old by the bookshelf runs over and throws himself against Michael's knees. "Daddy!" He's almost up to his waist. It's Tim. He looks up into his father's eyes and then buries his face in his thighs. "Daddy. Where you go? Where you go, Daddy?" Michael lowers his hand to his boy's head, surprised by how easy it is to reach; it was farther away yesterday. He runs his hands through the curls that twine around his fingers, a curlier, shorter echo of Sarah's hair.

If so much time has passed, how would Tim remember him?

The spell over the room has been broken and Greta looks up at Michael, her eyes flashing with anger and hatred. But she smiles. Sarah won't even look at him; she continues staring out the window.

It's Greta who gets her attention. "Sarah, your husband is home."

There's general whispering amongst the women. Sarah looks up in surprise and tears of gratitude fill her eyes. She gets up from the chair and walks over to him. Michael is startled and saddened to see that it's a different presence walking toward him. Gone is Sarah's solidness, her confident stride, her ability to command the ground under her feet. This skeletal, shadowy figure walks tentatively, frightened.

Sarah throws herself into Michael's arms and buries her face in his chest. He gently puts his arms around her and wonders if this is how it felt to greet loved ones when they had gotten out of the camps in World War II. So diminished from living through un-told . . . untold. She's at least warm to the touch. She looks him in the eyes and there, sunk in her sockets, surrounded by dark rings, shining in her green irises, which are mercifully unchanged, he sees love. And in that love, he recognizes Sarah and he knows she's still there.

She doesn't blame him this time. "I'm so happy you're home. I waited."

I didn't leave. I never left—and look at you. He whispers so only she can hear, "Thank you for waiting. I love you so." He smiles en-couragingly and her face is instantly nourished. The color rises to her cheeks, the shadows recede a little. But through her thinning hair, he can see her scalp. It saddens him, this woman withering from the lack of him.

Greta is still glaring at him with the imperious look of a disapproving matriarch. But he's done with her.

Greta addresses the women in the room, trying to ignore him. "Susan was telling us about her trouble with—"

Michael cuts her off too sharply. "I hate to interrupt your meeting, but could Sarah and I please be left alone?"

Greta rises. "I see. You can leave and when I take care of your wife and child for a year and you decide to come back I'm expected to suddenly disappear?"

A year?

Greta has a blackness to her eyes and a shrill tone to her voice that Michael hasn't heard before. The dank odor of mildew fills the air, the smell of a basement where something has died, long ago forgotten. This is Greta losing control. The women in the room are stirred by this change in her personality and shield their children, watching her anxiously. Sarah turns to face Greta, keeping Tim between herself and Michael. Michael's impressed to feel his wife straighten her gaunt body and square her bony shoulders to face this apparition.

With her every breath now, black matter seeps out of Greta's clothing and hangs about her like soot. The light and atmosphere have been sucked out of the room. The room is a black fog of dust, the others only dimly visible. The storm has snuffed out the noises of the children, the crying, the cooing and the fussing of their mothers. The cave-deep breathing as Greta seethes is the only sound remaining. Michael freezes beside Sarah, worried shielding her will increase Greta's wrath.

But then Greta looks at the women cowering, these dark forms around her. Some part of her, in the midst of this blackness, remembers a human side. Michael watches the shadows recede from her eyes as the light comes back into the room. He steps up to Sarah and puts his arms around her, looking for Tim, who is playing, oddly unaffected, in the corner with the other children. How could he not have noticed what happened?

Greta sinks down into her seat, looking more unsettled than Michael has ever seen her. She says, "I'm not going. Anywhere." Michael can see her try forcibly to breathe more carefully. Slowly, the sounds of the room come back, some of which Michael had forgotten in their absence. The traffic from outside, the ticking of the clock in the hallway, the creak of the floor under the chairs scattered around the room. And the children, some crying, others fussing. Michael hears Tim's life-affirming mantra, "Daddy. Daddy. Daddy."

The light from outside the window is so bright that it has him squinting. Michael feels exposed when Sarah extracts herself from him and steps forward toward Greta. He bends down and picks the boy up. He's notably heavier, but still light enough to wrap his legs around his father like a monkey, balancing his weight. Michael hugs the boy's new body to him, wiry, all pudge gone. He wants to touch each part of him, examine his growth, but he's worried about Sarah approaching that woman whose eyes still glow, obsidian.

Sarah's voice quavers, her fear showing to the point that Michael feels a surge of pride in her bravery. "Greta. I need to spend time with my husband now. To let him be with his boy." Greta appears to calm at the recognition of her own wording. Her eyes go gray and more human. But Michael knows she is still weighing her options.

Sarah looks around the room at the other mothers. "You ladies understand as well, yes?" Two of them burst out crying. "I didn't mean to offend any of you. But I know that if our places were reversed, I would want you to have any time you could find with your husbands. However little. I know you understand."

Greta sits, looking at Michael and Sarah in turns. Michael can see the moment at which she arrives at a decision and he's both alarmed and relieved when it happens.

One by one, the women disappear. Greta, never taking her eyes off Michael, goes last.

TEN

I t's the day before the funeral. Greta hasn't returned since that scene three days ago. Michael doesn't know what the funeral will mean, and Greta's cautioning him against it now holds more weight. Will she try to move back in when he leaves?

But whatever happens, whatever the funeral brings, he knows that he needs to take advantage of this last day, in case this is the last time he has with his wife and son. He and Sarah sit in the living room for ages, marveling at Tim. He's playing with a pile of foam-rubber trucks, driving them around the floor, making car noises. *Rrrrrrrrrr . . . rrrrrrr . . . rrrrrrr.* Michael sits on the floor opposite him.

Tim says, "Car, Daddy. Car."

Michael says, "That's right. A car. Where are you driving to?"

"To my room!" The boy goes up elephant-walk style, one hand driving the car, his other three limbs careening him across the room and down the hall.

Michael gets to his feet to follow him. Sarah stops him. "He's okay."

"Can he get into any . . . trouble? Did you child-proof the bath-room?" The moment he says this, he knows how absurd it is.

She laughs. "Trust me, he's okay."

Michael sits down on the sofa next to Sarah. He studies her more closely. She's wearing a dress he hasn't seen before, a vintage forties number, burgundy crêpe.

He says, "That's a nice dress."

She smiles. "Thanks. Couldn't fit into it before. I picked it up at that flea market in the park last year." She looks away, sad. Then she smiles at him and pats him on the knee. "I'm so happy to see you, honey." She pauses as if trying to think of something to say. "How's Caroline?" Has so much time passed for her that she has to make halting small talk?

He says, "Caroline's crazy."

She laughs. "What else is new. She still with Alana?"

He shakes his head, "Yeah. I don't know how she puts up with her. I mean, we do well together, but she gets so obsessive about her boots. Listening to that speech every morning when she put them on was seriously wearing on my nerves. *Survival is dependent on one thing only: keeping your feet dry.*"

Sarah imitates Caroline. "*Wet feet equal death for serious hikers.*"

Michael says, "And she's on this whole vegan thing, which is not only hugely inconvenient, but it's another subject for her to lecture me on."

"I can only imagine that one."

He says, "By the time she's done, I can't even look at my beef jerky."

They both laugh, but then go quiet, staring at the floor. It's like an awkward date, only he's not trying to figure out how to get her back to his place; he's trying to figure out how to tell her about tomorrow.

She puts her hand on his arm and squeezes gently. "What's bugging you?"

Well, you're dead, for one. "Sarah."

She twines her fingers in his and grabs his hand. "I'm here, honey."

Five things to say go through his head, but instead he inhales sharply and exhales. "I want to spend all night with you. You know?"

She laughs. "Well, I'd hope so. But let's wait 'til the boy is in bed."

"No. No. I mean, yeah, *sure.*"

She leans over so she can look him in the eyes and says, "What."

He meets her gaze. "I have to go somewhere tomorrow. And it doesn't matter where, but the way things have been going, I don't know. Can you . . . is there any way you can fight Greta off while I'm gone?" He wants to say, *She's dangerous, can we stop her? Is there some sort of armor, or holy water or silver sword?* But he doesn't want to frighten Sarah. He wants to be practical. Within her reality, what can they actually do?

She sits up stiffly.

He says, "I don't think she's good for you. Every time I find you with her, you're worse off. Just. Can you try. Try to keep her out of the apartment while I'm gone?"

She says, "Where are you going?" It's getting chilly.

"Honey, I don't want to talk about it." *Tell her.* He can't tell her. He doesn't know what's going to happen when they say whatever prayers over those coffins, but he does know that her worrying about it isn't going to help anybody. He says, "Look, forget about Greta. I. Now. I want to spend tonight with you. Talk. Hang out. We don't need food. We have each other. And Tim. We have Tim." He hollers for him, exhilarated. "Timmy!"

The boy answers with an insolent tone one would expect from an older kid. "What?" It's so incongruous with his age, that they both laugh.

Tim's on the sofa on his back. They've tickled him for a good ten minutes and it's clear that he's exhausted. Michael feels a little guilty, keeping the kid up too late just to spend time with him.

Tim starts to fuss a bit. Michael picks him up and rolls him into his lap. His head goes up to Michael's chin now, when they're sitting like this; yesterday he only came up to his chest. Tim spins around until he's facing his dad, his legs straddling his torso, his head leaning on him. Michael kisses the top of his head. The milky-sour odor of his babyhood . . . yesterday . . . has changed and Michael smells shampoo, salty kid head, peculiarly stinky feet with the faint odor of peanut butter underlying it. He tries to memorize the weight of his boy, the smell of him.

"Daddy, wheah you go?" Tim can't say his *r*'s.

"I'm right here."

Tim says, "Wheah you go *befowa* here?" His voice. It's husky and low, but has a quizzical squeak to it when he asks questions. Michael tries to listen harder. To memorize it.

He says, "Before here what?"

"Wheah befowa what?" The boy gets it: it's a game. He leans back, pulling at Michael's shirt.

"Oh, before *that*."

Tim absently pulls at Michael's belt buckle, waggling it up and down. "After befowa wheah wheah wheah?"

Michael looks down to see what Tim's up to and notices with alarm that his belt, once snug, has gotten loose enough for Tim to pull it out a few inches.

Tim turns his big eyes look up into his father's face. "Wheah, wheah, wheah?" His eyes are green and almond-shaped, like his mother's, but feathered with blue, from Michael. He has more of a nose now, and it seems to be taking on the form of Michael's, broad and flat, not small and tip-tilted like his mom's. Michael hopes he doesn't get that hook to his nose that plagued his teenage years. He's gotten used to it, but Tim shouldn't have to suffer. Then he remembers that teenage years probably won't happen for this boy. *Stop thinking. Look at him.*

The curls he can't explain. Both grandmothers have slightly curly hair, so maybe it's in there somewhere. Tim looks up at him, breathing heavily, but it's moved from baby breath to back-of-the-throat, stuffy nose breath. Michael grins as he realizes his kid is old enough to have bad breath.

Tim says, "Daddy? Daddy?"

Michael says, "Tim? Tim?"

"Wheah you go?"

He can't bring himself to answer the question. "I'm right here." He doesn't know how.

Tim's hands go up to his face and grab his cheeks, rubbing his two days' growth of beard. "Sandy face."

Michael laughs. He's trying like hell not to cry and he feels less and less able to prevent it. He's weaker and that underlying throb of grief is closer to the surface today. He mirrors the boy and takes his rosy, very soft cheeks in his hands. Where do they put the pores on kids? Tim's skin is perfect, soft, covered with a light down and glowing beneath, revealing a delicate framework of blue veins near his forehead. He's getting a smattering of freckles across his nose. Michael hugs him to his chest and the child relents for a moment before he starts to squirm.

He slips out of Michael's arms to the floor and barks, "Mommy! It's bed."

Sarah laughs and says, "Kiss your father."

Michael says, "I got him." He hoists Tim over his shoulder, stands a moment to steady himself, fighting off dizziness, and flies him down the hall.

Sarah follows them, cringing, as Michael steers Tim around the hallway haphazardly, nearly smashing him into the wall, the ceiling, to make the ride more adventurous. Michael is sweating and shaking by the time he gets to his room, but Tim squawks with laughter.

Michael and Sarah are lying in bed on their bellies, feet dangling off opposite ends of the bed, faces next to each other in the middle, hands entwined. He's looking at her. They've been reminiscing for an hour and have run out of things to say. Some things they talk about are not complete conversations.

He says, "Munich."

She answers, "Marcus."

He says, "Nut job."

"Do you think he misses us?"

"I'm sure thoughts of us fill his every waking moment."

She gets quiet. Then, "If you see my mom?"

He says, "Don't talk that way."

"If you see my mom? You have to tell her I'm sorry."

He asks, "For what?"

"I took the twenty bucks in junior high. The twenty bucks she thought the cleaning lady stole."

He laughs. "You're surely going to hell for that one." Sarah looks away, darkens a little. *Bad joke. Move on.* "Did she get fired?"

She says, "No, but Mom never treated her the same after that."

He says, "I'm sure that worry has weighed on her for years."

"Stop teasing me."

"Should I start writing things down?"

She says, "Tell Anna I broke her china shepherdess figurine."

"Oh for chrissake, now you're getting maudlin, you promised you wouldn't get maudlin." He's hoping his tone will keep her in a good humor.

But she's serious. "Tell her, okay?"

He says, "Did she also blame the cleaning lady?"

"The cat."

"Because the cat's worried about it."

She's welling up. "*Tell* her, okay?" He feels the stress, her realization that this is it. Her hands are turning cold in his, icy.

He tries to bring her down with something real. "Remember the flat tire?"

She says, "Which flat tire?"

"The worst one. Snowstorm. Jersey."

Her hands warm up. She teases him. "You thought you could change a tire."

He says, "I watched my mom do it."

She says, "You're lucky you didn't lose a limb."

He says, "Yeah, but that was the deciding factor."

"Of what?"

He moves around like the hand of a clock until he's parallel with her. He pulls her to him, playing with her hair as he continues, "I already knew I loved you. I knew I wanted to be with you. But when I saw you roll your eyes at me and take command of that jack . . . "

She giggles. "Oh, please."

"Seriously."

"Really?"

He says, "You were capable. I knew that you could take care of yourself and for some reason that was a major turn-on."

She says, "All I remember is wondering who the hell raised a kid in the country who didn't know how to change a tire."

"I was too busy collecting rocks." He pauses. "Can I go wake him up?"

"No."

"Just checking."

She scoots up and straddles his stomach, kissing his neck. "I'm not done with you yet." He loves her. More than anything. But she's bony and fragile and it's not the same. He kisses her back. It'll be okay. It'll be okay.

It's Sarah. It is.

———————

Sarah wasn't supposed to let him sleep. She won't for long. But he's so beautiful when he sleeps. And the way he was talking earlier, about going out? Not about his going out, but the worry in his voice, the way he wants to spend time with her. She's afraid. It's not a fear like she's felt with Greta, or the blackness, or Michael suddenly leaving. But a fear of something solid. Like the fear she felt when she first went into labor. The fear that it was time for something unknown, terrible, and unstoppable to happen. Where that fear eventually led makes her more afraid of this new feeling.

When he leaves this time this might be it. She buries her face in his neck and breathes deeply. She can smell him tonight. The sweat. The smell of Michael's ear. The musk of the sex they just had—that she couldn't feel. But when he came, he grabbed the back of her neck and pulled her face into his chest and she could feel how grateful he was. How wholly he had felt it. And that was enough for her.

She murmurs into his ear. "He walked around the world on his four fur feet. His four fur feet. His four fur feet."

He startles awake. "Sarah?"

She nuzzles in closer. "He walked around the world on his four fur feet and never made a sound-O."

Michael says, "Did I fall asleep?"

"Just a little."

"Don't let me fall asleep."

She kisses his neck. "It was only for a minute. You were so cute."

———————

They're in the kitchen. He's alive, he has needs. Maybe if he eats something he won't feel so heady. Spinning. He gets some garlic naan out of the fridge and the leftover tikka masala. He doesn't bother heating it up. Sarah's sitting at the kitchen table in a bathrobe. She doesn't usually wear her bathrobe, but Michael knows that she's self-conscious about her changing body. She's warmer and smiling, but the gaunt, starved look hasn't left her. Her eyes have lost a battle with her cheekbones and have receded. Her hair is lanky; her scalp shows when the light hits her right. He tries to give her a reassuring smile, as one does with the severely disabled. To let her know he sees *her*, the person under all of this decay.

She doesn't smell the same. He noticed. During sex. That musk, the warm Sarah-flesh smell that underlay every time they spent together in their lives has been replaced with something else. It has echoes of her scents, the shampoo is the same, the lotion, but the essence of Sarah has soured. Milk gone slightly off; not totally gone, but still not right.

She watches him eat and then sighs. "I miss food."

He says, "I'm sorry."

She says, "You need to stop being sorry."

"I'm sorry."

She laughs. Then she doesn't. "I mean it, Michael. It's so important to me that you're not sorry. Can you promise me that?" She doesn't normally address him by his name and when she does, it makes him feel scolded.

He asks, "What should I be instead?"

"I just said I miss food. That's all. You can listen. Be understanding. But it's not your fault I can't eat."

He doesn't know what she wants him to say. "Okay."

She says. "Thank you."

He thinks for a moment. He feels like the conversation is somehow keeping her with him, keeping her from getting vague. He asks, "Do you miss Indian food?"

She nods, watching him eat. "A lot."

"Pizza?"

"Painfully."

"What else?"

"The snap of a fresh carrot. Cucumbers in rice wine vinegar. Garlic. On anything. Chocolate. The smell of the fridge when you open it."

He laughs. "Trust me, you aren't missing anything good on that last one." The food doesn't taste right anymore. His chewing slows.

She says, "Still. Fresh-baked bread. Stinky cheese. Juice. Grapes. Ripe grapes, chilled. A juicy steak, done so rare, it quivers. Fresh lobster with butter and lemon in Maine, by the water, after a walk on the beach. Garlic fries. Garlic. On anything. And I never thought I'd say this, but, a proper Thanksgiving turkey dinner. Your mom's drunken sweet potatoes. Mashed potatoes. With garlic. Garlic, on anything."

"I'm sorry."

"Michael."

"I can't help it, this tikka masala is so good even cold, and if you could have smelled the saag when I opened it up."

She says, "What did it smell like?"

He says, "Coriander. Cardamom. Cinnamon. Allspice. Mustard. Cumin. That undertone of butter. Spinach. And. Warm."

She closes her eyes, remembering. "Thank you."

"I should have taken you out to more gourmet meals while you were pregnant."

She says, "Shoulda woulda coulda." She gets up and walks to him. It's awkward, holding the carton of food in one hand, the naan in another, but he opens up his arms so she can hug him.

She says, squeezing him, "I'm glad I'm here."

He says, "I'm glad you're here, too."

They quiet for a minute. The clock on their seventies stove does its weird electric grinding tick. The fridge kicks in. Michael can hear his breath coming through his nose as he swallows what's in his mouth. He reaches behind him to put down the takeout container, then the other way for the bread. He wraps his arms around his wife. Holding on.

It's dawn. They've stayed awake the whole night. Michael wants to fight back the rising of the sun as his fingers are wrapped in Sarah's, their legs twined around each other on their bed. He feels her go cold and the light dims. She must be having a bad thought to fill the room with such darkness.

He says, "What?" He rubs her arms and back. It's inadequate for fighting this chill. Her skin is so loose over her bones that he worries he'll rub it off her, that she'll disintegrate under his touch down to sinew, bones, dust.

She says, "I think you should feel free to remarry."

He laughs. He doesn't mean to, but the thought is so foreign and absurd.

She looks up at him with a scowl. "This is important."

"Sarah, this is ridiculous." He kisses her forehead and squeezes her gently. If he could cover all of her with his arms to keep her warm and with him, he would.

She maintains her scowl, but her eyes smile and she warms a bit. They pause.

He jokes, "Shall we solve world hunger while we're at it?"

She nestles in his arms and says, "I love you."

"That's all we need to think about now. Can I wake him up?"

She says, "No," reflexively. Then, looking at the gray light in the window, "Sure."

He looks at his watch. Six a.m. Two hours until his mother comes by with the car. He springs out of bed, hoping Sarah won't pick up on the fact that he's starting to panic. He feels slightly dizzy and breaks into a cold sweat. He imagines everyone at the funeral. Anna, weeping, Sarah's mom, the hundreds of people who are going to need to give him their condolences. He doesn't know how he will cope.

Tim. He'll get to Tim. Two hours is a long time, if spent right.

He opens the boy's door and finds him sitting in his bed, playing with his animals. The wood-framed daybed, used as a bench for grown-ups before, has become Tim's bed. The crib is where it was two days ago, when he was small enough to sleep in it. Tim's life has become a time lapse of movement and growth against a stable backdrop.

Tim looks up at his father and his face lights up with a mischievous smile. Surrounded by his dozens of stuffed animals, he looks like Max, king of all wild things. Michael dives into the boy's bed next to him, its wooden frame scraping the floor as its back hits the wall. The mattress is thinner than most and he feels his hip hitting the base of the bed. He pulls Tim to him. Where Sarah's wasting away, the boy is thriving. Michael buries his face in Tim's neck and blows, causing him to giggle. Timmy is filled with life, and squirming, and drool, and giggles and warmth. He's real. This is real. The boy protests, "Daddy, squish! Squish!"

Michael laughs and releases him. Tim turns and starts patting Michael's arm. "Daddy, squish! Squish. Squish. Daddy, squish. Squish."

Michael senses Sarah sinking to the floor behind them. They're quiet for a moment. Timmy tumbles out of bed onto the floor with a clunk and heads over to his toy bins. He starts getting out some blocks. Sarah climbs onto the tiny bed and wraps herself around Michael. They watch their boy play.

———

Half an hour to go. He's taken a shower and shaven. While shaving, he saw his gaunt face in the mirror, the rings under his eyes. His skin has gone sallow, jaundiced. Not all sleep deprivation, he knows. It's the tea. Sarah brings two cups into the bathroom while he dresses. He looks at the mug for a long moment. He picks it up and drinks it in quick gulps, even though he knows he shouldn't. He drinks it in hopes that maybe this won't be their last time together. He drinks it in hopes of keeping her closer, even though he is leaving. She mirrors his swift gulps, a brash dare or drinking game. She flashes him a wicked smile and slams the empty mug down on the counter. The tea churns in his stomach and he doesn't have the heart to laugh.

He won't wear black. That might frighten her. There's no law about wearing black and, alive or dead, Sarah wouldn't like it. He chooses a gray suit, a white shirt, a blue tie. Tasteful, somber, but not gloomy. Sarah comes in and straightens his tie. She looks at his face and saddens.

He reassures her, "I won't be long." *But I still don't know what happens now. What will happen once the prayers are said? Once the coffins are buried?*

There are still a few questions to ask her.

He clears his throat in an effort to sound natural, and says, "Uh. Honey. The safe deposit box?"

"Mmm?" She sounds contented and distracted as she dusts off his shoulders.

He says, "I never did have the key. I just wondered."

"It's in the apothecary." The Chinese cabinet that holds up the television set is in the living room, there are more than fifty drawers in it.

"Oh."

They don't talk as she goes into his underwear drawer for a handkerchief. He never owned a handkerchief before he met her, but Sarah always believed it necessary for a gentleman's suit. He doesn't know how to space these questions, but if she's gone when he gets back, he won't be able to ask them.

He says, "What are you and Tim going to do while I'm gone?"

That frost again. But she's working against it. She speaks quickly, with perky cheer. "I think we'll play this morning. Then, when he goes down for his nap I'm going to read a book. It's been so long since I've read a proper book, you know, a novel. And I've always wanted to read *Huckleberry Finn*. I never did read it. I was abroad when they read it in high school English and I loved *Tom Sawyer* so much. I think I read four books that talked about it in college. But I never read the book itself. I had one friend who said it was life changing. Can a book be life changing? I don't know."

She tucks the handkerchief into his pocket. It's blue to match his tie. She pats it and looks up at him.

He blurts, "What do we keep in our safe, anyway?"

She says, "Safe?"

"You insisted on buying one when we moved in, but I've never seen you use it."

She smiles, coy. "Oh, just some stuff."

He puts his arms around her, rocking her playfully. "What's in there?"

She chills again. She pushes away from him as she says, "The combination is in the apothecary." She walks away.

He feels awful. "I'm sorry."

"What did I say about saying that?"

He walks behind her and puts his arms around her. "I love you."

She says, "I know."

"I've always loved you." His chest is closing up now. He squeezes her gently and holds her.

She turns around to face him. "I know." She looks worried. "You need to kiss the boy."

"Why? I mean, of course I'll kiss him."

It's freezing. Like that. Sarah heads down the hall calling frantically, "Tim? Tim?" She turns on Michael, accusing, "You stopped watching him!"

He says, "He was napping. Remember the napping part?"

She slams open the door to Tim's room and Michael is behind her. Is she hard to see or is he dizzy from not sleeping? The hallway still holds the icy air, but the moment he rounds the corner to the boy's room, he hits a pool of warm air. Like swimming in a lake, he's immersed in a tepid pocket. He's moved from lost panic to a beautiful tableau. Sarah's sitting on the bed, reading to Tim in less time than it should have taken her to get there, farther into the book than she should be. The boy's in his underwear and nothing else. Spiderman underwear. His head hangs down between his knees, his legs wrapped around his arms in a position that's a comical echo of his placement in the womb. He rocks and wiggles as he listens to Sarah.

She reads, *"All sorts of dinosaurs eating their lunch . . . "*

The boy chimes in with her, giggling as she tickles him. *"Gobble, Gobble, nibble, nibble, munch scrunch bunch."*

The table lamp casts coziness, the floor is covered with blocks and bits of plastic toys. A pair of child-sized overalls is squished down like an accordion, still in the position where Tim stepped out of them. Michael sits and watches as Sarah turns to get another book.

He looks at his watch. It's time to go. He wants to be downstairs when the car arrives. He's not sure if he should say good-bye. Sarah's reading some Shel Silverstein and Timmy has scooched down in the bed, his head curled against her chest, relaxing into the rhythm of the her words.

Michael gets up and walks over to her, kissing her on the top of her head. For a little too long. But not long enough to freak her out. He kneels down and rubs noses with Tim, grinning at him. His kid, his *kid* smiles back and rubs his cheeks, whispering sleepily, "Sandy man." Michael kisses him once on the forehead, once on the belly, and once on the top of his head in those curls. For too long. Tim squirms to get a better view of the book and Michael gets to his feet, turns and leaves. He doesn't say anything. He doesn't look back. His chest clenches; he hears the blood rushing in his ears as he walks down the hall toward the front door.

He opens the door and stops. He does this every time he leaves the apartment, to make sure he has his keys. To make sure he hasn't forgotten anything.

He could *not* go. He could close the door and shut them all out. But they'd come. All of those people in town for the funeral. And they'd keep coming. And he'd be diagnosed as crazy and they'd lock him up and people would come into the apartment and wouldn't that be worse?

As if she knows he's weighing his options, Greta appears in front of him. She asks, "Where are you going?"

He's not surprised to see her. She steps closer. He tries to move around her, but she steps sideways to meet him, like a junior-high bully.

He says, "I need to go."

"No you don't. Tell them you were sick."

"Get out of my way." He steps forward and takes her by the arms, trying to move her. She does not yield like a human. She's taken on the density of solid marble.

He starts to feel helpless. "I have to go."

Greta says, "No you don't. Tell them you were injured. On the stairs." She seems to grow in size as she raises her arm to strike him.

The elevator dings. Greta lowers her arm. Michael's mother gets off and walks toward him. Can she see Greta? Can Greta hurt her?

When his mother looks up at him and smiles, he knows that Greta doesn't dwell in her world. He looks at Greta, who's furious. Her eyes have gone black and she's seething with anger. The temperature drops, black dust surrounds her, and the hall goes dark. His mother, oblivious, continues toward them in her well-lit world. Greta vanishes. The black dust falls to the ground, leaving a chill in its wake.

Michael steps through the dust quickly and goes to his mother's side, taking her elbow and kissing her on the cheek.

"It's freezing up here, Michael. You should tell the super." She looks at him, concerned. "Honey, do you feel okay? You look like you're coming down with something."

"I'm fine. I'm fine." *It's just this toxic tea I've been drinking. No big deal.* Is there any proof that it helps things? It helps Sarah, but what's it doing to him? He can't focus on this now. He'll think about this tonight. He has something to do now.

He steers her toward the elevator swiftly, to get her as far away as he can from the cold, dark patch Greta left.

"Mom. I forgot something. Can I—can I meet you in the lobby?"

"I can wait."

"I'll be just a minute. I . . . need the bathroom."

She pats his hand. A mother understands. Nerves. "I'll see you in the lobby. The car is waiting."

He waits until the door to the elevator closes to go to Dr. James's door. He could talk to him, but he doesn't want to get caught up. And he really doesn't want to talk about what might happen because of the funeral. He pulls a note from his pocket. He wrote it yesterday morning, while Sarah was napping:

DR. JAMES. GONE TO FUNERAL. CHECK IN ON THEM FOR ME, WILL YOU?

He rewrote it about four times to get the wording right. Two versions had Sarah's name and seemed too damning. What if someone else read it? The third note had made him giggle, reminding him of spy notes he'd written as a child. Then he wrote *their funeral* and tore it up. The next one was cryptic. Short. Self-explanatory. Version number four is the one he now slips under the good doctor's door.

─────────

Sarah hears the door close and she knows he's gone. It'll be okay. She'll stay here, with Tim. It may take awhile, but it'll be okay. He'll come back. Why did he seem so unsure about that? Why was he asking all of those end-of-the-road sort of questions about the safe deposit box? He didn't have another field trip, did he? No. He was wearing . . . he was wearing. She helped him with something he was wearing. But if it were a field trip, it'd have been his vest, his flannels, his good boots. He wasn't wearing that. It was something else. For going out.

Tim says, "Again, again, Mommy." He's pushing the smallish cardboard book, Dinosaur Roar *into her face, pressing it against her chin.*

"Not the face, Timmy." It's the first time she's called him Timmy. It makes her feel Michael's absence more.

Read the book. This is going to be a long wait.

She needs to relax and live each moment. That's the point of their being here, isn't it? To feel each moment. But that sense of foreboding hasn't left her. He's gone, what worse could happen? *She has to focus on the joy of reading a book, for the twelfth time that day, to her three year old.*

Tim hollers, "Dinosaur roar! Dinosaur squeak!"

Sarah feels a warm presence and smells Greta's perfume in the room. She won't look at her; if she does, she'll have let her in, and once she has a hold, it's hard to shake. Sarah knows that Greta is sitting in the rocker by the window. She can hear the clatter of her wooden bracelet against the wood of the chair, the squeak of boards under her feet as she shifts her weight.

Greta's voice is sonorous and convincing. "I thought you might like some company."

Sarah knows she's working hard to pull her in, and that knowledge gives her a little power. She keeps her eyes on the book in front of her, buries her face in Tim's hair to smell his head and to block out the patchouli, floral and fleshy, soporific sweetness that Greta carries with her. She says, "We're okay, Greta. Only reading a book, thank you for your concern."

Greta says, "Don't mind me, I could use a good story." She shifts, sinking into her seat, getting more comfortable.

Sarah closes her eyes. "Could you please leave us alone? We're doing fine. Michael will be back any minute."

She can feel the room darken and it gets bitingly cold. Sarah worries she's going to the Dark, but she realizes the cold is not emanating from her. It's coming from Greta. A noise rises with her, an abstract roar, not unlike what Sarah heard in the elevator shaft. She curls herself around Tim and breathes in his neck, waiting.

Tim doesn't seem to notice anything's wrong and says a bright but muffled, "Tent!" from underneath her.

There is a zap and Greta is gone. The room is still cold, but she's gone.

They can do this, wait for Michael. It'll be okay.

ELEVEN

The sounds in the lobby are jarring. It's been several days since Michael set foot outside the apartment. His dress shoes clomp on the marble floor beside the snipping of his mother's heels, and both sounds bounce off high-ceilinged, mirrored walls.

Phil gets up from his post, startled. "Mr. Gould." His voice echoes. Michael says, "Phil."

Phil watches them as they walk by, worried, sad, unsure of how to act. Michael braces himself: Phil is only the first of many.

Michael squints as he steps through the front door; the sights and sounds of the streets assault his senses after his apartment-encased existence. It's an unusually warm day. The pungent smell of garbage underlies the usual spring smells of exhaust, flowers, and new leaves. The sun hurts the back of his eyes and the warmth makes his skin contract, prickling the back of his neck up into his scalp. A sudden jackhammer down the street makes him put his hands to his ears. Even a beeping horn from two blocks over is surprising. Michael breathes in deeply; he will have to muscle through his re-entry into life.

The black town car is parked out front and the driver gets out to let them in. Michael gives him a polite smile and a hello.

The driver nods nervously and looks at the ground as Helen gets in. The shame of there having been a death is too heavy for small talk. Michael feels embarrassed by his hello, left hanging there, hollow and flat in the open air.

The door of the town car closes, creating a sound-proof bubble so pungent with new-car air freshener that Michael blinks from the smell.

Helen has chosen gray, too. She's wearing a trouser suit with a white shirt and her black cowboy boots. Michael smiles. He was tormented for his mother wearing her cowboy boots when he was in junior high in Jersey. The town he grew up in was not known for its sense of style. But when school let out each day, there she would be, leaning against the only topless Jeep Wrangler in town. He learned, only later, that it was actually cooler to identify with his mom than with his classmates.

Helen looks out the window, but he can tell she's trying to hide a nervous energy. For now, Michael will try to think only about where they are and not about where they're going.

Helen's voice flutters nervously as she chirps, "Monica did the flowers. They're lovely."

So much for that. Michael says, "Oh?"

Helen says, "She gave us a huge discount."

Someone's been planning this event. Putting work into it. There were flowers ordered. Invitations sent. And where was he? He should feel guilty, but he's relieved and grateful for these days he's had alone with Sarah. The idea of never having met Tim goes through his head. Not an option.

Helen says, "We go to the church for the funeral, then there are more prayers, later, at the site."

Stop. I mean, can you stop? But she won't stop. "Lunch at the club after, but that's only for one hundred of the guests."

It won't stop. This is it.

Only one hundred. An adolescent squeak comes into his voice, "Jeez, how many people are coming, Mom?"

She says, "Well, you know Sarah's family. That's why your wedding was such a to-do. Every family occasion commands the whole country club set. And people from work. Oh, honey, Dan and Chuck will be there. Rotten timing, but it'll be good to see them again."

This is happening.

He thinks of the parade at his wedding, the cousins of cousins and friends of Aunt Nancy, the group of suited biddies who cooed every time he walked past, and his father-in-law's entire office. His father-in-law had died five years before, but his colleagues remained and looked as if they belonged there more than Michael did. It was a joyful day and he was very happy to be marrying this woman who truly made him whole. But by the time he shook that fiftieth hand, he began to feel more like a product than a person. The son-in-law. Respectable job, looks good in a suit, could pass for WASP, although his mother was a recovering Catholic and he was raised without religion. He sat there at the bridal table. The entire crowd clinked their glasses, the command for the newlyweds to kiss. He remembers wondering how all of these people were so involved in the most important and intimate moment of his life.

Now they're all turning out to take part in his grief. The grief he hasn't gotten a handle on yet. Because Sarah's still here. *Oh, God, let her still be here.*

His mother is once again looking out the window. She respects his mood, but she nervously pulls at her jacket. He knows more is coming.

She says, "It won't be too bad. You should be home again by three."

Five hours. He was gone for only about half an hour for groceries. Months passed. He was gone five minutes, weeks. That one night he had gone to sleep without her, by the time he woke up the boy had aged one whole year and Greta once again had a hold. *Five hours.* It's better than all night. Maybe it won't be so bad.

His mother's voice startles him, despite the baffling from the leather seats. "Sarah would have hated all this."

"You're right."

She says, "Remember, you were going to elope? Barefoot in the woods or something."

He smiles. "We tried to get Dan to write away for that minister-by-mail thing."

"What stopped you?"

"Sarah felt bad for her mom. Seriously, she went through with that ginormous wedding just to please her mother." She's so incredible. And selfless.

His mother grasps his hand and pats it. She loved Sarah, too.

They're quiet for a few blocks. Traffic is slow, unusual for a Saturday morning. But Michael's in no hurry to get there. He stares at a smudge of something on the seat in front of him. Sticky. Viscous. He tries to think about what might have made this mark to get his mind off of Sarah on their wedding night when they were finally alone after the all-day shake-and-kiss-athon. How she got the giggles and couldn't stop. How she shed her enormous wedding dress like a skin and danced around in her ridiculously ornate underwear, jumping on the bed, shrieking, "I'm free! I'm free!" How she threw her arms around him and grinned, whispering, conspiratorial, "We're free." And then.

Has Greta come? Will Sarah be strong enough to hold her off?

Michael leans his forehead against the glass, inhales the new car smell, and focuses on the fruit market outside the window. The car has stopped at a light. Bins of colorful fruits and vegetables are overflowing under the green-and-white-striped awning. The sidewalk has recently been hosed down. Pears. Apples. Zucchini. Cauliflower. Garlic. *Garlic on anything.*

The car moves again and they're in front of the gray stone steps of the church. There's a blur of people outside the window. His mother reaches over and grasps his hand again. He keeps his forehead on the glass a moment longer.

She says, "Michael."

He can't look at her, but he turns his head toward her, focusing again on the smudge. Maybe where gum had been taken off. Or a sticker.

She shakes his arm to get his attention. "Mikey." He looks her in the eyes in response to his childhood name. He wishes he hadn't. She looks anxious, and for the first time he notices that she's been crying recently. Probably before she came to get him. She says, "I need you to remember something important." She has that *What I say next will fix everything* tone. It won't. "This is for her parents, honey. It's not about Sarah at all."

It does help. A little. She pats his hand again and the driver opens his door. He gets out to meet the masses.

The Cathedral of St. John the Divine. Sarah's mother never did anything halfway. They were married here. Betsy had to pull some major strings to make that happen. He cringes to think of what she had to do to get the space again, and how much she paid for it.

He steps out of the car into the warm spring air. The sky is painfully blue, and everything on the steps of the soaring cathedral is too bright. The edge of each particle in the stone steps cuts his eyes— quartz, gypsum, flecks of mica. He blinks hard and the people come into focus; each one of them slams him with their familiarity.

Sarah's roommate from college, Karen; their old neighbor, Doug; the Pittsburgh cousins—two of them are named Pam and it gets confusing. Oh shit, absolutely everyone from work is here. The Brooklyn Peters. Lucinda and Lucy, cute as ever and wearing matching black suits—exactly the right thing, of course. Miguel and Diana. Jimmy and Tom. Oh, God, there's Betsy, Sarah's mom. *Do I have to see her? Could I sneak through this thing somehow without talking to her?* She's crying into her handkerchief and not looking, but the crowd on the steps is parting to make way for him. The ripple will soon reach her.

He feels two strong arms around his neck and a warm cheek pressed fiercely to his. He's gripped in a hug he recognizes and Caroline barks into his ear, "Why don't you answer your phone, you ratfink?" He's worried she'll squeeze out his sadness and the tears will start, but just in time, she pulls away to look at him. Worry crosses her broad, tanned face. He wishes he could take her away from this and talk to her about everything. She'd have good advice. Caroline always had good advice. But his situation is beyond explanation.

She's wearing a lot of makeup, which looks strange on her. She's wearing a suit, which is also strange. Her blonde spiked hair is much the same. She smiles, but he can see that she's been crying. This shakes him more than his mother crying. Even with the countless hours spent traveling with her, even hopelessly lost in the wilderness with plummeting temperatures, he's never seen Caroline cry.

"Well." She smacks him on the shoulders with both her hands and searches his eyes. She has a lot on her mind and Michael is hoping she won't share any of it.

Helen steps in and hugs Caroline, kissing her cheek. "Caroline, how great to see you. Honey, your girl Alana looks totally abandoned over there; she doesn't know anybody and Michael has a few people he needs to talk to."

Caroline looks embarrassed. She looks at Helen, then at Michael, and clears her throat. "Right! Oh. I'm sorry. I. Once I heard, I felt so terrible. That I hadn't made a big deal about it when you kinda knew . . . " She trails off. Too much to talk about.

Michael rescues her by pulling her into another hug. Although she's been his friend and colleague for six years, he didn't know how grateful he was for her until now. He kisses her on the cheek, saying, "It's okay. I'm glad you're here."

Caroline puts on one of her most encouraging smiles, which comes off as a peculiar grimace. "See you after." She backs off and heads over to her girlfriend.

His mother takes his hand and leads him through the crowd and up the stairs, making a beeline for Betsy. She turns her head as they go and mutters, "Let's get this over with." God bless her, Helen always knows the right thing to do at these occasions.

Betsy's wearing a bold black-and-white-patterned dress and a black straw hat. She looks like she's dressed for Ascot. Apparently this is appropriate mother-in-grief wear. Anna's standing next to her, uncomfortable in a skirt suit and heels, looking irritated, concerned, and then irritated again. Her scowl disintegrates when she sees Helen and Michael approaching them. Michael never thought he'd take comfort in Anna's sharp features. But she understands how horrible this all is. And that helps.

Over there are Chuck and Dan. He loves them and he's so glad they're here, but they're shuffling their feet and talking quietly to each other, heads bent low. Chuck straightens his tie and looks at his shoes. They look lost. If they don't know how to behave, how's Michael going to get by?

Helen lays a hand on Betsy's black-and-white shoulder and Michael notices to his horror that she's wearing black, elbow-length gloves. As always with Sarah's family, he feels underdressed and out of place.

Betsy sees Helen and her face screws up, ready to bawl. Then she sees Michael. Impossibly, it screws up further. There are tears in her voice and she lets out a maudlin stage-gasp. "Oh, Michael!"

As she puts her arms around him, his face is scraped by her straw hat. *Sandy man.* Wet breath is at his neck, and he tries not to think of Tim. Betsy squeezes him tight, sobbing into his shirt. How she manages to avoid dislodging her hat is a mystery.

He's never felt comfortable with Betsy. This is awful.

Anna looks irritated with her mother. "Mother, give him a minute." She flashes Michael an apologetic look. He smiles, sheepishly, which helps him ward off the wave of grief coming out of this gloved, hatted, black-and-white-patterned, perfumed thing pressing herself to his chest. She's clearly not listening to her daughter. He sees Anna's eyes light up. "You'll ruin your makeup."

Michael flashes Anna a thankful look.

The grip loosens. Betsy pulls away. She dabs her eyes with her handkerchief and looks Michael over. He can't read what she sees. What does he look like? He seemed presentable, if gaunt, when he looked at himself in the mirror this morning, but he didn't pay much attention: is he looking appropriately grief-stricken? Numb? Or are they going to know that he hasn't said good-bye yet? That Sarah's still with him?

Or has he gone completely crazy and imagined everything? The apartment, the boy and the smell of his head, Sarah's withering, her glassy eyes; it all seems distant in the glaring sunlight on the steps of the church. All of the pressed suits, the black, the solemnity; the crystal clarity that the light gives each detail makes it all seem unreal. The resolution is too high and makes his family in his apartment feel dim and distant by comparison.

Betsy squeezes his arms in a bolstering grip. "We can do this, Michael. For Sarah."

What's he supposed to say to that? Anna saves him. "Of course we can, Mother. Let's go in, we need to take our seats."

Michael notices Chuck and Dan talking to each other, looking at him, uncertain of what to do. He feels like a bad host for putting them in this awkward position. Chuck gives him the chin-tilt greeting and he returns the gesture. Michael realizes that he's too surrounded by people close to Sarah for his buddies to feel comfortable talking to him right now.

He's startled to find that two of the Pittsburgh cousins were waiting for him to finish with Betsy and people have lined up behind him.

To his horror, a small queue of condolences has formed, trailing down the steps. He nods politely at the cousins, takes his mother's arm in his, turns toward the door and enters the church.

———

It's been a week now. This happened before. He explained. It was a year last time, but it was only one night. Sarah needs to be patient. This happened before. He'll come back. But why did it feel like he was saying Good-bye, not just good-bye? That feeling of certain badness, of unavoidable fate, hasn't dissipated; if anything, it has grown since Michael left. Her emotions have been so uncertain for so long that she can't trust them. Even before she died, during pregnancy, she was prone to sudden fears and creeping anxiety. She pushes the feeling down and watches Tim as he plays with his Lego on the floor. His legs are stretched wide, his back is straight, his brow furrowed in concentration.

Tim keeps asking about Daddy. "Where's Daddy this time?" His memory doesn't jive with his age or the passage of time. That time when Michael was gone for a year last week, Tim remembered him when he came back. She can't help but have that queasy doubt come over her. Tim has never lived. Is she raising her boy or is he something else entirely?

As if he knows what she's thinking, Tim looks up from his Lego on the floor and climbs up into her lap, burying his face in her chest. She kisses the top of his head.

Whatever it is, it's worth it, this time with him.

Tim grabs her face and looks her in the eyes. "Mommy, you miss Daddy?"

She smiles and grabs his cheeks, mirroring his hold on her. "How could I miss anyone with you around, buddy?"

Tim beams back with Michael's eyes and that smile that's both of them. He starts walking his fingers up her arm. "Creepy mouse, creepy mouse . . . "

She creeps her fingers up his arm and tickles his neck, "Creep all over Timmy's house!" He collapses into a gale of laughter and squirms.

Michael was doing okay until everybody sat down and it got quiet. The church. The cathedral is the same. Ridiculously large, cavernous, dark. The marble floor still holds the chill of the morning, and even though he's sweating in his jacket, his ankles feel cold. There's the faint smell of incense and candles and the strong smell of cold marble and polished wood. Lilies. They smell like death.

Two coffins. One large, blonde wood, absolutely covered in white-and-cream-colored roses and Easter lilies and calla lilies, surrounded by green leaves of various shapes and sizes. They make the coffin look as if its organs have exploded out of its center and now lie in twisted tendrils, draping down its sides. Next to it, a small white coffin, barely visible for its matching disembowelment of flowers.

Michael spent so much time worrying about those coffins, those empty coffins, that they aren't very shocking now. His lack of surprise surprises him. Tim is as real as Sarah and is as present as Sarah and as gone as Sarah, and the two coffins are only boxes standing in for them. It helps that they're so far away in this enormous space. Way up in front of the altar. Where he stood with Sarah when they got married. Twenty-five feet from where he sits now.

Anna's sitting next to him, fidgeting with her unfamiliar clutch purse, clearly bought for the occasion. She wears black and she's wearing an essential oils perfume, lavender and rose with an echo of patchouli. This makes Michael think of Greta, and he can feel an ominous echo of her presence in the space. A warning note from afar.

Anna whispers to him, "You okay?"

He gives her an incredulous look.

She says, "I mean you look like crap. More than you usually do."

Her sisterly ribbing doesn't play right, the timing is off. He pats her hand comfortingly. He doesn't have the right words now. No one does.

They decided against music because, Helen told him, Betsy said it would not be appropriate. Why they had to rent the cathedral, he doesn't know. There's a cacophony in the quiet. Programs rustle, people creak, moving in their seats, they sniffle and cough. There's the murmur of whispered conversation. He can't tell which coughs are genuine, which are awkward, and which are from people trying not to cry. He wants to look back at the crowd, but he knows that all eyes are on him right now.

Helen hands him a program. There's a picture of Sarah on it, a kick in the gut. The blood rushes to his head and his vision clouds. The sound of the rustling papers and sniffling grows louder until it hurts. Michael's mortified to realize that every person in this church has now seen this photo, this singular moment of Sarah, which he had always thought too private to share.

He took the photo their first summer together. They were traveling Europe on a Eurail pass and their stop in Munich for a few days turned into a month's stay. Crazy Marcus loaned them his apartment; how could they turn it down? They were at the *Englischer Garten* in the center of town, watching and laughing as locals threw themselves into the stream that runs through the middle of park. People in various states of undress would ride the current, past picnickers, down to the bottom of the hill, and then get out and ride the trolley back up. The kicker was that it was illegal. They just didn't care.

Sarah and Michael sat there for hours in the shade, warming various parts of themselves in patches of sun, watching the bizarre ritual, talking about life. The park smelled alive, baked grass, blooming flowers, the cool damp from the wood of trees and the earth beneath them. Michael was photographing one of the larger middle-aged male bathers when he wheeled the camera around at Sarah, focused it, and asked her to move in with him. She didn't look surprised or angry, as he worried she might. She smiled with a slow, revelatory glee; he pressed the button and the shutter clicked.

Michael didn't know that she'd given a copy of that photo to her mother. Or maybe Anna had pinched it while she was stealing children's books from their apartment. He feels his face flush at the photo and then sees her name written below: Sarah Margaret Lowell Gould, May 14, 1974–March 7, 2013. His mother, as if sensing his distress, places her hand in his. He can't cry. There are too many people. But there she is, looking at the camera with all of that love and youth and promise, and there are those dates, and his head goes down, the tears come and his shoulders shake. His chest seizes with an intake of air and then he begins to sob. The crowd stirs with an audible move of concern. A few *Oh*s escape and some sobbing ripples out, echoing his own.

He doesn't know how much more of this he can take. Father Peter's voice breaks the rustle of the hall, and Michael tries to pull himself together.

———

Six months. Today. Tim turned four two months ago. She's been patient, but she's starting to panic. What if Tim gets sick again? Michael was supposedly the reason he was able to stay, and to grow. So far, Tim appears well, grounded in the here and now. But she can't be sure this will last.

Sarah's surprised that she actually does have a say in Greta's presence. Greta had for so long swept in past her, despite protests. But Sarah finds that if she stands her ground, Greta will, after some dramatics, leave.

*The trouble is, Sarah's getting lonely. Tim's lovely, he is, but he isn't a grown-up. She'd kill for some adult conversation. They've read all of the books in the house twice (*Huckleberry Finn *wasn't life-changing, but it was worth it) and Tim's started to have frustrated tantrums. The other mommies were kind of desperate and horrible, but at least they were company. And they had things to talk about. And she wasn't alone.*

But now she's alone. And maybe he isn't coming back. Maybe what he couldn't tell her was good-bye. He was so upset when he left and she didn't want to ask. But he said he didn't know. That he'd try. When will she know if he's stopped trying?

Tim's working with some wooden beads at the little table in his bedroom. He's stringing them on a shoelace and singing to himself, "And you dream it all, and dreams dream a story do you know what you dream, you're the dream dreamer." *She laughs at his version of the lyrics. They probably make more sense to him.*

Sarah sits down in the preschool-sized chair opposite Tim. He looks so much bigger now that she's down at his level. He's concentrating on his beads and keeps singing, "When you was little, you dreamed you was big . . . "

She joins in, "You must have been something, a real tiny kid . . . "

He snarls at her, his chin in a pout, his eyes snapping. "No, Mommy. My turn. No singing."

Should she scold him for talking back? Is he too young? These seminal moments of motherhood get to her. Who exactly is she making this decision for? If he's never going to be a responsible member of society, does she have to bother with these daily parenting battles?

But what else is she there for? "Tim, honey, I'm happy to listen to you sing. But is there a nicer way to tell me how you feel?"

He looks up at her, struggling with the idea. He's only four. So many big emotions are new to him. He bursts into tears.

She laughs and leans forward, rubbing his back. "I know, buddy. You and me, both." *She pulls him out of his chair and into her lap.* "We don't know what to do with it all, do we?"

"Mommy, sing." *He snuffles into her neck, his hot breath making her want to cry for the joy of having him here. But it also makes her wonder if it's cruel to have him here. He doesn't have a normal life. He never gets to go outside. He doesn't have any playmates. He's never been to his grandmothers' homes. He's never been to a puppet show at the library. He'll never go to preschool. Have a birthday cake. Scrape his knee on the sidewalk. Ride a bike. She'll never be able to take him to the Met to see the mummies. Ever since he was conceived, that had been a fantasy of hers, taking her little boy or girl to see the mummies, watching his horror and glee at the brains getting pulled out the bodies' noses with hooks. What did they do with her body? It was just. Gone. And here she was. Is a part of her rotting somewhere on the other side of town?*

She can't think like that. She can only think about what Tim does have and what she can do for him. Maybe the mommies have playmates for Tim. But the babies never seem to be old enough for him. Why aren't there any others as old as he is? She starts to hum the song to him and rocks him a little.

Greta's voice startles Sarah. "A little lonely, are we?" Sarah jerks, but Tim stops crying, staring across the room with his wise, big green eyes.

Greta's in the rocker, knitting. Today her perfume smell is soothing, earthy. Sarah feels the comfort she did when Greta first appeared to her. It softens the edges of her thoughts and makes her feel safe. She's bothered, like she's forgotten something important, but she's grateful for the company.

Sarah says, "We're doing fine, thank you. Aren't we Tim?"

He waves enthusiastically, grinning. "Hi, lady!"

Greta gently corrects him. "Miss Greta, honey. I told you that before."

Anger flares up in Sarah at the correction, but dissipates when her boy runs to Greta and is taken in an embrace. At least it's somebody else. Tim needs other people, too.

Father Peter is an older priest in his sixties who married Michael and Sarah only five years before. His voice and the smells of the building pull Michael in all directions. Nostalgia, anger, separation, fear, loss, and love all swirl inside him. He stops crying, startled into a glazed stare. He knows he won't be able to get a handle on this; he only has to get through it.

Sarah stood there in that ridiculous wedding cake of a dress with a train the size and shape of Manhattan, and he'd been made to wear a morning suit . . . mourning suit? Complete with a top hat. It was the only time he felt sufficiently dressed for her family, but Chuck and Dan gave him all sorts of shit for their matching groomsmen outfits. Sarah grinned wickedly at him as she came down the aisle and then went all somber in an effort to make him laugh. It worked. She was gonna marry him. That was so huge.

To distract himself, Michael listens carefully to the priest, looking for mistakes. He hasn't seen Father Peter but once a year since he married them. *Let's see how much of Sarah he gets right.*

The priest's unctuous delivery fills the space as if it's been measured for it. "Dearly beloved, we are gathered here today, too soon, to remember one of our own."

She was mine. Is mine. Not ours. Okay, maybe Anna's and some friends' . . .

"Sarah Lowell was a vibrant, lovely young girl."

Sarah Gould.

The priest says, "I remember when she held her place as the second chair in the youth choir. In the fifth grade. She was the youngest to hold that chair."

She was in choir? Why didn't she ever talk about that?

"And ten short years later, I was marrying her off to Michael Gould." Father Peter shoots Michael a sympathetic look that makes him want to punch him. This helps him not cry. Anger is good. Irritation is better.

"I spent much of their earlier marriage badgering them to have children."

When was that? When you saw us once a year at Christmas service?

"So when the news came of Sarah's pregnancy, I was overjoyed."

You need to shut up now.

"At last, Sarah could have the baby of her dreams."

Shut up. You have no idea what she was thinking. She was terrified. Maybe she knew . . . oh, God, maybe she knew.

"But this child . . . "

Oh, for chrissake.

The priest pauses. Michael looks up with a challenging, *what next?* glare in his eyes. He doesn't mean to scoff; it slips out. It's not his fault that it echoes. His mother grabs his elbow in the corrective way she used to at public events when he was small. She pats his hand. It'll be okay.

The priest has taken off his glasses now and dabs his eyes with a crumpled blue handkerchief he's retrieved from God knows where. Do those vestments have pockets?

Is it okay to walk out of your wife's funeral? Why does he have to be here, anyway? Can't they put the bereaved in the crying room reserved for babies? He could suffer in privacy while getting all of the benefits of the funeral. Whatever those are.

He needs to leave.

Father Peter says, "I'm sorry, Michael, I'm so sorry."

Please do not talk to me. If you don't want me to kill you, don't talk to me.

"This beautiful woman, this child, were both taken from us. We don't know why, Lord, we only ask that they are at peace, in your bosom."

They are *not* at peace. They're waiting. In the apartment. And the only bosoms around belong to a psychopathic possessive ghost demon-y thing. *Why can't I go home? I shouldn't have come.* The past forty-five minutes have passed so slowly for him, he's certain an eternity has passed for Sarah and Tim. Tim's probably shaving by now.

Someone has started wailing in anguish several rows back, which distracts Michael from his own concerns. He won't turn around to look; he doesn't want Chuck and Dan and Caroline, all of them to see his probably swollen nose and eyes. The wail sounds like it belongs to a woman and echoes throughout the church, of which even the two hundred and fifty only fill a sixth or so. It sounds so alien, so separate from his own grief, that it allows him to go on.

It's the first time in several months that the mommies come into the apartment. Sarah doesn't know any of them and she wonders where they go when they go. Thinking about this gives her a creeping bad feeling, but she can't define it. She wonders why she doesn't go where they go. She doesn't want to go, but it does seem odd to be the only constant. Aside from Greta. And Tim. Why is Tim the oldest? It's getting awkward, the difference. But none of the mommies seem to mind. They look on Sarah as the more experienced mother and ask her questions that make her feel needed.

The chatter of women, the babble of babies—it's nice at first. Tim is so excited about the babies, even though none are old enough to play with him. He goes around the room peering into their faces and grinning madly.

Small talk feels so much better than the silence of the empty apartment.

"Oh how sweet, how old is she?"

Tim is standing near the woman named Doris. She has a bubbly, nine-month-old girl straddling her knee and wriggling. Tim makes faces at the baby and she squeals delightedly. Sarah tries not to pay attention to the dour woman in the corner fretting over a bundle wrapped in a shawl. She doesn't know if the bundle is an actual baby or a substitute, but she doesn't want to find out.

This can't be wrong. Letting Greta back in. It's company for them and it will help pass the time until he returns. When is he coming back? It's been too long. Maybe he won't come back. But he said he wanted to . . .

She can't think that way. She turns her attention back to the people she's with. The people who fill the room with their warmth and conversation.

They've at least reached the funeral part. Michael's been to three funerals in his life: both grandmothers' and his father's. One grandmother was Catholic and so was his father, so the text was different. He was only five when his father died, so he can't remember much of that one. This service seems longer than his grandmother's. More serious. Sinister, almost. But he takes comfort in the rhythm of the words as the ceremony begins.

The priest says, "I am the Resurrection and the Life, saith the Lord . . . "

Michael tries to go to that sleepy listening place where the words have no meaning, only rhythm. But Sarah grew up in this church. Sang in the choir. How do these prayers correspond with her beliefs? Maybe if you believe it, it's real to you. She stopped going to church every Sunday, mostly because of him. Guilt washes over him. What else has he taken away from her?

The priest says, "Blessed are the dead who die in the Lord."

But she didn't die in the Lord. What did happen?

" . . . Grant them an entrant into the land of light and joy, in the fellowship of thy saints . . . "

Michael thinks of the dark company she keeps. Those mothers. Greta. What is he keeping her from? *Oh, God. Don't think that way.*

He was so secure in his beliefs before she died. Well, before she came back. Nature ruled, God made the world and it was good, and who knows what happens after that? Who cares? You're dead, you won't notice. When you die you're going back to nature—unless, of course you're living with your unborn son in an apartment on the Upper West Side.

The priest says, "God is our hope and strength, a very present help in trouble."

Why has it never occurred to him to pray? He prayed a lot when he was little, thanking God for an especially beautiful day, praying for his dog to live when she was ailing (fat lot of good that did), praying to get a microscope for Christmas. But when he became a man, he put childish praying aside. He thought of a deep breath of the wilderness and digging into the earth as his prayer. Talking to God seemed silly.

He prays silently. *God. God, if you can hear me . . .*

The priest continues, "Be still then, and know that I am God; I will be exalted among the nations, and I will be exalted in the earth."

These words make God an even more distant, impersonal force. Michael stops praying. To God. He closes his eyes and thinks very hard, to Sarah. *Don't leave. Sarah. Sarah. Don't leave. I can't live without you. Please don't leave.* A heavy pool of shame fills his belly and floods up his chest to his head. He should let her go.

There is a distant murmuring, an intonation of some sort, and Sarah gets a sick feeling in her stomach, a pull. The voice is not coming from this room, and she can't make out the words, but it pulls at her from elsewhere. It's the most physical sensation she's had since she died. It reminds her of that terrible empty rumbling that happened when she came down with food poisoning in her prior life. Bad shrimp. Grumble.

"Sarah." Greta calls her again sharply, "Sarah." When Sarah looks up at her, she sees genuine concern on her face.

"Tim." Sarah has to get to the boy. She needs him with her. Suddenly his place across the room seems very far away. She gets up and stumbles a little. She feels weak. She panics. "Tim."

She walks across the floor, which seems to be made of jelly. Each footstep pulls her dangerously down until she springs up with the next. Tim gets farther away. Sarah's stomach and head rise and fall with each step. "Tim!"

Michael thinks about what happens in the movies. They tell them to go into the light. The priest moves over to the coffins. They're only boxes. It can't mean anything.

He says, "Give rest, O Christ, to thy servants with thy saints . . . " These words sound so final, so absolute.

The congregation responds, "Where sorrow and pain are no more, neither sighing, but life everlasting."

In their murmured unison, they are all working against him now, and Michael's getting angry. He clenches his eyes shut again. *Don't go, Sarah. I need you. Don't go, Tim. I'll say good-bye. We'll have a little more time.*

The priest continues, steadily, terribly: "Into thy hands, O merciful Savior, we commend thy servant Sarah, thy servant Timothy. Acknowledge, we humbly beseech thee, sheep of thine own flock, sinners of thine own redeeming."

What does he mean sinner? Tim wasn't even born, for God's sake. *Don't go, Sarah, don't. Keep Tim with you. Don't go.*

The words don't stop and a chorus of voices join in. She can make out the intonations. "Life everlasting . . . " What does it mean?

Greta has started talking in that slow, commanding voice. "Sarah, you're not feeling well. It's okay. Tim's right here, see?" This helps ease the pull in Sarah's stomach, but she doesn't like that Greta's holding Tim now. And she doesn't know why.

Greta commands, "Ladies."

They know their cue. Had they discussed this beforehand? "Sarah. Sarah, honey. It's us. We're here." She's known these women all of half an hour, but they mutter in the same comforting voices of the women in the previous mommies groups.

Greta says, "Come get Tim, honey."

But he looks too far away and her stomach starts pulling again. She can't get to Tim. She has to get to Tim.

Can Michael make the priest stop? They are sending her away and there are things he hasn't said to her. He told her he loved her. He asked her where the key to the safe deposit was. *Idiot.* But if he's going to send her away, say good-bye to Tim . . . Tim . . . how can you forbid someone to live in this world? Kick him out? Tim's only life has been in this sort of in-between place, so to say good-bye to him would be ending him.

Don't . . .

The priest says, "Receive them into the arms of thy mercy, into the blessed rest of everlasting peace, and into the glorious company of saints in the light."

Don't go.

The prayer mercifully comes to a close.

The congregation says "Amen" and Michael slumps in his seat, exhausted.

Anna takes his hand now. It's slightly damp, she's crying.

He pulls his hand away and clenches his eyes shut, trying to sense if Sarah's still there. He knew she was in trouble from thousands of miles away; can he sense it from the three miles to their apartment?

His mother grabs his hand, but he keeps his eyes closed. *Sarah, are you still there?* He has no idea. Would he know if she disappeared? Would he feel it?

Anna tugs on his arm. He yanks it away from her.

Sarah?

Only when he sees his mother and Anna's expressions of surprise and concern does Michael start to process his surroundings. The family is walking out of the pew and he's expected to follow. As he turns, he knocks his knee against the missal holder at the back of the pew. It hurts and he stumbles. His mother grabs his arm and walks him into the aisle. He realizes that he's following the priest who's following the coffins, which are on chrome metal gurneys. The coffins, now in motion, look like eviscerated aliens being wheeled into autopsy. He sees Chuck and Dan walking next to Sarah's coffin with two other guys he can't recognize by the backs of their heads. Anna catches up to Tim's coffin and walks alongside. On the other side is Chrissie, one of Sarah's bridesmaids. He hasn't seen her since the wedding. The empty boxes need company.

As Michael follows the procession toward the door, he sees that everyone is looking at him, concerned, worried, wanting to share something. He doesn't know if there'll be enough of him left to accept that sharing.

Someone opens the front doors to the church and, to his relief, the blazing sunlight puts the faces of the congregation in the dark. He focuses on the front door, gently shakes off his mother's arm, and walks out into the light.

Once his eyes adjust, he sees he's standing next to the empty gurney. A bizarre contraption, no platform, only a too-shiny frame with joints for folding. He watches the boxes being carried down the steps of the church by the pallbearers. Chuck and Dan. Michael recognizes Sarah's cousin Doug and his brother Steve holding the other side of the coffin. No wonder the guys were nervous. What a grim task. At least the boxes are empty.

Michael sees two limos behind the hearse and remembers they aren't done yet. They have to go to the cemetery. The committal. Where is the cemetery? He hadn't even thought to ask.

TWELVE

*S*arah's brought Tim to bed with her. She's not sure what happened in there with the mommies and Greta: the feeling in her stomach, not being able to get to Tim. Then she was sitting in her chair, Tim on her lap and the ladies were all discussing breastfeeding. Again. She finished nursing so long ago that her joy in being needed swiftly turned to irritation. She did sympathize with them, nursing had a huge learning curve, but picking up on their anxieties and little worries only made her want desperately to be somewhere else. What bothered her most was that they weren't discussing what had just happened. Hadn't they seen it?

It isn't the feeling in her stomach that's keeping her awake tonight, or the horror when she couldn't get to Tim. Sarah feels like she's forgotten to do something. It's the feeling of apprehension she used to get at work when she showed up to a meeting she hadn't been prepped for. What paperwork had she not filed, filled out? What protocol had she not followed?

At the moment Sarah felt ill, Greta seemed to go into combat mode. She took over the room with such command and made the women all . . . what were they doing? All they did was call her name. But then there she was,

*Tim on her lap and a feeling of missing something beyond missing Michael
and worrying about him.*

*She kisses Tim's forehead and pulls him toward her. She's here, now.
He's here. The rest is all time passing. Thinking about Michael will get her
panicking again, so she nuzzles Tim's neck and breathes deeply, the salty,
doughy smell of boy calming her.*

———————

Michael's in the car with Chuck and Dan. He was surprised when
he got into the back seat and his mother didn't. But when he heard her
call out "Betsy!" in a solicitous greeting and walk away, and then, when
Chuck and Dan slipped into the car, he realized that he'd been rescued
from the mother-in-grief once again.

The guys don't say much at first. It's awkward. They look out the
window as if settling in for a ride together without words is completely
normal.

Michael knows he has to talk first but he doesn't know what to
say. These are his best friends from college. He's played foosball with
them for hours, gotten drunk with them, tended to them when they
couldn't hold their liquor, gone rock climbing. They've all helped each
other through various physical, academic, and romantic traumas. They
stood up with him at his wedding.

Michael looks out the window. "Where the hell are we going
anyway?"

Chuck laughs, Dan hits him. Michael laughs. Dan laughs. The
pressure's been released.

Chuck reaches into his pocket for the program. Michael looks
away. He doesn't want to see that particular image of Sarah's face right
now. He closes his eyes briefly and sees her face as it was this morning:
sunken eyes with their worried glint, patchy hair. He opens his eyes and
looks out the window at the city going by. Buildings, garbage cans, life

going on. A woman pushes her two-year-old son in a baby carriage as he wails and squirms in a tantrum. Real-life baby. A doorman is hosing down a sidewalk. The limo is turning down residential streets headed in the direction of what he thinks will be the Henry Hudson Parkway.

Chuck says, "I don't understand. Sleepy Hollow Cemetery. Are they kidding? I mean, is there such a place? Or was the story named after a place? Or was the place named after the story?"

Michael sinks back in his seat. He is extremely relieved to be sitting down. "Ha." Sarah laughed about this place. It's where her father's buried. She joked about how it was made for haunting. That her father would come back headless, on a horse, demanding the correct kind of brandy. He knows how she dealt with his death. Humor. How will he deal with her death? Death. Not the right word. Not now.

Sarah still missed her father when Michael first met her. And she missed him at holidays in the years after. Maybe they'll be together. If that's how it works. *God, don't let it have worked! Sarah, I will come back. As soon as I can.*

They're only empty coffins. Where are the ashes?

But Chuck asked him a question.

Michael answers, "Place, then story, then place."

Chuck says, "What?"

Michael says, "Old churchyard, legend. Washington Irving wrote the story. Or made the legend. I can't remember. The cemetery next door was named the Tarrytown Cemetery, but in honor of Washington Irving's request, they changed the name of the cemetery posthumously."

Chuck is interested. "Is he buried there?"

"Yep, along with a few Carnegies and one or two Rockefellers."

Dan doesn't seem interested. His leg is jiggling and he's looking around shiftily, working himself up for something. He vaguely acknowledges the conversation. "Weird."

Michael continues, "You should see the gift shop. T-shirts reading, 'I lost my head at Sleepy Hollow.'"

Chuck likes this. "I want one!"

Dan finally looks at Michael and blurts out, a little too loudly, "How are you doing, man, like, really? I mean, you don't look so good. Like worse than you *should* be looking."

Chuck smacks his arm. "Dude. Not smooth."

Dan says, "Seriously, shouldn't we be asking him how he's doing? Isn't that what friends are supposed to do?"

Chuck glares at Dan, Dan raises his eyebrows, Chuck concedes. Michael hates all of it, but he loves these guys. He's so tempted to tell them everything, about Sarah, all about Tim. His son. He knows this isn't possible. Anything to say on the subject that goes through his head sounds completely whacked out. *She's dead, but I've been living with her for several days now. I'm drinking some supernatural nasty tea that makes me sick so I can be more "aware" of her. We still get to have sex. It's kind of cool. And sad. But cool.*

He tries to keep it abstract. "It's a day-by-day thing. The funeral was fucking awful."

Chuck laughs. Dan hits him. Chuck insists, "Seriously. I mean, I've been to a few funerals, but that was *crazy*."

Michael agrees. "It was so . . . *serious*."

Dan is irritated. "Funerals should be funny?"

Michael adds, "And endless."

Chuck is amped up now. "Endless! And what's with the graveside thing? I've only seen it in movies, that graveside stuff. They took my dad away in the hearse and that was all she wrote."

Michael tries to imagine ahead. Dirt on the empty coffins. Probably more dire words. Will the burying finish them?

Dan starts, "That seems . . . "

Michael finishes, "Easier."

Chuck says, "*And* a reception. It's like a wedding—"

Dan hits him, but Chuck already realizes his mistake. "I'm sorry, man."

Michael shakes his head. "It's fine. Seriously, it's fine. Of course you'd think of it, and I've already thought of it, so don't worry."

Weddings take hours.

Does he have to go to the reception? Can't he claim he's prostrate with grief or something? He doesn't understand all of these obstacles the grieving are expected to hurdle. They should be allowed to curl up alone in soft fuzzy rooms and be fed comfort food for several months before having to see anyone. Instead, Michael's confronted with hundreds of people wanting a piece of him. A piece of Sarah. And there's not that much left of her.

Doris stops coming to the mommies meetings, and when Sarah asks Greta about it, she sees a cloud flicker across her face. Then the forced smile.

Greta says, "Doris moved to New Jersey to be closer to her husband."

This seems to placate the ladies, but Sarah fights to hold on to why this doesn't work. This doesn't work because they're dead. And if they're dead, how do they find Greta? Do all of these people live in this building? Where do they come from?

But Greta has started again and things are getting fuzzy. "I think Sarah needs to share with us, I mean, she's had so much experience—Sarah needs to share how she got her baby off the breast and on to solid food. Sarah's done such a good job with Tim." Every time Greta says Sarah's name, another blanket falls over the thoughts she was trying to string together. "Sarah, can you tell us? Did you shift to milk first or formula? How did you do it?"

There was something about Doris. About Doris. And New Jersey. Something's wrong in New Jersey.

Maybe it was that recall on the lettuce. New Jersey lettuce. It doesn't make it to New York. Not to Fairway. They get their lettuce from Connecticut. And California in the winter. The recall was in the summer.

There's a knock at the front door. Greta stops. The ladies look up.

Greta answers the door. Sarah used to take issue with her doing this; after all, whose apartment was this? But after a few months, she resigned herself. It's not like it's a door she can ever use again.

When the mommies and babies start disappearing around her, she takes notice. Some fade. Some disappear instantly.

Tim shouts, "Pop!"

He starts making a game of it, clapping his hands each time another one disappears. "Pop! Pop! Pop!" This would have been cute when he was four, but he's nine now and has a dangerous sparkle in his eye. There's anger in his final "Pop!"

Sarah needs to reprimand him, but she needs to know who's at the door. She says, "Greta?" Greta stands in front of the open door, blocking Sarah's view with her broad back. But there's a cloud of darkness around her and Sarah can feel that she's angry. Best to leave her alone. But maybe he's come home! Sarah leaps to her feet and runs to the door. Sarah says, "Michael?" She stops a few feet shy of Greta, who's become a dark force that She can't get past. She's talking to someone.

Greta addresses the someone, "You don't belong here. You need to go."

Sarah squints to see past her, but the blackness around Greta has blocked her view. She can barely make out a muffled voice. It is male. It's not Michael.

He says, "I'm here to speak with Sarah."

Greta says, "You have no business with the dead." Sarah can feel the anger emanating from Greta's shoulders. She wants to make her stop, push her out of the way, but when she reaches out her hand to touch Greta's shoulder, it burns with cold. She withdraws it quickly.

The male voice is clearer now. "I beg to differ, madam. Will you step aside? I need to speak with Sarah. Her husband insisted." Sarah thinks she recognizes the voice from a long time ago.

Greta's blackness grows, her anger grows, but the darkness falls to the floor, surrounding her like water, and the bulky woman disintegrates into black matter and lingers for a moment in a cloud-like mass. Then the black matter collapses and dissolves through the cracked, wooden flooring. Greta's gone and Sarah can see Dr. James's startled, sweating face in the doorway. He's breathing quite heavily, and, given his large frame, he appears in danger of having a heart attack.

She cries out, "Dr. James!" She's so happy to see him. It's been what, five years? His living presence gives her an inexplicable hope for Michael.

Dr. James stutters himself into manners. "Good. Good morning."

Morning? The same morning? Or is this a different morning? Does he know? Which morning? Did Michael talk to him?

He's staring at the floor where Greta disappeared. He says, "What . . . who was that?"

Sarah says, "That was Greta." She looks down at her feet and pushes her toe around where Greta once stood. She feels a cold graininess beneath her bare foot, reminding her of snow dust blown into the entryway of a rental house in the mountains when she was small.

He says, "Michael asked me to check in on you."

Thank God. "How long has he been gone?"

The man doesn't seem to hear her question He looks up and says, "Sarah?"

She looks up at Dr. James, who tentatively puts his hand out to her arm, pressing it, as if to make sure she's there. She doesn't know why he bothers. He's shaken her hand before. He's looking her over with incredulous pity in his eyes. She starts to touch her hair, unsure of how she looks. But mirrors aren't exactly working for her these days.

Dr. James guides Sarah gently into the apartment and steps over the threshold. She steps back, giving him room to pass and she closes the door.

The gravesite is under a weeping willow. Betsy has spared no expense. A bumblebee buzzes in Michael's ear and brushes his cheek. He hears birds chirping and a warm wind ruffles the trees. Michael can't get enough of the smells. Grass, trees, blooming flowers from the well-appointed flowerbeds, dying flowers from the graves, fresh, damp earth. He wants to reach his arms out and take hold of the nature, take off his shoes, fall to his knees and grab handfuls of grass. He wants to seize this life that has been shut out of his apartment. He wants to take it home for Tim. But the people start turning around to look at him: Betsy, the cousins, Caroline and Alana. Michael will have to settle for the satisfaction of soft grass under his dress shoes. Only about fifty came to the gravesite. The rest will be killing time until the reception.

It's only when the group of people parts, revealing the dark holes in the ground, their sharp angles incongruous with the mounding nature around them, that he realizes the source of the earthy smell. One large rectangle. One smaller. The coffins are already hammocked above them, held by webbed fabric straps that remind him of rock climbing gear. Michael can get through this part. Tim and Sarah clearly aren't here. He will focus on the grass beneath his feet. He bows his head reverently as Father Peter begins his sonorous intonation. There's a whole lot more ceremony to do before they are done.

Look. Ants.

On the way back from the cemetery, Michael made Chuck and Dan promise not to abandon him at the reception. They walk up the large marble staircase of the Manhattan club together, their six solid dress shoes thudding heavily as they go. They move through the dark-wood arched doors as a force. Michael stops at the top of the stairs to catch his breath. He's breathing heavily again. With his friends by his side, maybe he can get through this. But the moment Betsy approaches, Chuck and Dan melt into the crowd with an annoying swiftness. Michael tries glaring at them, but they're making themselves busy at the buffet table.

What a spread. The bar only offers fruit juice and other non-alcoholic fare, but there are multitudes of dip, cheese, seafood, and a lot of fruit. Cold cuts and various bakery breads and rolls and crackers. Foie gras. Michael wonders how the propriety of funeral foods is decided. Salad, shrimp, four kinds of dressing. The flowers are white and simple. The dessert table might be a bit more demure (no chocolate, but lemon bars and blondies and oatmeal cookies), but this is basically the same spread as Michael and Sarah's engagement party, minus the dripping swan ice sculpture and the chocolate fountain.

This walnut-paneled, opera-chaired, oil-painting-covered, and corniced-ceilinged, chandeliered club has a long history of *something* in New York. With the family. Or New York history. Or New York families. Michael has always tuned out Betsy's ramblings on her pride for the place. Sarah dismissed it as, "my parents' snooty watering hole," and for Michael, it had been a place where he and Sarah misbehaved. They had done so much bonding through their insubordination here: groping each other in the alcove outside the ladies' washroom, eating smuggled snacks in the library, where food is strictly forbidden, and giggling at various family events. Here, they had been scoundrels.

Here without her feels stuffy and uncomfortable.

Betsy has recovered from her emotional upheaval at the church and is behaving the way she's meant to. Always appropriate, she's somber, keeping steady gentle tones in her voice, saying the right things. She walks up to Michael and kisses him gently on both cheeks. Despite the alcohol-free bar, she smells of high-call gin. He wouldn't have figured Betsy for a closet drinker, but he can't blame her.

The gin odor makes him soften to her a bit. This woman lost her daughter. He looks into her eyes and takes her hands. "How you holding up?"

Tears come to her eyes and she smiles before she extracts herself. Michael's touched as he realizes that she is also too overwhelmed to talk right now.

She says, "Come, we need to do the rounds."

He says, "Of course."

Michael is whisked off into a grim echo of his wedding day, shaking hands and being given condolences instead of congratulations by a network of cousins and family friends and, yes, again, his deceased father-in-law's workmates.

A paper-dry, old-lady hand clasps his with the appropriate amount of pressure. "I'm so sorry for your loss."

A beefy older gentleman in a navy blazer presses Michael's palm with a slightly sweaty hand: a warm steak. "Michael, is it? Yes. I'm so sorry. Beautiful girl. Terrible loss."

A tiny, beak-nosed, librarian-looking woman presses her icy cold hand into Michael's and squeezes too hard. In a fluttery voice, she says, "She was so lovely, I'm so sorry."

The Pams from Pittsburgh coo and aw, each moving her stemmed glass of Diet Coke into her left hand (two lipstick marked straws apiece) before taking Michael's hand briefly, in turn. Only long enough for a squeeze, each quickly withdrawn. One gets off a furtive, "We're so sorry," before they retreat. That wasn't too bad.

Michael doesn't understand why alcohol isn't served; he could certainly use a drink. He's not sure if it would be gentlemanly to ask Betsy for a sip from wherever she's hiding hers.

A tall, lanky older gentleman takes Michael's hand and holds it for too long in his bony, shaking one, looking sincerely at him with gray, red-rimmed, watery eyes. He has a look that Michael recognizes but can't place. Betsy tenses as the moment becomes uncomfortably long and interjects. "Thank you, Tom." Tom says nothing, but nods understandingly and lets go, heading for the bar. Michael suspects that he, too, will be upset by the lack of drink.

Betsy steers Michael toward another part of the room, whispering in his ear, "Tom lost his wife last year. Hasn't been the same since." Now Tom's look makes sense—he's haunted.

Betsy squeezes Michael's arm. "It takes time. It just does." She stops him for a moment and looks up at him. "Bill did so love this club." She smiles. He hadn't really thought of Sarah's parents in terms of being a couple. She says, "I hope Sarah and her father are together at least. They always did get along so well."

Betsy continues walking and Michael looks around the crowd wondering how many other people here are carrying losses.

Betsy says, "Watch out, we'll do this group quickly. Vultures." Michael smiles and brings his hand up to hers. He's never seen this side of her. He realizes that Sarah can't have come from nowhere. Her spirit, her humor, and even her capacity for loving him came from her mother. He has underestimated Betsy and feels a sudden pang of regret. Maybe Sarah would have wanted him to put in more of an effort.

Don't go there. Watch the vultures. Vultures. Vultures. Focusing on the word, he anchors himself and musters his best, appropriately grieving smile as Betsy re-introduces him.

"Of course you remember . . . and her sister . . . and Sarah's first friend's mother . . . and . . . "

Michael nods graciously and shakes each of these ladies' hands. Dry and Warm. Damp and Fleshy. Dry and Cold. Too Many Rings.

"We're so sorry for your loss."

"Such a lovely girl."

"We're so sorry."

Too Many Rings holds his hand firmly and says solicitously, "If there's *anything* we can do." Her sudden need for involvement is an uncomfortable reminder of Greta. This fills Michael with dread and, taking Betsy's cue, he allows himself to be steered away to a group of gentlemen.

"Terrible. Terrible. So sorry."

"We're so sorry."

He has to get home.

"Lovely girl, so sorry."

They smell of gin, too. Perhaps there is a gin closet in this club of which he is unaware.

"We're so sorry for your loss."

"Such a lovely girl."

Michael is increasingly puzzled by the fact that no one mentions Sarah's name. He's grateful for their condolences, but he does find it odd. Maybe if they don't mention that it's Sarah about whom they're terribly sorry, she will still be there when he gets home. A superstitious and childlike thought; he pushes it from his mind.

He notices that the people he has not greeted yet are eyeing him fearfully. He looks at the people he's shaken hands with and they seem relaxed.

Michael almost laughs. They were dreading this more than he was. Each mourner is doing what is required and is eager to get done with it. Rather than making him angry, this frees him. They're no longer his burden. He is theirs. He thinks about how Sarah would laugh at the stir she's caused, the ripple through her parents' society.

When they were wading (the gifts covered every spare space in the living room) through their hundreds of wedding presents, Michael kept muttering, "They shouldn't have . . . ," and Sarah laughed at him.

She said, "Oh, honey, you don't understand. They *had* to." She unwrapped the industrial-strength KitchenAid in its Breast-Cancer-Society pink and laughed wickedly.

Michael was embarrassed. "*Sarah.*"

With those snapping and beautiful and lively—they were so alive—green eyes, she gazed at him with mock pity and explained for the inexperienced, "Honey. They're just paying mother back for all of the gifts she doled out over the years for their debutantes, brides, and babies." At that point, Michael realized he'd married into a tribe different from his own.

And now, he knows he's undergoing a ritual of this tribe for the last time. He's not sure what part of him feels sentimental about this, but he knows that it's best not to question his emotions right now. Betsy steers Michael over to what he thinks is another group of people, but turns out to be the door.

She leans in and kisses his cheek, giving him back his arm. She says, "Now, go. You've done more than enough for today."

Grateful, he reaches in and gives her a solid hug before taking off down the stairs. He makes sure not to run until the staircase goes around a corner and he knows she can no longer see him.

Sarah isn't doing a good job explaining everything. Dr. James seems to understand the problem with time. But she's having extra trouble describing Greta and he doesn't seem to understand. He keeps shooting questions at her that make her anxious. What can she say? Greta helped when no one else was there for her. She seems to know how everything works and, when everyone else disappears and Sarah feels lost, Greta is there to bring her back, with tea, or words, or comfort.

She helps mothers in need.

But the more Sarah tells Dr. James about Greta and how helpful she is, the more concerned he looks.

He asks her, "Was she there before or after . . . I mean." He stops. Something new occurs to him. "Sarah, what happened when you died? What was it like?"

This turn in questioning brings a little relief. Sarah wonders why talking about Greta gives her such an ugly feeling of betrayal. Greta's never told her not to talk, but Sarah feels like a snitch whenever she mentions her name.

She looks down and sees that Dr. James has his hand on her arm and she has a sudden yearning to feel that hand, that intimacy with another person. She puts her hand gently on top of his and there it sits. Or at least she can see it there, so she must assume it is there. Her bony hand (when did it get so old? so sallow?) is resting on the thick flesh of the florid man's hand, which must be warm.

He says, "Sarah."

Or is it clammy? Sometimes big guys like this have clammy hands. Particularly when they're nervous. Michael's hands were never clammy. Always warm.

Dr. James repeats, "Sarah."

She murmurs, "You were asking me something."

He sounds surprised, agitated. "Ten minutes ago. I wanted to know if you remember what it was like when you died. What happened?"

When the labor started, Sarah thought it was the usual Braxton Hicks contractions, but then her water broke and she called Anna, who got her to the hospital. It was so hard to breathe and labor hurt beyond any of her expectations. At the hospital, they hooked her up to a fetal monitor and everything seemed to be going fine. She got an epidural for the pain, but it was getting harder and harder to breathe. Then Tim's heart rate went down and they prepped her for a C-section. Her arms wouldn't stop shaking, so they had to strap them down beside her outright, making her feel even more helpless.

She had a birth plan, she knew how to do labor, she was going to do this, but they took all control from her. There she was, strapped to a table, laid out for sacrifice, and her hands were so far away at the ends of her long pale arms, shaking like they belonged to someone else. She felt so cold. Anna was sitting at her head, behind the raised sheet so she wouldn't see the surgery. She murmured, "Everything's fine, Sarah. This'll be over soon."

All of the voices in the room were calm and procedural, but suddenly the monitors started beeping and everyone around her was getting worried and agitated. She felt her body jerking strangely, rocking back and forth, and then Anna was gone. There were beeping machines and a deafening noise and then everything went completely silent.

She was in the Dark—complete blackness—and she could hear a baby crying somewhere in the distance, but she couldn't get a handle on anything. She heard women's voices, talking, talking, talking. They wouldn't stop talking and she wanted to walk away. There was someplace she had to get to and the darkness was broken by a patch of blinding light. She squinted to see it, but it wasn't clear, and the women went on talking and one woman was chanting in an ancient language. It all seemed to grow and grab and pull at her, and then the patch of light was gone and she was in complete blackness again.

And then she was in the apartment. On the sofa. And Tim was in the bassinet. And things were different. She didn't have time to think about things because the baby was crying and she knew she was supposed to be doing something.

Dr. James calls her name. "Sarah!" Why is he so distraught?

She says, "I don't remember." She's starting to feel frightened of something and she doesn't know what it is. She begins to cry. She looks up and notices Dr. James looking at his hand in alarm, flexing his fingers. It looks very, very red. Are those blisters? When did he take his hand away?

The doctor is saying soothing words, but his tone is vexed. "Are you okay? I'm sorry. I won't ask any more questions." His words sound warble-y at first, but then she begins to make them out. "Tim. I would love to see the boy. Sarah, can I see Tim? Can you show me Tim? Where is the little man?" He sounds desperately cheerful.

Here's Tim. She's not sure why, but the doctor seems frightened by him. Dr. James breathes in deeply and Sarah sees that he's trying very hard not to sound nervous. "Hello there, young man. How are you doing?"

There's a loud thudding, shattering the quiet.

Dr. James says, "Don't worry, I won't answer it. Stay with me, Sarah. Michael will be home soon and I know he wants so much to see you."

Thud. Thud. Thud. She knows it's the door. Things start to shimmer and she looks at Tim and puts her arm around his waist, but he pulls away. He's getting too old to cuddle all the time now. He has to be in the mood.

The doctor shouts in the direction of the door, "Go away!"

And Sarah is in blackness again. Tim doesn't stay with her when this happens now, he wanders off. He's there, but she can no longer take any comfort from his presence. She's frightened. She hopes Greta comes soon.

THIRTEEN

The car can't go fast enough. Out there: at the church, at the cemetery, at the reception, surrounded by people, someone else had taken control of the time and he couldn't do anything about it. It's not like he can do anything about the car and how fast it's going, but now that this is only about him and not all of those other people, he feels responsible for not being home immediately.

Thank God for his friends. Dan held his shoulders and delivered a very sincere pledge of help and lifelong friendship before he left. Michael thought he smelled gin. Chuck just punched him in the chest and pulled him into a bear hug. Then they went back to their lives and left him to his. His life right now is about getting back to the apartment to see Sarah. It's clearly not happening fast enough.

It's that strange part of the afternoon in Manhattan, when the sun has moved behind the buildings, casting early evening on pockets of the island, but it's only about four p.m. The quickening of the darkness adds an air of urgency to Michael's predicament. As they pass each numbered street, sunlight flashes into the car from the west and disappears just as quickly, making Michael's head hurt.

He can't imagine what might wait or not wait for him at the apartment. The possibilities flash through his mind in circular repetition with the dizzying sunlight. He rolls down the window of the sealed car. He's tired of closed environments.

Michael closes his eyes and breathes in deeply. Trace of dog shit. Spilled alcohol. Garbage bin. Candle shop. Indian food. He opens his eyes and smiles as he sees his favorite local Indian place. He needs to go back there. For all of his being out and about today, he hadn't felt like he was anywhere real: the cold, marble-and-stone church, the impossibly warm, green, floral cemetery, the rarified air of the club.

Too late, too soon, the cab arrives at The Harrowgate. He doesn't have to settle up with the driver. This was on his mom. Michael tells the driver, "Thank you." He's not sure about tipping with limos, but he didn't bring any cash. He'll make sure Helen takes care of it on the bill.

The driver turns around and looks back at him. "Wait, I'll get the door."

Michael says, "No time."

The driver stops him with a, "Sir?"

"Yes?" All he wants is to get up to the apartment.

The driver says, "I know it's hard to believe right now. Hard to hear. But rest assured. Another girl will come along. And other children, too."

I don't want anybody else, asshole. Forget about that tip.

It's been a long time, this time in the Dark. Tim keeps wandering off, which makes her worry.

She's also worried about the tree, which has turned to a sapling hurling a cluster of branches upward. It looks fragile—in a winter stage, bare and surrounded by a swirl of something black. Is it smoke? No. A cloud of black dust whirls in a silent maelstrom around the fragile tree, which looks in danger of being uprooted by the wind. Its vulnerability and size distress her with a thrumming sort of anxiety over her inaction. There's something she should be doing, working toward. She can't remember what.

Despite his wanderings for this past . . . week? Day? Month? Tim's leaning against her back in the dark—so tall already, that his head reaches her neck—talking. It helps the time pass.

He says, "So the Romans?" He's obsessed with the Romans. They've spent more time talking about them than the Egyptians, even.

She says, "What about the Romans?"

"Well, if they were so smart and everything, and inventive. Why the lions? Why all that murder?"

Sarah sighs. "Humans are complicated, honey."

Tim says, "Not like aliens. Aliens are simple."

She laughs.

He continues. "Because they don't have lions."

"Right."

He says, "They'd be feeding people to geworniaks."

She says, "The fierce, evil geworniak." They laugh for a minute. She thinks she's off the hook.

But Tim says, "So why the lions?"

Sarah says, "I don't know, honey. People were pretty savage back then. Killing was like nothing."

Tim says, "Romans invented money, plumbing, writing."

"They didn't invent writing, honey. They were just good at it."

"You know what I mean. Why the killing?"

She sighs. "Like I said, most people were pretty savage back then. Death was sort of an everyday thing. So was brutality. I think their brains developed, but it took their souls awhile longer to catch up. So writing, art, *architecture, that was all happening. But that 'don't kill or hurt your neighbor' common sense hadn't developed yet."*

Tim sits quietly, processing this. Sarah's pretty proud of her answer. Not too bad for on the fly. It's so nice to be able to have conversations about bigger things than dinner or puppies or dinosaurs.

She wishes she hadn't used the word "soul." Tim has quizzed her on everything from ancient civilization to biology to death. But for some reason, in all of their time together, even in this dark, empty place with the backwards tree, he's never asked about their circumstance in particular. He's never asked why they're dead. Or if they're dead. Or where his father's gone. Or why they come here. Sometimes, she thinks it's because he's oblivious. Other times, she thinks he knows, but he doesn't want to think about it too much. Shouldn't he want to know?

And like that, they're in their living room, sitting in the same position on the floor. She's going to get out that Time-Life book about the Vikings. Tim will like the Vikings. When Michael gets home he'll teach Tim so much. He'll be so pleased at how he's grown.

Tim's on his feet and turns around to help his mother up. He's grown even more in the Dark. His face is catching up to his complex thoughts. He grabs hold of her hands, and as he pulls her to her feet, he winces. She wonders if she pinched him accidentally. Tim looks into her eyes and she realizes that he's almost as tall as she is. But his expression is worried, frightened.

He says, "Mom?"

"What?"

Tim breathes deeply, as if resigning himself to something, shrugs, and turns away. "Nothing."

Nothing never means nothing now. But it does mean he won't talk about what crossed his mind, even pressed. Did she hurt him somehow, when he helped her up? Is it something about how she looks? If he's changed so much in the Dark, has she?

She puts her hand up to his face but stops herself before touching him. Preadolescent boys need their space. She says, "I have a book I wanted to show you."

But he keeps his back to her, heading down the hall. "Later, I'm going to my room."

"But it's about Vikings. You're gonna love the Vikings."

He waves. "Awesome. Later."

His door closes and she looks at her hands. She gasps. She touches one with the other and is alarmed by their lack of flesh. Her skin has gone all strange, wrinkled but tight at the same time. She looks down to her feet, but a quick glimpse tells her to stop looking. She can't help how she looks, but she can find the book. She'll find the book.

As the elevator labors to a stop at the fourteenth floor, Michael takes a deep breath.

When the elevator door opens, it lets in a blast of shockingly cold air from the hallway. That can't be good. Every nightmare scenario he thought of in the limo comes back to him.

Dr. James sits in an armchair outside Michael's door in the hallway, reading a book by the light of a lamp Michael recognizes from his living room. He's wearing a sheepskin coat and a blanket is draped over his shoulders. His hand is wrapped in a bandage, and he's got an incongruous, bright-orange Knicks hat pulled down over his ears.

The lamp's power cord trails back inside the door to Michael's apartment, and it casts a yellow light that makes the hallway look strangely like someone's living room.

Michael is relieved to see Dr. James, but his surroundings are unnerving.

The doctor, startled, looks up. He relaxes only when he sees that it's Michael. He didn't look this frightened when he came about Milo. When Michael gets closer, a searching look of concern crosses the doctor's face. He's seen it a dozen times today: *you don't look so good, buddy.*

But the doctor says, "Thank God."

"What happened?" It looks like Dr. James is guarding Michael's apartment. Is he keeping him out?

"I'm not . . . I'm not sure. Have you encountered . . . this Greta person?"

"Have you seen Sarah?" He has spent the past five hours missing her, needing her, calling her. He can't worry about Greta now.

Dr. James looks saddened by the mention of her name. "Yes, Michael. I saw her. We talked."

Michael says, "How is she?"

"Not the same." The doctor doesn't offer any more. But he saw her and that much is hopeful.

"Is she in there?"

"Not at present. But." He stops.

"And why are you out here?"

Dr. James says, "That Greta person, Michael. She's not good. I don't know. I've been doing some research." He holds up his book. "And I can't pin her down, but I don't think she's a ghost. She's something else entirely."

Michael nods to the book the doctor's holding. "What have you learned?"

He says, "Ghosts don't give off that . . . dust. That blackness." It takes him a slow creaking moment to get out of the chair before he continues. "She was the first person Sarah saw after she died. She helps new mothers."

Michael, irritated, says, "I know. What else?"

"Ah. But that part's important. It means she's attracted to a specific kind of person. Sounds like a sociopath, right?"

How does one do psychology on the non-human? Michael asks, "What does she want?"

Dr. James sighs and pauses a moment, closing the book. He says, "When we find the answer to that, Michael, we may be able to get somewhere."

The doctor comes close to Michael and peers into his face, examining him like a medical doctor. He says, "Look up." He raises his finger for Michael to follow.

He obeys for a moment but then turns away from the doctor, saying, "I know, I don't look so great." He doesn't want to tell him about the tea. He knows that if he does, he'll be admitting that it was a stupid thing to do. And it was. The doctor didn't need any tea to see Milo. Greta's doing something to him.

The doctor says, "You look ill, Michael, jaundiced. Something is affecting your endocrine system." He frowns. "How much have you been seeing of this Greta? Has It given you anything to eat?"

Greta has ceased being a she.

"No." It's not a complete lie. *Is he out here because of her?* He asks, "Is she in there?"

Dr. James shakes his head and turns to switch off the lamp. "No. No, my boy. Not that she didn't try."

"What happened?"

"A flower delivery arrived. Sarah disappeared. Your boy, such a fine strong young man . . . " He trails off, his brow furrowing in concern. "Michael, we need to talk about your boy."

Young man. "How old was Tim when you saw him?"

The doctor says, "You didn't tell me how bad the time slippage was."

"How old?"

The doctor says, "I'd guess about ten."

Michael's heart sinks. Too long has passed.

The doctor continues, "He and Sarah disappeared. I brought the flowers in and then it—that thing—Greta appeared. I had seen her when I first arrived, but only briefly. It was odd, this time she knocked on the front door. She tried the friendly approach, but when I told her to get out, she went all . . . well, septic. I've never seen anything like it. I'd seen the black stuff when I visited Sarah, but the *anger.* I hate to use such a strong word and in my profession we try to avoid it, but . . . I think Greta's evil."

Michael doesn't want to know, but he needs to. "Is Sarah okay?"

Dr. James considers the question a moment. "You might want to prepare yourself."

"How bad is it?"

"She's . . . diminished."

Panic strikes him, but he can't do anything about that now.

He says, " Greta went septic, the temperature dropped alarmingly, it's only now warming up." If this is warm, they're in trouble. "But then she left. I didn't want her coming back, but I didn't want to scare Sarah, so"—he shrugs—"Here I am."

Michael doesn't know what to do. All of his energy had been geared toward getting back to Sarah, and now she's not here. He remembers that it's not him Dr. James is trying to keep out. He wants to be alone in the apartment, but clearly they have much more to talk about.

Michael picks up the lamp and gestures inside with his head. "Come inside. Please."

Dr. James gathers up his effects.

Once through the door, Michael says, "How long has it been since she left?"

Dr. James says, "About, two, three hours?"

Maybe she's back.

Michael strides quickly down the hallway to the bedroom. Empty. Nursery, bathroom, back to the living room. Kitchen. Empty.

It was worth a try.

The doctor has taken off his coat and his hair sticks straight up from removing his hat. He rubs the top of his head back and forth with his hand.

Michael can't make her come back. But he and the doctor have time to talk. He says, "Tea?" and the doctor *hmms* his approval.

Michael goes into the kitchen and starts the kettle. He takes off his tie and jacket. The apartment looks so strange after his brief time out. Part of him is relieved to be home, the other part feels the walls and familiar smells close in around him, like that old plaid blanket he had a love-hate relationship with one depressed winter in college.

Dr. James sits at the table and lays out his book. He looks up at the wall. "Ha! Rosie the Riveter. I like your Sarah more, the better I get to know her."

Michael asks, "What happened to your hand?"

Dr. James holds up the bandage and considers it a moment before answering. "Only a little run-in with a ghost." He flexes his fingers a little, wincing with pain.

Milo's getting violent. Michael doesn't want to ask. He's exhausted, but too antsy to sit. He goes to the kettle, which is a long way from boiling, and then leans against the counter by the sink. He asks, "Is there anything else you can tell me about Greta? Anything at all?"

Dr. James takes off his glasses and puts them on the table, their frames clacking a little too hard on the Formica. He rubs his face with his hand.

"No," he said apologetically. "I just know that the power that thing has over Sarah is frightening. She, that thing means her no good."

Exasperated, Michael says, "But what does she want? And why is Sarah getting worse? Why is Tim growing so fast?"

The doctor runs his hand through his hair, agitated. "Why does Milo keep coming back? Why, whatever I do, does it always end the same way?"

How can he find answers if the doctor is as baffled as he is?

He goes to the cabinet for the tea. He reaches up without looking and then feels the old, green tin in his hand. *No.* He pushes it aside and gets down the PG Tips.

Dr. James keeps working at it. "We can only go at this from a logical standpoint." The doctor sits at the kitchen table.

"Yeah, because it's making so much sense." Michael sits down opposite him.

"Bear with me. What do we know? Sarah is here. She has your boy with her. He's getting older. There's this . . . thing . . . Greta. We must assume that It has some ulterior motive for helping these other mothers. And we can only presume they are ghosts as well."

As he listens, Michael sips his tea, which tastes bland and flat, a dull echo of tea. He tries to put the green tin out of his mind.

"The mothers change," Michael offers, thinking the doctor might not know that. "The second meeting was the same, but when Tim was older, they were all . . . new."

"Interesting. And Sarah's staying longer, or so it seems. She's here, we believe, because of Tim or because of you."

This makes Michael deeply uneasy. Is he culpable in some way? He gets up from the table and paces over to the counter. "Or because of Greta." Even as he says it he knows the doctor is right. Sarah's here because of him.

Dr. James says, "But one must assume that ghosts are not an everyday occurrence. If people didn't pass on . . . to somewhere, we'd be bumping into them all over the place."

This makes Michael think of the reception. Of Tom and Betsy and their ghosts.

The doctor says, "There has to be some reason for their staying."

"And the reason Milo stays?"

The doctor's head lowers. "My punishment."

"And Sarah?"

———

He's home.

———

Michael's chest constricts suddenly and he can't breathe. Ice-cold iron braces wrap around his back. He yells.

The doctor lets out an "Oh!"

Michael looks down and sees a head pressed to his chest. A definite scalp, leathery and spotted like a dinosaur egg, wisps of blonde hair clinging to it in spots.

It takes a moment for him to understand that it's Sarah. He resists the urge to register his horror, shove her away.

But the glimpse of that mole, the one that dwelled in Sarah's hairline now fully exposed on an open terrain of mottled hide, brings the knowledge home with terrifying certainty. The coldness of her, which burned through his clothing at first, fades and she heats up with such swiftness that now she feels feverish and sweat breaks out under his suit.

He says, "Sarah. Sarah."

The doctor looks at them with a sadness and pity that makes Michael feel exposed and defensive. Dr. James doesn't get to decide what this is.

He turns Sarah from the doctor's view and rubs her back so gently that he hardly moves the fabric of her dress. The peach-colored Batik now hangs like a sack from her shoulders. He could count her ribs with his fingertips. Having so recently been consumed with memories of the living Sarah—his own and others—he can't bear to look at her yet. He looks up at the ceiling, holding her, and tears fall from his eyes.

Dr. James rises from his spot, taking his book and creeps sideways past Michael, not wanting to interrupt. Michael doesn't know if he can do this again. "Don't go."

Quietly, the doctor says, "Whatever you do, don't let that *thing* we talked about in again. I've my own to attend to. I'll come back . . . " He pauses for a long moment, pain deep in his eyes. "After." Dr. James slips out the kitchen door into the back hallway.

Michael's left with Sarah and he's terrified of seeing her face, what she's become. He takes her by the arms and pushes her, very gently, away from him. It reminds him of extracting a beetle from his finger when he was small; the bug's pincers had a painful grip on his flesh, but he knew that if he pulled too hard, it would lose a limb. Sarah loosens her grip and complies.

It's bad. Worse than he thought. Her eyes are sunken, beady doll-glass, barely held in place by the skin of her lids. There's no underlying flesh holding the skin secure; instead it has adhered and puckered around the edges of her eye sockets like that of a corpse. Her cheeks have sunken in so that he can see the outlines of her teeth through the skin next to her mouth. He looks for signs of Sarah, and while there's still a flicker of green around the edge of her pupils, it's small; the pupils have taken over. There's next to no flesh on her arms.

He tries to control his countenance, tries to look like he's happy to see her, but she can tell. Her wispy eyebrows furrow. "I'm awful." Her hand drifts up in front of what is left of her face and she turns it over, studying it as if it's a foreign object. "I can see it in my hands, I just don't . . . do mirrors. You know?"

He says, "I love you. So much."

She says, "I know I'm awful. I wish . . . " She drifts off. The chill comes swiftly.

Michael asks, hoping to ground her, "Where's Tim?" and as quickly, the chill is gone.

Sarah smiles and he wishes she hadn't; the skin around her mouth puckers, and when her lips part, her receded gums are exposed and she's the grinning ghoulish stuff of childhood nightmares. "Wait 'til you see him, he's such a fine fellow." She calls for him. "Tim!"

There is an irritated "What?" from the living room. A surly teen-age sort of response.

Sarah leads Michael and he cringes as he sees her shoulder blades stick out like a cat's, or the wings of a plucked bird. Most of her hair is gone and the outline of her head is alarming as it perches high on her neck, the upside down V of its join visible. Michael focuses on the apartment and then the sofa. Tim's reading a battered paperback, his feet up on a nearby chair. His hair is shaggy, the curls looser, and while his cheeks still have the smoothness of boyhood, Michael can see in his fully formed nose (yes, beakish, like Michael's) and his growing jaw an echo of the man he will become. Michael's heart swells and he shyly approaches this boy that has grown from a small child to a free-thinking individual in the course of one day.

Michael has no idea what to say, how to start a conversation with this being who seems to know so firmly who he is. He says, "Hey."

Tim looks up. Michael can see in his eyes that he's a little shy, too. But then he grins with his big-boy teeth, so fine and straight, and he's on his feet. He walks over to Michael cautiously at first and then throws his arms around him, hugging him with a big kid's strength. Michael grabs his head, now up to his clavicle, and holds him, living, warm, and so grown. He doesn't know why, but his rocking instinct and kissing instinct have abated. He finds himself thwacking the boy's back to emphasize the hug. It gives off such a satisfying *thump*. He sneaks a kiss on the top of Tim's head before he pulls away.

Tim's voice cracks when he shoves him on the chest and says, "I missed you."

This kills Michael. Did six years pass? Were they six real years for Sarah? Does Tim understand time? Did Michael miss out on six years of development or have they been in some strange holding pattern?

Michael says, "I missed you, too, Tim." However she looks, however uneasy he is with the reason for their being here, he wouldn't have missed this moment with his son for anything. He feels weak and sinks to the sofa. The boy sits with him. Michael says, "Whatcha reading?"

The boy rubs the top of his curly shag and scoffs, "A book."

Michael laughs. "I got that. Any good?"

Tim shrugs. He still has freckles. His head has grown into his eyes and Michael imagines girls must be going wild for him. Only they're not. Because he's stuck. But they *would*. Oh, God this is awful.

But he wants to keep Tim talking. He says, "You like it?"

Tim nods. "It's pretty cool, I guess."

Sarah is drifting over near the bookshelves, watching them. Her face looks as warm as it can. Michael tries to keep her in the corner of his eye, to sense her as her vibrant soul, not as the wraith that it dwells in.

He asks Tim, "How've you and your mom been?"

Tim scoffs again. It's a necessary noise from a ten-year-old. It seems like every sentence Tim says causes him anxiety and embarrassment. His very attitude takes Michael back to fifth grade. He remembers that his walks alone in the woods got longer around then.

Tim says, "We've been, . . . okay, I guess. We missed you. It gets kinda boring. And then sometimes it's just weird." Michael wonders what Tim has to compare things with in order to come up with the word *weird*.

He has to ask. This isn't a small child, whom he could frighten with scary ideas. This is a sentient being with emotions and fully formed thoughts about his circumstance. "Has Greta been around?" Michael startles to see his son's brow darken.

Tim starts, "We-ell . . . "

His mother stops him with a cautionary, *"Tim."*

Michael looks over at Sarah. His feeling that she was drifting is not far from the truth. She sways, her fingers tracing the bookshelf behind her, running past the antique, wooden, straight-backed chair that's pushed against it. When she gets to one end, she sways back the other way. The repetition of touching the books is doing something for her. Grounding her?

The boy whines, "Mom, if we can't talk to Dad, who *can* we talk to?"

Michael finds himself upset by his son's tone. He's about to reprimand him when the corner of his eye catches something odd. He looks back to Sarah to find that her swaying has left the ground. She's crouched on the chair like a spider, bobbing.

She says, "We can't. We can't. We can't. We can't." She's pulling a wisp of her hair in front of her eye and looking at it. "We can't. We can't. We can't."

Michael breathes in and feels cold air, although there's still warmth coming from Tim.

Tim mutters, for comic effect, but full of sadness, "And there she goes." He flops back onto the sofa and picks up the book.

Michael asks, "How long has she . . . been like this?"

Tim flashes him a, *you're kidding, right?* look.

Michael tries to bring her back. "Sarah."

But she doesn't answer. She's started muttering to herself, still crouched. Michael takes the opportunity to sit next to his son. The warmth and weight of him breaks his heart as he asks, very softly, "Has Greta been around . . . a lot?"

"Yeah. Mom sent her away, but she keeps coming back."

Michael asks, "Do you like her?"

Tim shrugs. "She's all right, I guess. She calms Mom down sometimes, when she's like, you know, totally out of it."

"Has she ever . . . " He feels like he's asking his son about a pedophile; he's not sure of the right words to use to not freak him out. "Has she ever. Asked you . . . anything weird?"

Tim says, "Like what?"

To go with her somewhere. To do something to your mother. To leave. To stay. What does this woman want?

But he can't think of the right question, because he doesn't know what he's dealing with. He feels a chill to his right and Sarah's there, crouched on the sofa next to him.

"Mom." Tim's clearly embarrassed. "We have *company.*"

When did Michael get relegated to company? Was it during the funeral, the burial, or the reception? Was he gone one year or three before Tim categorized him?

Sarah lowers herself to a sitting position, putting her feet on the floor, crossing her legs demurely, and smoothing her dress over her skeletal figure. Michael looks at her to give her a reassuring smile and then fixes his eyes on the carpet in front of him, trying to keep her bare feet out of his eyeline.

Sarah asks carefully, "Tim, could you leave your father and me alone, darling?"

Tim scoffs.

Michael says, "Sarah. It's okay." He likes the weight of his boy, his presence. The lump of lead in his belly lets him know that they are nearing the end of all this. He doesn't want Tim to go.

But the boy gets up and takes his book. "I'll be in my room."

Sarah and Michael sit in an awkward silence, like a couple on a first date. Michael can hear the dim horns from traffic passing outside. There's the distant clunk from the icemaker in the kitchen. Sarah's breathing is quick and shallow now, blowing through her nose like an anxious animal. This adds an urgency to their not talking.

Michael tries. "I'm sorry I had to go, honey. It was unavoidable."

Sarah doesn't respond.

Michael says, "There are so many people who loved . . . love you. You should know that."

She leans her head against his shoulder. He's happy for the weight of it, although it's noticeably lighter. He resists the reflex to kiss her head and is grateful that he doesn't have to look at her to talk. This is a familiar talking position for them.

She feels comfortable enough to attempt normal conversation. "How's my mom?"

How much does she know about where he was? "Your mom, honey, she's pretty terrific. I wish I'd known . . . " *before you died.* "She does love you." *And miss you. She would have gotten such a kick out of Tim.*

Her breathing is slowing, calming. "And Anna?"

"She's a strong girl. I get the feeling she's finally going to get her act together. No more excuses."

Sarah exhales sharply out of her nose. He can't tell if it's an expression of irritation or sadness.

She says, tentatively, "You're home now."

"Yes, yes I am."

She puts her hand on his knee. He lets his rest on top of hers; he doesn't want to clasp it for fear it will crumble. There's no flesh, only bone and skin. But Sarah always had cold hands, so that much is familiar.

Sarah says, "We need to think about the future, how it will work. We can't keep going on like we have been."

Michael starts to feel truly uncomfortable. This is like one of Sarah's old heart-to-hearts she'd put him through every year or so. He'd be going forward, day to day, in their life, oblivious, and she'd have a *talk* with him in which she'd reached some conclusion about their relationship or something lacking in their life. They were uncomfortable conversations, but usually ended up somewhere good. There was one about deciding to let her mother throw the big wedding. One about needing to spend more weekends doing nothing (tired of flea markets and chores for the apartment, he'd enjoyed the outcome of that one). One about having a baby; he doesn't wish they hadn't had him—he loves Tim—but what if that conversation hadn't happened? The way she's beginning this conversation does not feel like it will have a happy outcome. The only options are her going away or her staying. Her staying seemed like a good thing, but now staying means the bony hand underneath his and something evil lurking right outside.

Years of living together have provided him with the best response to her raising a point: "What's on your mind, honey?"

She says, "When you go away, it's for so long and I know it's not long for you. How long were you gone this time?"

He says, "Around seven, eight hours."

She sits up to look at him. "Six years, Michael. Six."

His chest feels tight. "I'm so sorry."

She laughs and leans back on his shoulder. Her laugh resonates in a different way, insulated by less flesh. It sounds wheezy, thin. She says, "What did we say about the sorry part?"

"I'm sorry." They both laugh hollowly. The lead in his belly is spreading to his chest.

Sarah says, "I think you need to stay here, Michael. You can order food in. Stop having company over. They'll think you're grieving, anyway. I have enough in CDs, and if you cash in your 401K, that will support us for a year." How does one support the dead? He supposes she means the apartment.

Sarah's voice is picking up in speed and excitement. "You can spend time with your son. Get to know him better. You missed so much of his life. His sense of humor, his wonder, and he's a big thinker, honey. Big thoughts about the world. He needs his father to talk to him about things I can't. He's getting old enough that you should talk to him about sex."

To what end?

"I can't help but think . . . " She tapers off and looks sadly into her lap, he knows this by the position of her head on his shoulder.

Michael says, "He's incredible, Sarah, I get that."

She says, "And if you spend time with him, get to know him . . . " She raises the hand he isn't holding and looks at it. "I don't know why I'm this way. But when you're around, it doesn't seem to be so bad, does it?"

He doesn't want to look at her. She brings her hand up to his head and turns it.

"Does it?" Her eyes are not so beady, there's more green there and there's some color to her skin that makes it look less . . . mummified. But the sunken eyes, the lack of flesh and hair, this is not something that will be remedied.

A husband knows the right response when it comes to a question of looks. "No, not so bad."

This satisfies her. "I was thinking you could teach Tim about geology. Your passion for rocks and you have all of those great books. I tried to get him to read some, but coming from you, it might hold more interest."

How can he teach his son about geology if Tim can't even go outdoors? How can he teach him about sex if it's something that will never happen for him? What, is he going to start dating ghost girls? Maybe Milo has some friends.

Sarah sits up cross-legged on the sofa to face him and continues. "I want to show him so many movies, too, you know? He'd love the Marx Brothers. How can a ten-year-old boy not have seen *A Night at the Opera*?" She does Groucho's voice. "'Make that three hard-boiled eggs.' And the books, honey, we're running out of books, but . . . you know the library delivers? It's a service for shut-ins. You could order us movies and books and we could spend this time together. As a family."

The more she talks, the more he knows all of this is impossible. He doesn't know what will happen; he only knows it won't be what she's dreaming up.

"Maybe you can show him some websites. I can't work your computer, but with you there, he could see the whole world from your office. Those Time-Life books were good for photos of the world, but for him to see pictures from your field trips would really be something." She gets wistful. "He did so love the photos from our wedding."

Oh, God.

She goes on, "And there are videos on there. I can't see the computer, but things seem to work differently for Tim. He says he can feel stuff, you know?" Could she not feel stuff? How were things working for her? He hadn't thought of that. He'd only thought of what she was like for him. Could she feel his embrace? His hand on hers? His kiss?

Sarah looks at him fervently. He doesn't know what to do. But he needs to see Tim. Tim is a good thing.

He hollers. "Tim?" Sarah doesn't mind. Maybe she's expecting him to start showing the kid his view of the world right now.

The boy shuffles into the room and says, "Yeah?"

"Come hang out for a little, will you?" Michael pats the sofa next to him. This stilted gesture makes him feel like he's acting out some pre-written role of Dad.

The boy complies and plops down next to Michael, hugging his knees, facing him. He's so long and thin and tall. His head is so big and his presence so tangible. He looks at his father with his wide-set green eyes and Michael is shot through with a pang of missing Sarah as she used to be. Tim looks at Michael expectantly. He realizes that he has no idea what to say. "How's school?" is the standard question for a kid his age. He can't ask him what video games he's been playing. What are his favorite foods. Or television shows. Or can he? They've already had the reading discussion. But any question that comes to mind is relative to a normal boy's life, one with a working knowledge of the real world.

Michael says, "You're so big." It's all he can think of.

Tim smiles and shoves his dad on the chest. Such a hearty shove, so full of life, force. Why does Sarah shrink as Tim grows? Are these two things related? Is the son going to grow his mother into oblivion?

There's a knock at the door. Michael grabs Tim's knee and looks at Sarah. But they stay. He goes to answer it. If it's Greta, he'll send her away. If Dr. James could do it, he can, too. He slows as he approaches the door and looks back at his son, just in case. Tim has slouched down in the sofa and stretched out his legs to put his feet back on the chair. Sarah's curled up around him, anxiously petting his hair. He tolerates it and smiles up at his mother. There's so much love there. That can't be wrong.

Michael looks out the peephole and is relieved to see Dr. James. He opens the door.

The doctor stands there, looking older than moments before, tears in his eyes, but smiling.

Michael stands back, holding the door wider. "Please, come in."

Dr. James grabs Michael by the elbow as he closes the door. He pulls him close and speaks softly. "He's gone."

Michael hears Tim and Sarah in the next room, making the happy sounds of mother and child chatting about nothing in particular. He pulls Dr. James down the hall toward the nursery. Tim's room. Whatever it is now. They speak softly.

Michael asks, "What do you mean, gone?"

"He said good-bye."

"I don't understand."

Dr. James says, "I don't either. But he didn't kill himself this time."

"That's good."

He continues, "It was the same. He threatened. I pleaded. He went into the bathroom and I waited. But this time he came out again, undamaged, and sat on the bed. We talked. I told him I was sorry that I didn't do the right thing. Sorry that I couldn't fix him. I always tell him I'm sorry and it never changes anything, but this time he listened. He touched my face." He gets distant and tears well up in his eyes.

Michael waits for him. There's no right thing to say right now.

"Michael, it wasn't only about me. Why he was here. He'd been going to his parents, too. He'd been coming and going."

Michael says, "And Sarah stayed."

"And Sarah stayed. But Milo. Milo had to apologize to his parents. He had to do that before he could hear my apology."

This stops Michael. He knows it's not all about Tim. Or not all about Sarah. What is the exchange that needs to happen before Sarah can move on?

The doctor says, "But that's not important. But what is . . . he told me that you and Sarah need me more than he does."

Michael says, "Sarah?"

"He said that where he goes, she must follow. And I'm to help you."

"But how?"

The doctor shrugs. "Milo said the right thing will happen at the right time. I asked him about Greta, but he only looked at me with those giant sad eyes." He thinks a moment, then says, "But they weren't entirely sad; he looked like he knew a secret. A very happy sort of secret. He turned away, told me I'd figure it out, and he was gone."

"Did he . . . " Did he disappear? Was there a doorway? Did he ascend into white light and was there a chorus of angels? Michael asks, "What did you see?" He needs to know something good comes after.

The doctor says, "He stood up and sort of . . . walked away."

"Did you see anything else?"

"No. He faded and I knew that, that he's okay. You know? He's okay now." Tears form in his eyes and soon he's crying freely. "I can't believe it's over." But he's smiling. "Five years of that, over and over and over, and it's finally finished."

Michael pats the doctor, anxiously looking over his shoulder. He doesn't want Tim to see this old man cry. He wants to shelter him from anything complicated or ugly.

But it's too late for that now, isn't it?

FOURTEEN

They're playing Monopoly. Michael doesn't know who had the idea. After he made the doctor some tea and they ate some heated-up remains of Indian food, they sat on the floor of the living room and started a game. The doctor believed firmly in Milo's words that the right time would come. And there was really nothing else to do. At least it gave him a little more time with his boy.

Michael is entranced by Tim.

His son is moving the little silver boot around the board, seven spaces. After quite a take, landing on Free Parking during his last turn, he now lands on Park Place. His face glows, victorious. "Ha!"

Sarah shifts between being an attentive player and staring vaguely and sadly at her feet. Michael tries not to look at her too often, but, every so often, he puts out his hand and gives her back a reassuring, very gentle rub. He tries to ignore the new sensation of her beneath his hand, a pile of sticks wrapped in something rubbery.

He asks Tim, "Do you have enough money?" He knows he does, but in the past hour of playing, Michael has already learned the parental prompts that keep a child on task.

"Do I? Do I?" Tim gets up his wad of cash and counts out $350, which he hands to Dr. James, the banker for this game.

The doctor appears to be having fun. "Thank you, sir. And your property . . . " He hands the boy his card.

Michael picks up the dice to roll, saying, "Wait 'til you get a hotel on that property."

Tim grins, "Donald Trump's got nothing on me."

Where, in the world of their apartment, did Tim get the concept of Donald Trump? The more fascinated and filled with love Michael is, the more uneasy he is over Tim's being here at all.

Michael's conscience is pricking him in the same way it would when he was a child: right and wrong were elusive, but still, the conscience would speak up. Although he hadn't been taught differently, he knew instinctively: it is not okay to take that gum from the store; it is not okay to disturb the bird's nest and touch the eggs no matter how interesting they look; it is not okay to pick the tulips, for they won't grow again until next year. It is not okay to let Tim go on growing like this, and it's definitely not okay to let Sarah continue to wither. She shouldn't be here, and as beautiful and amazing as Tim is, he shouldn't, either. Michael knows this with growing certainty.

There's an overwhelming odor of patchouli and flesh and something dark and sinister in the room. They all look up and there's Greta, sitting on the sofa, knitting, like some grandmother watching the younger folks play after dinner. The beneficence on her face speaks only of evil, and Michael resists the urge to fly at her and yell questions.

He puts his arms protectively around Sarah. He feels her stiffen.

Greta knits and says nothing. Dr. James looks at Michael, questioningly. Michael shrugs.

Sarah extracts herself from Michael and squares her shoulders, saying, "You're not welcome here anymore."

Michael swells with pride over his wraith wife's inner strength. Her voice is less resonant than when she was closer to life, but it's determined. Sarah does not turn to Greta, who keeps on knitting as if nothing has been said.

Michael keeps his eyes on the Monopoly board and says, "Please leave."

Greta, undisturbed, continues her knitting.

Dr. James looks around the room as if weighing his options. Michael wonders if he's looking for weapons. With a wheeze, the doctor rises to his feet and stretches.

He walks over to the chair adjacent to the sofa and sits down, leaning in to Greta. "What are you doing here?"

Greta keeps knitting. "Biding time."

"Until what?"

She doesn't answer, but her needles start to click as she picks up speed.

The doctor's not going to give up, and Michael is grateful as he forges forward. He feels he's been dropped into an important mission without instructions. "Are you merely a lost spirit or do you have some *purpose*?"

Still clicking, she says, "I'm a caretaker for mothers who need me."

The doctor considers her a moment, then says, "What . . . what did you do when you were of this earth?"

The knitting stops. Michael expects something terrible to follow, but Greta looks up at Dr. James and smiles, remembering fondly. "I've always taken care of lost mothers. It's my vocation. It is what I was put on this earth to do. There is nothing so beautiful as that bond between mother and child."

Michael's startled by the sound of his own voice. "Weren't you a doula?"

"And a lactation consultant. Giving where I was needed."

Michael continues, "How did you die?"

She resumes her knitting and doesn't answer. The temperature in the room drops. Michael reaches over to touch Sarah and he feels that she's not the one causing this atmospheric change. She's looking at the hem of her dress, smoothing it and re-smoothing it, muttering to herself like an oblivious child.

Tim pipes up, still playing. "I have Park Place now. Proceed at your own risk. Your turn, Dr. James."

How can he be so untroubled by the tension in the room?

Dr. James sits up straight in his chair and his voice has a forced confidence. He says to Greta, "What do you want from this family?"

With an obnoxiously beatific smile, Greta looks over at Michael and says, "I want to keep this family together. A family deserves to be together." These simple, seemingly lovely words terrify him.

Michael says, "No, we don't. We do, I mean, but we shouldn't. This"—he gestures to Sarah—"This is wrong. Look at her! Why is she like this?"

Greta shrugs and goes back to knitting. "Perhaps a side effect of staying? Her body has forgotten her. But your boy, Michael, look at your boy. He's only now learning to live." The steadiness and certainty of her voice makes Michael sleepy. He looks over to his son who smiles at him with those intelligent green eyes. He smiles back. She's right. Look at him. She continues in steady tones. "The most important thing is for a mother and child to be together. To stay together and to grow. No mother should have that taken away from her." She's right. "No father should be denied his wife and child." Her words resonate, hitting a chord deep within him, and the feelings of illness that he's been fighting for days now wrap around him as something else, a calling. A comfort.

Michael feels a righteous anger of agreement rise in him—a single-minded need to curl up in a blanket with Sarah and Tim. A need to take hold of them and let the world disappear around them.

Michael can hear Dr. James's voice in the distance. "Did you have that taken away from you? Did something happen to your child?"

Greta laughs. Clearly the doctor is not even close to the right answer. The room is colder and it gets dark. Michael looks over, straining to see through the darkness, this ringing stupor. Greta is no longer holding her knitting. She's standing, facing Dr. James who has come to his feet as well. She's angry and the room is feeling that anger's effect. He sees Sarah creep sideways across the floor like a crab, never taking her eyes off Greta. With Greta no longer next to him, the cloak of need and certainty thins a little. Sarah goes behind Tim and puts her emaciated limbs around him protectively. Tim looks frightened. Michael rises and the world twists around him as he joins the doctor. Sarah and Tim cower behind them next to the sofa.

Dr. James asks, "How did you die?" Michael knows it's the wrong question, but he doesn't know the right one.

Greta laughs in a creepily human way. "I don't die." She turns to Michael, speaking in her calm, soothing, human voice. She says, "The most important thing in the world is for a mother to be with her child. You can't get in the way of that bond. That bond goes across time and space, life and death. That bond is pure energy."

The doctor braces himself. "You're not welcome here. You have to let this one go."

Greta says, "Oh, they all go. Those babies, those innocents . . . they always move on." She smiles like she's having a wistful memory. "The mommies, they're mine. All of that longing, that love. Them, I can keep."

Greta looks back at Michael. Her eyes are gray and the weight of her gaze makes him drop his head to look at her feet. She's wearing a long, Indian peasant skirt with brass bangles sewn on. Her boots are beige suede. Her voice now takes on some urgency, and he can smell nervous sweat mixing with her perfume. It makes her smell more living than she has before. He knows now what it was about that flesh . . . what made her smell so awful . . . decay. Michael knows she's still looking at him, but he doesn't look up.

Greta says, "This one—Sarah—is different. She came with a living husband who *believes*. You feel it now, Michael don't you? I can tell."

She lifts his chin with a burning cold hand and looks into his eyes. "You know the right thing to do." He jerks his head away, but she smiles as if she's won something. She continues. "She waited for him. He came. He's keeping her here."

Wait.

Greta says, "And his boy. His boy hasn't gone like the others. He hasn't moved on. His boy is growing up."

Wait. No, wait.

Greta's boots vanish. She has transported herself to somewhere else in the room. Michael, the weight, the clutch on him slightly loosened by Greta's distance, wheels around to see her sitting on the sofa, right near Tim and Sarah.

Sarah turns to Greta. "No, it's not true. I *want* to stay." She looks at Michael, her glassy, doll eyes imploring. "I want to stay."

As Greta talks, Michael walks around the far side of the sofa to be near Sarah and Tim. He's ready to . . . ready to do whatever it is that he can think of. What can he do? All he wants to do is hold them, keep them close, go away somewhere.

There's more than one way to go away. If he joins them, if he goes too, maybe they'll be free. Maybe Sarah will stop . . . withering. A kernel of an idea burns in the pit of his stomach.

Pride fills Greta's eyes as she says, "I got to see a child grow *up*. I almost had a family." She looks at Michael and that pride fades. She never did have him. She reaches out and tousles Tim's hair. "And this one. Maybe. Maybe this one I can keep."

Wait. Keep. What does keep mean?

Greta looks up at Michael.

Sarah says, "No. No, no, no."

Michael steps in front of Sarah, and Sarah and Tim slide back a few feet behind him.

Greta says, "He has lived here so long, it will be harder for him to find his way. His time is almost up." She turns her head to Michael and looks at him with terrifying obsidian eyes. Her command rings deep inside of him. "Look at him!" Michael has a deep compulsion to turn around and look at Tim, but won't. He will look at him when he gets rid of this . . . thing. He will not do anything that this evil being wants. What does she mean *keep*? And what does she mean about the mommies being hers?

He makes his voice as strong as he knows how. "You are not wanted here. You need to leave." *Get rid of Greta. Deal with everything else after.* He feels like he knows what to do after. The kernel has grown to an urgent plan. He feels foolish for not seeing it before. But Greta—this thing—cannot be part of their hereafter.

Sarah's thin voice sounds farther away than she is. "You can't have him." Michael looks over and sees her hands flying about Tim, touching his hair, his shoulders, as if casting a protective spell. She's crying. "I only wanted to be with Michael. To watch Tim grow."

Greta, rises to face Michael. He feels the chill and the darkness coming off her, and the black dust cuts his nose when he breathes. He looks directly into her black silt eyes. Although he wants to, he doesn't yell. He remains calm. He says, "Leave. My. House."

The fury seeps into her eyes, the blackness swirls, and she seethes. Greta says, "The boy is mine." She's not growling, exactly, but a roar of some sort seems to be emanating from her. It's so cold that Michael's eyes burn and the inside of his nose crackles. But this anger and his plan give him newfound courage. He knows now that he has some say in this. He motions for Sarah and Tim to move farther away. Greta never takes her black roiling eyes off his.

He's louder this time. "You can't have them. Leave. My. House."

The noise, the roar and the growl, stop. Michael didn't realize how hard he was breathing until it becomes all he can hear. Greta seems frozen for a moment until Michael notices the rising and falling of her shoulders. She's breathing, but her face bears no expression.

Slowly, the light returns to the room. Michael can now hear the doctor's wheeze; he sounds as if he's coming off some form of strenuous exercise.

Greta's face softens as she watches Michael, and he sees color return to her eyes, bringing with it a deep sadness. Are those tears? Greta looks around the room. She looks at Tim and Sarah. Then the doctor, then Michael. Michael holds his ground, staring intently. Greta's skin seems more fragile, less supple, blotchy. It makes her look sadly human, exposed.

Michael doesn't know what she's looking for in his eyes, but he steels himself to make sure that she doesn't find it. She doesn't. She lowers her head. Then she is over by Tim, squatting down before him. Michael steps toward her, but Sarah holds her own, her arms around her son, fierce, vigilant. Greta looks at Tim, who looks up at her. He's crying. This has finally gotten to him. Greta reaches out and pushes his forelock off his head. She runs her hand under his chin, but he jerks his head away.

There's the sound of a baby crying in the distance. It's not a sound in the apartment, and it doesn't carry like a sound from outside or in the hall. It's *elsewhere.*

Greta's head jerks up. Eyes still watery, she smiles, the sound filling her with joy. She rises to her feet and begins to hum. She turns away from all of them as if they've ceased to exist. She starts singing softly to herself. "Hush little baby, don't say a word, Greta's gonna buy you a mockingbird . . . " She sashays toward the front door, but before she reaches it, she dissipates, leaving a faint black trail of dust in her wake.

And she's gone. And the room warms. The urgency in Michael slows to an abstract need. What was he thinking about? Something important.

Michael looks over to see Sarah, still curled around Tim on the floor. She's crying and kissing Tim's head. He was going to do something. What? He looks at Dr. James, who pats him on the shoulder and turns to leave. The doctor stops for a moment and turns back toward Sarah and Tim. He crouches down and looks at Sarah, saying, "It'll be okay. I promise. It's a better place. I know that now." Frightened, she clutches Tim closer. But she nods. She knows.

The doctor's words cut through this fervent cloud that had grown in Michael. He looks at Sarah, so frail. So *not* Sarah. He did this to her. His plan fades as his certainty grows. He did this and it's wrong.

The doctor presses Michael's arm as he goes, and Michael says, "Thank you." He tries not to collapse when he hears the door close behind him. He walks over and sits on the floor, leaning against the sofa next to Sarah. He can't help the tears. He says, "I'm so sorry, honey. I didn't know."

She asks, though she knows, "What?"

He says, "I didn't know it was me. My fault."

"What?"

He did this.

He says, "I couldn't. I couldn't let you go. And look at you, honey. Look what I've done."

Tim is looking frightened now. This is harder to bear. "Dad?"

Michael says, "Tim."

Tim's voice cracks, betraying his fear. "Dad?"

Michael holds his arms out and Sarah gives Tim one more kiss on the head before letting him go to his father. The boy curls up in a ball against Michael's belly and the father wraps his arms around him, trying to get the full sense of his weight and smell, sweaty, earthy, older. He kisses the boy's curls and he can hear Tim sniffle. Michael says, "I love you, little man."

He says, "I'm scared, Dad."

Sarah says, "Michael."

Michael looks up at Sarah, her face peaceful now. There are tears trickling from her diminished eyes. She presses her lips together and nods. Despite her withered condition, she seems more Sarah than she's been since he got back from the funeral. She comes to her knees next to them and breathes in deeply. Her hand goes out to Tim's hair, and she says, in a voice stronger than he's heard in a long time, "It's okay, baby. It's time."

Michael says, "I'm here, Tim. And it's time to go. Go with your mom now."

Tim says, "Where?"

Michael says, "Wherever you're meant to." He kisses him. "It's okay. Go."

The boy feels lighter in his arms, skinnier. Michael pulls his face away and turns Tim's head to him. He's younger now. Maybe eight. All elbows and knees. One of the years Michael missed. He tries to memorize his face, but then he's smaller still. His strong Michael-like nose recedes a little, the frightened look in his eyes becomes bewildered, and then he calms. Michael kisses him again and looks up at Sarah. She puts her hand out to touch her boy. Tim is on his dad's lap at about five now, head up to his chin. He smiles and says, "Mommy!" holding out his arms to her. He's four and Michael has room to reach out a free arm and pull Sarah in. Now he's three and full of joy, happy to be with his parents, and starts singing in an atonal, "Ba, ba, ba, ba, ba."

Sarah's flesh is filling in and her hair is coming back. This is frightening, but feels right. Tim's not shrinking so much as distilling, becoming more himself, less an aberration. He is two now and starts rubbing Michael's face, laughing. Sarah's peachy glow is back, her freckles take on their old life, her hair is full. Her cheeks are still hollow, but she smiles at the boy, pulling him onto her lap. Michael puts his hand on his Tim's face, so supple, so full of life. That drool-y breathing is back. He leans in and kisses Sarah's head, smelling her. He had missed her. Tim, eighteen months or so, makes a pterodactyl squeal and Michael and Sarah laugh together.

Sarah's tears are gone. She's kissing her baby of six months, who sits on her lap kicking and squealing joyfully. Michael wants to slow this. He knows he can't and he knows that it's right, but he wants to stop it, right here, for a moment. He puts his hand on Tim's belly and feels his squirming, his breathing, the vibration when he babbles and squeals.

Quickly, before they go, Michael says, "I love you, Sarah." He's crying freely, now. "I love you, Tim."

Sarah looks up at him and flashes him a smile. "Best thing ever?"

He says, "Best thing ever."

Tim is a smaller baby, squirming in Sarah's arms. And then he's an infant, wizened face yawning.

It all stops. For now. Sarah is Sarah again, and Michael smiles for the sight of her. He wipes his face with his sleeve.

Sarah looks down at Tim, holding her finger in his outstretched little hand, which clamps shut around it. "Look at you, little man!" She's the smiling mother of a newborn, astonished by the tiny enormous yawn. He doesn't know if Sarah can remember anything, if that was part of the process. He knows that she's here with her baby and they're happy and he won't disturb that. She looks up at Michael, so proudly. "Look what we made."

Michael holds his hand out to the boy's peach fuzz head and pets it, his skull so warm and fragile. He runs his finger down his tiny pearl of a nose and then rests his hand on his belly. He kisses Sarah on top of her warm head, breathing in. She smells whole and alive. His little family.

He gives Sarah a squeeze. She looks up at him, smiling with such love, and kisses him, long and firm. It's good-bye. He smiles and says, "It's okay." And he sees in her eyes that she knows this. He breathes in his wife and his son one last time. They fade away too quickly. The warmth on his chest is all that remains of them, his shirt separates from his chest where they rested.

Michael stretches his legs out, his foot kicking over a clatter of the Monopoly game's metal pieces and plastic houses. The shoe that Tim had chosen. The little dog for Sarah.

He's too empty to weep any more. The noises from the street seep through the antique windows. A siren. Jackhammers. Traffic. He's not sure if those sounds were missing while Sarah was with him or if life was too noisy for him to notice them.

He moves his leaden limbs and slowly gets to his feet, walking over to the window. He pulls on its heavy sash, gives it the usual wiggle and shove with his shoulder, hefting it upward and it rumbles open.

The sun is setting and the air carries the chill of night. A kid yells something in the distance. The apartment buildings across the street are bathed in the purply blue glow of evening, while a wayward streak of sunlight escapes through a space somewhere between the Harrowgate and the river to the west, laying a pink stripe on the sidewalk. There's a warm updraft from the street, baked pavement, warmed leaves and dirt; the traces of a spring day now past.

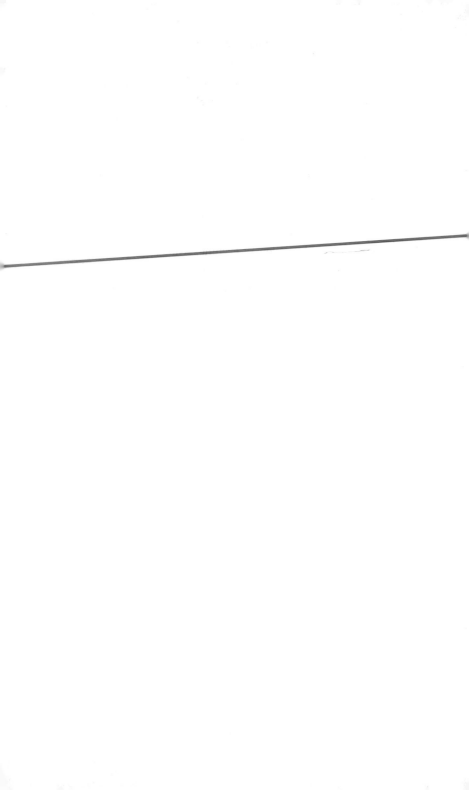

ABOUT THE AUTHOR

GLORIA VILLEGAS

Kate Maruyama writes, teaches, cooks, and eats in Los Angeles where she lives with her husband and two children.

Her fiction has been published in several literary journals in print and online and she holds an MFA in Creative Writing from Antioch University Los Angeles. In 2009, she co-founded the literary website Annotationnation.com with Diane Sherlock, which publishes interviews and articles about the craft of writing.

Acknowledgements

This story has been dogging me in one form or another for almost twelve years. Thanks to Stephen Gates, Dana Scanlan, Caroline Macaulay, and Matt Bierman, who helped me with its prior incarnation. Encouraging words and solid notes are the fuel that keep writers going, and I am forever grateful for their time and support.

Several years later, the five pages at the end of that incarnation that wouldn't leave me bloomed into the beginning of a novel, and I was buoyed by encouraging words and solid notes once again, this time from my very first workshop at Antioch University Los Angeles. Thanks to Jonathan Berzer, Neal Bonser, Janine Coveney, Gloria Gibson, Gleah Powers, and Tisha Reichle, who were generous with their notes and patience, and to Rob Roberge, who was gracious enough to lift the cone of silence to allow me to ask questions of this group. In that workshop, I figured out how my twenty pages of beginning would yield a novel.

To my generous mentors of that program, Dodie Bellamy, who gave me my legs in writing, Gayle Brandeis, who allowed me to run with them, and Rob Roberge, who has done more for this book than he probably knows. They are all fine writers and constant guiding voices in my head every time I sit down to write, and sometimes still live voices when I need them.

Thanks to David Byrne, a sympathetic artistic soul who gave me permission to use "Dream Operator," which had become central to the fabric of this novel.

Thanks to Wendy Hudson, who unwittingly changed everything.

Thanks to Diane Sherlock, a generous writer, friend, critic, business partner, and sounding board. Thanks to Marian Halpin, Stephanie Westphal, Jae Gordon, Richard Rushfield, and Angela Brommel for their considerate reads. To my writer peeps, especially David Davis (who was the first), Lisa Brown, and Yuvi Zalkow, whom I consult regularly in all things about the literary world. To my Antioch peeps and especially the rest of my Sages without whom I don't think I could face my writing life every week.

Thanks to Ko, for more reasons than I can count. And to Jack, who gave me most of Tim.

Thanks to Kit and Joe Reed, who taught me everything I know about narrative and raised me in a creatively open spirit that I have only recently learned is missing in so many writers' childhoods.

Thanks to the tireless and brilliant John Silbersack. With his careful notes and constant encouragement, he helped me to shape this novel into a real book. There were times he had more faith in my characters than I did, and that is a rare thing in an agent. He would not give up until this novel found a home, another thing that I have learned is rare in an agent.

I'm extremely grateful to Jeff VanderMeer, who only made things better.

And an enormous thank-you to Alex Carr and the team at 47North for their enthusiastic collaboration in bringing the book to fruition.